KT-569-294

Eddy Shah started out as a writer but was sidetracked into various business enterprises. As the founder of a group of provincial newspapers, he rapidly became one of Britain's most successful entrepreneurs. He founded *Today*, Britain's first all-colour daily paper, but sold his interest in newspapers in order to return to writing. His previous three novels, *Ring of Red Roses*, *The Lucy Ghosts* and *Manchester Blue*, are also published by Corgi.

FALLEN ANGELS

Eddy Shah

CORGI BOOKS

FALLEN ANGELS
A CORGI BOOK: 0 552 14290 5

Originally published in Great Britain by Doubleday,
a division of Transworld Publishers Ltd

PRINTING HISTORY
Doubleday edition published 1994
Corgi edition published 1995

Set in 10/11½ pt Linotron Times by
Falcon Graphic Art Ltd

Corgi Books are published by Transworld Publishers Ltd,
61–63 Uxbridge Road, Ealing, London W5 5SA,
in Australia by Transworld Publishers (Australia) Pty Ltd,
15–25 Helles Avenue, Moorebank, NSW 2170,
and in New Zealand by Transworld Publishers (NZ) Ltd,
3 William Pickering Drive, Albany, Auckland.

Reproduced, printed and bound in Great Britain by
Cox & Wyman Ltd, Reading, Berks.

To Ronnie Bloom

An unsung warrior of our time
A friend to be trusted when alive
A friend to be warmly remembered now gone.

BACKGROUND STATISTICS

In the 1980s a 3 Infantry Brigade Army captain, Intelligence (Armagh, Northern Ireland), was asked to prepare a most secret plan.

The brief was simple.

To organize a concerted attack on the Provisional IRA. To arrest or take out its most dangerous members; to capture and destroy all arms and explosives; to hit the PIRA so hard that it would take many years for it to regroup. Its true purpose was to force the IRA to lay down their arms and enter discussions for a peaceful solution.

The report also asked for a conclusion as to how such an action would be regarded by other friendly, and unfriendly, allies.

The plan was prepared and the document circulated to a few at the top of the security chain of command.

It was turned down as being too risky and one that would isolate the British government from the rest of the world.

Since then, and before the start of the peace talks between the Irish and British governments in November 1993, there have been in Northern Ireland:

791 deaths which included **486** innocent civilians in security-related situations.

9730 injuries which included **5598** innocent civilians in security-related situations.

4841 shootings and **6692** armed robberies in security-related situations.

4971 persons charged with terrorist offences.

The figures above do not include the deaths or injuries of any PIRA or other Republican groups or any of the deaths and injuries suffered by people on the mainland, including Warrington and the City of London bombings.

In that same time **1873** people died in road accidents in Northern Ireland.

It is a common belief that the reason the IRA declared a cease-fire in 1994 and joined the peace talks between Britain's Prime Minister John Major and Ireland's Taoiseach Albert Reynolds was that they realized that further terrorist acts would not help the nationalist cause any longer.

This was further highlighted by the huge response by the British public to the imprisonment of a soldier from 3 Para, Private Lee Clegg, who was found guilty of murder when he opened fire on a car driven by joyriders in Belfast's Glenn Road and killed one of the occupants. When Private Clegg lost his appeal on the charge of murder, nearly two million signatures were received on petitions to the Home Office supporting the young soldier. Most felt he had simply been doing his duty and had not set out, unlike the Provisional IRA, to deliberately maim and kill innocent bystanders. This furious reaction brought about a realization that most Britons still saw the IRA as terrorists in spite of the peace declaration and subsequent cease-fire.

Should the peace talks fail, there is little doubt that some would want to take the law into their own hands, just as the IRA had done in the past.

This book, written prior to the cease-fire, is based on a Plan that was put forward to be used against the IRA, but never instigated. The response to Private Clegg's unfortunate incarceration for murder shows that many of the public would support any such defensive action against future terrorists, should the peace talks break down due to the intransigence of any one side.

Like many, I hope peace prevails, and there will never be the need for individuals and groups to react for vengeance and retribution.

As John Lennon sang '*All we are saying is give peace a chance.*'.

BOOK ONE

THE START OF THE JOURNEY
[The mid-1990s]

Central Intelligence Agency
Langley
Virginia

Francis Duggan grinned with satisfaction as he watched the small television set in the corner of his small office.

The cause of his delight was the man coming down the steps of the US Federal Building court-house in New York, laughing and waving.

Tim Flaherty. Provisional IRA terrorist. Released by a federal court after two years of being held for extradition to Great Britain for crimes committed in the UK; crimes that resulted in the death of eleven civilians in a spate of indiscriminate bombings on the British mainland between 1991 and 1993.

Tim Flaherty. Irish Republican soldier and hero, decorated by the IRA. A man with a dream and a country to free. Born and bred in the Falls Road; brought up throwing rocks and bottles at British soldiers since he was nine, in a city where violence was the only currency and manhood was bar-mitzvahed when you kicked your first Prod unconscious.

Tim Flaherty. At twenty-five a champion to some, a corrupt and vile gangster to others.

Tim Flaherty. Freed from jail on a technicality and free to kill again.

It wasn't that Duggan approved of violence; in truth he was a conscientious CIA analyst who believed in law and order and put his duty before all else. He was a member of the CIA's Counter Terrorist Center which brought together analytical, operational, communications and technical support personnel, drawn primarily from the CIA but with participation from the FBI, Army, Navy, Air Force, Marines and Treasury.

But Duggan was also of Irish descent. And like many of his fellow countrymen he instinctively saw Ireland as a repressed nation, ruled against its will by the British; ruled with the gun and a Chieftain tank. It was how he had been raised; by Irish immigrant parents from Belfast, with strong Roman Catholic beliefs, who passed their nationalistic views on to their son. He didn't agree with terrorism, but felt an instinctive and hereditary pleasure in knowing a Republican freedom fighter had escaped capture. It was not something he would let be freely known, certainly not amongst his colleagues.

'I'm a free man', Flaherty was saying with a Northern Irish brogue, on the screen, 'because of American justice. This is the land of the free because of the battle your forefathers fought against the British. It's my aim, and every free Irishman's, to make all of Ireland as free as this great country of yours. For that I'll endure torture and beatings and death at the hands of the British government, even if it means going back to the concentration camps of Long Kesh in Belfast. Whatever it takes to be free. Long live the Republic of America. Long live the Republic of Ireland.'

10

'What are your plans now?' asked a reporter.

'That's up to the Army Council. I'm a soldier. I do as I'm ordered. And that is to attack British military targets. And unlike all them false stories about me, all that British propaganda, I don't believe in indiscriminate bombings.'

Duggan, for all his emotive support, knew lies and propaganda when he heard it. In the end they were terrorists, and he suddenly felt guilty. Flaherty, a member of the IRA's 3rd Battalion, B Company, had done wrong; there was no justification for the Provos' indiscriminate attacks on the British mainland, especially the recent rash of bombings that had shaken London and other British cities. He thought of his cousins back in Ireland, probably rejoicing at the news. They were all staunch Republicans, believers in the cause. There was a sudden sadness in him that Flaherty had escaped justice for the crimes he had committed.

Duggan shrugged off his own contradictions and remote-switched the set off. His last view was of Flaherty climbing into a stretch-limo that was parked under a sign for 'Tim Flaherty Corner', a street recently named after the terrorist by the New York City Mayor. Such was the power of the Irish Americans; so important was their vote.

Francis Duggan, at thirty-seven, was not how you would imagine the all-American spy. He was tall, with rounded features under a thick red unkempt thatch. It wasn't that Duggan was uninterested in his appearance, just that his wiry hair was impossible to control. Duggan had a 'Deputy Dawg' sort of face, tired and worldly, which was not a true reflection as he had done very little with his life except live in the comfort zone of middle-class America. He was a detached man, uneasy in the company of others. But he was a committed Agency man with a sharp mind that analysed most European terrorist situations faster than the two computers that

11

sat on his desk. That was the main sphere of his responsibilities; the analysis and dissemination of information on all terrorist activities in Western European countries.

Francis was actually preoccupied with thoughts far removed from Tim Flaherty and the Agency. His divorced wife, Carmella, had refused him visitation rights to see their two daughters, Samantha, seven, and Natalie, nine, over the coming weekend. Her reasoning was that her new fiancé was bringing his own son and daughter to meet Carmella's family that weekend and it would 'just be so gross and unfair if you turned up and ruined our time together'.

He hated her for that; for making him feel their daughters would soon have a new Daddy, a new family. He hated her anyway. *God knows what anyone else sees in her*. He was further upset by the fact that he had missed his daughters a fortnight earlier when he had been called away to listen in on a United Nations conference about the exchange of information between countries who were in the front line of terrorism. Which, as Duggan reminded his boss, Rob Volger, America wasn't. But the ploy didn't work; Volger had wanted a first-hand report on the meeting. All this meant Duggan was now a month between seeing his daughters. Another month for that bitch to cement their relationship *with their new father*. He spat the last word out. That's what she'd said, 'their new father'. The images of his girls with another man, teaching them, loving them, them loving him, were too much for Duggan.

He slammed out of the room and went for a walk down the long, endless corridors that meander around Langley.

He wasn't in his office when his direct superior rang to inform him that Tim Flaherty had walked free from a New York court and was now under the constant surveillance of the FBI.

12

Charley O's Bar and Grill
33 West 48 Street
New York

Tim Flaherty knew he was being tailed by the FBI. He didn't mind; it guaranteed his safety.

The party to celebrate his release was being held at Charley O's Bar and Grill, one of New York's many Irish restaurants, complete with oyster bar and fish and chips. It had been organized by an American group called the 'Friends of Tim Flaherty'. The restaurant was packed; supporters, hangers-on, press and whoever else was passing by. An Irish band played in the corner, its bouncing jig reflecting the celebration of the moment.

Flaherty, the centre of attention, stood at the bar with a Guinness in his hand. He was surrounded by well-wishers, exuberant and noisy in their praise of the Irishman. Flaherty wasn't a senior member of the IRA; he was simply a foot-soldier, and not a very bright one at that. But now he was a symbol, a celebrity that could be marketed. Tim Flaherty had become an important man.

Jed Geraghty, the twenty-nine-year-old NORAID officer standing next to him was aware of Flaherty's new status. For NORAID, the Irish Northern Aid Committee, it was an important victory at a time when North American funds for the PIRA had almost dried up, dropping from over eight million dollars in the 1980s to below one hundred thousand in 1993. With the correct publicity, NORAID could once again raise support from the Irish-American community; IRA members like Flaherty would be seen as freedom fighters and soldiers of honour instead of the gangsters and terrorists the American press had recently portrayed them as. The recent indictments of three Irishmen, including a priest, for being involved in an $8 million armed robbery at the Brinks bullion plant in Rochester, New York, had not helped the IRA's cause. All three men had active connections with the Republican movement and the IRA had taken the unusual step of denying any involvement with them. It was a sensitive time for Irish-American relations and Geraghty knew he had a real opportunity to improve the situation using the appeal of the JFK look-alike, Flaherty. It was all about presentation with the Americans. And the curly-haired Flaherty, with his wide winning smile, was a promoter's dream. As long as he held back on the juice.

'Give the man some space,' Geraghty told those who were hemming Flaherty in. 'Give him a chance. He's been locked up for long enough. Let him enjoy his freedom.'

'I'm fine,' said Flaherty. 'I'm enjoying myself.' He winked at a girl who had attached herself to his right arm. 'Careful, girl, that's—'

'My name's Anna.'

'. . . Anna. That's my drinking arm you're hanging on to.'

Geraghty leant over and whispered in Flaherty's ear. 'Ease up on the booze.'

'I'll be OK. But I'm not going to have a wake on my first night out.'

Geraghty laughed. 'All right, Noddy.'

'What's that supposed to mean?'

'Big Ears had never seen Noddy so aggressive before.'

'What the fuck's that?'

'You're just Noddy in Toytown. You may be important in here, Tim. To these bums. But to half of them, this is just a free party. They'll be drinking someone else's booze tomorrow. They won't even remember you. The men in Belfast want you doing what's right for the cause. And that means making sure you're sober for a television interview later on. Remember that. Don't believe your own publicity. Otherwise it won't be the Brits who'll take you out.'

'I said I'm OK,' came the belligerent reply. 'I'll be

fine for when we do the interview.' He turned his attentions back to Anna and the crowd that pressed forward to shake his hand and pat his back.

Someone let off a party-popper in another part of the restaurant. Geraghty tensed, then relaxed. They were safe here. Nobody was going to shoot them in New York. Not when the FBI were following them. Even the crazy Prods weren't crazy enough to come shooting up the streets of an American city. He relaxed; maybe he was being over-sensitive. Flaherty deserved a moment of relaxation. God knows he'd had little of that in the last two years, being locked up in the overcrowded and noisy Metropolitan Correction Center.

Geraghty took a glass of wine from a passing waiter. Things were going well. After years of NORAID being shunned by the American public, the recent February visit of Sinn Féin leader Gerry Adams had made support for a free and independent Ireland popular again. Adams had attended a special peace conference in New York and been well received by senators, congressmen and the media. He'd played his cards well, blaming the British government for not moving the Anglo-Irish peace talks along. Sinn Féin and the IRA had grasped the initiative from the British and, in spite of their recent bombing outrages in Belfast which had killed ten innocent passers-by, were now the peacemakers in the eyes of the gullible American public.

Geraghty sipped his wine slowly and looked round the room. Plenty of money here, plenty of support. After years in the wilderness, he could once again tap the rich American source to pay for the struggle in Northern Ireland. There were millions of dollars already raised since Adams's visit. Flaherty's popularity would definitely keep the fund-flags flying.

'Hey, I heard the Catholics don't get the vote in Northern Ireland?' an American man asked him. 'Is that shit true?'

15

Geraghty nodded. 'It's the truth,' he said, shaking his head sadly. 'It's a sad world, but that's how it is.' He chuckled inside. *They really were gullible, these Yanks. Thank God. It certainly made fund-raising easy when they believed crap like that.*

Raphael picked up the pay phone, slotted a quarter into the machine and dialled long distance. As he waited for the line to connect he watched the entrance to the restaurant.

'Everything's in place,' he said when the phone was picked up.

'Are you sure?' came the answer; an older man, English.

'It's the only way to go now.'

'I agree. But I want to make sure you feel the same.'

'I do.'

'If you're caught you're on your own.'

'I won't be.' He didn't need to add that if things got out of hand he had already decided he wouldn't be taken alive. 'It'll be done correctly. The way we're taught.'

'Good luck, Raphael.'

The phone clicked dead, but Raphael held the receiver next to his ear, as if he was still talking, not wanting to draw attention to himself. He'd already picked up the two FBI men who were watching over Flaherty; they stood near the entrance of the restaurant. Raphael had been waiting outside the court-house three hours earlier to see who was protecting the PIRA man. He was surprised to see there were no police; but then who genuinely expected trouble in New York? As soon as Flaherty had entered the restaurant, Raphael had surveyed the entire area before he was satisfied that the two FBI men were all there were. Apart from the crowds inside the restaurant. And the TV cameras. And the photographers.

He smiled. He would use them to his advantage.

He had eaten in a small restaurant across the road, then sat at the bar and waited. He knew that Flaherty would soon be leaving for the television studio; the station had been advertising the interview all afternoon.

There was a sudden surge of movement outside the restaurant and Raphael hung up the receiver, then quickly skipped through the light traffic and crossed the street. He saw the driver of the limousine that had brought Flaherty from the court-house to the restaurant get out of the car and move round to open the back door. The photographers were spread across the pavement, blocking off the FBI men, as Raphael reached the limousine and joined the crowd. He pulled the hood of his anorak over his head and yanked the cord tight to hide his face, just leaving enough of an opening to see clearly. He didn't look out of place; it was a cold evening and a fresh chilling wind blew across the city. He slipped his hand into his coat pocket and felt the Glock 19, polymer-bodied, 9mm pistol; found it comforting to touch as he waited for Flaherty.

He would have preferred the usual reliable Browning High-Power hand-gun, but he was on foreign soil and the lightweight Glock was easier to carry. He had gone up to Harlem, got in conversation with a street-corner drug dealer and offered him $1,500 for a Glock and twenty rounds. The dealer, pleased to make a quick $1,000 profit, had taken him to a gun store and, while Raphael waited outside, had gone in and bought the gun. The deal was consummated down the next alleyway, where cash swapped hands for the weapon and the bullets. There was some difficulty in communication between the two men for Raphael spoke with a thick Northern Irish accent. He imitated the brogue well, something he had picked up in his years in the province.

As the excitement built in the crowd, so the tension

rose in Raphael. He tried to block it out, to think only in technical terms about the task in hand, but it had been some considerable time since he had been in the field. There was a sudden panic; *what if it goes wrong, what if I fuck up?* June and the kids flashed through his mind. He'd always been faithful to her. If she hadn't divorced him, he wouldn't be here now. He'd be with the kids, where he wanted to be. She'd left him because of his career; she couldn't take the pain of knowing he might not come back alive. That was the trouble with American women. They didn't have the fortitude of the British army wives. But it didn't take away the pain, the love he had felt for her. All he'd ended up with was a green card as her spouse so that he could work in America. The end had been inevitable; he'd come home to Basingstoke and found she'd left for America with the kids. The house was empty of personal belongings; only the furniture was left in 'Mary Deare' fashion and a note informing him that he was on his own for the rest of his life. Damn. The Army was the only job he had ever known, the only life he had ever understood. *Poor June. Poor kids. Poor Raphael. Shit. What about Flaherty?* He suddenly recalled the outrage he had felt when the newspapers reported weeks ago that Flaherty would probably escape extradition. He remembered the people, innocent passers-by who had no truck with Flaherty or the IRA, who were killed and maimed by the bombs that Flaherty had left in the streets of London. It calmed him; thinking of what the Irishman had done; what he deserved. Raphael took deep breaths, slowly bringing his anxiety under control. He recalled what he had said on the phone only a few minutes earlier. 'It'll be done correctly. The way we're taught.'

Then the tenseness in his shoulders and the knot of worry in his stomach evaporated as he saw Flaherty come through the restaurant door with a smiling, waving, 'Look what a great man I am' attitude. The Irishman had a girl on his arm and was flanked by the NORAID man, Geraghty.

Raphael released the safety-catch of the already cocked pistol in his pocket and moved closer to the chauffeur. He didn't worry about the flashing camera lights; he knew he was safe within the concealment of his anorak hood.

Geraghty pushed through the crowd towards the car as the chauffeur opened the door. He stepped back, let Flaherty and the girl get in, then followed them. The chauffeur shut the door and made his way round to the driver's door. Raphael saw the two FBI men stride away towards their support car to follow the limousine. With his left hand he took out an orange armband and slipped it onto his sleeve. Then he leant forward and knocked on the door. The window was wound down as the chauffeur started the car.

'What is it?' Geraghty asked.

Raphael mumbled through the anorak hood as he tried the door handle.

'What do you want?' Geraghty asked again. There was no alarm in his voice; the last thing he expected was trouble.

The handle unlatched and Raphael swung the door open. He pushed Geraghty back into his seat, ignoring his sudden protests. As Flaherty, sensing danger, rose towards him, Raphael slammed the door shut behind him with his left hand as he pulled the Glock out with his right.

The girl, seeing the gun first, screamed, but it had no effect on Raphael. He shot Flaherty in the throat, then spun round and shot Geraghty in the temple. Then he pushed the girl, hitting her hard across the mouth as he did, and jammed the muzzle of the gun into the chauffeur's neck.

'Drive, you bastard,' he shouted. 'Just drive or you're a dead man.' He saw the driver hesitate, so he prodded him with the gun again. 'GoGoGoGoGo!' He turned and hit the girl once more, this time knocking her out.

The chauffeur snapped out of his terror and slammed his foot down on the accelerator. The car careered away from the pavement and hurtled down the road, cutting across traffic as other cars squealed and honked in protest.

The whole thing had taken eight seconds.

'Left, left now,' Raphael yelled as they approached the first corner. The car swung round and drew away from the traffic. Two hundred yards further on he told the driver to pull up. When the car stopped, he knocked the safety-catch on, then threw the Glock onto the thick-carpeted floor and stepped out into the road. He ran across it and disappeared down an alleyway. As he ran he tore off his anorak and threw it down, the orange armband still round the sleeve. At the end of the alleyway he slowed to a walk, joined the passing crowd and disappeared into its bustling anonymity.

The girl, Anna, was too frightened to remember anything that could help the police.

The chauffeur had his back to the gunman at all times. 'What the hell do you expect?' he grumbled. 'Would you turn around with a gun rammed in your neck?'

The first FBI man to reach the limousine ran down the alleyway where the chauffeur told him the assassin had escaped. All he found was the discarded anorak with the orange armband. There were no labels on the jacket. It took a long time before they traced its owner, a doctor from whom it had been stolen eight days earlier from a restaurant cloakroom.

'Did you report it?' a policeman had asked the doctor.

'You've got to be joking,' came the reply. 'It's so old I couldn't give it away.'

*　　*　　*

20

For all the photographers and television cameras, for all the witnesses outside the restaurant, nobody could give a decent identification for a photo-fit.

There was one camera shot, a full frontal of the assassin's hooded face, that was enlarged to show the colour of his eyes.

It was no good. The technician in the photo-lab said the man under the hood was wearing reflective sunglasses.

'We didn't agree you should take them both out, Raphael,' the English voice said on the phone.

'It seemed expedient. They were both evil men.'

'Agreed. But next time try and stick to orders.'

'Yes, sir.'

'Time for you to go home, Raphael.'

'I'll be on the first available flight.'

'You did well. The unit is proud of you.'

'Thank you, sir.'

'And don't forget to contact the authorities just before you go through the gate.'

The CIA's Director of Operations rang Francis Duggan and told him to attend a meeting at the Old Executive Office Building in the White House the next day. He also instructed him to prepare a short report on the IRA, the Ulster Defence Force, the Ulster Freedom Fighters and any of the latest information the CIA had on these and other paramilitary groups.

They traced the gun to the store in Harlem where it had been sold.

Then they traced the drug pusher who had bought it. He told them the gun was stolen from him. They knew he lied and threatened to run him in on a false drugs charge. Even though it would be planted evidence, he knew the charge would stick. He valued his freedom, so he stuck to his story that the gun had been stolen. But he gave them a good, truthful description of the white man who had 'stolen' the weapon from him.

They wanted to believe him; there was no reason for him to lie. The bit that really excited them was when he told them that the white guy had a strange accent. Not American, but still good English. They played him some actors' voices with different accents.

The drug pusher recognized the Northern Irish accent.

That's when they finally believed him.

Old Executive Office Building
The White House
Washington

'All I want to know is, is this a one-off, or are we about to get involved in a terrorist war?' The President's National Security Advisor looked round the table. There were five people facing him, two from the CIA and one each from the FBI, Justice and State. He took his time before continuing. 'We've managed to keep terrorists out of this country. If one group gets away with it, the rest could follow. Baader-Meinhof, the Red Brigade, Direct Action; it'd be open season for any of those organizations.'

Francis Duggan sat behind the CIA's Director of Operations, Clifford McNabb, and listened to the NSA. Duggan wouldn't normally attend such a high-powered meeting, but the NSA had insisted that McNabb bring along an expert in Irish terrorist action. The phone had rung, catching Duggan on his way out of the house in the morning; he was going to detour via Carmella's house and insist that the children spend some time with him over the weekend, *new Daddy or not*. His frustration was now at its peak as he listened to the

NSA; his mind was in a frenzy as he realized he now had little chance of seeing his daughters. He tried to block them out and listen to the NSA. *Bloody crazy Irish*. That's all it would be. One violent group trying to knock out another.

'. . . orange armband, probably for the Protestants . . .' the NSA continued.

'That's SAS,' Duggan interrupted instinctively.

'What?' asked the NSA. Everyone else at the table looked at him.

'British Army Special Air—'

'We know who the SAS are. What's an orange armband got to do with them?'

'They wear an orange armband. When they go out in civilian clothes on a shoot-to-kill operation.'

'You sure?' asked McNabb.

'Yes, sir. That's how they do it in Ireland. To identify themselves as regular troops. That way, if a British patrol turns up, they know they're SAS men.'

'Jesus,' sighed the NSA. 'That's all we need.'

'Doesn't mean it was them,' came in Hank Mickleton from the FBI. He wasn't happy to be present. After all, the FBI dealt with terrorism and any attacks on US soil was the Bureau's responsibility. Except it had been taken out of their hands this time. 'Hell, it could be any crank. Orange is the Protestant colour, isn't it? I mean, if they were SAS, why leave the evidence behind? And why drop the gun in the car?'

'What type of gun was it?' Duggan asked.

'A Glock 19,' replied Mickleton. 'Don't you read reports before coming to meetings?' The fact that the CIA had two men there added to his discomfort. After all, this was an internal affair, on American soil, nothing to do with the spook team from Langley.

'That's the standard SAS hand-gun. And I didn't get a report. I was only asked to attend this—'

23

'Let's not start squabbling,' interjected the NSA.

'I thought the SAS used the Browning High-Power,' stated Mickleton.

'Used to,' replied Francis. 'Some still carry them. But the Glock's become their main hand-gun.'

'It's the sort of slick, military killing you'd expect from the SAS,' said Jim Lacelle, the State Department's representative. 'I think we should move this thing onto a regular footing. We're not going to find anything between the five of us. We need to set up a new counter-terrorist centre to deal solely with this problem.'

'That's the President's view.' The NSA took control again. 'To show we're doing something about it. Immediately.' He didn't need to add why the White House wanted to be seen reacting quickly. They all knew. The recent American visit by Sinn Féin President Gerry Adams had sparked a conflict between the President's men and the security services. Both the FBI and CIA knew that any acceptance of the IRA by the government, even in allowing short-stay visas, would be cynically used by Republican supporters as tacit support for the Provisionals. It made the American counter-terrorist operations more difficult as the Irish-American lobby pressured the President towards IRA support. The British government had always backed the Americans, especially during attacks on Libya and after the Lockerbie disaster. Any official recognition for the Provos would weaken that link; not something the security forces wanted as fundamentalists and other potential terrorist groups turned their attention on the USA. By reacting quickly, the American government would be seen to be holding a neutral line. The NSA turned to the man from the Justice Department. 'What's been released to the Press?'

'Nothing yet,' was the reply. 'Just that Flaherty, whilst awaiting a formal response from the Immigration Service as an illegal alien, was shot by persons unknown. The killing was professional and we're following all potential leads.'

'No mention of the gun?'

'No. Or the orange armband.'

'Any ideas?' The NSA turned to Mickleton. 'However crazy they are.'

Mickleton shook his head. 'Nothing concrete. Our counter-terrorist task force has been concentrating on the IRA's efforts to buy hi-tech arms. We've pulled our special agents off that and onto the surveillance of Irish-Americans and other groups that support the Provisionals. But I think we could be closing the stable door too late. We're also concentrating on those who support the Ulster Defence people.'

'Protestants?'

'Yes. But there's not too many of them. The more powerfully backed terrorist organizations, like the IRA, have other nation-states that are willing to supply funds. That doesn't apply to the Prods, as they're known. Most of their money and support comes from within Northern Ireland. They concentrate on bank robberies and extortion and even porno videos to keep them going. The IRA gets support from American nationals, Libya and probably Iraq. The head of the task force also tells me we should be examining the arms suppliers. He reckons the IRA might have reneged on a deal and somebody decided to teach them a lesson.' Mickleton paused, took a deep breath before continuing. 'It could even be the Mafia.'

'What?' exploded an alarmed NSA.

'Always a possibility.' Mickleton felt a pleasurable glow of smugness inside. He doubted it was the Mafia, but it sure as hell got the NSA jumping. *Why the hell didn't they leave this to the Bureau? It'll probably end up on my desk in the end.*

'Why?'

'You remember the Brinks Inc and Hudson Armoured

Car robberies? Thieves took around fifteen million dollars from two heists; one in Rochester, New York, and one in Brooklyn. We know it was IRA-inspired to help mount a fresh wave of terror attacks in Britain. We've been working with MI5 and the RUC Special Branch in Belfast. We've even had input from the Garda Síochána in Dublin. It was with their help that we got the indictments over here. If organized crime senses the IRA are muscling in on their territory, they'll hit any Irishman who has links with the IRA, however tenuous.' Mickleton suddenly realized his earlier prod at the NSA had some basis; this thing *could* extend to organized crime. He shifted uncomfortably in the chair but was saved from any further explanation when a secretary walked in and handed the NSA a note.

'OK,' the NSA told the secretary when he had finished reading it. 'No answer.' As the secretary left, the NSA turned back to the room. 'This was received twenty minutes ago by the *Washington Post* news-room. The message was taken on the phone.' He read aloud from the note. '"The execution of the murderer Tim Flaherty was in accordance with the Rules of Engagement as laid down by the Irish Republican Army. In an attempt to fight fire with fire, as the only means now left open to resolve the question of Irish terrorism, Soldier Raphael, under orders of the Highest Command, carried out the execution of the criminal Tim Flaherty and his supporter Jed Geraghty. Should the acts of violence by the Republicans continue, then the Highest Command will have no alternative but to order quick and terrible retribution against those who are the enemies of a peaceful and just solution for the Irish situation."' He put down the paper.

'Who the hell is the Highest Command?' asked Justice of no-one in particular. 'And who the hell is Raphael?'

'That, gentlemen, is what we had better find out. And quick.' The NSA slid the paper across to Lacelle from

26

the State Department. 'Let's get copies of that. It must be time to activate a counter-terrorist centre. At the CIA in Langley.' He turned to Mickleton. 'No offence, Hank, but let's play this one by the book. The rule is that the CTC is based at Langley. We need some of your people there, but we'll run it along the established guidelines. That means the CTC reports to Jim Lacelle as its chairman. Operational centre will be Langley, but all reports to the committee to be in the SitRoom.' The Situation Room was below ground level in the West Wing of the White House, divided by a narrow street from the Old Executive Building.

'I think we should keep the interagency group small,' added Lacelle, now taking charge of the meeting. 'Low-key, but with availability to whatever resources we need. I'll handle any links with the Press myself.' He pulled a sheet of paper from his file and held it up so he could read from it, his eyeglasses balanced precariously on the end of his nose. 'You all know most of this stuff, but I want to go through it so that we all understand the rules we're going to play by.' He sniffed; he could sense a cold hovering somewhere in the deep recesses of his throat. 'The aim of the CTC is to concentrate, in one place, all the ingredients needed to create operations likely to have the greatest impact in countering terrorist attacks against American interests.'

Duggan stifled a yawn and the CIA Director of Operations looked warningly at him, then winked. It was typical of Lacelle to textbook this operation.

'Location, as I've said, will be at Langley,' continued Lacelle. 'Participants to include State, CIA, Treasury, FBI, Defence, military services including all special forces. And, on this one, I want the cream of the crop; the most prescient and best-informed analysts, the sharpest and most creative operations officers, the most imaginative communications and technical support people and the most effective paramilitary personnel.'

'Do we really need all this?' asked Mickleton. 'I mean, we're going to be so muscle-bound with experts that we won't be able to move fast enough.'

'That's the way we want it to be,' the NSA intervened. 'By your admission, the field could include the Mafia, the Ulster Protestants, the British government, drug barons . . . Hell, the only people not under suspicion are the FBI and CIA.' He snorted. 'Up to now, that is.'

'I agree with Hank,' said the CIA Director. 'Too many people will slow us down.'

Lacelle fought to keep control of his position. 'We have to be visible. The American public need to see we're on top of this.' He cleared his throat. The last thing he wanted was a coughing fit at this moment. 'I just want to add that the President expects this to be the highest priority. He wants some headway within a few days. He doesn't want to be seen hindering any solution to the present peace talks between the British and Irish governments. Let's face it, those guys are all working towards peace. It's the Provisionals who're holding back by continuing their activities. And refusing to hand over their weapons.'

'Somebody should've thought of that before they decided to invite Gerry Adams to New York,' Mickleton muttered to his CIA counterpart.

Lacelle heard him and swung round. 'Listen, the IRA always thought they could bomb their way to the peace table. In part, they succeeded. But if they don't come to the table soon, they'll lose all their support. We don't want to be seen backing any group that refuses to take part in a peace process. That's why the State Department agreed that Adams come over here.'

'We're playing to a hysterical media.'

'That's how it has to be,' confirmed the NSA, irritated. 'Dammit, we need answers. For all we know it could even be the IRA taking out one of their own men so that they can blame the British and bring an end to any peaceful solution. They'll do anything to win back the publicity war now that they've continued their violence while the British and Irish governments are trying to forge a peace.' He turned back to Lacelle. 'Go on, Jim.'

'I don't want too many secretaries.' Lacelle looked round the room, but none of them bothered telling him that there were few secretaries in any CTC operation, that everyone did their own reports because it was a joint operation with as little paperwork as possible. 'Security is of the highest importance. The CT room is to be split into two groups. Analysts on one side, operational support on the other. I want the telephone system restricted to within the CT Center, to certain offices within the CIA and to provide encrypted communication to other telephones enjoying compatible encryption capability anywhere in the United States Government and throughout the world.' He felt the cough coming and collected his papers to close the meeting.

Duggan knew Lacelle was reading straight from the CTC operations manual. It was a waste of time, but State always liked to cover its own tail. If the terrorists were to be frustrated, if they were to strike again, that is, which Duggan frankly doubted, then it would not be due to anyone in this room.

Elgin Place
Hammersmith
London W6

It was a sunny, sparkling sort of morning, crisp and chilly. Sam Richardson sat at the window and watched the old man in the street below. Military in stance, black-suited, with starched tie, bulled black shoes and carrying a bowler hat under his arm, he rolled along the pavement. It *was* a roll, rather than a walk, due mostly to the fact that his right leg was bowed inwards from the hip down to his ankle, almost as if a truck had run into him and dented him permanently. Sam thought of his dad; if he'd lived he would probably have ended up like the old man down there.

'Watching the girls go by, are we?' said Andrea from behind, as she brought his hot toast to the table.

'No,' replied Sam, his Mancunian accent heavy in spite of living in the South for more than twenty years. 'Just an old soldier.'

'He looks very smart,' she said, looking out of the window.

'Probably on his way to some old comrade's funeral.' Richardson wondered if any old comrades would be concerned about him when he died, wondered if any would care. That was the trouble with his life. He wasn't meant to exist. Even if the Government had now decreed that the Firm, as MI6 was known, was accountable to Parliament. Everyone knew that was only to satisfy the media.

Sam Richardson was thirty-five; a short man, wiry, with the sort of looks and wavy thick hair that fifties matinée idols made their fortunes from. His chiselled jaw and 'seen-it-all-before' eyes gave him the look of a professional hard man people took care not to anger. He had lived with Andrea for nearly five years; it was a relationship that suited them both. They loved each other, but both enjoyed their respective careers and had made a pact not to marry and have children. A trained nurse, Andrea was now an operating-theatre sister at one of London's biggest private hospitals.

'Remind you of your dad?' she asked.

'You don't miss much, do you?' He smiled, turning and putting his arm round her.

'Don't smudge my lipstick.' She giggled, brushing his lips softly with hers. 'I've got to get off to work.'

He watched as she slipped on her coat and picked

up her briefcase. She was beautiful and he knew he was lucky to have found her. She was the type of woman men automatically made passes at; they confused her honesty and friendliness with wantonness, her direct gaze with flirtation. She was essentially a one-man woman, and he never gave her cause to doubt her trust. Over the years she had become his best friend as well as his lover. 'Are you late tonight?'

'No.'

'Shall we eat out?'

'Let's stay in. I'll get something on the way home.' She put a packet of Benson and Hedges on the table. He pulled a similar packet from his pocket and handed it over to her. She opened it. The packet was empty. She put it in her handbag.

Richardson opened the packet she had put in front of him and counted. There were ten cigarettes. 'Used to be easier in the days when you could buy ten Woodbines,' he said.

'You've done well. From forty a day down to ten.'

'Bloody patch,' he swore and pulled his shirt-sleeve up. It was stuck on his upper arm.

'You don't have to smoke all ten,' she said. 'Try harder. Nine or even eight a day would be a start.'

'Easy for you, oh ye who have never smoked.' He deliberately ignored her suggestion, knowing she was right.

She went out into the hall. 'I love you,' she shouted as she opened the door.

'Love you, too,' he returned, then heard the front door close.

He turned back and saw the old man in the black suit roll round the corner and out of sight. Would that be him one day, or would he go the way of his father, a violent, bloody death where no-one cared? His old man had been killed in Oman in January 1959, in the Jebel Akhdar campaign. A member of the so-called

31

British Army Training Team, his father was, in truth, a member of 22 SAS, part of a small unit that had fought off more than three hundred rebels. On his way back to Mirbat in the south he was shot by a sniper. He was dead before he hit the ground. His wife, pregnant with Sam, had been as stoic as could be expected of an army wife. The Richardsons came from a long line of professional soldiers, all NCOs, who saw death as part of the everyday business of living. Sam, as he grew up, always knew he would follow in the family tradition.

The Manchester lad joined the Cheshires, then the Paras. In time, because of his family history with the regiment, as well as his ability, he joined the SAS and served in the Gulf War and Northern Ireland. He worked undercover, was enlisted in the intelligence unit, the 14 Int, and served with honour after a rigorous and intensive training in mobile and static surveillance techniques. But, for all his experience, Richardson remained a creature of habit and true to his roots. He always voted for the Labour Party, even when the 'Loopy Left', as he called them, controlled the politics. He supported Margaret Thatcher, but couldn't make himself put an X next to his local Conservative candidate's name. Someone once asked him why he bothered voting if he disagreed so vehemently with the Labour Party's schedule. 'Because there's no point in having a vote and not using it,' he had replied. To Richardson, voting was a duty that was demanded in a democracy. The same democracy his father had died for, that he now put his life on the line for. And Sam Richardson was definitely a man of duty. He never discussed politics, didn't feel he needed to because of his commitment to his roots. It made being a professional soldier easier; his duty was to his country and what it had been, rather than to personalities and what they promised.

On one of his leaves in London he met Andrea and moved in before he reported back to duty seven days later. It was an instinctive and immediate attraction for both of them. They met at a dinner party thrown by a colleague of his; she was escorted by an investment banker who thought he knew all the answers. The banker was so infatuated with himself, he never realized his companion was interested elsewhere. He escorted Andrea home, and was surprised not to be asked in for a nightcap. Richardson watched him drive off, then went and rang the bell of her flat. She had slipped him her address at the dinner party.

They knew they were right for each other from that moment. Their love-making had not been explosive, but certain and somehow inevitable. Their relationship was sure-footed and they demanded little from each other, yet felt as if they were one. He moved his few belongings in before he returned to Ulster for his next tour.

She realized what he did, but never pressured him to give up his duty. Two years earlier, when MI6's role was being questioned after the collapse of the Soviet Empire, the Specialist Intelligence Service expanded its counter-terrorist role. Richardson was quick to apply when he found they needed experts who had field experience. He was seconded to the SIS and became part of the Joint Liaison team that handled the Belfast situation; it was a mixture of MI5, MI6, the Ulster Constabulary, the Army, the Northern Ireland Office and the Foreign Office. Classified CT/(I), Counter-terrorist/Ireland, he fell on his new role with relish. As an analyst with undercover field experience, Richardson was a valuable member of the Joint Liaison team. It also meant he could live in London, now that he was a desk-wallah, and spend more time with Andrea.

He was on to his third slice of toast when the phone rang.

'Hello,' he answered, wiping the butter that had run down his chin.

33

'Have you any appointments today?' came the clipped tones of Richard Carter, his Section Head.

'No.'

'What're you working on?'

'Operation Beaver.' Richardson referred to an arms shipment that according to intelligence had been stored by the South Armagh Provisionals.

'I'll get that passed on to someone else. In the meantime go along to the library and read whatever you can about the Irish incident in New York ten days ago. I don't want anyone else in the Firm to know what you're up to. Then I'll meet you at the Club. At twelve. For a bite of early lunch. I'll be paying. By the way, any ideas on the bombings last night?'

'Bombings?'

'Three fire-bombs, all at Victoria Station. Timed to go off when the night-club crowd were on their way home. Nobody killed, a couple of minor injuries. The PIRA have claimed responsibility. No serious damage, thank God. Anyway, catch you later.'

Richardson put the phone down and groaned; Carter wouldn't be pleased that he wasn't in touch with the news by now. It had been a lazy sort of morning; he and Andrea had woken up and made love and not worried about the rest of the day too much until they had satisfied each other and she had rushed off so as not to be late. The *Daily Telegraph* and *Daily Mirror* had lain unopened by the side of the bed; they hadn't even bothered to put on the radio.

The meeting with Carter sounded like an emergency. For all his training, Sam hated emergencies, liked things in their natural order. The Irish incident Carter referred to was obviously Tim Flaherty's assassination. The newspapers had been big on coverage but short on facts. Flaherty was shot outside a New York restaurant after he had escaped extradition to Britain. The hit had been professionally planned and the Yanks had no idea

34

as to who had executed it. Most of the people in the security services were secretly pleased; someone else had wiped out one of their problems. A rumour had spread like wildfire that one of the British security forces had been responsible for the assassination, but it was soon discounted. The British were unlikely to antagonize the Americans on their own turf.

He suddenly felt the shiver of apprehension in his spine, just like it used to be whenever he went into a dangerous operation. If there was a red alert on, that meant the Yanks had run dry on their leads. They could be asking for help. And if Carter didn't want anyone else at the office to know he was involved, that could only mean some form of covert action being planned.

Dammit, don't stick me back in Belfast. Not after all this time . . . I can't face that again . . .

He switched his mind off the fear that had suddenly flared in him, finished his breakfast, smoked his first cigarette of the day which tasted bitter, and went to the library.

On the way he thought about his father and wondered whether the man he had never known, except through his mother's words, had ever felt fear.

O'Connell Street
Dublin
Eire

Penuel waited in the lobby of the Gresham Hotel until 11 a.m. before picking up the public phone, inserting a pile of coins and dialling the Miami Beach number.

'This is Penuel,' he said when the phone was answered. 'I've decided on Bewley's Café.'

'Why?' asked the English voice at the other end.

'Easiest place to leave the shipment. A lot of people constantly moving in and out of the shop. And it's got a number of floors, so I'll reconnoitre it completely before making the delivery.'

'When will you make the delivery?'

'About three-thirty. It's at its quietest then, after the lunch-time rush.'

'We don't want any innocent casualties.'

'I know. I'll trigger it when it looks clear.'

'Good. Well, we warned them after Flaherty. They shouldn't have scorched Victoria Station last night. At least we'll show them we respond immediately. Remember, if caught, you're on your own.'

'Not forgotten.'

'Best of luck, Penuel.'

Penuel hung up the receiver and left the Gresham, crossed O'Connell Street and went back to his hotel a quarter of a mile away. He'd picked a busy, modern hotel where he could be lost in the crowd. The trouble with small hotels was that you were easily remembered.

And that was the last thing Penuel wanted.

**Somewhere in Knightsbridge
London**

Sam Richardson rang the buzzer on the solid front door.

'Can I help you?' came the usual polite query over the small speaker-phone by the side of the push-button.

He looked up at the TV security camera that was above the door so that he could be identified. 'Sam Richardson.'

There was a buzzing sound and the electric click of a lock being opened. Richardson pushed against the door and it swung open; he let himself into the hallway and heard the door swing shut behind him.

'Hello, Mr Richardson,' a girl shouted from the small office on the right.

36

'Hello, Claire,' he replied as he took his overcoat off and hung it on the open rack of coat-hangers on the left. He wore his usual outfit; a double-breasted blazer with double vents at the back, a Cheshire regiment's badge displayed proudly on the breast pocket and a 22 SAS tie, dark blue with the small azure, winged daggers. His trousers were cavalry twill, with turn-ups crowning deep brown brogue shoes, burnished with a lustre after years of careful polishing. His alternative outfit was a Cheshire regimental tie with grey flannel trousers and equally highly polished black brogues. On Saturdays, when he went supermarket shopping with Andrea, he changed into mufti, always a sports coat, sometimes with dark blue jeans. He never allowed himself in public with an open collar or without his brogues. It was the way Richardson liked it. A uniform gave you a sense of belonging, a sense of knowing your place.

'Has Mr Carter arrived?' he shouted to the unseen girl.

'Five minutes ago. He's up in the bar,' came the chirpy reply. No outsider who ever visited the Club noticed the ex-service doorman who monitored the entrance at all times. This was not a place for ordinary members of the public and was as secure as a bank vault.

Richardson climbed the stairs, the walls lined with pictures of military heroes, many who had given their lives in the service of the Allied cause behind enemy lines during the Second World War. The place always impressed him.

The Special Forces Club had been formed for the original wartime Special Operations Executive, the group that paved the way for the SAS and other specialist military and intelligence groups. Most of the members were retired, although the place was occasionally filled with younger, active members who found themselves in London. Richardson remembered once sitting next to two elderly ladies with their Harrods shopping bags who had both seen service with the SOE in France.

One of them had been captured and tortured by the Gestapo. He had eavesdropped on them only to find their discussion was of grandchildren and birthday presents and speculation about their pensions.

Carter, a Martini in hand, was standing under the big picture of the Queen Mother when Richardson walked into the bar. To Richardson, Carter was the most unlikely looking spy chief. He wore a loud check waistcoat stretched tight over his ample belly. The waistcoat was covered by a cavalry twill jacket which didn't match the dark green corduroy trousers and brown brogues. A big, round chap, weighing nearly twenty stone and standing 6'3", Carter was known for his lack of dress sense yet, for all his appearance as a jolly pub landlord, he had one of the sharpest operational minds in SIS. Richardson always felt dwarfed in Carter's presence.

'Do you mind if we go straight in to eat?'

'Of course not.' The small dining-room adjacent to the bar was the most private room in the club. Sam followed Carter into the restaurant and sat down at a small table by the window that had a RESERVED sign on it. The only other diners were an elderly couple at a table across the room.

'Our friends over the water have got themselves into a bit of a fix,' Carter said after they had given the waiter their order. 'Funny lot, really. I mean, they're all walking around shooting at each other in the streets with guns they can buy in any shop, yet they panic as soon as they think the terrorists are moving in.'

'Is that what they think?'

'I don't know. All I know is that they're worried this thing could escalate. You've read about the immigration lines and everything being searched at American airports.'

Sam nodded. All the flights going into American cities were subject to delays as the customs and immigration officers over-zealously searched all baggage. It was causing chaos to an overcrowded system, not helped by shortened tempers and children crying as they waited with their parents in line. 'It was the same after the Lockerbie Pan-Am disaster,' he said. 'We take it for granted over here, what with Belfast and all the terrorist groups in Europe.'

'You see from the papers that no-one has any idea why Flaherty was taken out.'

'Bit of luck for us, I thought.'

Carter grinned. 'Not officially, of course. Still, it was a naughty thing to do. Just go in and hit a terrorist who's been freed by an American court.'

'They must have some theories on what's going on.'

'Plenty of theories. Absolutely nothing concrete.' Carter shook his head and clucked. 'They're even putting Mad Dog McGlinchey down to this lot.' Dominic 'Mad Dog' McGlinchey, the ex-commander of the Irish National Liberation Army, was one of the most notorious Republican paramilitary figures and earned his nickname after going on a barbarous killing spree in the 1980s. Having boasted that he personally was responsible for more than thirty deaths, he was finally gunned down in front of his son in February 1994. No organization had claimed responsibility for his death.

'He was slotted with a 9mm,' said a thoughtful Richardson. 'As was Flaherty.'

'That similarity has already been noted. Anyway, what concerns us is that the Americans think our people could have been involved.'

'Are we?'

'Of course not. The Prime Minister wants us to convince the Yanks that we're not. We're an obvious suspect. Especially after the recent Heathrow bombings.' Carter referred to the attacks in March 1994 when the IRA managed to shell the airport's runways and terminals with mortar bombs, none of which exploded. The IRA had said this was deliberate, although the explosives men who checked the devices were convinced the bombs had been badly constructed. 'I needn't tell you that the public is clamouring for a stronger retaliation from the authorities.'

'That doesn't give the Yanks the right to think we are involved.'

'Unfortunately everything so far points over here. First of all, the killer wore an orange armband, which was then found in an alleyway by the police. Second, a Glock 19 was used. Which, as you know, is the Force's favourite at the moment. And, lastly, the gun was traced to having been bought by a man with a Northern Irish accent.' Carter pushed a carrier-bag under the table to Richardson. 'All the papers we have on the subject, all the correspondence with their CTC in Langley is in this. Keep it safe at home. I don't want anyone else to know you're involved.'

'Why not?'

'It's how our friends want it. They're worried that if someone in British intelligence is involved, we wouldn't tip them off.'

'The Americans can't really believe we'd take out an IRA man on their turf, surely?'

'In the absence of all other evidence, they see it as a strong possibility. In their suspicious little minds.'

'It sounds like a set-up by the Provos to me.'

'Explain.'

'Leaving evidence around, the armband and the gun. Also making sure the gun was traced. Too easily by the sounds of it. It's what you'd expect from the IRA, going out of their way to embarrass us.'

'And killing one of their own men?'

'Flaherty wasn't an important soldier to them. The extradition case was, but not Flaherty. He bungled quite a few jobs in his time. Small beer in the scheme of things.' Richardson sat back as the waiter arrived and served their food, beef curry for Carter and steak

40

and kidney pudding for himself. He continued once the waiter had gone. 'Flaherty was expendable.'

'But still useful to them.'

'Immigration was going to throw him out. The IRA knew we'd catch up with him eventually.'

'Are we certain about that?'

'Yes. That information came from the Circle.'

Richardson accepted it as fact; the 'Circle' was a chain of contacts within the intelligence community who worked by mutual trust. Like Freemasons, within the Circle a favour asked was a favour given – with no questions asked. Someone in the CIA or FBI would have provided that little morsel.

'Are you convinced it was the Provos?' Carter asked.

'No. It could just as easily have been the Protestants. Dressing it up to look like it was us. Or just dressing it up to confuse everybody.'

'What about some third force? Independents?'

'Could be,' replied a thoughtful Richardson. 'Only I've not heard of anything. Have you?'

'No. There's nothing the SIS, MI5 or Army intelligence has picked up. We've even been through the SAS computer data record at Hereford. You know how difficult they can be. But this time they co-operated immediately. Nobody wants to be seen as being unhelpful while these talks are going on between our people and Dublin. Nothing, no link to Raphael, nothing on the Glock, nobody with excessive bad feelings towards Flaherty. It all points to some sort of independent group.'

'Where do I fit in?'

'You're one of our main analysts on Northern Ireland. You're a member of the Joint Liaison Committee. You've been on the ground in the province, and you know many of our soldiers over there. And probably quite a few Provos, and the UDA, by sight. You're the best man for the job.'

'There are others with more up-to-date knowledge,' countered Richardson.

'Not since the crash at Kintyre,' Carter referred to the recent disaster off the Scottish coast on the Mull of Kintyre when a giant RAF Chinook helicopter crashed in fog killing twenty-five of the most senior intelligence chiefs. All the victims, Northern Ireland terrorist experts, had been on their way to Fort George for a high-level conference aimed at resolving the Ulster problem in the wake of the recent Anglo-Irish peace talks. 'It's left us a bit light on the ground. Rapid promotion, in some cases, of people who aren't ready for the increased responsibility,'

'Where am I to be based?'

'London. You're to be seconded to help the Americans' Counter Terrorist Center. One of their people is coming over. They feel they need a man on the ground over here. You'll work with him, find out what you can. I mean, we're giving them all the official support we can. But we need someone closer to the ground. You've got good contacts from your field days. Use them to find out what's happening.'

Richardson felt a rush of relief and, to avoid Carter noticing, he bent over and started to eat. *No more Belfast. No more facing the awful monsters inside his head.* Carter hadn't even suggested he get his weapons skills sharpened. But then, Carter knew he was always at the range, that he prided himself on his fitness. 'When?' Sam asked eventually.

'As far as the office is concerned, you're on a special research project.'

'A bit sudden, to just switch operations.'

'It'll be all right. I'll deal with it myself. The other thing is that they're playing this thing as close to their chests as we are. The reason we're agreeing to this is because they obviously think we might be involved. So we're playing the white man.'

'Who'm I responsible to?'

'Let their man feel he's being listened to. But you're on your own. Unless you feel you're being compromised. Then call me.'

They ate in silence. Then Richardson asked, 'Who do you think's behind this?'

'I really have no idea. Too many permutations.'

Richardson believed Carter. 'And if I find it all leads straight back to one of our own security services?'

'Then sever the lead. By whatever means available. You're not out there just to help the Yanks, you're also there to protect us.'

'By whatever means available,' Richardson repeated.

'Yes,' said Carter as he lifted another spoon of beef curry to his mouth. 'Even if it's on American territory. When the Prime Minister says he doesn't want us compromised, he means just that. That's why we're treading on Five's territory.'

'I wondered about that.' Richardson knew how zealously MI5 protected their own turf, which included Northern Ireland.

Carter stuffed the curry into his mouth and grinned at Richardson. 'Good food, eh, Sam? The best in London.'

**Adams Morgan District
Washington, DC.**

Duggan had always liked the house, a three-bedroomed, white-boarded home he had chosen with Carmella when they first got married.

Situated in the fashionable leafy suburb of Adams Morgan, surrounded by diplomats and government movers-and-shakers, he expected to spend the rest of his life in the area. The birth of his two daughters, Samantha and Natalie, had made him believe that the American Dream was his, all for the taking. Good home, good neighbours, good job and good family. What else could a man ask for?

The bitterness rose in him as he recalled his dream. All shattered now by that bitch Carmella. He cursed her and his own misfortune as he climbed the steps to the house and rang the bell.

'What're you doing here?' Carmella asked angrily, surprised to see him as she opened the door.

'I want to see the girls.'

'I asked you not to come this weekend.' Her face was red; he'd forgotten how red it became when she lost her temper.

'I've got no choice. I'm going away tomorrow.'

'Where?'

'Out of the country.' He could tell she didn't believe him, that she was convinced he was lying just so that he could spoil her weekend. 'I can't tell you where,' he said, exasperated. 'But it's the truth.'

'Playing little games with your spy friends, I suppose.' She knew her mother had been right; she should've married a dentist or a lawyer. 'You can't see them.'

'Carmella, I *will* see them if I have to push past you and find them, new boyfriend or not.'

She'd seen him that determined before. 'OK, but I'll get them. You'll have to wait in the dining room. At least let them finish what they're doing before I send them through.'

He knew why she'd insisted he wait in the dining-room. The table was laid out for a special meal, the best cutlery and dinnerware he'd bought sitting and waiting for someone else. Carmella knew that would hurt him. He ignored the table with its folded napkins and went to the window.

The girls were there, playing a game of basketball with the new man, *God he looked ugly*, and his two children. He was shorter than Duggan, stockier. He was sweating in a T-shirt that stretched tightly across his paunch, and his thin legs and arms were matted with black hair. *It probably comes out of his nose and his fucking arse too. Serves her right to end up with a gorilla.* Natalie saw him at the window and waved. Duggan smiled and waved back. She went on playing, immersed in her game, not aware of the pain she caused him by not rushing into the house.

The trip to London had been totally unexpected. He'd been called into a special Counter Terrorist meeting in the Situation Room in the West Wing of the White House. This special room was equipped for visual displays and had stands to house maps and other gathered intelligence. This time there were no maps, there was no gathered information. The place was bare, apart from the men who sat disconsolately at the table.

The National Security Advisor had been present, as had the CIA Director of Operations, Mickleton from FBI and Lacelle, the State Department man heading the team. Duggan was surprised there were so few attending; the last two meetings had included Justice, Defence and the assistant Secretary of Defence for 'Low Intensity Conflict' troops which handled the Army Special Forces, Navy Seals and other highly trained attack units.

'We're not getting anywhere,' started the NSA. 'It's been ten days since Flaherty was hit. With all the analytical intelligence from CIA, FBI, diplomatic and overseas posts, as well as Army, Navy, Air, Marines . . ', he flicked a finger to emphasize each service as he spoke, '. . . State, Foreign and even the Treasury, we haven't got one fact to show for our efforts. Apart from an orange armband, a Glock and the contact from Raphael. That name, as well as the "Highest Command", has drawn a complete blank on all our computers and field investigations.' He paused and surveyed the room. 'There is one further lead. Before I reveal it, I want it understood that any further stages in this operation are strictly between those of us in this room.' He looked round at the others before continuing. 'I want our normal CTC operation to continue. Four days isn't that long and we've still got ground to cover. But, like I said before, it's also important that we're visible on this. OK. Hank,' he said to Mickleton, 'you can take it from here.'

'The call to the *Washington Post* was made from Kennedy Airport,' said Mickleton. 'The *Post* has a "who called" system, just like you've got at home. If somebody rings, the number they're calling from is flashed up on your handset. We traced the number. It's a call-phone, right next to the British Airways departure lounge. Now, you know that each major airline into Kennedy has its own terminal. So, it's unlikely the caller was flying some other airline. Unless he wanted us to think that he was flying to Europe.' Mickleton referred to a sheet of paper in front of him. 'The call was timed. We checked the flights out of there. There was a BA flight to London Heathrow thirty minutes later. The call was made just after the final announcement for late passengers for the flight. Our investigations with the staff show that one passenger was very late, in fact only minutes after the call to the *Washington Post* came through. We checked his name from their lists, then confirmed he'd been on the flight. Then, with the CIA's help, we contacted our embassy in London.

'This is where it gets sticky. As you know, officially, we have no CIA operatives in the UK. Now we all know that's not true, that we do have a skeleton operation over there, looking at politicians and any other sections who could be a potential threat to the USG. We also have an FBI man there, to help the Brits on drugs and stuff like that. He works as a legal attaché at the Embassy and also has an office in New Scotland Yard. Anyway, we checked the name through both our sources. Daniel Morrison. He's a captain in the British army. We found out he serves outside the UK. The concierge in his apartment block said he spent a lot of time outside the UK. He mentioned that Morrison sometimes spoke of visiting Northern Ireland. Grosvenor Square thinks he might be SAS, but we have no certain way of confirming that. They don't publicly advertise their SAS men.' He turned to the NSA. 'That's about it.'

'I'm not saying it's the case,' said the NSA, 'but we could be involving another government. I doubt the British security services are involved, but we can't take the chance. Who knows, some English Ollie North working in the background without the government aware of his tricks. Hell, the IRA have brought this on themselves. They screwed us when Gerry Adams came over here promising peace, then went back and dropped mortars on the runway at Heathrow Airport to show their good intent. In view of the sensitive nature of any such British covert action, we've decided to set up a secondary operation.' He turned to McNabb, the CIA Director. 'What've you come up with?'

'Hank and I spent some time on this, looked at all the variations,' said McNabb. 'We both feel we need a physical presence over there. But our operative can't go in alone, he'd stand out like a sore thumb. He wouldn't know where to start anyway. Any such exercise would also go against the spirit of co-operation we have with the British. So we've asked them for help. They've already pledged themselves to give us any support they can. We've said we'd like to send one of our analysts, not a field man who could make them suspicious, but a top analyst to liaise with them, to be an extension of our own CTC.'

Duggan realized why he had been asked to attend. He was being sent into the field. As he looked up he saw the others eyeing him; he was being asked – no, ordered – to be the sacrificial lamb. His brain suddenly pounded in dread, but his expression remained impassive.

'They've agreed to our request,' McNabb continued.

'Including the fact that we want the whole secondary operation to be undercover.'

'Do they know about Morrison?' asked Duggan, his usual inquisitiveness overriding his fear.

'No. Nor do we want them to. That's our link. If it is the British authorities who're responsible, I don't want them warned off.'

'It's up to you to find out about Morrison,' Mickleton said to Duggan. 'But don't trust anyone. The MI6 guy they're sticking you with . . . he could be a front. That's what we'd do if the situation was reversed.'

'Have you had any field training?' Lacelle asked.

'I've spent time at the range and also at the Farm.' Duggan referred to the CIA training and interrogation complex in Maryland.

'But no field experience?'

'No.'

'Don't you have any analysts with operational experience?' Lacelle asked McNabb.

'Yes. But no-one who understands Northern Ireland like Duggan. I'm happy with him going.'

'So am I,' added Mickleton. If there was going to be a screw-up he didn't want it landing back on the FBI's desk.

Lacelle shrugged. Sending inexperienced men into the war zone wasn't something a 'by-the-book' man like Lacelle understood. But he had made his point; he was covered if things went wrong. 'When?' he asked, turning to the NSA.

'As soon as possible,' replied the NSA.

'He'll need a day at the Farm to re-acquaint himself with some weapons drill.' McNabb smiled at the others; he was relieved his own staff were involved. After the recent Ames fiasco, when a high-ranking CIA official in charge of the ex-Soviet desk was detected as a Russian agent, the CIA looked for any opportunity to absolve itself of its past. 'I would think he can be on a flight tomorrow night.'

'OK. We'll leave the final details to you.' The NSA turned to Duggan. 'Remember, if things get out of hand, you don't take any unnecessary chances. You break cover, then you're on your own. No embarrassment to the Government. Find Morrison, get the answer, then get out. That's all we expect of you.'

'Unless . . .' added McNabb, '. . . you find yourself in a situation where you can get any additional intelligence which could help USG.'

'Use your own judgement on that.' The NSA picked up his papers and stood up. 'Just make sure you don't compromise us.'

As the NSA and McNabb walked away from the SitRoom, Duggan asked no-one in particular, 'How come I didn't get a chance to volunteer?'

'Daddy, what are you doing?' Natalie cut across his thoughts. He had sat down on one of the dining-room chairs and had been staring at the wall.

He stood up and turned round. 'Hello, baby.' He held out his arms. She ran to him and he hugged her, swung her off her feet. 'Where's Sam?' he asked eventually, putting her down.

'In the kitchen with David.' *So the gorilla had a name.* 'She's coming.'

They didn't know how easily they could hurt. 'With David?'

'Mummy's new husband.'

'Not yet.' He regretted his snap reaction. 'Do you like David?'

'He's nice. Not like you, but he's very nice. Spends a lot of time with us, Daddy.'

Samantha came into the room, followed by Carmella. Samantha was more distant; she had never trusted him after the marriage had disintegrated. She listened to her mother's complaints and believed that Duggan had deserted them. When Carmella's new beau came into the household, Samantha had taken to him quickly. She needed a father, and if Duggan wasn't there, she'd turn to the first available substitute.

'Hello, Sam,' said Duggan.

The small girl smiled back at him, her mother holding her hand and protecting her.

Duggan held out his hand to her, but she stayed where she was. 'Come on, baby.'

'I told you today was a bad day,' Carmella cut in.

'Tough. I wanted to see my children before I —'

'You're lying,' she screamed back at him. 'You just want to spoil my life.'

'Why should . . . ?'

Samantha drew back and started to sob.

'Don't shout at Daddy,' Natalie shouted at her mother.

'See the problems you've caused,' Carmella accused. 'You always do it. Always screw up everyone. You're a monster. Bastard, bastard.'

'I just want—' Duggan replied helplessly.

'What's going on in here?' boomed a man's voice over Carmella's shoulder as the hairy gorilla came through the door.

'Butt out,' warned Duggan.

'You arse-hole,' came the reply. David put his arm round Carmella's shoulders and turned her away, then beckoned to Natalie. 'Come on, let's get back to what we were doing, Natalie, Sam. Let's go.'

'I said butt—'

'I know your visitation rights, arse-hole. Cause problems and we'll dump you in front of a judge before you can blink.' He beckoned Natalie again. 'Come on, Natalie.'

She looked up at Duggan. 'Daddy?' she asked plaintively.

'Right in front of a judge, arse-hole. I promise you.'

Duggan pulled back. 'Go on, baby. Go with your mother. For now.'

The girl, suddenly confused and beaten, fled from the room, followed by her mother and sister.

'Get out,' David said. 'Before I change my mind.'

Duggan, in his shame, put his head down and pushed past, keeping his eyes averted in his moment of defeat. By the time he was in the street the tears were running down his cheek; he half ran, half walked away from what had been his home.

Emotions ransacked, he suddenly thought of McNabb and his crazy plan. He wasn't an operational man. The last place in the world he wanted to go was London.

**Grafton Street
Dublin**

As Penuel watched the girl walking towards Bewley's Café, the small sports-bag in her hand, he thought back to his meeting with the Irishman three weeks earlier.

Martyn Darcy had been nervous; he hadn't heard from Penuel for years and the sudden phone call arranging to meet him by the statue on O'Connell Street had startled him. The statue and fountain, a modern interpretation representing James Joyce's Anna Livia, had been donated to the city by an international Irish businessman and become known amongst Dubliners as 'the floozie in the Jacuzzi' due to its strange design. The shopping list that Penuel had given him, as they mixed with the office workers on their lunch-break, made him realize his fears were founded.

* A Frequency Scanner – brand Regency
* A CB transceiver – make Marconi
* An amplifier/decoder/firing circuit board

* A MemoPark keyring timer
* Two clear plastic boxes
* A length of fine black multi-strand wire
* Two 6V 996 lantern batteries
* Hot melt glue and glue gun
* Small soldering iron and solder
* A circuit tester
* Adhesive tape
* Plastic lunch-box
* Two three-inch oval nails
* A small length of plywood

'What're you using this for?' Darcy asked when he had scanned the list.

'That's my business.'

'Not here in Dublin, surely?'

Penuel laughed. 'Shouldn't worry you boys. London or Dublin, what's the difference?'

'You're crazy. The Provos will never—'

'Who's going to tell them?' Penuel cut harshly across Darcy. 'You? You're going to risk them finding out about you, that I handled you, that you were responsible for us knocking out six IRA operations and killing three of your operators. No, Martyn, I don't think so.'

'Have you got the putty?' Darcy asked, changing the subject.

'No. I don't need to put that on the list.'

'How much?'

'Five pounds. Semtex H.'

'That's a big explosion.'

'It is, Martyn. But don't worry. There'll be no innocent bystanders.'

'Anything else?'

'I need it within a few days.'

'That's pushing it. I mean, things've changed since you were last here. I mean, the radio kit control and transmitter, as well as the multimeter and circuit test bulb, are all supplied direct to us now. We don't individually store them, or make them, like we used to.' Darcy watched Penuel closely, but realized he wasn't getting any further. He pushed on, his voice now higher. 'I'll have to get those items out of the PIRA logistics system. Not easy, not at all. I mean, I'll have to raid a hide myself, then try and compromise it so that the Gardaí find it after I've taken out what I need. It's the only way the boyos will know nothing's been stolen.'

'However. But as soon as possible.'

'I'll see what I can do.' Darcy put the list into his coat pocket. 'It could take longer,' he warned again.

'I know you can get your hands on the stuff. Dammit, you'll have radio equipment and other specialized stuff down in Dublin from Belfast for repairs. I know how the system works, Martyn. I know you'll be able to get your hands on the stuff. You'll have it stashed all over the city, in one of your hideaways.'

'What about the detonator?'

'Got it.' Penuel had smuggled the Czech Z1 electric detonator through customs in the hollowed-out heel of his Reebok fashion trainers, too low for the security metal detectors to pick up. 'It's a Z1.'

'Not the best. You'd be better off with a Canadian CIL or American IRECO.'

'You offering one?' Penuel realized that Darcy had unwittingly let it slip that the PIRA had both types of detonators in their possession. That was something the authorities would have to know about.

'No,' said Darcy, trying to cover his mistake. 'Just stating the obvious.'

'The Z1 will be fine for our requirements.'

'Are you anything to do with Flaherty's death?'

'No,' lied Penuel.

Darcy watched him curiously. 'Are you sure? You can tell me.'

'I said not.' Penuel realized Darcy needed closer

control; the fear of being discovered as a supergrass wasn't enough. 'I'll need some companionship, some cover, while I'm in Dublin. And also someone who can contact you quickly and without suspicion.'

'Like who?'

'Sally. You still see her, don't you?' He could tell Darcy wasn't happy; Sally had been his girl for years, but for some reason they had never married. She was a plump-faced girl with thick black hair and long legs; sexy in a sort of obvious way. 'She can stay at the hotel with me. If anyone wants to know where she is, just say she's gone to see her relatives. I mean, I presume she still lives on the other side of town to you.' He knew she did; he had already checked in the phone book.

'She may not—' Darcy started to whine.

'I'll make it worth her while. And . . . I won't touch her, Martyn. She's not my type.' *Like hell, she wasn't.* He'd spent time with her before and used the information she'd given him to turn Darcy into a supergrass. That wasn't something Darcy knew.

'I'll talk to her. What's in it for me?'

'Money and silence.'

'What ID do you want on the bomb?'

Penuel knew that every bomb-maker had his own method, his own style. Experts could tell who made individual bombs; they were as distinct as fingerprints. 'Yours.'

'No chance.'

Penuel grinned. 'I'll assemble it. It'll be a Provo ID.'

'What're you lot up to? Vicious crowd, you SAS.'

'Better you don't know. It'll keep you alive.'

'I need to get away before someone recognizes me.' He looked round nervously. 'Can't understand why you wanted to meet somewhere so public.'

'It suited me.' Penuel didn't add that he wanted to make sure Darcy hadn't brought along a colleague. After all this time away from the Irishman, he wanted to be sure he could still trust him. 'When you've got everything, I want it at my place to test. No funny business, because Sally will be standing next to me when I put it together.'

'You're a bastard.'

'It's what keeps me alive. I want to assemble it myself. Just make sure I get all the bits on the list. And I want all the serial data and batch numbers scratched off the components. Oh, I'll need some surgical gloves for assembly too. Don't want them to trace me too easily.'

Sally had come to the hotel two days later, smiling and coy and, as usual, ready for bed.

'You're a dirty bugger,' she said when he finally spurted over her breasts. 'Why don't you like coming inside me?'

'That's Darcy's space,' he lied. He liked degrading them, dismissing them with his spent effort; it made him feel in charge.

Three days later Sally went to see Darcy and returned with the components, packed in amongst goods in two large Brown Thomas shopping carriers.

Penuel took his time unpacking them, keeping Sally next to him. He didn't think Darcy would double-cross him, but he still wasn't prepared to take chances. All the materials were there, just as he had directed.

'Did Darcy say anything?' he asked her as he examined the Semtex wearing his surgical gloves.

'Wanted to know if I fucked you.'

'And . . . ?'

'What do you think? I told him you had a bigger cock than him.'

He chortled. 'Anything else?'

'No.'

'Did he fuck you?'

'No,' she lied.

'You're lying.'

'He wanted to.'

Penuel looked at her and she blushed. He always knew when she lied, through all those years when he handled Darcy and spent his spare nights with her. 'Go and scrub yourself out, you dirty cow,' he said.

She turned quickly and went to the bathroom. She was excited now; knew he would rough her up. It was how she enjoyed it: no beatings, no marks left on her, just sexual violence that made her feel wanted. She loved it when men lost control.

Penuel assembled and tested the bomb; it worked as he had expected it to. He was an expert in his work and he gave it the ID he had been instructed to. The insulation tape was blue and he held a section, about twelve inches long, then bit it before tearing the strip off with his hands. He laid the torn segment on the bed, then carefully rolled the remaining tape back onto the spool and slipped it into an envelope which he put in his pocket. He used the tape on the bed to bind the transmitter.

When he finished, and while he waited for his next order, he spent his time between Sally's thighs or in the exercise room in the hotel. He also took long walks with Sally in the countryside far away from Dublin. The bomb was always near him, though, buried in a sports-bag under his training gear.

He heard on the radio about the three fire-bombs in Victoria Station. That was when he rang Miami Beach to get clearance to continue.

Sally sensed then he was near the climax of the operation. That night his sexual excitement was at its peak; it was the most exhilarating experience she had ever known. There was a desperation to their love-making, increasing in intensity, increasing in his degradation of her as the night went on. He would nap between sessions, his hand always holding on to the sports holdall that was on the floor beside the bed as he slept. Then he would wake and fall on her again, forcing himself into all her openings, frantic in his efforts to satisfy himself and cleanse himself. And she took it all, loving his extremes, holding him as he slept and believing as the night wore on that she loved him and that he needed her.

At ten that morning, Penuel rang reception and asked them to send up some Panadol, said he had a most terrible headache. He instructed the cleaner not to clean the room as he would spend all day there because of his illness. He and Sally stayed in the room until one, when he suddenly announced he was going out and would return in an hour. He left the DO NOT DISTURB sign on the door and took the sports-bag with him. He made sure he left by the rear entrance, had already worked out his exit from the hotel when he didn't want to be seen.

'Where've you been?' Sally asked when he returned two hours later.

'Working.' He smiled at her. She was sprawled on the bed wrapped in an hotel towel. She flipped it off and opened her legs. It had no effect; his mind was on his work, the professional had taken over. 'Later,' he said, the smile still on his face. 'Get dressed. We're going shopping in O'Connell Street.'

She got up, excited. They'd been shopping before and Penuel had spent considerable money on her. He watched her dress, waited patiently, the warmth still in his smile.

They left through the back door twenty minutes later. She was laughing and girlish; he was warm, looking after her, holding her arm.

They walked down O'Connell Street, across the river and on into pedestrianized Grafton Street. The streets were half empty now that the office workers had returned to work. When they were nearing Bewley's he slowed down and checked the area. No-one had followed them, there were no Gardaí present. She sensed something was wrong.

'I want you to deposit the sports-bag over there.' Penuel pointed to Bewley's.

'I thought we were shopp—' Sally stopped suddenly. In her eagerness to go shopping she'd forgotten how excited he'd been last night, how she suspected he was about to trigger his plan of action. 'Why me?' she asked, suddenly frightened.

'That's how Darcy and I agreed it.'

'He never said.'

'Where do you think I was earlier?' He took a wallet out of his pocket and held it up for her. She recognized Darcy's wallet. 'He gave me this so that you'd know we were working together. When this is over we go back to Darcy, give him his wallet, and his girl, and I leave Dublin.'

'I'd forgotten how good it was with you.'

'You were always Darcy's. I don't even belong in this country. However strongly I feel for you.'

'You do care, don't you?' she asked, wanting to believe him.

'Of course. What do you think last night was about?'

She moved towards him and he held her off, then slipped the bag into her hands. 'Do it now. Next to the lift.'

'It'll kill people. I know what you and Darcy do, but I never saw anyone killed before.'

'The place is empty. Even the basement is closed off today. Just put it down and walk out. Walk away from me, down towards the opposite corner. When you're clear, Darcy'll let it off.'

'Darcy?'

'You don't think I'd risk standing here with a radio in my hand. Darcy's around somewhere, he can see us. He'll trigger it.'

She nodded, safe in the knowledge that her man would never hurt her. 'Where do I go?'

'I'll see you back at the hotel.' Abruptly he turned

and walked away, then stopped and looked in Marks & Spencer's window as any tourist would. Out of the corner of his eye he saw her cross the road towards Bewley's.

Now he swung round to follow her. Sally went through the open archway, past the bread and cakes counters to the lift. There weren't many people about; some customers left over from the lunch rush-hour were sitting in the main central area, and the staff were enjoying a break before the next burst of customers round tea-time. She bent down and placed the sports-bag under a table near the lift.

As she stood up she saw Penuel across the road.

She didn't understand; he'd said he would meet her back at the hotel.

Then she saw the radio transmitter in his hand.

There was no apology in his eyes.

She started to run towards the entrance.

He pressed the transmitter button. The radio signal's audio tone encoded the integrated circuit which triggered the detonator and exploded the Semtex H packed with nails inside the plastic lunch-box.

Sally opened her mouth to scream but the sound of the explosion overtook her. One of the nails that had been packed inside the device hurtled into the back of her neck, sliced through her brain and killed her before the explosion ripped her body apart.

Penuel raced away from the explosion as the glass from the café's windows blew out across the road. He wasn't conspicuous as he ran, one of a number of screaming pedestrians fleeing the bomb blast. He threw the transmitter into a refuse-bin as he passed.

Inside Bewley's, the explosion carried upwards, consuming the lift and throwing flames up the stairway. Part of the roof was now a blazing inferno. Customers, some with minor injuries, escaped out of the front and side entrances, while people on the higher floors at the front of the building jumped through the blown-out windows. Apart from Sally, no-one was killed.

When he reached the hotel, Penuel had a shower and went back to bed. Two hours later he cleared up the room to his own high standards. He wiped away all fingerprints, put Sally's clothes and accessories into a smaller second suitcase, then cleaned away the remains of bomb construction; wire off-cuts, tapes, packages, glue, solder and anything that the Semtex had come into contact with. He worked for nearly seven hours before he was satisfied. Then he went out for a walk and dropped the left-overs of his handiwork into the River Liffey. He would have preferred to incinerate them in a furnace, but could not find one where he would have easy access. He finally went to bed after midnight; it was only then that he thought about Sally. He was sorry he had killed her, but it was no more than she deserved in the end. He knew she had often carried explosives for Darcy and had been indirectly responsible for the injury and death of many bomb victims. She, like so many other people in Ireland, was herself a victim, of circumstance, of living in the wrong place at the wrong time. Then he switched his mind off, in that detached way he had, and went to sleep.

The next morning Penuel booked out of the hotel and caught the Aer Lingus flight to Paris. Just before the flight was called, he went to a phone box and called the *Irish Independent*. When he was put through to the news-room he spoke from the prepared statement he had committed to memory. 'The device that was exploded yesterday afternoon at Bewley's Café was in retaliation for the fire-bombs detonated at Victoria Station by the IRA. This was in accordance with the Rules of Engagement as laid down by the Provisionals. Once again, in an attempt to fight fire with fire, Soldier Penuel, under the orders of the Highest Command, carried out the bombing in Grafton Street. Should the acts of violence by the Republicans continue, then the Highest Command will have no alternative but to order quick and terrible retribution against those who are the enemies to a peaceful and just solution for the Irish situation.'

Then Penuel put down the phone, picked up his hand-luggage and started to walk towards the gate. He suddenly remembered Darcy's words and went back to the phone. He dialled another number and waited for the phone to be answered.

'Don't hang up. This is an anonymous call. The enemy have a large selection of IRECO and CIL detonators in Dublin. They also have three explosives caches at the following addresses.' He calmly gave out three addresses, then put down the phone. The call took fourteen seconds, not long enough to be traced; he knew all calls to that number were traced within sixteen seconds. The information he had calmly given them had been extracted out of Darcy in a far more painful manner. That hadn't concerned Penuel too much. He knew Darcy had reverted back to the PIRA now that he felt safe from his past indiscretions; safe until Penuel arrived back on the scene. He walked through to board his plane. The two suitcases, containing his clothes and those of the bomb-carrier, Sally, were already packed and waiting in the hold of the big jet.

He flew to Paris, changed planes and then went in to Schipol Airport in Amsterdam. An hour later, he caught the evening flight to New York. He felt an ironic satisfaction as the Boeing 747 lifted off the runway; the 'Amsterdam Connection' was the preferred route for the IRA to enter Canada or the USA without attracting too much attention from the security forces on either side of the Atlantic.

That night, as Penuel enjoyed his meal in clear skies over the Atlantic, the Dublin Gardaí discovered Darcy's body under a pile of rubble on a building site, a deep knife wound in the base of the neck. They also found severe bruises on his body. His lips had been cut away from his mouth, then gruesomely placed over his penis.

'Bye, cocksucker,' Penuel said as he left the body. His orders had been to confuse the police, and he'd certainly done that. When detectives searched Darcy's clothing they found his wallet and cash missing. They presumed he had been robbed before being murdered. It was only after they had entered his fingerprints into the computer that they learned he was an active member of the PIRA bombing squads. They also found a roll of blue plastic insulation tape in his pocket. It was soon matched with some tape found wrapped round the transmitter which Penuel had dropped into a refuse-bin in Grafton Street. A technician matched the tear-point of the roll and the segment found on the transmitter. There was no doubt it was the same tape.

By then, Penuel had landed in New York and transferred to his next destination.

Heathrow Airport
London

It had been an uncomfortable journey for Duggan, trapped in Club Class between a cowboy-booted, Walkman-plugged rocker on one side and a shifting, excited schoolboy returning from holiday on the other. The Boeing 747 had bumped across 3,500 miles of turbulent sky before thudding down on Heathrow's Runway 27 on an equally bumpy landing.

Flying had never worried Duggan; he simply settled down, ignored his close-quarter neighbours, ate his not-quite-first-class food and watched the movie. His mind raced furiously, a farrago of confused emotions and crisp logic. He tried to concentrate on the task he faced in London, on Daniel Morrison and his role in the affair, but the shame he had felt in Adams Morgan kept surfacing and reminding him of his own feebleness. Duggan stayed awake for the whole flight and arrived as red-eyed as the RedEye Special, as the overnight transatlantic flight was popularly known.

The newspaper headlines on the news-stand was the first he heard of the Dublin bomb explosion, although he didn't connect it with his own assignment at that stage.

Richardson picked him up as he came through the customs hall; the CIA had already faxed him a picture of Duggan.

'Hi, Francis,' he called, appearing as though they were old friends. As Duggan came through the barrier, Richardson, with a big smile across his face, leant forward to take the American's suitcase. 'Let me take that. You must be shattered.'

'Hi, there.' He was already annoyed with Richardson. The British hadn't told him who would be meeting him and he was at a distinct disadvantage. But he smiled back, joining in the charade.

'We're in the car-park,' continued Richardson, leading the way. 'Good flight?'

'Fine.'

'Great. How're Carmella and the kids?'

How the hell did . . . ? 'They're great,' he replied. *Who the hell had briefed this guy?* He watched the smaller, broad-shouldered, flat-bellied Englishman and could tell he was extremely fit. Soldier type. *All blazing guns and flash bang wallop.*

Richardson led Duggan to his car, a maroon 1955 Fastback Bentley Continental S1. It was the Englishman's pride and joy, bought cheaply fifteen years earlier and lovingly restored. He opened the small boot, squeezed Duggan's case into it, then unlocked the passenger door and slid across to the driver's seat, beckoning Duggan to climb in. 'Sorry about that, but these cars never did have a lock on the driver's door. Safety, I think. To stop people getting in from the road.'

As Duggan settled himself he cursed McNabb back in Washington. The Englishman was a clown, all hooray-henry and gin and tonics – even if his accent wasn't plummy like the rest of the Brits Duggan had met over the years. Shitshitshitshit! While he was stuck here that bastard gorilla would be at home worming his way into his kids' lives. 'Who're you?' he asked as he shut his door trying a touch too hard to slam the nightmare of Adams Morgan out of his mind.

'Careful with that door. She's an old girl.' Richardson stuck his hand out. He was going to be pleasant even if he didn't like the look of the Yank; all ex-sixties hippie with that shock of hair. 'Sam Richardson.'

Duggan shook the Englishman's hand. 'Who briefed you about me?'

'We got a fax-photo through and a short bio. Just age and kids' names, that sort of thing.'

'I'm divorced,' snapped back Duggan.

'You should tell your superiors. As far as the fax was concerned, they must think you're still married.'

'Where're we going?'

'My place. It's the best place for you to stay.'

Neither man was happy that they were to be billeted together; both felt it was an intrusion, but each was trained to follow orders. The journey was completed in silence, apart from two short exchanges.

'This car's a bit obvious, isn't it?' stated Duggan.

'Meaning?'

'If we go anywhere we're going to stand out like a sore thumb.'

Richardson decided to ignore the comment. As if he would use this car on a surveillance. He'd only brought it along because he thought the American would enjoy riding in an old car; it had been a way of breaking the ice with him.

'There was a bomb explosion in Dublin yesterday,' Richardson said as they drove towards Battersea.

'I saw the headlines. Who did it?'

'The Highest Command.'

'What?' said a surprised Duggan. 'Why didn't you tell me?'

'Thought we'd settle down to business when we got home.'

'Could you tell me now?' Duggan tried not to show his annoyance. He couldn't understand how the British worked; there always seemed to be a time and a place for everything. *Nine to bloody fivers*. He listened as Richardson took him through the bombing. One woman killed, considerable damage to the café, call had been identical to the one made to the *Washington Post*, except this was made by Soldier Penuel.

'Raphael and Penuel. What the hell kind of names are those?' asked Duggan when Richardson had finished.

'No idea. Code-names, but we can't link them to anything.'

Duggan didn't say anything else. This latest action made it an international problem; it wasn't just about the USA any longer. Maybe they'd call him back now that it was on a wider stage. Then he remembered Morrison and his reason for being there. It was because they didn't trust the British. He shut his eyes and tried to sleep for the rest of the journey.

The apartment was spacious, but without the natural sprawl associated with large living areas. Everything, the furniture, the ornaments, the fittings were precise in their display, almost military in their formation. There were few pictures around, most of them of military people, many from an earlier period. They were mostly of ordinary soldiers and NCOs; Duggan realized Richardson came from a military family, but the tradition was of a blue-collar background. One of the photos was of

Richardson in sergeant's dress uniform. He didn't look a lot older now; the only difference was that his hair was cropped as short as Velcro in the photo. The adjoining picture was of an older man in an identical uniform; Duggan guessed it was Richardson's father. The third picture of the trio was of a black woman, young and very beautiful.

'You can catch some sleep if you want,' suggested Richardson as he showed Duggan into the spare bedroom.

'No. Just need a shower to freshen up. Then I'd like to get on with the investigation.'

'We don't have a shower,' Richardson said apologetically. 'Bath. After the Army and all those cold showers I decided there was nothing like luxuriating in a foamy bath.'

He left Duggan to unpack and went into the kitchen. 'Coffee?' he shouted.

'Yes, please,' came the reply.

'Decaffeinated?'

'Perfect.'

Richardson smiled and was smugly delighted that he had picked up a jar of unleaded coffee. He knew Duggan would be a decaffeinated man. That's the type he was, a desk analyst who found himself in the front line. Then he realized he was nothing more than a baby-sitter. That's all Carter had wanted. A bloody baby-sitter. He decided then that he would follow this thing all the way. The assignment was what he made it. And maybe it did lead somewhere in this crazy maze of retaliations.

The phone rang and it was Carter. 'Two bits of info from the Box.' The Box was the nickname for MI5, or Post Office Box Number 500, which used to be the official address of the security service. 'The girl who died in Dublin. Darcy's girlfriend – Sally Dillon.

We can presume she was the carrier. According to the forensic chaps in Dublin, who asked for help from our Northern Irish chaps, the device had the hallmarks of a Provo device.'

'Doesn't make sense.'

'I agree. Especially as the fingerprints on the debris, and its ID, led the investigators straight back to Darcy. They say it had all his personal hallmarks on it. Including some tape which matched a roll found in his pocket.'

'Very convenient.'

'That crossed my mind.'

'Was it radio-controlled?'

'Yes.'

'He was an experienced man. I can't see him making such an unstable device.'

'It didn't matter. According to the pathologist, Darcy had already been killed before the thing exploded. He wasn't the triggerman.'

'What do I tell our visitor?'

'Just that. Keep him busy. I'll contact his people.'

Duggan came into the kitchen half an hour later, his hair still wet, his cheeks shiny after the hot bath. He pulled up a stool at the counter. 'Thanks,' he said, gulping down his coffee. 'I needed that. So, where do we start?'

'You tell me. This is your operation.'

'Have your people come up with anything yet?'

'No. Not a sniff.' Richardson then told Duggan about Carter's phone call.

'What's your instinct?'

'I don't have one. Yet. Now that this thing's gone beyond the boundaries of the US, it's a new game.'

'Will your people notify Washington about this latest development?'

'They're passing it on. I would think they'll also be involving Trevi.' Trevi was the Economic Community's joint structure on international terrorism and violence. Richardson paused; they were both getting nowhere, too polite. 'I suppose some of your people think it's the British security forces.'

Duggan didn't respond immediately, just sipped from his cup. 'We'd be stupid not to,' he answered eventually.

'If it is, I don't know about it.'

'You mean it could be?'

'I doubt it, but I can't guarantee it. Just as you know it could be your lot.'

'Why?' Duggan was genuinely surprised; the possibility had never entered his mind.

'That judge slipped up, letting Flaherty go. Your own security services wanted him brought back here; they don't want America seen as a safe haven for terrorists.' Richardson laughed. 'Give me your poor, give me your needy, give me your terrorists. No, any of your security organizations could have eliminated Flaherty. To stop anyone else having the same idea.'

'And then we bombed Dublin as well,' came the cynical answer.

'No. But it made you think. This thing runs very deep. And we could both find ourselves in the middle of—'

'A squeeze play.'

'Yeah. Pips in a bloody orange.'

'What're you getting at?'

'That we pool our resources. Stop being quite so touchy with each other. Work on this thing together and make something of it.'

'I don't know you. I'm just here to do a job.'

'You mean you don't trust me. I don't trust you, either. But we are stuck together. We may as well make the most of it.'

There was the noise of the front door opening. 'I'm back,' Andrea shouted from the hall.

'In the kitchen,' Richardson shouted back, switching

the kettle back on to make another coffee.

'Hello,' said Andrea as she entered. 'You must be Francis Duggan.'

'Hello,' he replied, standing, recognizing the woman from the picture he had seen earlier.

They shook hands. 'I'm sorry I'm still in uniform,' she said, slightly embarrassed to be wearing her nurse's outfit. 'I've been on night shift.'

'No problem. Glad you can put me up.' Duggan looked across at Richardson as Andrea went over and kissed him. The blue-collar soldier suddenly went up in his estimation. He wasn't as hard-hatted as Duggan had thought, not if he was living with a black girl.

They left Andrea to sleep and Richardson, on discovering that Duggan had never been to London, only to Ireland, took him on a quick tour of the West End, this time in Andrea's smaller Vauxhall Astra. After the customary view of the Houses of Parliament, Buckingham Palace, the Thames and Admiralty Arch, followed by the MI5 Headquarters in Gower Street and the American Embassy, Richardson turned north up the Edgware Road towards Kilburn.

'This is the heart of the Anglo-Irish community,' he said as they drove down Kilburn High Road. It was, as usual, jammed with single-lane traffic, and he had plenty of time to point out the pubs and places which the IRA and the PIRA used. 'You see, if we wanted to, we could take out a crowd of them here. We wouldn't have to do it in America and risk ruining our relationship with you.'

Duggan didn't respond. 'I want to go to Dublin,' he said, changing the subject.

'OK. In the meantime, I've got a meeting with a grass later on. Do you want to come?'

'Grass?'

'Informer. One of my contacts.'

'Yes. What about?'

'He's one of my sources. He didn't have anything on Flaherty, but he might have heard something on the grapevine about the Dublin bomb.'

'When?'

'Tonight. After we've eaten. Then we'll arrange to get over to Dublin.'

Duggan didn't say any more. He still had no idea how to trace Morrison.

When they were near Richardson's flat, Duggan asked if Richardson would drop him off, he wanted to walk a little and get some fresh air. Richardson pulled up and gave Duggan instructions on how to find the flat. After he'd driven off Duggan set about finding a phone box. Within minutes he was through to the American Embassy.

He gave an extension number. 'Duggan,' he said when the phone was answered. 'Any news on Morrison?'

'Nothing yet,' replied one of the Embassy's legal attachés. 'We know he's not in Germany or any of the other European centres where we and the British have military personnel. Could be here or in Northern Ireland. We found his home number and kept trying it. There's no answer day or night. He doesn't even have an answerphone. We spoke to some neighbours; he lives in a big apartment block, but all anyone knows is that he's in the Army and that he's away from home quite a lot. Couldn't ask too much without sounding suspicious. You heard about Dublin?'

'Yeah.'

'How much?'

'I know about Darcy and the girl. And the involvement of their employers. I believe the device was meant to look like his handiwork.'

'You heard he died before the—'

'That's right. I've got the same story.'

'Any messages for home?'

70

'Yeah, tell them I'm going to Dublin, probably tomorrow. And that I'll be meeting one of their Irish moles over here.'

'OK.'

Duggan put down the receiver. He didn't see Richardson behind him, watching him from the street corner.

It was a simple meal, the sort families eat when they sit down together in the evening. Duggan appreciated that; the family environment and simplicity of human contact was something he had missed for a long time.

The discussion had been general; none of it concerned the reason that had drawn them together. They only touched on it when Richardson mentioned that many British people, and the media, although publicly disagreeing with the retaliation attacks, were nevertheless secretly pleased that something was finally being done and the battle was being taken to the IRA. Duggan didn't comment, nor did he mention that his roots were still firmly in Ireland; but he understood the reaction and why it made even Richardson quite 'gung-ho!' The Englishman spoke of his background and upbringing in Manchester; it was a life that Duggan couldn't comprehend. Where he had been brought up with dishwashers, baseball, hot dogs and constant television, Richardson had played in the walled backyards of the terraced houses in Salford, a world of outside toilets and 'a clip round the ear' from the local bobby when you did wrong. Duggan noticed how quiet Richardson's voice went when he spoke of his father's death, the man he had loved and never known. Duggan had been right; the third photograph was Richardson's father. Richardson spoke warmly of his days in the Army and his tour with the SAS. Duggan could tell he wasn't happy about being stuck at a desk in MI6, but also sensed that there was a secret fear in Richardson about his early days, something he did not want to discuss. The American didn't volunteer any information on his own career; there was little point. Unlike Richardson, Duggan had had little experience in the field; he was an analyst by nature and vocation, having earned his stripes because of his university degree in civil engineering and European politics rather than on any grounds of experience.

Andrea captivated him, not just by her beauty, but also with her sincerity and ability to join in most discussions. The picture on the mantelpiece hadn't done her justice. The daughter of a Somali diplomat, she had the high cheek-bones, almond eyes and delicate features that symbolized her race. When her parents left London, she stayed on as a schoolgirl, then went into modelling where she had some modest success. But the irregular life didn't suit her and, because she was still an alien without a work permit, she applied to join a nursing college for further education. She developed a vocation for her new career, applying for citizenship and a work permit as soon as she was qualified. As the meal wore on, Duggan realized that her delicate nature and apparent vulnerability excited him tremendously; it was a spiritual and loving feeling he had not had for another woman since the break-up of his marriage. He also saw there was a deep affection between her and Richardson; they acted like a married couple.

After the meal he insisted on helping her wash up.

'Ease up,' warned Richardson jokingly as Duggan carried the plates into the kitchen. 'Go on being a New Man and you'll make me look bad. I never do the washing-up.'

'You should help more than you do,' replied Duggan, immediately regretting his words. At least his host was making a go of his relationship, which was more than Duggan had achieved. He knew he sounded priggish and smiled weakly. New Man had met Mister Macho.

When they had finished, Richardson announced they had to leave for a meeting. Andrea, used to his erratic hours, said she was going to bed to catch up with her sleep; she started a new day shift the following morning.

It was nine forty-five when they drove off in the Bentley. Both men had mellowed considerably towards each other, but the warmth was on the surface; they both were more than aware that they had jobs to do which might put them in confrontation with each other.

Richardson parked the Bentley by the side of the Victoria Embankment, next to the *Tattersall Castle*, a former Humber ferry-boat that had become a well-known floating bar and restaurant.

'We're not eating again, are we?' asked Duggan, his belt already tight after Andrea's superb meal.

'No. Just a few noggins.'

Richardson led Duggan across the gangplank and onto the ship. They crossed the main deck and descended to the lower deck bar called the Wardroom. Duggan was impressed by the polished wooden surrounding, as Richardson knew most Americans were, and started to relax in the ambience of the bar.

'What're you having?' Richardson asked as he sat at the bar.

'A diet soda, if they've got one. A Coke.'

The barman raised his eyebrows, then reached under the counter and pulled out a can of Diet Coke. 'The usual, Mr Richardson?' he asked in a Northern Irish accent, as he poured.

'Please.' Sam waited until he had received his Scotch and soda and the barman had gone to serve another customer before he continued. 'They're not used to people drinking pop here. This is for the heavy drinkers.'

'Why here?'

'Look around. Not just tourists. Mostly MoD, ex-Army Ruperts. Just round the corner from the MoD in Northumberland Avenue, even though it's £2.85 down to expenses for a large gin. This is one of their favourite haunts, even if they all bugger off home at four o'clock. It's nicknamed the Belgrano.'

'Yours?'

'When it suits me. I prefer it to the sort of place where you get tired and emotional business types partnered by equally tired and emotional secretaries. There're more secrets kept here than practically anywhere else I know. And I don't mean extra-marital.'

'You reckon we could get a lead here?'

'Not from that lot,' he waved his hand to encompass the room. He swung round and called to the barman. 'Can we have some cashews when you've got a minute?' He turned back to Duggan. 'Notice his accent?'

'Irish.'

'Northern. Belfast. Sandy Row, to be precise.'

Duggan watched the barman out of the corner of his eye; about forty, black hair cut in a short military style and a soft-skinned, plump face. 'So?'

'Protestant. Although his name's of Catholic origin. Was with the Red Hand commandos. One of their top hit-men. Then he was promoted to commander of the Mid-Ulster Brigade UVF.'

Duggan knew all about the Red Hand group, Ulster paramilitaries who had been founded in 1972 by John McKeague after he was thrown out of the Shankhill Defence Association, one of Belfast's most violent Protestant vigilante groups. 'I thought those organizations were outlawed by your government.'

'They are. But they exist.'

'What's he doing here?'

'There's an enormous Irish influence in the catering trade. That includes IRA and other groups. I mean, what a great way to get information. In places like this, serving drinks to loosen people's tongues.'

'And your security people allow it?' Duggan was amazed.

'It's one way of keeping our eye on them. Out in the

open. Anyway, Sean's past all that now.' He waited as the barman approached them, a fresh bowl of cashews in his hand. 'Need to talk, Sean,' Richardson said in a soft voice as the barman put the bowl on the bar-top. 'Later. Usual place.'

'Was there anything else, sir?' replied Sean Coyle.

'No,' Richardson smiled back. 'About midnight.'

'That'll be fine, sir. Give me a shout when you need a refill.'

Richardson smiled. 'I will. Any new ones for me, Sean?'

'Just one, sir. What do you call a girl with one leg shorter than the other?'

'No idea.'

'Eileen.'

Richardson laughed, a large guffaw which made those nearest look at him. 'That's terrible.'

'And what do you call a Chinese girl with one leg shorter than the other?'

'Go on.'

'Irene, sir.'

He turned and walked away as Richardson continued to laugh. 'Irene,' he said to Duggan. 'Bloody Irene.'

To Duggan the joke had not been all that funny, it wasn't even good barrack-room humour. 'Is he still with the Red Hand?' he asked when Richardson had quietened down.

'No. He likes the quiet life now. I'm sure he still passes info back to them. But it'll be soft stuff, the sort you can read in the newspapers.'

'How come he didn't go to prison?'

'Never got caught.' Richardson didn't add that the Protestant paramilitaries got away with far more than the Catholics in the early days of the Troubles.

'You trust him?'

'As far as possible. Don't forget, we know everything about him. His habits, his family, his contacts.

When they're squeezed that hard, they tend to do as you ask.'

Duggan looked over at Coyle. It was hard to imagine the soft-skinned man had once been a vicious killer; for all he knew still was. Then he surveyed the inhabitants of the room. All involved in some form of skulduggery, all up to no good. Then he thought of himself. No different from them, sitting here on the bar-stool, pretending to be above it all, drinking his soda-pop.

Richardson spun round and grinned at him. As the Englishman's coat swung open, Duggan saw the flash of a gun handle sticking out of a shoulder holster; a big wooden handle signifying a large-barrelled gun.

'Sorry,' said Richardson as he fastened the coat.

'Expecting trouble?' asked Duggan.

'Always. Want another pop?'

The Puzzle Palace
NSA Headquarters
Fort George G. Meade
Maryland

The complex, known locally as the Puzzle Palace, lies halfway between Washington and Baltimore. Covering over 1,500 acres, it is the nerve-centre of the USA's largest intelligence-gathering organization, employing over 60,000 people with an annual budget that is larger than the CIA's and FBI's combined.

The National Security Agency, started by order of President Truman in the forties in a single office in the Old Munitions Building in Washington, was now an antennae-bristling complex of twenty vast buildings with links into satellites and any other paraphernalia of modern-day snooping that could read a number-plate of a car parked next to the Red Square Metro. Signals Intelligence, or SIGINT by its better-known name, has rapidly become the first line of the USA's intelligence, much to the chagrin of the CIA and FBI. The NSA is linked to receivers all over the world, from Turkey to Australia, from Puerto Rico to Antarctica, in addition to numerous satellites circling the earth, solely designed to intercept radio signals and other telemetry. The organization had to admit to regularly intercepting and reading the secret communications of over forty countries after defectors to the Soviet Union exposed it in 1960.

Intercepting and recording a simple phone call on the transatlantic airwaves from Dublin to Miami Beach posed no serious problem to those at SIGINT City. It was one of thousands of calls that were recorded daily by satellite on an automatic machine tuned into the transatlantic frequency. These calls were then routed into a special recording room at the Telecommunication Center in the NSA. Each coding machine could read over 500,000,000 characters a second, more than four hundred, 500-page novels.

The duty operator, sitting in the low-lit TCOM room, one of a group of men all in front of their individual computer work-stations, looked at his schedule, then ran a routine check on the calls, his FIND code searching for key words he had punched in. In that way, the call made three days earlier was located.

The words he punched in on his FIND code were: 'IRA, PIRA, Provisional, Provo, Prods, Republicans, Bewley's, Café, Penuel, Raphael, Flaherty, Bomb, Device, Detonator, SAS, Darcy, Sally, O'Connell Street'.

The result came up within seven minutes. There were innumerable calls with the word 'IRA', but they were unimportant, just part of general conversation between parties. The computer picked up the word 'Bewley's' and found sixty-three conversations relating to it, most of them once again commenting on the explosion in O'Connell Street. While it isolated those calls, it searched for its next word, 'Penuel'. That homed-in on one call, the one made by Penuel to Miami Beach. The computer also linked the word 'Flaherty' to the same phone message.

As it flashed up on the screen, the operator hit another button for a full audio-copy of the call as well as a print-out.

Fifteen minutes later the conversation between Penuel and his link-man in Miami Beach was on its way to the CIA Director of Operations at Langley.

Five men listened to the tape in the CTC.

'Who else has got this?' asked Lacelle.

'Just this one copy,' replied McNabb, holding up a print-out. 'And this printed copy. Although I think the British will probably know about it as well.'

'Why?'

'GCHQ.' He referred to the British SIGINT centre in Cheltenham, which enjoyed a very close and secret partnership with the NSA. 'They monitor everything coming out of Ireland on radiotelephony with their Goonhilly Downs receiver.'

'Have we traced where the call was made to?'

'Yes. Miami Beach. A phone booth in the street.'

'What the hell . . . ?' Lacelle stopped. He'd presumed the Dublin explosion had taken any future terrorist acts off American soil. He'd presumed Flaherty's murder had been a singular incident. He realized he'd presumed wrong. 'Will GCHQ pick that up?'

'Almost definitely.'

'We've got a local agent looking around,' said Mickleton. 'Don't expect much. Not much there, just a phone kiosk outside one of the art deco hotels. No obvious links. We're checking to see if any Brits with military records live near by. I should add that the whole Miami Beach area has hundreds, if not thousands, of Brits living there, either permanently or with holiday homes. We're also running a voice check on both men. But it sounds like they're genuine English accents, not Americans faking. The call made to the *Irish Independent* was, we're told by their Gardaí, made from the airport. Apparently there was a Tannoy in the background as Penuel spoke.' Mickleton sniffed; he wasn't happy reporting to Lacelle. 'We're also checking all the passenger manifests out of Dublin to England and the USA. Seeing if we can find any names that link up with the one out of JFK to Heathrow.'

'Like Daniel Morrison?'

'It would be nice to be that lucky.'

'I suggest we pass all this on to the British. Through official channels,' said McNabb.

Lacelle nodded. 'Guess so. And you better tell our man over there. Duggan, isn't it?'

'Duggan,' McNabb confirmed.

'Has he had any luck yet?' Lacelle asked impatiently.

'Not yet. He's only been there twenty-four hours.'

'As long as he's not sleeping on the job. This whole thing is getting out of hand. I'd like something more concrete before I report to the NSA.'

Hampstead Heath
London

Duggan was tired now; totally jet-lagged, fighting to keep awake as Richardson drove him through the town centre of the north London suburb of Hampstead Heath.

The Bentley swept up the hill, past the newly opened McDonald's, and out towards the Heath itself. As they crossed the Heath pond near Jack Straw's Castle public house, Duggan looked at the Englishman. It was a scene from a fifties film; Richardson imitating George Sanders at the wheel of this old, powerful car as it swept through the night, its headlights cutting swathes of light across the openness of the Heath it now approached. *What the hell am I doing here? Where the hell am I going with this crazy guy?*

Richardson pulled the Bentley into a grass lay-by and switched off the lights.

'Do you want to stay here or come with me?' he asked.

'I'll come,' said an exhausted Duggan. He climbed out of the car and closed the door as Richardson came round to his side. 'Where the hell is this?'

'Hampstead Heath.'

'Some kind of park?'

Richardson laughed. 'You could call it that.' He opened his jacket and loosened the holster clip that held the hammer of his pistol.

'You licensed to carry that?'

'Of course.' Richardson pulled the hand-gun out of the holster and held it up in the moonlight for Duggan to see. 'Colt Python. 357 Magnum. Stop a gorilla on heat in a banana factory.'

'I know the weapon.'

'I got it off a German who was supplying arms to the Provos. Gave it to me as a bribe. Thought I was one of them.' He holstered the gun, then took out a pack of cigarettes, took the last one out, crumpled the pack and flicked it at the large refuse-bin in the lay-by. 'Damn,' he swore as the pack missed the bin; neither man moved to pick it up. 'It's my last one today,' Richardson said as he lit up. 'My tenth. Hope I can stick it out.'

'You expecting to use the gun?'

'No. Just like being prepared.' Richardson leant against the Bentley's wing and looked out over the Heath and towards the night lights of London. 'You ever hear of the Bois de Boulogne?'

'In Paris, yeah.'

'It's where the transvestites and hookers run round in the undergrowth getting laid for a few hundred francs.'

'So I've heard.'

'This place is the same. Only it's more specialized. And still got amateur status.'

'Meaning?'

'Just listen. Just hear nature's night-life.'

Duggan kept quiet and listened. It took some time before he acclimatized to the silence. Only it wasn't silence. There was movement in the bushes all around; not just the swish of branches and trees, but gasps and grunts and the odd shriek. He knew it wasn't animals, knew it was people. About fifty yards away he heard someone laugh, then there was a shrill, short scream from another area. He realized there were a lot of people out there, all buried in the secrecy of the night.

'Doctors, lawyers, judges, office clerks, probably even policemen,' said Richardson cynically after five minutes. 'Bum-boys. Sodomy on Hampstead Heath. Nice world we live in, eh?' Richardson inhaled, enjoying the last drags from his last cigarette. A small BMW drove past slowly towards the castellated pub. 'The pub we passed, Jack Straw's Castle, its car-park is the start of the cruisers' territory. Whoever's in that car will leave it there, then charge down the muddy paths into those deep woods. It's known to the bum-boys as the Jungle. They're all strangers to each other. If they walk past someone they like, then they give him a long hard stare. Conversations like, "Hello, do you come here often?" are considered soppy amongst these characters. If they fancy you, they walk past you a couple of times, then head for the bushes. You do the same and wham, bang, thank you, Mister.'

'You're kidding me.'

'Like hell. They have different areas for different thrills. There's the leg-of-mutton pond for oral sex, the Vanilla Path and YumYum Trees for orthodox sex, and even an Orgy Bush for sado-masochists. One guy, about three years ago, was kicked to death. His last words were, "Is that all you can do? Do you call yourself men?"' Richardson paused as another man went past. The stranger, a respectable middle-class man in his forties, stared hard at Richardson, and on getting no response, hurried past. 'Hurry, sweetheart, before your wife misses you at home,' taunted Richardson.

'Fuck off,' said the respectable man as he scurried into the bushes.

'You know a lot about what goes on here,' commented Duggan.

'Had to research it. Some of the PLO Arabs used to come down here. It's not only the IRA we have to watch. In the summer there's five hundred people a night up to no good in there.' Richardson nodded towards the woods. 'One night when I was here on surveillance, a woman walked past, crying for help because she'd lost her dog. About thirty guys came out from the bushes, some still dressed as bimbos, and helped her look for the animal. They found it twenty minutes later.' He threw away his last cigarette and turned to Duggan. 'You don't approve of my attitude, do you? Not politically correct, I guess.'

Duggan made no comment. Then he saw another man approaching from the wooded area to his left. He recognized Coyle, the barman from the restaurant. He wore a long, raglan-sleeved wool overcoat. When he got close to them, Duggan realized the man's face was fully made-up with mascara, lipstick and panstick. It all looked bizarre under the short-cropped haircut.

'Mr Richardson,' Coyle said when he stood between them. 'Who's the Yank?'

'With me. He's secure.'

'You'll want to know about this Flaherty job. That's why he's here.' Coyle indicated Duggan.

'You got anything on it?'

'No. Lot of gossip, but nothing else.'

'What sort of gossip?'

'Every sort. Some say it's the IRA after a sob-story

about how badly they're being treated. Others say it's the UDA and UFF. The SAS are also being fingered. There're those convinced it's the Government taking out the Provos. You name the organization and there'll be someone pointing the finger of suspicion at them. Hell, the Prods back home are pleased as punch.'

'What about KAS?'

'Come off it, Mr Richardson. Just 'cos I used to help them out. No, I don't even think they're in business any more. Victims of the recession.'

'Who's KAS?' asked Duggan.

'They were a private security organization set up by the founder of the SAS, Colonel David Sterling. All ex-SAS men. With people like Sean helping occasionally.' Richardson turned back to the Irishman. 'Name Penuel mean anything?'

'No. Nor does Raphael.'

Richardson was silent for a while. 'What do you think, Sean?' he asked eventually.

'For what it's worth, I'll put my money on the Republicans.'

'Why?'

'They need some public support. If they could make it appear that they were being terrorized and openly killed by the British government, they reckon they could pull back some of the grass-roots support they've lost. I mean, the Brits will be the gangsters in the eyes of the world, won't they? Kill off any peace initiative. Proving what a nice bloke that Gerry Adams is.' He turned to Duggan. 'And you lot are the biggest bastards of all, funding them to blow the rest of us up.'

'Cut it out. We're on the same side,' warned Richardson.

Coyle shrugged, then continued. 'Flaherty was a clown. Always in trouble, botched up more than he got right. By taking him out they created a martyr. Talk about making a silk purse out of a sow's ear.'

'But you've nothing concrete?'

'The fellow Darcy who was found dead.'

Richardson's interest sharpened. 'What about him?'

'You think he was the bomber, don't you?'

'We think so.' He didn't disclose that Darcy had been already dead when the bomb exploded; that information had remained classified.

'I think he was taken out by his own mob.'

'Go on.'

'Then they told the girl to go and plant the bomb. Only they detonated it before she could get away.'

'Why would they do that?'

'Gets them maximum publicity. They're not the villains any more, only the victims. And it gets rid of one of their big problems.'

'What problem?'

'Darcy. He was a supergrass.'

Richardson looked at Duggan in the stunned silence that followed. 'Who says?' he asked.

'I do. When I was with the Mid-Ulster Brigade, I once followed Darcy. I was going to hit him when I saw him have a secret meeting with another bloke. Near City Hall. They passed one another, then, when they were sure they weren't being followed, nipped down a side-street. They were only down there a couple of minutes. The guy he was chatting to wasn't a Republican. I'd seen him before. He was Army. SAS man. Intelligence. Darcy passed him something, then went back towards Ballymurphy, where he lived.'

'That's a Catholic area,' Richardson informed Duggan.

'I followed the SAS man back to barracks,' Coyle went on.

'You recognized him?'

'No. Saw him a couple of times. But I minded my own business. I guessed he was handling Darcy.'

'How do you know he was a supergrass?'

'Because the next day they hit a safe house in Short Strand. Took out an ASU unit waiting to go to the mainland.' Coyle referred to the IRA Active Service Units, usually no more than three people who were responsible for bombing and other terrorist activities in the British Isles and Europe. 'Darcy sometimes hung round that safe house. Only he wasn't there when the Army went in. I saw it happen. One of the officers leading was the man Darcy had met the night before.' Coyle heard someone shriek in the bushes and turned to see what was happening. There was nothing visible and he swung back to Richardson. 'I reckon the Republican Army Council found out about Darcy and decided to do him in. While they did that, they made sure they were clear of the whole thing. Kill two birds with one stone.'

'Does the name Captain Daniel Morrison mean anything?' Duggan asked.

'No,' replied Coyle cautiously. 'Why?'

'Just a name we had on our files,' lied Duggan, immediately regretting his impetuosity.

'Well, never heard of him. Not when I was there, anyway. Anything else, Mr Richardson?'

'That was a terrible joke, back at the *Tattersall*,' said Richardson. 'Next time give me a funny one I can really laugh at.'

'Sorry, it's the only one I could think of. Didn't expect to see you in.'

'Go on, fuck off and have a good time.'

'Yes, sir.' Coyle opened his coat and displayed a naked body underneath, apart from two trouser legs which were held up at the knee by string. The body, like the face, was plump and soft. Coyle giggled, then wrapped the coat round him and walked back onto the Heath.

Duggan, shocked, noted the mischievous smile on Richardson's face. The Englishman laughed, then climbed back into the Bentley. Duggan joined him and the car pulled away from the lay-by.

'You must be tired,' said Richardson.

'Very. Did you know Darcy was an informer?'

'No. But I'll get onto it tomorrow. Who's Morrison?'

'We checked all flights out of JFK to London after the hit on Flaherty. Just after the call was made by Raphael, the flight to Heathrow took off and included a British army captain. Daniel Morrison.' He decided not to tell Richardson that the FBI had traced the call to the British Airways terminal. 'Just a hunch. To see if it had any effect on Sean.'

Richardson sensed Duggan was holding back, but decided not to push it. He'd follow up on Morrison; he knew the American would have to go through him if he wanted to get at army records.

'You must have other contacts as well as him?' Duggan continued.

'Spoken to most of them before you got here. Got nothing out of them.'

'Why concentrate on Sean?'

'Because these gay boys put it around with each other. Doesn't matter to them what religion the arse is they're screwing. He's got the widest selection of contacts. Including bloody IRA sympathizers. You'd be surprised what people give away when their minds are occupied elsewhere.'

They drove back in silence. Richardson swore because he didn't have any cigarettes.

The glow of London's night lights reddened the sky ahead of them.

Duggan was in a deep sleep when Richardson shook him awake at eight the next morning.

'Time to get up,' he said as he watched Duggan struggle out of his somnolence. 'Things have moved on since we went to bed. There's a coffee ready for you in the kitchen.'

Duggan lay there for a minute after Richardson had

gone, collecting his thoughts. He recalled climbing into bed at 1.17 a.m.; the bedside digital clock had told him the exact time. But he was overtired and found it difficult to sleep. When he did doze off, his mind nightmared onto the scenes at the Heath; a plump, pink, naked Coyle kneeling on all fours as others crowded round him and took turns mounting him. As Coyle screamed in anticipation and pain, his tormentors ignored him, chatted amongst themselves as they waited, as if in a queue at the check-out counter of a supermarket. The sheer depravity of it all turned Duggan's stomach and he shouted for them to stop, but they ignored him. Then the sound changed and Coyle and his friends faded from his mind, to be replaced by Andrea, shouting and waving at him. He ran towards her, his feet pedalling furiously, trying to propel him forward, but for all his effort he remained where he was. When he woke, sweat across his brow, the sound continued, faint at first, then growing louder, the sounds of love-making coming from the next-door bedroom. He imagined Andrea under Richardson, squirming and turning and wanting more; it upset him because he found her so attractive. *What the hell did she see in Richardson?*

Richardson looked up as a shaved, bathed and yawning Duggan came into the kitchen. 'Breakfast?' Richardson asked.

'You got any cereal?'

'Special K?'

'Fine.'

Richardson opened a cupboard and took out a packet.

'How's the smoking?' Duggan asked.

'Terrible. I've already had two this morning. Bloody phone woke me at six-thirty.'

'So what's the latest?' Duggan enquired as Richardson put the cereal on the table.

'Last night. At the Red Lion in Parliament Square. The IRA hit back.'

Duggan's spoon paused on the way to his mouth, then continued its journey. 'Jesus, it never stops,' he said through his mouthful.

'About eleven-thirty, while we were driving up to Hampstead. The Red Lion is where all the politicians hang out. You could call it their local; it's right across from Parliament. Anyway, as some of them were coming out at closing time, two black taxis pulled up, going across the road and blocking the traffic. Two gunmen got out, each one the driver of the cab, and sprayed semi-automatic pistol-fire towards the MPs. Nobody got seriously hurt; one of the MPs got hit in his elbow, another twisted and fractured his foot as he tried to run away. There were policemen running towards the terrorists and one of them was armed and fired into the air to distract the gunmen. Anyway, they disappeared down a side-road where there were two motorbikes waiting for them. They were last seen heading into the West End. The bikes were found an hour later in a multi-storey garage. Both had been reported stolen yesterday afternoon.'

'Rush job,' said Duggan, always the analyst.

'Sounds like it. No real planning. Hit a target that's soft and always available.'

'They're reacting to Penuel and the killing of Darcy.'

'And Dublin.'

'No. If it isn't the PIRA behind that, then Darcy was always the object. Think about it. Penuel, his organization that is, wanted to teach the PIRA a lesson. That's why nobody was killed when the bomb went off.'

'The woman, Sally.'

'Linked to Darcy. Penuel's sole purpose was to kill a PIRA man.'

'Except he was a supergrass.'

'I don't think the PIRA knew.' Duggan's certainty surprised Richardson. 'I'm convinced about that, after last night's fiasco at the Red Lion. The Provos hit back fast; a badly planned operation. They did that because they wanted to retaliate quickly. And be seen to do it.'

'So what's that tell you?'

'That Penuel came after Darcy. For two possible reasons. Either to teach the PIRA another lesson after Flaherty. Or . . . ' Duggan paused. '. . . because he knew Darcy was an informer and wanted to shut him up. Because . . . ' Duggan saw that Richardson agreed with the logic of his argument, '. . . Darcy knew who Penuel was. Maybe had even worked with him before.'

'You're moving into dangerous territory.'

'Yeah. Well, that puts the ball in your court. It's either someone who knew Darcy and was trusted by him – or it was one of your security services. And that sorta makes it official.'

'They hit the girl because she was close to Darcy and probably knew what was going on.'

'Hell, it's unlikely she was sharing his bed and didn't know what he was up to. Elementary, my dear Watson.' Duggan suddenly believed that Richardson had no idea if the authorities were involved, that he had been put in to determine the truth.

'But you still have no theories who it was?'

Duggan shook his head. 'All I believe is that it wasn't the IRA.'

'Not what Coyle said. And he's close to it.'

'That's his Protestant instinct. Always blame the enemy. You know, it could be his people, the Protestants.'

'Could be anybody.' Richardson drained his coffee. 'I've booked a flight to Dublin later this afternoon. We need to leave here at four.'

'What you got planned before then?'

'Nothing. We're trying to trace Morrison. Should have something later on. Do you want to use the phone?'

'No.'

'It's not bugged.'

Duggan laughed. 'Wouldn't expect it to be. No, I'm going to get some fresh air. Could do with stretching my legs.'

'OK.' Richardson crossed to the key-rack and un-hooked a spare key. He slid it across the breakfast counter. 'Use that. Then you can let yourself in and out.' He grinned mischievously. 'Can I leave the washing-up to you?'

'Of course.' Duggan refused to be rankled.

Richardson left the room and Duggan picked up the *Daily Telegraph*. He read the headline story on the Red Lion attack; although the item took more than half the page it said little more than what he had already been told. Apart from the fact that the PIRA had claimed responsibility immediately after the attack and blamed the Dublin and New York 'atrocities' on the British government. The caller had accused the Prime Minister of personally giving the go-ahead for the retaliation attacks: Too cowardly to face the IRA directly on the battlefield of Northern Ireland, having realized they cannot win that battle, the British Cabinet has now made a policy decision to attack them on foreign soil. It's time people listened to the real peace initiative as laid down by Gerry Adams instead of the lies of the British government. Surely, by freeing Tim Flaherty and allowing Gerry Adams into New York, even the American government sees the truth for what it is. It's time the British government did the same.

Duggan didn't take it seriously; if that were the truth, the last people to know would be the Republicans. What concerned him was that the tone of the paper was bullish about the New York and Dublin attacks; its view was that other countries could now see what the British people were going through because of terrorist attacks, and possibly they would understand how dangerous the IRA had really become. And the continual references to Gerry Adams's visit to New York was proving that the American government could be embarrassed by the situation unless the matter was resolved quickly. Which, at the end of the day, was his reason for being in London.

He threw the paper down, did the washing-up, grabbed his coat and went for a walk.

He watched to see if he was being followed, but didn't spot anyone.

Richardson, in an old duffel coat, baseball cap, battered Reeboks and a pair of glasses, knew Duggan hadn't recognized him. He followed the American past the phone box where he had made the earlier call and on to another one three streets away. *Smart*. Just in case the first one had been bugged after his previous call.

He waited for Duggan to finish his call, then followed him while Duggan retraced his steps back to the flat. Richardson went up the back way, entered through the fire-escape and changed back into his normal clothes.

Duggan went straight to his room. His call to the Embassy had been fruitful. The legal attaché informed him that SIGINT City had traced a transatlantic call from the Gresham Hotel in Dublin to Miami Beach. The call was made by Penuel the day before the bombing. The Miami Beach receiver was only a public pay phone in a normally busy public area. The FBI were following that up, and also combing the hotel registers, airlines and car-rental firms to come up with something on Morrison. No, they hadn't traced his whereabouts in Britain yet. The attaché's last words were that the British, through their Cheltenham aerials, were probably aware of the call from Penuel to Miami Beach, and the fact that both men on the phone, from their accents, appeared to be English. He added that Langley would be informing the Joint Liaison staff in London about the intercepted call later on in the day.

As Duggan lay on his bed, his hands behind his

head as he pondered the latest news, he heard the phone ring and someone answer it.

'Sam,' said Carter as Richardson picked up the receiver.

'Yes, sir.'

'More information for you.' Carter relayed the contents of the taped transatlantic call between Penuel and Miami Beach. 'Cheltenham came up with it,' he said when he'd finished. 'Do you want me to go through it all, again?'

'No.' Richardson had an excellent retentive memory and easily logged the contents of the short conversation. 'Where was it traced from?'

'The Gresham Hotel. Are you still going over there?'

'Aer Lingus at 18.25 out of Heathrow.'

'No point sending anyone over to dab for fingerprints. The phone is in the lobby and there'll be hundreds of prints around it. And if he was a pro, he would've wiped the handset anyway. We also put a tap on all the working phone boxes around your area, as you suggested. Your man rang his Embassy legal attaché. He's already been informed about the Penuel call. Maryland picked it up. Exactly the same conversation. He's still interested in Captain Morrison. There's more there than meets the eye.'

'Have you traced him yet?'

'No. Got to tread carefully where the Army's concerned. And we don't want Five jumping up and down, demanding to know why we're involved in their territory.'

'I thought we had their agreement?'

'Only in that we're looking after the Yank at the Americans' request. Don't worry,' he added, 'this line is scrambled for cleartalk.'

Richardson took that for granted. 'Does that mean I could be out on my own?'

'Possible, but unlikely. Only if this thing traces back

to Five, or even Special Branch. Or even MoD security. They have been known to tell the others to get stuffed. If that happens, then we go direct to Downing Street. That's our remit. Anyway,' he continued, 'Darcy was a supergrass. Not by Five, but run by the Army. We'll find out who handled him. It'll take time; there was probably more than one handler over the years. When I told my oppo at Five, it nearly blew his socks off.' Carter chuckled. 'Only a handful of people knew. He was one of their top informers. He came out with some tremendous stuff, although it dried up within the last three years. Five have promised all the help on that.'

'Shame half the UDA knew about Darcy.'

'Yes. That's what shocked Five. My chap wouldn't discuss it any further on the phone; we had to meet at Harrods' restaurant for coffee before he confirmed it. Your contact's certainly stirred up a hornet's nest there.'

'Is he safe?'

'Yes. Even I don't know who he is.'

Richardson was relieved that Coyle was safe. 'Duggan believes the target was Darcy all along.'

'I agree. They obviously spent time setting up the Dublin operation. They would have had a definite target all along.'

'He's convinced it isn't the Provos.'

'Why?' Carter listened while Richardson went through the arguments Duggan had put forward. 'Not necessarily correct,' he said when Richardson had finished. 'It's unlikely that one of our services, or a group of ex-employees, would knock out a supergrass who was on our side. Doesn't make sense, that.'

'You did say he'd dried up as a source.'

'Put into cold storage would be more like it.'

'Unless his handler, or someone who had access to Darcy, didn't want us to find out what he and Penuel had been up to.' A thought suddenly came to Richardson. 'Unless . . .' He paused.

'Go on.'

'I'm trying to think this through. That telephone call – Penuel says he's made the decision to hit Bewley's. Yet he was already in Dublin; must've been for some time to get the bomb prepared. You don't just walk in with something like that off a plane.'

'Which means he understood the use and transport of explosives.'

'If they'd already decided to hit a building in retaliation, then it would've been planned. Not done on a last-minute decision, like Bewley's was. They'd planned it, but the location of the bomb wasn't too important, as long as they didn't hurt innocent passers-by. What they had already decided was to take out Darcy and the girl. That's obvious now. Duggan's right. He was the target.'

'Because he knew who they were.'

'He certainly knew who Penuel was. That could mean Flaherty was also planned well in advance.'

'It'll all out in the end. There's one more bit of information. I think this should be for your ears only.'

'OK.'

'My Harrods friend also told me that Penuel, or at least they *presume* it was Penuel, made a second call about the same time he rang the *Irish Independent*. He rang the Army Confidential Line in Belfast, and gave them three addresses which turned out to be IRA arms and explosives caches. Two in Dublin and one in Dundalk. We informed the Gardaí and they came away with quite a haul. We've asked them not to publicize that success.'

'Did they trace the call?'

'No. Except the only people who use that line are informers and our own intelligence groups, including the Army.'

'This thing just gets closer.'

'Well, we'll see. When you get to Dublin see what you can pull up on Darcy.'

94

'I don't want the Gardaí involved.'

'I'll leave the logistics up to you. I'm sure you'll use your own sources. You'll need a portable.' The portable handsets used by SIS operatives allowed cleartalk through a scramble system that went via a satellite to GCHQ at Cheltenham. 'I'll get Despatch to deliver one immediately.'

Richardson told Duggan about his conversation with Carter, apart from the information on Darcy. They sat at a corner table at the Crown and Anchor, just round the corner from the flat, and enjoyed a pint and a ploughman's lunch. Richardson watched closely for any expression from the American when he told him about the intercepted transatlantic phone call.

There was nothing; Duggan simply listened to what he was told.

'Our people are going to pass that on to your CTC,' added Richardson.

'Good. I guess our SIGINT unit will also have picked it up.'

'Ring your people when we get back, just in case they didn't.'

'I'll do that.' Duggan sipped his pint of bitter; he had asked the disapproving barman to half-fill the glass with ice. They both settled down to eat in silence.

'You're of Irish descent,' said Richardson eventually.

'Yeah. But Florida born and raised. Just north of Miami.'

'How did you get in the Agency?'

'I came out of college with a civil engineering degree and the Agency approached me. They like their people to come from a variety of backgrounds. Not like the FBI, who just go for lawyers.'

Richardson started to sing. 'A wild colonial boy – Jack Duggan was his name.' He stopped sharply and said, 'That's an Irish hero's name, Duggan.'

'I know. Before you check, my full name is Francis Jack Duggan.' Duggan emphasized the word 'Jack'. 'My parents emigrated from Ireland in the fifties.'

'North or South?'

'North. Belfast.'

'You been there?'

'Twice. And once to Dublin.' He ate another mouthful before continuing, more than aware that Richardson had suddenly developed a keen interest in his heritage. 'My parents were killed five years ago in an auto accident outside Vero Beach. That's in—'

'Florida. I know.'

'They'd retired there. Anyway, they always wanted to be buried back in Belfast. That was my first trip. To the Milltown cemetery for their burial.'

'You're Catholic.' Richardson knew the cemetery was in the centre of Belfast and was the oldest and most traditional resting place for the Catholic community.

Duggan nodded. 'It's what they wanted, the least I could do. A big Irish funeral.'

'The IRA hold some of their paramilitary burials in Milltown.'

'I've seen the pictures on TV. My parents didn't get that sort of a send-off.'

'Lots of your relatives attend?'

'Plenty.'

'Made friends?'

'Some.'

'Tell them you were CIA?'

'Of course not. They think I'm a journalist, working for the Government. Public relations in the State Department.'

'Americans like to retrace their roots, don't they?'

'Doesn't everybody?'

'And you went back for a second visit?'

'Yeah. I like my family. And I still keep in contact.' He leant forward, an aggressive movement towards

Richardson. 'I'm not a sympathizer. Maybe most of my relatives are. But I'm not. I work for the Agency. I carry that responsibility seriously. Above anything else. OK?'

Richardson smiled, then went on as though he hadn't pushed Duggan. 'Fine. You're lucky. To have family. My dad died before I was born and my mother looked after me until I went into the Army. She died six weeks later. I think it was of a broken heart. She never looked at another man. But always spoke about Dad, as if he was alive. It didn't matter once I was in the Army; being looked after, as she put it. She'd done her job and she just wanted to join him. I've been a loner ever since, until I met Andrea.' He looked at his watch. 'We'd better get a move on. We've a plane to catch.'

They finished their meal in silence. They both knew there was a barrier between them, and neither man was particularly anxious to break it down.

IRA Army Council
Seán McDermott Street
Dublin

It was the death of Darcy that had brought them together.

Seven of them with one singular purpose. How to respond to the sudden attacks they found themselves under by persons unknown; attacks that had resulted in the death of Tim Flaherty and Martyn Darcy.

The troops in the Provisional Irish Republican Army would look towards them for guidance; after all, they were the Officers Commanding, the Army Council.

The PIRA. The violent arm of the Republicans that grew tired of the old IRA and its Marxist philosophy and unleashed a fierce violence never before seen in Ulster in the seventies. The Provisionals rejected the values and 'old-man thinking' of the IRA and, under the control of the Army Council, declared war on the British. They were the defenders of Catholics against the domination of the Protestants, and the Ulster police force they saw as the iron fist of the Prods' majority. The formation of the PIRA split the Republicans, but, in time, the Official IRA accepted that the Army Council ran the PIRA, and with it the force that could finally break the will of the British. The two lived in an uneasy truce, side by side. But the Army Council was all-powerful; it controlled the Provisionals, and through them controlled the Catholic areas of Belfast.

Each member of the Army Council was safe in the knowledge that the British security forces and the Irish Gardaí Síochána could not prove a thing against them.

Each member of the Council was therefore rarely seen with known terrorists.

But each member was open to attacks on their lives by other paramilitary forces or even imagined attacks by the authorities.

Which is why the Army Council operated out of Dublin as its main base, met as rarely as possible, and was always surrounded by wingers, or bodyguards, who were usually local sympathizers called in to protect it.

Michael Griffin, chief of staff, led the discussion. He was a tall, bearded man in his late forties, a veteran of the bomb squads and terrorist attacks both in Belfast and the mainland. In the years of internment he had spent long sessions in Lisburn's Maze prison, but nothing had ever been proven against him. Griffin was also a fearsome general to his own troops, known for his rigid discipline and brutal temper, not a man to be ignored when he demanded something.

'Flaherty could've been a one-off. But Darcy's death means they're orchestrating a campaign to hit us outside of the six counties.'

'They're coming after us where we've little or no protection,' cut in Séamus McAteer, the director of organization. He was inexperienced in his supervisory role, having only been in charge of operations for six months since the conviction and imprisonment of the previous director who now languished in the Maze. 'That's because they're an independent group, not the British authorities.'

'Then how come they discovered the arms caches?' questioned the grizzled, white-bearded Father John O'Malley, the Army Council's adjutant-general. 'That wasn't the work of any private organization. That's someone with inside information. Authorized information.'

Father O'Malley had long been excommunicated from the Catholic Church. His zeal as a Republican supporter had embarrassed the Vatican and he was duly defrocked in the early eighties. But to his supporters and ex-parishioners he would always remain 'the Father'. As adjutant-general, Father O'Malley was responsible for overseas finance and logistics; he had just returned from Amsterdam where he had arranged the purchase and delivery of MemoPark timers and Marconi CB transceivers. Although the subject of countless British army intelligence reports, in fact he had the dubious distinction of having the thickest file of any Council member, Father O'Malley had never even been interned. This gave him the ability to travel freely without fear of being arrested, not only in Europe but across the United Kingdom. His frequent trips into Ulster were always undercover; he feared the death squads of the Protestant organizations far more than he did the security services.

'Are you saying we've got an informer on the loose?' countered McAteer. He spat out the word 'informer'; to the Republicans there was nothing lower or more despised than a grass.

'I'm just bringing it to your attention that Martyn

Darcy knew where all the explosives stores were. But I'm sure he wasn't the informant. Otherwise he wouldn't be dead now.'

'One of our contacts with the Gardaí thinks that Darcy had been tortured before he was killed,' joined in Fergal Baxter, director of intelligence. Of southern Irish extraction, unlike his fellow members of the Army Council, the thirty-five-year-old Baxter had a good relationship with the Eire authorities.

'What other rumours are they coming up with?' asked Griffin.

'That the detonator had Darcy's trademark all over it.'

'How can that be?' jumped in O'Malley. 'Why would he want to let a bomb off in Grafton Street? And with his own woman still attached to it?'

'I'm just repeating what's been said. It's not like normal, this time. The Gardaí have clamped down on any information over this. Top Secret stamped all over it. Chit-chat's all I've got to work with.'

'Then push harder,' ordered Griffin.

'We are,' defended Baxter. 'But not so that we frighten off our contacts.'

'Listen, this is more important than anything we've faced before,' flared up Griffin. 'This time they've thrown away the rule-book. Whoever they are. That means they're coming after us at every opportunity, and it doesn't matter where it is. It's not just our money they're after this time.' The others knew what he meant as he looked round the table. Over one thousand police in England and on both sides of the Irish border had raided more than forty addresses the previous April in an operation against IRA fund-raising. Operation 'Madrona', co-ordinated by the RUC's C13 anti-racketeering squad, was designed to halt the eight-million-pound-a-year income that fuelled the IRA. A dozen people had been arrested and the police had seized substantial quantities of drugs, money and stolen property. The haul had included computers and documents with details of bank and building society accounts. 'Let them get away with this, and they'll be after us in Belfast, directly attacking our people. Shoot and run, and if a few innocent Catholics get hurt, so what? That's the game they're playing. And we need information to stop it. Fast.'

'I'll put some more pressure on.' The intelligence chief backed down.

'The one thing I'm certain about is that we're fighting an organization. This is no renegade individual. Not hitting us first in New York and then quickly in Dublin. Jesus, it's like they're trying to bomb us to the peace negotiations. Playing us at our own game. Well, it won't be that easy for the bastards. They can only carry it on for so long. We can go on for ever.'

'If there's any of us left,' commented Father O'Malley ominously. 'If it's not the Brits, then I'd like to know where they're getting their finance.'

'Aye. These'll be expensive operations.'

'A lot of money, illicit money, to take out men in New York and Dublin. And if they retaliate against our attack at the Red Lion, then we'll know they're heavily subsidized.'

'That was stupid. Too bloody hasty.' Griffin looked at McAteer. As head of operations, the attack had been his responsibility. 'The last time we did that it led to the Balcombe Street siege. We're lucky we didn't lose some of our soldiers.'

'The Council asked for quick retaliation. That's what we did,' McAteer said defensively.

'You should've killed one of them politicians.'

'Just bad luck. That's what you expect when you force us to rush something.'

Griffin turned his attention back to Father O'Malley. 'Do the Prods have that sort of money?'

'Not up to now, not unless their illegal rackets are

taking off in a big way,' answered Father O'Malley.

'Sod them. We'll stuff them, however much money they get.'

Liam Russell, quartermaster general, changed the subject to avoid it degenerating into an emotional brawl. 'We still haven't resolved what Darcy was up to.' He paused as the others looked at him; at fifty-seven he was the elder statesman in the Council. 'Let's say there's something in the rumour that it was his trademark on the bomb. The questions that need answering are: one, why was his girl carrying a bomb that was detonated, rather than going off by accident; two, why did he arrange something we had no knowledge of; three, should we presume that the bomb was made of parts from our stocks, which we can't verify because the Gardaí raided our dumps and confiscated our supplies; and four, what the hell was he doing planting a bomb in Dublin when we've agreed not to commit any actions in this town?'

'We need facts,' said Griffin. 'Otherwise we're just playing Scrabble without any vowels.' He rounded on Baxter again. 'Put pressure on them, your bloody Gardaí contacts. Call in every favour you've got.'

'I've said I'll do that,' replied a nervous Baxter; he was frightened of his chief of staff and knew how easily he could erupt once his fierce temper took hold. 'I'll get results for you. It's not so easy since Reynolds started talking to Major. I mean, because we're not quitting our actions against the Brits, the Irish government has turned the Gardaí against us. It's not as easy as it used to be.'

'It was never easy. But we'll not be told how we're to win this war, by Sinn Féin, or anybody. Not when we've come this far. It's the gun and the bomb that brought them to the table – and it'll be the gun and the bomb that'll keep them there. When they've had enough, then we'll get all we want, including our lads released from the

102

Maze.' Griffin paused, knowing this was not the time for political speeches. But he was like a dog with a bone; the Anglo-Irish peace talks had brought its own pressures on the leadership. 'We can't be distracted from that end. While Sinn Féin are keeping pressure on the British by asking for clarification and dragging it out, we've got to be seen as strong in resolve as ever we were. The British Prime Minister's weak; he's shown that already by the way he's acted over other matters. I'm telling you, we keep the bombings going and he'll weaken and capitulate to Sinn Féin's demands to persuade the Unionists to become part of the Irish Republic. He's gone this far because of us. Now let's give him a little shove to go the whole way. And anyway, even if we go to the peace talks, at least we'll walk away with honour in the eyes of those who've put their trust in us.' Griffin leant back in his chair, his diatribe fading away.

'I agree with you,' said Russell, trying to move the meeting on. 'But we've got to find who's out to harm us. As I see it, there's only three possibilities – the Prods, the Brits or an independent group supporting one of those two.'

'Or the Yanks with the Brits,' added Baxter.

'Why them?' asked Griffin.

'The FBI would love to bring us under control. They've always supported the Brits. And they don't want us on their soil. That's why they've got their own counter-terrorist group. It's us they're really after. If they're into covert operations with the Brits, under some new policy we know nothing about, then we've got to ease up chasing funds and arms in America to get them off our backs.'

'Afraid they'll send you back from your holiday?' joked Father O'Malley softly under his breath.

'What the fuck are you talking about?' snapped Griffin, picking up the comment.

'Sorry.' Father O'Malley smiled apologetically.

'I'm going to Disney World,' answered Baxter sheepishly when Griffin turned on him. 'To Florida. With the family.'

'Bejesus!' Griffin shook his head, his neck reddening. But he didn't attack Father O'Malley; the ex-priest had his own terrible reputation and was not someone Griffin would willingly tangle with.

'A small sense of humour now and then doesn't go amiss,' said Father O'Malley.

'There was also the rumour that Darcy was an informer.' Baxter spoke, then stopped as everyone in the room swung round on him.

'That was an old rumour. Been going for years.'

'Like Liam, I'm just bringing up any possibility.'

'But Martyn Darcy never let us down. He was the best explosives man we had. I think those rumours were started by the British authorities. To make us suspect our own. He never did anything that even came near being suspicious in my eyes. And I don't think he'd be dead now if he'd been a grass.'

'I agree with Father John,' cut in Griffin. 'But, in view of the fact that we know nothing at all, I don't think we should completely discard it. What I want is two things. First, I want a report from everyone as to what they think are the possibilities of who it is that's hitting us. However silly your idea may seem, I still want to know what it is. Then, Fergal, you put them all together on one report so that we can study it. And second,' Griffin pointedly looked at McAteer, 'I want to make sure that we're ready to hit back if they follow up on the Red Lion attack. This time make it count. I want casualties. I want the Brits, and their fucking press, to be so horrified that they won't be so cock-a-hoop about this new lot taking us on. I want to make sure that they know we're fighting back all the more.'

He looked round the room. 'All in favour.'

Six hands rose and joined Griffin's upheld arm.

Richardson was already in the bar, beer in hand, when Duggan joined him.

'Room OK?' Richardson asked after Duggan had ordered a Diet Coke. They went to a corner seat away from the others in the bar.

'It's fine.' Duggan leant back and watched Richardson light up. 'How many today?'

'Eight. I've got two to go.'

'You don't *have* to smoke all ten.'

'I know. But I'm just following the instructions. It says smoke ten, so I'm smoking ten. She's packed me off with enough supplies to last me eight days. Four packs. She's put a different crayon colour on each batch of ten fags. Blue for Monday, green for Tuesday, and so on.'

Duggan shook his head. 'Your lungs. Anyway, I've had some thoughts. I'd like to know where these guys get their finances.'

'You mean, if it's an independent group?'

'Whoever it is. Operations on this scale cost a lot of money. Travel, pay-offs, guns, bombs. It's all top-drawer stuff. Expensive. If we were running an operation like that we'd be looking at tens of thousands. If they're going to sustain it, they're into the hundreds of thousands.'

Richardson nodded. 'I agree. We've looked at that. It's either a great deal of money, or an existing organization that has contacts in these places.'

'Or offices.'

'That's right. If it's not the IRA, or the authorities, or the UDA, then it's private, with vast funds or an existing structure they can use without drawing suspicion to themselves. Like . . .'

'Like what?'

'Like a security firm.' Richardson realized Duggan

had already come to that conclusion before he had come down for a drink. He'd led the Englishman into that surmise, almost arrogantly in that he pretended Richardson had discovered the possibility himself. Richardson played along with Duggan's game. 'Yeah. Except there's thousands of them.'

'A lot of them staffed and run by ex-security and military types. Hell, that's what they all do when they leave the services.'

'You saying it's private action by a security firm?'

'No. Just that, if they haven't the money, then a large private security company could set something like this going. Even in conjunction with the proper authorities. We have the same thing in America. Ex-CIA spooks and FBI gendarmerie setting up advisory or security firms. Let's face it, these guys know all the contacts, all the secrets, all the places the bodies are hidden. And it avoids any embarrassment to the authorities if they're discovered.'

'I'll run that through our people. Call them tomorrow.'

'OK. I already rang Langley. They're seeing what the computer comes up with.' He picked up the portable that Richardson had lent him and handed it back. 'Thanks for the use of the scramble line, but I rang direct and Langley ran their own scramble.'

They sat back and enjoyed the show out of the window; dark night and passers-by scurrying along, their clothes and hair being tossed by the brisk wind, girls' skirts flaring, men leaning into the gusts. The sort of night you sat by the fire and felt safe in the comfort of your own home.

'You said your dad died before you were born,' Duggan said eventually, his natural inquisitiveness once again taking over.

'Yes.'

'Is that how the family history runs? In the services?'

'Army. Lancashire Regiment, some in the Cheshires. All NCOs. That's—'

'Non-commissioned. We have the same. How did he die?'

Richardson told him of his father's death in Oman. He took his time; it was a quiet part of the evening and he always enjoyed talking about his dad; sort of kept him alive, brought them closer together.

'SAS, huh?' said Duggan when Richardson had finished. 'You kept it running in the family.'

'It's in my blood. Family tradition. Holier than the Holy Ghost is the Army to the Richardsons. When Gabriel blows that trumpet, we automatically stand to attention and get out and fight for Queen and Country.'

'And Andrea?'

'You mean what am I doing with her because she's black?'

'Unusual. Don't expect that in England.' Duggan trod carefully.

'Listen,' Richardson grinned. 'We're not as puritanical as you Yanks. We've had a mixed population for centuries. Came with the Empire. It's only you Americans who think you've got a mixed society. Yet there's far more bigotry on your side. I remember when the Iranian hostages from your embassy were released. The last one, and the youngest to come out, was a young black marine. He was a hero, and they got him up to the White House for a presentation. We saw it on TV over here. He brought his wife along. Blond hair, blue eyes, not what you'd expect him to be married to. I remember some American friends of mine were shocked. Jesus, they were a mixed couple and no-one knew till they stood in front of the camera. It didn't have the same effect over here. We're more broad-minded, you see. Even us parochials from the north of England.'

'That's not fair.'

'The truth never is.'

'You always going to keep running us down?'

'Why not? It helps pass the time.' Richardson didn't know why he was annoyed; it was an instinct. He put down his half-finished beer and stood up. 'I'm sorry. I'm tired, I guess.'

'What's with you? We're meant to be working on this thing together.'

'Are we? I'll tell you what pisses me off. I'm nothing more than a fucking nursemaid. And you're sitting on things, like this bloody Captain Daniel Morrison thing, and not telling me what's really going on. We're just wasting each other's time. And we're going on doing it, because we've been ordered to. Shit, isn't it? A waste of breath.'

He turned and left the bar. He was angry with himself for losing control, but Duggan irritated him. Then he suddenly grinned as he climbed the stairs. He always had the ability to get over his tempers quickly. What made him smile was the fact that he had also kept secrets from the American. *You're a two-faced bastard, Sam Richardson. That's what happens when you get out of uniform and become a spook.*

He went to bed and dropped straight off to sleep after ringing Andrea and telling her he loved her.

'How many cigarettes?' she had asked.

'Eight.'

'That's good. You don't have to smoke ten every day just because—'

'. . . it says it on the packet. I know.'

His last thought as he blanked out was of her; the smile on his face attested to that.

The phone's warble woke Richardson three hours later.

'It's Francis,' said Duggan. 'Can I come and see you?'

'Of course,' he replied, looking at the bedside clock. The red digits showed 1.14 a.m.

He went to the door, unlocked it and clambered back into bed. He was sitting up with the bedside light on when Duggan let himself in. The American was wearing a dressing-gown and carried an unopened can of beer and a can of Diet Coke. He set the beer next to Richardson, pulled up the wooden chair in front of the dressing table and sat down. The room was in total contrast to his own. Whereas he had left his clothes vaguely folded where they had dropped, Richardson's clothes were meticulously in order, the blazer and trousers in the Corby press, the soiled cream shirt folded ready for the laundry bag. Richardson's brown brogues had already been polished and positioned, smart as sentries at attention, at the foot of the Corby.

'Don't worry,' he said. 'I'm not here because I'm gay.'

'I got the impression you weren't. From the way you were eyeing Andrea up and down.'

'That obvious, huh?'

'Eyes on stalks. They swivelled every time she left the room.'

'I'm sorry. But she is attractive.' Duggan held up his Coke can. 'I would never try anything.'

'I didn't think you would.'

'Is that why you're angry?'

'No. As far as Andrea's concerned, I know I'm lucky to be with her. We suit each other. If she decided to move on, then there's nothing I could do about it. I'd regret it. But it's her life. And while she shares it with me, I'm grateful.'

'And very lucky. So what did annoy you?'

'Anybody ever told you you're a patronizing, arrogant bastard?'

'Yes. My ex-wife.'

'She's a good judge.'

Duggan grinned. 'Probably. Aren't you going to drink that beer?'

'At one in the morning? No, I'll keep it till tomorrow.

Anyway, that would set me off wanting a smoke. And I kept to eight.'

'Good for you.'

'Don't patronize me.'

Duggan held his hands up in mock apology. 'I'll try harder, Sam.'

'So what brought you here this early? Or this late, whichever way you're looking at it.'

'To apologize.'

'What for?'

'I don't know. For whatever fucks you in the head regarding me.'

'Apology accepted.'

'And because you're right. We don't share everything. And I guess we should. On one understanding.'

'Go on.'

'That if we pass confidential stuff to each other that we've been instructed not to, we keep it to ourselves. And don't spill it to our own departments.'

'OK.'

Duggan explained why the CIA was interested in Captain Daniel Morrison. Richardson listened; then decided not to tell the American about Penuel's phone call on the Army Confidential Line which resulted in the discovery of the IRA's Dublin and Dundalk arms caches. Neither did he pass on the information that Darcy had been tortured before he was killed. He felt he had no choice but to continue the deceit; the last thing he wanted to do was discover that Morrison led straight back to the British authorities. He remembered Carter's chilling words; the responsibility to stop that happening lay at Richardson's door. If Morrison was involved officially, then Richardson would have to take him out before any further progress was made by the American. He felt himself break into a gentle sweat; danger loomed and he remembered the face of the running soldier, shouting at him, appealing for help.

'That's why we need to see Morrison,' concluded Duggan.

'As soon as we know where he is we'll go and interview him.'

'I also called the CTC in Langley. They ran the tapes on Raphael, the person he spoke to, Penuel, and his contact in Miami Beach. Raphael and Penuel are not the same person. But they both spoke to the same person at the other end. The voice prints on both tapes matched; identical, no doubts. All three were English. Our experts say that they were not Americans putting on false accents. Or Irish. One of them, Penuel, may have had some Scotch—'

'Scot. Scotch is the whisky.'

'Whatever. He had a trace of Scottish in his accent. While I was running a mental analysis on that information, I remembered your remark about the Holy Ghost and Gabriel blowing his trumpet. That triggered something off so I called Langley back and spoke to the chaplain.'

'You've got the CIA praying for a solution?'

'Not yet,' Duggan grinned. 'I remember the names Uriel and Phanuel. Ever heard of them?'

Richardson shook his head.

'Phanuel is a secondary name for Uriel. As is Suriel. And, my chaplain informs me, so is Penuel.'

'Are you going to tell me?' asked Richardson impatiently.

'Archangels, Sam. There were four of them. Gabriel, Michael, Raphael and Uriel. Like I said, Penuel is a name often used for Uriel.'

'Jesus!' said Richardson softly.

'He wasn't an Archangel.'

'I thought I did the bad jokes.'

'The Archangels were messengers of God. Also angels of blessing, guardians and protectors. They were also looked on as agents of judgement.'

'I've heard of Michael.'

'He fought Lucifer in Heaven and won. Lucifer was banished to Hell, where he became the Dark Angel. He is the principal overthrower of Satan and, so my chaplain tells me, there are over seven hundred churches in England and Wales named after him.'

'Wow!' Richardson saw that the sarcasm had no effect on Duggan. 'I was joking. What about Raphael?'

'He was the healer. He was sent to heal Tobit's blindness in the Apocrypha. Then there's Gabriel, who's the chief messenger.'

'And Penuel?'

'Uriel. He's linked with the other three as one of the Angels of the Throne. Milton, in *Paradise Lost*, said he was always nearest the throne, ready to command. He was the symbol of perfection and completion.'

'You've forgotten one.'

'Who?'

'Lucifer,' added Richardson. 'He started out as an Archangel.'

'OK, maybe there's five.'

'Tomorrow I'll ring London and find out if there's anything linking to Archangels, or Angels. Code-names, aliases, special operations. I'll get it run through the computer. I suppose you've already done that.'

'Mr Perfect, that's me,' shrugged Duggan. 'They're running it through now. As will the FBI, State, Justice, Immigration, Customs, you name it.'

'Raphael and Penuel have already struck. They haven't retaliated to the Red Lion shooting.' Richardson leant over and picked up his ten-cigarette pack; there were two left in it. He took one out, hard-eyed Duggan and dared him to make a comment, then lit it and took a deep drag. 'If your theory's correct, then there's three of them out there waiting to cause trouble. Michael, Lucifer and Gabriel. I wonder which one's going to bring us the glad tidings of comfort and joy.'

The prosperous suburb of Buitenveldert
Amsterdam
Holland

Gabriel nestled the rifle-butt against his cheek, balanced it on the single-support bipod that enabled the marksman to keep a close eye on his mark for long periods without having to take the weight of the gun.

He knew he would only have time for two, possibly three, quick shots. With two targets on his list, he couldn't afford to make a mistake.

Gabriel had rented the small one-bedroomed apartment three weeks earlier, about the same time that Penuel had arrived in Dublin. The house he watched, a neat two-storey corner property, had been known to the authorities for years as one of the PIRA safe houses organized by the Ierland Komitee Nederland. The IKN, founded after a visit by the Provisionals' Séamus Loughran in 1975, not only raised funds for the IRA but was their European base for the ASUs who attacked British military personnel in West Germany, and linked the organization with the various socialist terrorist organizations throughout Europe. In more recent times, the IKN and its sister organization, the Ireland Information Group based in Utrecht, had also organized routes into and out of Schipol Airport for Republican terrorists who had committed violent acts on the British mainland and needed a quick escape route. Although Amsterdam's heyday as the capital of European terrorism was over, there was still a residue of disparate anarchists waiting to strike when conditions were ripe once again for a new counter-culture.

Gabriel's apartment was across the road from one of three safe houses in Amsterdam. Each house was occupied by members, or supporters, of the IKN. Gabriel, in his three weeks of observations, determined that there were four occupants living there. A young married couple and two children aged around nine and eleven. He had identified the male as Adrian Velling, a history teacher who was a member of the IKN's main committee. His wife, Gilda, had been a journalist who had actively campaigned for better conditions in Armagh's women's prisons as well as being a prime-mover in setting up the H-Block Komitee Nederland during the 1981 hunger strikes. She had once been interrogated after throwing a petrol-bomb at the British Embassy in Paris, but had escaped conviction due to a lack of hard evidence. The bombing had resulted in the near death of a passing postman who had suffered major burns and never led a normal life again.

Gabriel left the apartment every day to wander round Amsterdam. His cover was that he was seconded to Holland on a business consultancy and, so as not to gather suspicion, he gave the appearance that he went to work each day. At weekends he stayed in the flat, spending his time watching the corner house from behind net curtains. He'd already worked out his plan when he heard the news about the Red Lion attack. The next morning he drove into Amsterdam, went to the Memphis Hotel on De Lairessestraat and dialled long distance.

'Need to talk. Forty minutes. Fort Lauderdale.' Gabriel put down the phone and spent the next forty minutes window-shopping before he found a street phone kiosk on Prins Hendrikkade. He dialled a number of a phone box in Fort Lauderdale, Florida, and waited to be connected.

'Operation is go,' said the voice that answered.

'They've got company,' said Gabriel. 'An Irish friend. Been there three days.'

'Friendly type?'

'To them, yes. Definitely unfriendly to the rest of us.'

'Nice to have a bonus. Take him instead of the woman.'

'What about her?'

'Only if you have time. The other two are now your primaries.'

'Have a nice day.'

'Don't be cheeky.'

Gabriel grinned and put down the phone. He drove back to the apartment and prepared himself. The room was already clean of fingerprints and any other clues that could lead to him. His clothes were packed in his suitcase in the boot of the car.

The gun, an Accuracy International PM L96A1, was packed in a second suitcase, a double-locked, hard-cased Samsonite. The rifle had been bought years earlier and stored in England. Gabriel, on his way to Amsterdam, had stopped off in Manchester, picked up the gun, re-packed it in the Samsonite wrapped with extra clothes, and travelled on by car-ferry to Holland. The car, an old Ford Granada, had been bought for cash from a newspaper advertisement in the *Manchester Evening News*. With false insurance papers, and with the European Community having adopted a single frontier policy, Gabriel drove off the ferry without having to make a declaration at customs and continued on to Amsterdam. It was the easiest he had ever smuggled a weapon into a country; there was little risk, which made him realize how simple it would be for terrorist attacks in the future.

He assembled the gun; it was the best for the job, having been developed by Olympic gold medallist Malcolm Cooper together with Accuracy International. Using 7.62mm ammunition it could be accurate up to 1000 metres. The 200 metres from his apartment window to the front garden of the corner house made his task easier.

He checked the rifle once he had assembled it. Some organizations preferred semi-automatic at this range because of the ability to rapid-fire, but Gabriel liked the single-shot bolt action. He zeroed the scope, went through the adjustments on its sighting range, then pulled out the bipod-rest at the front and balanced the rifle on a table he had pushed up against the window. Then he loaded a single 7.62mm round into the breech and snapped the bolt-action shut. He put three more rounds in the box magazine, then pulled out the secondary, single-rest under the butt of the gun and set it on the table.

The gun now rested on three legs some six inches above the table. He sat in the chair, pushed the nose of the rifle through the slightly opened window, its barrel just appearing through the net curtains. He aimed it at the front door of the corner house, then adjusted the bipod until the rifle was fixed on its stand aiming directly at his target. He re-focused the scope, then stepped away from the table. It would be another half an hour before the couple returned from school with their children. He knew the Irishman had gone out with Gilda and presumed he would also be with the group.

He made himself a cup of coffee and waited. He thought about the boys and felt the heat in his loins. The club he'd gone to last night had been the best on his visit to Amsterdam this time. The hostess had escorted him to one of the small private booths; there was a red velvet circular couch round a circular table which had a television set on it. He'd waited while the hostess brought him a photo album and he'd flicked through it before picking out two pictures. They were the simplest pictures, not yet spoilt by rouge and lipstick and years of neon night-life. When she brought the boys through, one fair, the other dark, both no older than eighteen, he had nodded approval and beckoned them to sit next to him. They were both in jeans, wore no shirts and showed no embarrassment. The waiter put a bottle of champagne on the table; Gabriel paid with American Express, then closed the curtains on the trio.

He gave them both a drink, asked them their names, then fondled them both. While he gently sucked the blond boy's nipple he was helped to undress by the other. He loved their freshness, their tight fluid skin. The television flickered on and he saw two men making love, both very young, no more than eighteen— he recognized the dark-haired boy as the one who sat next to him. The three were now naked and he got the dark-haired boy to duplicate the actions he was watching on the screen. Gabriel lay back as he felt himself enter the boy's mouth, soft inside, fresh and young. As he watched the boy and his television image perform the same act, he pulled the other down to him and started to kiss him, gently at first, then brutally. There was no adverse reaction; the boy was a professional. Gabriel spent two hours in the club before he was sated.

Gabriel slipped his trousers down as he waited for the Vellings to come home. He thought of the boys he had fucked, and masturbated to relieve the tension. Then he cleaned up, dragged the chair back to the window and waited. He was calm now; there would be no tension in him when the moment to act came. To pass the time, and to control his thoughts, he reminded himself of his tour with the SAS. They would've been surprised at his antics in the Amsterdam night-club. The SAS subjected special operations people to the most rigorous vetting; homosexuals usually didn't last long in the service. But he had kept his secret from his superiors, had even slept with the enemy at times. How the hell else did they think he got his grasses to do what he wanted?

The familiar blue Volvo estate pulled up in front of the corner house.

Gabriel flicked the bipod back into the butt and took the weight of the Accuracy International on his shoulder. He was wearing surgical gloves and he eased his finger round the trigger.

Gilda Velling was the first adult out. She had been

117

in the passenger seat.

Gabriel lined the scope on her head and ensured the focus-ring was set exactly to his vision. He could see the blond strands of her parting quite clearly with the scalp underneath.

Adrian Velling climbed out of the driver's seat as Des Campbell, PIRA gunman, pulled himself out from the rear passenger door. It was a lucky move, both Velling and Campbell were on Gabriel's side of the Volvo; they wouldn't be able to duck behind it.

Take your time. Don't rush. Wait till they're both away from the protection of the car doors.

Velling slammed his door, put his arm round Campbell's shoulders, pushed the rear door shut and joked with his guest. They moved round the back of the estate car.

Beautiful, beautiful, beautif— Gabriel held his breath and squeezed the trigger just like the training manual said.

Campbell never heard the end of the joke because Velling never finished it. The top of his head exploded into a bloody mess.

Gabriel snapped back the bolt, ejected the spent cartridge, then rammed in the second bullet. His eyes were still looking through the scope which had now swung to Campbell. The Irishman reacted instantly and tried to break away from Velling and take cover the other side of the Volvo. But Velling's arm gripped Campbell in a death reaction, stiffened round the Irishman, held him as Campbell tried to free himself, tried to run with the dead IKN member trailing behind him.

Campbell wasn't fast enough. The second bullet cut through his neck and threw him backwards onto the pavement. He didn't die instantly, the blood still spurted from the bullet-hole. He was dead by the time the ambulance arrived nine minutes later. His death, unlike Velling's, had been a painful one. It was what Gabriel

118

wanted. At 200 metres, with such a powerful and accurate sniper's weapon, it was as easy as shooting a six-foot wall close up with a shotgun.

The woman, Gilda, screamed, then stood and hurled defiant obscenities at the invisible attacker.

Silly cow! He remembered the burnt postman, then slapped the third bullet into the breech, and silenced her. She was a bad-un and deserved all she got so far as he was concerned.

He ignored the children screaming and running round in circles sobbing, panicked and not knowing what to do.

He quickly dismantled the rifle, put it back in the Samsonite, picked up the spent cartridges and slipped them into his pocket, made one final check of the room and left the apartment block by the rear entrance.

By the time the ambulance and police arrived Gabriel was two miles away, heading into the centre of Amsterdam, just another car in the swirling city traffic. He circled Amsterdam on Einstein Weg and drove south on the motorway to the border town of Breda. He stopped, two hours later, before crossing into Belgium and rang *De Telegraaf* newspaper in Amsterdam from a local phone box.

He repeated the words he had committed to memory to the news editor. 'Please take this down as I will not repeat myself. "The assassination of the terrorists, Adrian and Gilda Velling, two Dutch members of the Ierland Komitee Nederland, and the PIRA gunman Des Campbell who was in a safe house in Buitenveldert, was in retaliation for the attempted murder of innocent politicians at the Red Lion pub in London by the IRA. This was in accordance with the Rules of Engagement as laid down by the Provisionals. Once again, in an attempt to fight fire with fire, Soldier Gabriel, under the orders of the Highest Command, carried out the assassination of the three terrorists. Should the acts of violence by the Republicans continue, then the Highest Command will have no alternative but to order quick and terrible retribution against those who are the enemies to a peaceful and just solution for the Irish situation." He hung up before the news editor could ask any questions, then got in his car and drove across the unattended border.

He continued for thirty-five kilometres into Antwerp, then turned east and took the E313 to Liege. He stopped for a coffee and late-evening meal, then continued through the night eastward on the E40 to Cologne. By this time he had discarded the sniper's rifle and its associated ammunition, buried them deep in a soft-earthed forest on the outskirts of Maastricht. He stayed overnight in Cologne, then swept south to Mannheim. He put the Granada into a lock-up garage on a year's lease, then hired a Mercedes 190 from the local Hertz office, this time paying with a MasterCard credit card.

The papers he read told him that the only clue the police had solved was that Gabriel was connected with Raphael and Penuel; the link between the names of the Archangels was now headline news. 'Angels of Death'; 'Angels of Retribution'; 'The Death Angels'; 'Angels of Vengeance'; these were just some of the headlines as every newspaper tried to outdo the others. They had also traced the call from Breda, and the assassin was presumed to have escaped across Europe. He read his landlady's description; dark-haired, blue-eyed, tall. He grinned. He'd washed the Grecian 2000 out of his hair and had tossed the blue contact lenses out of the car near Cologne.

He settled down in Mannheim and waited for the call that would instruct him to go home.

Mickleton came into the Situation Room late. He carried a red folder under his arm and he threw it down angrily on the table as he took his seat.

'Sorry,' he apologised to the others round the table.

'Join the clan,' said Lacelle. 'I guess you're thin on good news as well.'

'I haven't got *any* news,' snapped back Mickleton. 'That's the shit of it.'

'Well, let's run through what we've got,' said the NSA. 'You want to kick it off, Hank?'

Mickleton opened his file, took out some sheets and spread them in front of him. 'Angels. We've run every computer we can, all over the country. Police files, payroll files, motor licence files, you name it, we've run it. I've got more angels than Heaven. Prize-fighters, Irish organizations, racing-drivers, policemen, drug pushers, angel-dust is even used as a name for a drug, politicians, Mafia hoods, saloon-owners,' he shook his head. 'We found angels everywhere. Only none of them linked to a terrorist organization or to any bomb-making, explosive or sniper activities. Just a fat zero, as far as the Bureau's concerned.'

'Same with us,' said McNabb. 'Nothing abroad, nothing from the British or any of the other European agencies. I also called Moscow. The KGB checked their records and found nothing.'

'Military and immigration came up flat as well,' added Lacelle.

'The Dutch authorities presume he went into Belgium. The call to the paper was made from Breda, a border town with Belgium. Except there's no real border these days. You don't need passports or visas, there's no customs barriers. He could've gone on to Brussels, west to France, east to Germany, even doubled back into Holland. *Where the hell do you start?'*

'The Press are heating things up,' interjected the NSA. 'We have to come up with something. The President needs answers.'

'Just say it's an international conspiracy.'

'That's fine. Except the phone calls from these *Angels*,' he spat out the word, 'end up in America.' He turned to Mickleton. 'What about your Miami Beach investigation?'

'Nothing. I've sent extra Bureau agents down to assist the local office. Up to now they've found no links. Apart from the fact they think they've uncovered an Irishman who could be under a false passport and who fits the description of a gunman that the British have circulated. We're interrogating him, but I don't think there's any connection with this little caper.'

'Do the Brits know we've got him?'

'Yeah. All they said was, "We hope"' Mickleton mimicked an English accent, '"you manage to get this one extradited. Otherwise don't waste your time."'

'Shit to them,' cursed Lacelle.

'It's the truth,' said the Director. 'If Flaherty hadn't been released, we wouldn't be involved in this mess.'

'Except it's traced back to Miami Beach. That automatically involves us.'

'Let's cool down,' interrupted the NSA. 'That was a good lead about their names from your boy in Dublin,' he said to McNabb. 'Pity the name thing blew immediately after he worked it out. We might have had some extra time before they realized we knew their code-names.'

'At the moment he's our strongest card. He's hoping to have a meeting with Captain Morrison soon.'

'Good. I also ran this thing through the banks. To see if there were any major accounts in the names of

122

Angels. A lot of religious orders, charity accounts, that sort of thing. But, up to now, nothing to link the name with where they're getting their finances.'

'Duggan thinks they need a considerable sum to mount the operations they're hitting us with.'

'I guess so.'

'How about the KGB?' asked Lacelle.

'No,' said Mickleton. 'Those guys have got enough of their own problems without taking on the IRA. Our surveillance teams on their diplomats over here are reporting very little movement. They're just burying themselves into their embassy. Hell, we've even looked at the drug barons to see whether they're hitting the Provos so that they can take over their operations and use them for drug distribution. Another theory was that the PIRA hadn't paid the Colombians for the drugs they were selling on the street to boost their funds, and that's why they were being hit. But it's all theory, all pissing in the wind while we're waiting for something more concrete.'

The phone rang and Lacelle picked it up. 'Bring it down now. Make four copies,' he barked after he listened to the message. He put the receiver back on the cradle. 'SIGINT City identified something new. Could be relevant. They're faxing it over now.'

The men talked of more general matters until a clerk delivered the fax. Lacelle looked at it, then handed the copies to the others. 'It's a phone call made from Prins Hendrikkade . . .' He had difficulty pronouncing the name. 'It's a street in Amsterdam. What you've got is a transcript of the conversation. It was a transatlantic call. The search operator dug it up when he listed all the calls with the word "Irish" in them.'

'We should get this to the Dutch authorities,' said the NSA.

'I'll do that,' said Lacelle.

'Where was the call made to?'

'Fort Lauderdale.'

No-one spoke for a while.

'That definitely puts the ball in our court,' said Mickleton eventually. 'What about the accents?'

'They're checking the voice prints now. First impression is they're both English. The man in Fort Lauderdale appears to match the same one Raphael and Penuel spoke to. The voice print should confirm that.'

'This transcript shows they had already planned to take out the Vellings. The Irishman, Campbell, he was just a fucking bonus to them.' Mickleton leant back in his chair. 'We're dealing with a large, well-oiled organization. These boys are pros. With plenty of resources behind them.'

The phone rang and Lacelle answered it. He listened then passed it over to McNabb. 'It's Langley.'

The CIA Director listened, then thanked the caller and passed the receiver back to Lacelle. 'That was our Embassy in Holland. They say the ballistics officer with the Royal Dutch Police has identified the rifle used in Amsterdam. They inspected the bullets in the bodies. It's an Accuracy International PM. One of the best.'

'Who uses that?'

'The British.'

'Who else?'

'Not a lot more. Most special forces prefer a semi-automatic, it gets more shots in. This is a single-shot, bolt-action gun. It's a favourite with SAS sniper teams. In fact, I think they're about the only special team that rely on it.'

The four men looked at each other.

There was a heavy silence in the room, no-one knowing what to say.

In the end, the NSA summed it up. He balled his fist and smashed it into the table. 'I'd better go and see the President. Shit! This is all we need.'

Duggan opened the lunch-time paper and saw the 72-point headline. REVENGE OF THE ANGELS.

He quickly read the story while he waited for Richardson in the lobby of the hotel. He slapped the paper shut when he had finished. He hoped Langley didn't think he'd made up the story after the news just so that he could look good. He crossed over the lobby to reception and asked for a morning paper. The story was headlined on the front page, though it was sketchy and dealt with the death of a PIRA man and two Dutch nationals, all shot at long range. He realized that the authorities had decided to keep Gabriel's message secret, too late for the morning editions.

'Francis,' he heard Richardson call him from across the lobby. Richardson had a companion, a man, about forty-five, wearing a blue trench coat. As Duggan walked over he saw the man wore police uniform trousers and well-polished shoes. Duggan held up the paper as he approached them.

'I know,' said Richardson. 'I've seen it.' He didn't mention that Carter had already rung him with the news last night after Duggan had left him. He introduced the man next to him. 'Chief Inspector Tack Monaghan of the Gardaí. Bomb Squad. He's an old friend of mine.' He paused while the two men shook hands. 'Tack and I go back quite a way. I trust him and he trusts me. When we do business, it's always just between the two of us.'

'What he's trying to say', said the craggy-faced Monaghan, his teeth gleaming under his walrus moustache, 'is that he's got something on me and I've something on him. So neither of us can afford to tell tales.'

Duggan laughed. 'Nice to meet you.'

'Tack's going to show us where Darcy lived. And

whatever else he thinks may help.'

Monaghan led the two men out of the hotel by the back entrance. 'No point making ourselves obvious,' he said. 'There's always a pair of eyes waiting around a corner somewhere in this town.' There was a dark grey Vauxhall Cavalier waiting further down the street. As Monaghan approached it, the driver got out and opened the passenger door. Monaghan signalled the other two into the back and slid into the front seat. 'This is Jed,' he introduced the driver when he was back in the driver's seat. 'Mr Richardson, you know,' he saw Jed nod at Richardson in the rear-view mirror, 'and an American friend from the CIA, Mr Duggan.'

'He doesn't look like a spy,' commented Jed.

'None of us do,' smiled Monaghan. 'Seán McDermott Street. Where Martyn Darcy used to live.' The car pulled into the traffic stream. 'Seán McDermott Street is a no-go area,' Monaghan continued. 'It's a bit like Belfast, except there's no Catholic–Protestant war. It's where the small-time crooks live. Everyone's either on the dole or on the fiddle, usually both. The flats and houses are boarded up with iron doors and iron grilles over the windows. Even the Post Office has got a high-barricaded wall with barbed wire running round it.'

Richardson was aware of Duggan's warning look. 'What's the matter?' he asked.

'Is he worried about me, Sam?' added Monaghan.

'I think so.'

'He's very polite.'

'Strong silent type.'

Duggan ignored the ribbing. 'Is this an official escort, Chief Inspector?'

'Call me Tack,' said Monaghan. 'Sam and I, and this reprobate driver next to me, are on the same side. It's us against the terrorists. The only thing that gets in the way are the governments. If we didn't have them to contend with, we would've sorted this mess out a long time ago.'

'Damn right,' added Richardson. 'There wouldn't be any PIRA because there wouldn't be any left.' He jabbed Duggan with his elbow. 'Don't get carried away, we're not the Angels. We don't disagree with their methods, but it's not our style.'

'Over the years there's been a few of us who've passed information on to each other,' Tack continued. 'That's our way of fighting back. It don't matter what our governments are up to, as long as *we* keep talking to each other. Do you understand that, Francis?'

'Yes,' replied a subdued Duggan. This was the shadow-world, his first contact with that elusive group of field men who made up the intelligence services and played by their own rules.

'We're not asking you to break your commitment to the CIA. Any more than I would to the Gardaí, or Sam would to his people. All we ask is that you don't inform on us.'

'Don't forget, Francis,' reminded Richardson, 'we're only helping because you asked.'

'You can be assured I won't take this any further.' Duggan knew he sounded pompous and regretted it. 'No sweat. Like you said, we're on the same side.' He remembered talk of the Circle and wondered if this was it. He remembered the phrase, 'A favour asked is a favour given – and no questions asked.' Then he realized it wasn't just one Circle. There were many, smaller concentric rings bringing together people with a common bond, that somehow joined up and became a bigger ring. He knew that members of his own organization, both retired and active, were part of this unofficial structure. As were FBI members, Special Forces, probably even members of State and Justice. It was natural that those who worked in security should sometimes trust each other more than those who controlled them. He suddenly wondered if the Angels were part of the Circle, a small renegade band doing what the others wished they had the freedom to do.

'Good.' Richardson seemed genuinely pleased. 'Just so you know, Tack and I go back more than eight years.'

'Too bloody long,' moaned Monaghan.

'He came over the border into Belfast to spend some time with our bomb disposal people.'

'Unofficially, of course. I don't think the British and Irish governments were getting on all that well, if I recall.'

'I was with the group that picked him up at the border and brought him, undercover, into the city. The trip was arranged by one of our majors; he and Tack had become friends in London after some European CT conference. Anyway, we got on, and we kept in touch. Occasionally I'd let some information get to him, sometimes he'd do the same for me. We both caught a few outlaws crossing the border that way.'

'Aye. We don't want them any more than the Brits do.'

'Where are we going?' asked Duggan.

'We told you. To where Darcy lived.'

'With his girlfriend?'

'He didn't live with her. His cover was that he was a single brickie.'

'Bricklayer,' translated Richardson.

'That's what most of them do,' went on Monaghan. 'They go from building site to building site. Difficult to keep tabs on. And they've always got a good reason for moving around.' He leant forward and opened the glove compartment, took out a box and handed it to Richardson. 'This OK? Couldn't get a holster, but it's already loaded.'

Richardson opened the box and picked up a Browning 9mm pistol. He checked it over, then slipped it into his coat pocket. From a smaller box he took out two more loaded clips which he put in his coat top pocket. He handed the empty box back to Monaghan. 'I'll return it before we go back to the mainland.'

The Cavalier pulled up next to what looked like a condemned building, part of a terraced block. The three men got out, leaving Jed to watch the car, and walked up the short path. Duggan was last and he looked down the street; it was as Monaghan had described it, a shabby, underprivileged area with burnt buildings and run-down homes and apartment blocks that would never see better days. Monaghan knocked on the peeling door and waited. When he had no reply, he knocked louder. 'Come on,' he shouted. 'I know you're in there. It's Gardaí business. And you'll not be wanting me breaking the door down.' He turned and grinned at Duggan. 'It's a rat-trap, but they always leave someone in charge. Like a housekeeper. She feeds and looks after—' He stopped as the door opened.

'Well, what'll you be worrying an old woman like me for?' said the grey-haired woman. She was in her sixties and wore a faded grey floral housecoat.

'We'd just like to look around. Where Mr Darcy used to live.' As he spoke, Monaghan pulled out his warrant card and showed it to her.

'It's about time you took your flags away,' she admonished. 'We'll need to be renting the room out again.'

'We will,' he said, pushing past her. 'We will.'

The house was like a squat inside. The carpet, although clean, was threadbare and showed the wooden floor through it. The paper was peeling off the walls and half the stair banisters were missing. Monaghan led the way upstairs and the woman, grumbling to herself, went into a back room on the ground floor.

'She'll be making herself a cup of tea down there,' Monaghan said. 'That's where they eat when she cooks for them.'

'How many people live in a place like this?' asked Duggan.

'Five or ten. And they're not people. They're animals.'

Monaghan stopped on the second landing in front of a door that was sealed off with a POLICE – DO NOT ENTER plastic banner. He pulled one side loose, let it fall to the floor, and pushed the door open. It was a small room, no more than ten feet by ten feet square. Like the rest of the house, the decoration would be classed as squat shabby. There were three mattresses side by side on the floor, all made up with sheets and blankets. 'All home comforts,' he said as he stepped over the mattresses.

'Looks like they're being used,' commented Richardson.

''Course they are. You don't think a wee sign like that's going to stop them sleeping here, do you?' He put his feet between the mattress on the right and the centre one, then pushed them apart. He leant down and turned them both over, letting them fall away in a heap. Then he bent down and pulled at the floor; three floor-boards came up in his hands. 'See that?' he said. 'That's where we found one cache. I'm surprised he kept it where he lived, which means he was probably into a rush job.'

'Any explosives?' asked a surprised Richardson.

'No. Although we did find remains of Semtex H. There was a 6V 996 lantern battery, a circuit tester, some fine black multi-strand wire and a glue gun. Forensic also found traces of hot-melt glue. We went over the rest of the house. There's storage places like this on every floor. But nothing in them. This was the only place we found any evidence of explosive materials.'

'What's that tell you?'

'That it was a secret job. Darcy wouldn't risk bringing stuff here, unless he had no choice. I think he kept it under him so he could always watch over it. I'm convinced this is the store for the materials used in Grafton Street.'

'That could also mean the Army Council didn't know what he was up to,' said Duggan softly.

'Aye. The one place they wouldn't think of searching

for anything was right under their most trusted bomber's arse. Which ties in with the phone call to the Belfast Confidential Line.'

'What call?' Duggan picked up quickly.

Monaghan looked surprised, then turned to Richardson. 'Sorry. I thought he knew.'

'Knew what?' insisted Duggan.

'Penuel,' said Richardson. 'After he rang the newspapers, he called a special informant line we have in Belfast. He told us where three explosives and arms stores were. We informed the Gardaí and that's how they discovered them.'

'That's not been reported in the press.'

'No,' cut in Monaghan. 'We wanted it that way. Just in case some of the boyos came back looking for their equipment.'

'Why didn't you tell me?' Duggan asked Richardson angrily.

'Have your disagreements elsewhere, will you?' admonished Monaghan. 'We've more to do.'

Monaghan led them out of the building, having once again secured the bedroom door. As they shut the front door they heard the old woman yell, 'Good riddance to you.'

'I guess we're being watched,' said Duggan as they got into the car.

'Aye. Those bastards have got eyes everywhere.'

They drove to the Dublin Forensic Centre, eating a quick McDonald's on the way. In the Centre, Monaghan introduced Richardson and Duggan to the forensic scientist who spent an hour explaining how the bomb had worked and why they believed it had Darcy's trademark on it. The transmitter was the key; it was exactly the same design Darcy had used before. The blue insulation tape was a bonus and could well have been planted on the body. Except that the transmitter was definitely Darcy's handiwork. At the end, as they left the building with Monaghan, both men were convinced that Darcy had designed and built the device. Monaghan dropped them back at the hotel arranging to meet them at seven that evening.

'You should've told me about the phone call,' Duggan said to Richardson as they got into the lift.

'My mistake.'

'Anything else I should know? Or do you look at this as a one-way information trade?'

'I said it was a mistake. It won't happen again,' came the grumpy reply.

Both men went to their rooms; there was now an atmosphere of tension between them again.

Richardson picked up his portable and called Carter. He informed him of all that had taken place, without naming Monaghan. Carter didn't push him; he knew how the Circle worked.

'Unfortunate,' said Carter when Richardson told him about Duggan's annoyance at not being informed about Penuel's Confidential Line phone call. 'Still, these things happen. You can cheer him up later. Tell him we've found Morrison.'

'Where?'

'Belfast. 3 Infantry. He's Weapons Intelligence Staff Officer at Brigade.'

'High-ranker.'

'Good man. Came up from the ranks. Not one of your normal Ruperts. Earned an enviable reputation as an ATO.'

Richardson knew the value of such men; Ammunition Technical Officers, more commonly known as bomb disposal experts. It wasn't something he could have done, defusing a device that could easily blow up because it was unstable or had been booby-trapped. 'Can we see him?'

'Only in Belfast. With this latest rash of attacks, they need every man they've got.'

'Duggan may want to go in there.'

'Try and dissuade him. It's MI5 territory and we would have to clear it through them. I don't think they want the Yanks seeing some of our more covert and unpleasant operations. Ask him for a set of questions that we can pass on to Morrison.'

'And if he insists on going?'

'I told you. Dissuade him. Has he come up with a reason as to why he wants to see Morrison?'

'No,' lied Richardson.

'Try and stop him going there.'

'Anything on the Angel name?'

'Nothing. We've talked to the Langley CTC and they've drawn a blank as well. The only Angel we found with terrorist connections was a Black Angel.'

'Where?'

'Angola. 1976. He was a pretty vicious UNITA military commander.'

'Have you traced him?'

'He's dead. Drove his four-wheeler over a land-mine. Blew him and his girlfriend up. The story was that UNITA dumped him because he was getting out of control.'

'Who ran him?'

'Reggie Flowers.'

'Never heard of him.'

'Before your time. I remember him. I was a new boy in those days. He was a Grade 3 operations man. Damn good. Ran part of Africa. Dead now. Died about ten years ago. Couldn't take the retirement, someone said.'

'I doubt this has got anything to do with Angola.'

'So do I. We're also checking all the retired specialist teams.'

'Good idea.' Richardson suddenly realized that each hit had been carried out by a separate specialist. The close-quarters killer in New York, the explosives expert

133

in Dublin and the sniper in Amsterdam. That's why they had been so successful, so expertly carried out. Each man was a trained practitioner in his own specialized field. It was how the Army worked. It was how the SAS worked. He didn't make any further comments; even if the line was cleared through GCHQ, there would be a recording made of it and he didn't want to be heard saying that the suspicion went beyond just retired ex-servicemen.

'They're also hitting other nationals now,' continued Carter. 'Not just the IRA. Killing the Dutch couple means they could be going after any supporters of the Provos. That'll worry the Americans. They still have citizens with links into the Republicans. Which reminds me. The NSA traced a call from Amsterdam to the jolly old USA. Fort Lauderdale in Florida. From Gabriel. Voice prints show he was British and also the person he was speaking to matched the other conversations. It looks like the whole thing's orchestrated from over the pond.'

'Except they're British personnel.'

'Yes,' replied Carter drily. 'Bad news for us. Very sticky.'

When Richardson finished, he undressed for a shower. He knew why he was sweating even though the room was quite cold. It was the thought of going back into Belfast, into that city of his worst nightmares. He tried to block out the face of the running soldier; he could've been no more than nineteen, fresh-faced with soft unstubbled skin, running towards him, crying with fear, knowing that Richardson could—

He pushed it from his mind and went into the shower where he turned the water so hot that it burnt him and helped him forget the torment that was his alone to bear.

Duggan had relaxed when they met later and Richardson told him that they had traced Morrison.

He wasn't quite as relaxed when Richardson told him where he was. 'Belfast! Can we get him out so that—' He stopped as Richardson shook his head. 'Can we go in?'

Richardson said he would ask Carter, although he felt the American should also clear it with Langley. He explained the possible difficulties with MI5. They both knew that Belfast was considered the British mainland and the CIA were not expected to have operators on the ground. London had been OK, but Belfast, with all its itinerary problems, was another matter. 'The best way is for you to prepare some questions, and we'll get them passed on.'

Duggan had returned to his room to call America. Before he dialled Langley, he tried the house in Adams Morgan. It was his sixth attempt of the day and there had been no reply. This time there was. It was Martia, the maid who cleaned twice a week.

'Is Carmella there?' he asked.

'No,' came the unco-operative answer. She had never liked him, had always believed Carmella's constant complaints about him.

'Where is she?'

'They've gone away.'

'All of them?'

'To his parents. In Arizona. He wanted them to meet his parents.'

He felt the panic rise in him. 'When will they be back?'

'She didn't say. Soon, they've got to go back to school.'

'I'll – ask her to—'

Martia cut across him sweetly; he could tell she was being extra polite. 'They went,' she oozed, 'because he's thinking of moving them all to Arizona. That's where his family business is. Bye, Mr Duggan.'

The phone went dead and he slammed it down. *How the hell could he visit Arizona every weekend?*

135

When he eventually calmed down he called Langley. He told them he wanted to go to Belfast, that he didn't want to interview Morrison by questionnaire. The Director of Operations mistook his brusque anger for coolness. He said he would ring Grosvenor Square and try to get the visit arranged.

While Duggan fumed, Richardson told Carter that Duggan was insistent that he wanted to go into Ulster. 'I tried to dissuade him,' he said. Carter eventually agreed to contact MI5, but pointed out that if the American crossed the border, it would be MI5, not Richardson, who would be handling the operation.

'Make sure you've got the portable with you if you go out,' reminded Carter.

They met Monaghan at seven; he led them out through the back entrance once again. This time they drove to Westside. It was an area of Dublin that had long since seen better days, yet tried to lift itself into the present. The former Kilmainham prison stood at its centre. Built in 1798 it had been home to most of Ireland's political prisoners including the signatories of the 1916 Proclamation of the Republic who were shot in the yard by a British firing-squad. It is now a museum, restored magnificently to its former depressive condition.

It was dark when they drew up in the car-park of Quincey's Bar and Restaurant. Jed left the engine running and went into the pub. He returned five minutes later, accompanied by a woman of about thirty, all tinsel and fake, her short, tight skirt wrapped indecently round her skinny legs as she wobbled on six-inch high heels. Monaghan got out, asked Duggan to sit in the front, took the girl's arm and pushed her into the back seat and slid in after her, squeezing her between himself and Richardson. Jed got back in and drove out of the car-park.

'Hello, Mary,' said Monaghan. 'I see you're dressed for a busy night.'

'I'm not doing anything wrong, Mr Monaghan,' she replied primly.

'You're always doing something wrong,' he snapped; she jerked at the harshness of it. 'We can talk while we're driving or we can call in to the Gardaí HQ on Blackhorse.'

'I'd rather not be seen going into the police station, if you don't mind.'

Monaghan nodded. 'These two gentlemen are friends of mine. They'd like some answers.'

She looked at Duggan then at Richardson and gave a weak smile. 'Always ready to help.'

'It's to do with Martyn Darcy.'

'I didn't know him that well,' she replied, too fast for her own good. They knew she was lying. 'Not too well, anyway.' She tried to repair the damage.

'Sally Dillon was your best friend.'

'She was. And it was a tragedy what happened on Grafton Street.'

'Who did it, Mary?'

'I don't know. On the Pope's grave, I don't know.'

'But you'll have heard something.'

'Nothing.'

'Nothing?' asked Monaghan. Then he gripped her elbow and squeezed it viciously between his thumb and index finger. She shrieked. Duggan looked away, but Richardson watched her closely; he'd seen her sort before. He knew she had a good idea of what was going on. It was part of the pillow-talk that went with her profession.

'There's all sorts being said. In truth no-one knows nothing.'

'Tell me, Mary.' Monaghan leant menacingly towards her again.

'The only thing I know for certain is that they had a visitor.'

'Who?'

'I don't know. Except Martyn and Sally both knew him. And Martyn was doing a job for him.'

'Was he Republican?'

'No. Not one of the regulars, anyway. That's all I know,' she said defiantly.

'A Belfast man?'

'Not at all.'

'Not with Martyn. He was a Republican through and through. Let's get to the station, Jed,' Monaghan told the driver impatiently.

'No. You said not,' cried Mary.

'I need a statement.'

'But *they'll* see me.' Who the *they* were was left unsaid, but they all knew to whom she referred. 'It was dangerous enough you coming in the pub.'

'You've not told us everything.'

'I have,' she cried, with one last defiant refutation.

'Then we need a statement. At the station.'

Her back-street instinct told her any further denial was pointless.

'All right. There was one thing. Sally knew this bloke well. I mean, she – you know – they shared a bed regular.'

'Did Martyn know?'

'He'd kill her if—' She stopped, realizing that Sally was already dead. 'They both knew him from way back.'

'Belfast?'

'I think so. Sally raved about him.'

'Was he English?' asked Richardson.

'I don't know.'

'If she raved about him, then – girls' talk. Was he English?'

'He was.'

'Was he Army?'

She nodded. 'That's why Sally knew him from Belfast. When he was serving there.'

'Was his name Morrison?'

'No. She never said.'

'Never. Unlikely, isn't it?'

Mary shook her head.

'Even with you two being so close? Come on – like I said, girls' talk.'

'Why should she tell me? The name meant nothing to me, did it? It could've been Jimmy or Peter or anything. It wasn't important.'

'She must've called him something when she referred to him,' interjected Monaghan.

'He was just her SAS man.' She stopped sharply.

'SAS, was he?'

'That's what she called him. That was all.'

Richardson believed her. 'Did you know Martyn helped the Brits?'

'Nobody knows that,' she replied incredulously.

'But you knew?'

'Sally told me. It was a long time ago.'

'How long was the Brit here for?' cut in Monaghan.

'About three weeks.'

'And did Sally go to a hotel and see him?'

'Yes.' Almost a whisper.

'Where?'

'I don't know. I, honest to God, don't. Sally was scared, in case the Provos found out. Then they would've killed her and Martyn. She didn't say where. Except it was near the city centre.'

There was little else she knew and they dropped her near the pub.

'I'll start a check on all the local hotels,' Monaghan said as they drove back to the Gresham. 'He probably registered under a false name, but if he stayed in one place for three weeks we might narrow the field.'

'He was SAS,' reminded Duggan.

'Maybe,' said Richardson. 'Every soldier I know tells a bird he's trying to pull that he's with the SAS. It's the ones who don't say anything that usually are.'

The encrypted portable phone rang and Richardson clicked it on.

It was Carter. 'Your man can visit. Their legal attaché's been on to Five. They don't mind as long as you keep him close to you. They'll have instructions for you when you go in. Remember, it's their territory. Make sure he understands that.'

Richardson broke out in a sweat. It was the last place he wanted to go. 'I don't want to go by air.'

'I understand that.' Carter knew that Richardson could be identified if he passed through the airport. It wasn't only Special Branch who ran surveillance teams on who came in and out. 'I suggest the Casacom. Work out the times and I'll get you picked up.'

'Tomorrow?'

'Whenever you're ready. How did your meeting go?'

Richardson gave Carter a brief résumé of the meeting with Mary. 'Involving the Army. I don't like the sound of that,' said Carter and clicked off.

'We're going to Belfast,' Richardson told Duggan. He turned to Monaghan. 'Can I keep the Browning?'

'No problem. How're you going over?'

'Casacom. On the Concession Road.'

'I'll make sure we haven't too many patrols out that way at the time you go through.'

Monaghan joined the two men for a drink at the Gresham's bar.

Duggan listened quietly; he was tired and the effects of his Atlantic jet-lag were catching up with him. He decided to have an Irish whiskey; Monaghan had suggested it would help him sleep better.

The whiskey, a Jamesons Crested 10, was just starting to take effect; Duggan was forcing himself to keep his eyes open when Monaghan casually mentioned the Plan.

'Could be someone's activated the Plan,' said Monaghan.

'That's a rumour. There's never been any substance to that,' replied Richardson.

'Oh, it was real, all right. I saw a copy. Our boys were ready to be involved.' Monaghan lit a cigarette and offered one to Richardson who shook his head.

'I've had nine. I'm saving the last one for when I go to bed.'

'Ach, you're wasting your time. You'll be back puffing these terrible things within weeks of giving up.' Monaghan took a deep drag, blew out the smoke and continued. 'It was all because of our own Ulster invasion. The one in 1970 that never happened.'

He referred to the Irish government's secret plot to invade Ulster using the IRA as guerrillas. In an attempt to isolate the Marxists from the 'old' IRA, the Government laundered money through four secret bank accounts to finance a group that eventually became the Provisional IRA. The Finance Minister of the time, Charles Haughey, later went on to become Prime Minister. The invasion was meant to have started with the PIRA gaining strategic positions in Newry, Derry and Belfast, thus thwarting the British forces while the Irish army moved into positions behind them. An old army camp in County Donegal was used by the Government for training in guerrilla warfare, and more than thirty men from Londonderry went there in 1969. While they were being trained, money, in the form of cash, was smuggled north over the border to help set up the manning of barricades in the Catholic areas and for the smuggling of guns into Belfast. In the end, the strategy, which was known as 'Doomsday', was never instigated, mostly because the Irish government realized they did not have the resources for a major civil war which would leave Eire and its people devastated.

'The Irish government came close to cutting their own throats at the time. Hell, most of us in the south don't even want Ulster as part of Eire. I mean, who wants those problems? The last thing I want is a bunch of crazy Protestants running loose with their bombs and guns down here.'

'Tell me about the Plan?'

'Well, after news of the invasion plan got out, some of your people in Army Intelligence were told to draw up counter-measures. Just in case. I don't know who prepared it, but it was presented to the British Cabinet.'

'What did it specify?'

'That a special Task Force be set up. The Doomsday Team, I think it was called. Not very imaginative, but effective. The idea was that the British intelligence services knew where most of the terrorists were. The SAS, Paras and police were going to move in one quick sweep and take them out.'

'Fully?'

'Aye. No prisoners. Just wipe them out and face the flak from the world afterwards.'

'I still think it was a rumour.'

'It wasn't. I was approached about it. It was only a few years back.'

'Why you?'

'By my own people. The Irish government were worried that their involvement in the original Doomsday would come out. So, they said they were prepared to help your lot. It was a trade, to keep the Irish government in power. There was an election coming up and they didn't want egg over their face so close to voting.' Monaghan looked over at Duggan, who appeared to have dozed off. 'The whiskey's working. We should get him to bed.'

'Tell me what happened,' insisted Richardson.

'The Gardaí were going to knock any known PIRA terrorists over the head if they crossed the border, those that lived in the south, that is. Then we were going to hand them over to your military. On one condition.

That we never knew what happened to them, or how you disposed of the bodies.'

'You agreed that?'

'Aye. Only the Plan was never implemented. I think your Cabinet blew it out.'

'Shame. It would've stopped a lot of headaches.'

'It would. But they weren't thinking of that. All they were worried about is how many votes it could lose them.'

'You think someone could be using that Plan now?'

'Well, I know that it had all the locations, personnel and logistics of the Provos. Some of the details are out of date now, but as a strategy, it's all in place.'

'Somebody might even have gone on up-dating it. Just in case.'

'That thought had also crossed my mind.'

'I'm not going to mention it till I get back to London. Even on a scrambled line, you don't know who might be listening, at our end.'

'Well, I'm just telling you there was a Plan. What you do with it is up to you.'

They shook Duggan awake. After he and Richardson had said their goodbyes to Monaghan, the two men went to their rooms.

'You heard all that, didn't you?' asked Richardson in a matter-of-fact way as they climbed the stairs.

'Yes. I was about to drop off when he mentioned it.'

'Keep it under your hat. You never know when we might need it.'

'Why did Monaghan discuss it in front of me?'

'You're in the Circle now. You, me and Monaghan. That's our Circle. Remember, no favour refused, no questions asked.'

'Except in the line of duty.'

'Except in the line of duty.'

Richardson rang Andrea when he entered his room.

'Hello, darling,' she said in a sleepy voice.

'You in bed?'

'Hmm.'

'Tough day?'

'Haven't been off my feet. Three major surgeries.'

'Go back to sleep.'

'No, talk to me.'

'I'm going into the old place tomorrow.'

'Where?'

'To the north of here.'

'That's not fair!' She was suddenly wide awake.

'Just for a few days.' He knew she was worried, but he had to tell her. She'd once made him promise to keep her informed about when he went into dangerous situations. 'No sweat.'

'With Francis?'

'Yes. He's doing an interview.'

'I wish you were here.'

'Don't tempt me. You'd better get back to sleep.'

'I won't. I'm worried now.'

'You always told me to tell you.'

'It's the way I want it. Are you all right?'

'Yes. Be glad when it's over.'

'So will I.'

'Go back to sleep.'

'I love you.'

'I love you.' Richardson put the phone down gently, held it as though it was Andrea.

Then he undressed and went to bed. He lay watching the ceiling for nearly an hour before he dropped off. Sleep before danger had never come easily to him.

It was an emergency meeting, called by Griffin, in the aftermath of the Buitenveldert assassination.

They met in one of the back rooms; they were safe there with the armed wingers positioned outside the door and in the bar.

'This time I want something that's going to make them all sit up and take notice. No more soft targets. Not like the Red Lion shit.' Griffin glared at McAteer. 'Have you come up with anything?'

'No,' replied the subdued director of operations. 'I've got all the section commanders searching for the right one. Hell, Michael, we were only asked for a report less than forty-eight hours ago.'

'Hit the Queen. Or one of the royals,' said Father O'Malley. 'That'll concentrate their minds.'

'Couldn't guarantee that in time. It's like the Mountbatten thing. Has to be planned properly.' He looked round the table. 'Unless you want a suicide squad. Then we can have a go. Even at the Prime Minister.'

'No,' said Griffin. 'No suicide squad. They're too messy if they go wrong.'

'The Dutch massacre's having a bad effect on us already,' continued Father O'Malley. 'People I was dealing with abroad, trying to raise more weapons, have just gone quiet on us. They're not saying no – they're just not saying.'

'We mustn't be seen to be weak, to be backing down. We can't even get Darcy's body out of Dublin for a military funeral. The pathologist insists on a full examination. At least Flaherty's back from America. We want a double funeral, get maximum publicity.'

'We're double-checking Flaherty's body before it goes into the coffin,' said Baxter. 'We'll do the same with

Darcy.' The IRA had become neurotic about coffins being bugged during official funerals since the writer Frederick Forsyth had included the possibility of such activity in a best-selling novel. Since then, they searched all coffins and cadavers as well as the ground and head-stones round the area in which the grave was dug. 'Des Campbell's body is going to take longer to get back. That's down to the Dutch authorities. We can have a second military funeral with honours when he's finally brought back.'

'I can step up operations in Belfast. Take out a few more Prods, hit the soldiers harder.' McAteer felt on safe ground; increasing Provo activity in the city was always an easy option.

'That's not where the battle is. It's on the mainland. That's where we've got to step up.' He swung round to Baxter. 'Have you had any more intelligence reports on who's behind this yet?'

Baxter shook his head. 'All we've got is that Monaghan from the Gardaí went down to Darcy's dwellings. He had two men with him, both foreigners. The old woman who looks after the house says one was a Brit and the other sounded like an American.'

'Did you get pictures?'

'Aye. They're being developed now. But that's all we've picked up.'

'Are you still going on holiday?' McAteer asked Baxter, eager to take the heat off himself.

Baxter nodded.

'You can't do that,' said Griffin.

'It's booked.'

'I don't bloody care.'

'The wife'll go berserk. She's been looking forward to—'

'I said I don't bloody care.'

'I've paid my money,' Baxter said indignantly. IRA men might have enjoyed job satisfaction, but their

146

take-home pay was minuscule, even for members of the Army Council. 'I won't get it back.'

'Let him go,' interrupted Father O'Malley. 'Let him go, Michael. It's only a week.'

'Nine days.'

'Let him go,' appealed Father O'Malley again. 'God, we could all do with a holiday, sometimes. It won't make a difference. He's got a good intelligence network. They can report to me or Séamus if anything comes up. And in an emergency we can always fly him home.'

'At his own cost,' said Griffin. 'Bloody Disney World.'

'Ach, the kids are looking forward to it,' shrugged Baxter. He decided to change the subject with some good news. 'Our contact at the Gardaí tells us he thinks whoever reported the position of our ammunition stores made the call to the Confidential Line in Belfast.'

'That's an SAS line.'

'It's a military line. Also used by their intelligence services.'

'Then that's where we hit them.' Griffin swung round to McAteer. 'Hit them where it hurts. Amongst their own kind. That's the operation you'd better put together.' He next addressed Baxter as head of intelligence. 'I want all the information you've got on any covert actions the Brits are running. In Belfast and in Armagh.' The next statement he addressed to all those in the room. 'Angels, my arse. We'll soon clip their fucking wings.'

BOOK TWO

NIGHTMARES WITH HAPPY
ENDINGS

N1
The north road out of Dublin

Richardson hired a Ford Escort the next morning and
waited for Carter to ring. The call came through at
eleven; the northern route had been set up and Richardson was given his final instructions. He thought about
ringing Andrea at the hospital, but decided against it;
she'd be in theatre by now.

They booked out at just after eleven and left the
city to the north, along the N1 coast road. It was a dry,
crisp day with the sun occasionally breaking through the
high cloud. Richardson told Duggan how they would be
going into Ulster. He explained why it was impossible
for him to go in by plane; he could not take the chance
of being recognized by an old enemy who might try to
take revenge. He pointed out some of the landmarks
as he drove, keeping the car within the speed limit,
not wanting to draw any extra attention to himself.
His heart pounded as he got closer to the border; it

had been a long time since he had driven into the face of danger.

Duggan was also nervous. This time he wasn't a tourist, but an agent going underground into enemy territory. That confused him; there was family in Belfast, known Republican supporters. He was being asked to take sides, yet it wasn't his fight. He asked Richardson about his days with the SAS, about how they had been trained. 'I hear they used to put your head in a sack full of snakes,' he said. 'Is that right?'

Richardson laughed, pleased to be taken out of his fearful thoughts. 'They weren't poisonous.'

'Hell, even so. How long for?'

'Twenty minutes, maybe half an hour. Brought out all the deep-rooted phobias you might have had. Worse was when they'd squiggle up your nose or try and burrow into your ear.' He grinned as he saw Duggan react with disgust. It wasn't all true; it had all taken no more than five minutes. He remembered giggling his way through that particular exercise. Fear wasn't something he had understood in those days. The young soldier's desperate face flashed into his mind and he tried to ignore it. 'You ever hear about the Killing House?' he asked.

'No.'

'That was built for Special Projects. It was a house with a single room, set up to represent a hostage situation. The hostages, all SAS men, were mixed with the guards. Only the guards were shop-window dummies. We were the live dummies,' he laughed. 'The idea was that a team of three men would enter the room from different areas, two from separate windows, one through the front door. They'd carry stun grenades and semi-automatic weapons. The room was in darkness. On a signal, they'd come through their entry-points, throw the stun grenade, then with live ammunition, take out the guards. All in four seconds. I tell you what, you needed fast and accurate reactions to avoid killing other SAS men instead of the dummy guards.'

'They do that at the Farm. Only we use film projection.'

'So do we now. In the Killing House. Three years ago an SAS sergeant was shot in the head when he was acting as hostage.'

'Not good.'

Richardson shrugged. 'I'm surprised no-one got hit before that.' He remembered how callous some of his colleagues had been; how sitting in one of those hostage chairs became like a game of 'chicken', how they all knew someone would get killed one day and how it gave them all a high.

'How long were you undercover?'

'About a year.'

'That's long, isn't it?'

'Yes. I never tried to be Irish. Took another Manchester boy's identity. He was killed in a mining accident in Pennsylvania. I was a Catholic, like him, so I understood all the lingo. He'd been a Marxist supporter, so I came here and pretended I was bringing the revolution to Belfast. They all thought I was a nutter. Certainly acted like one.' Richardson chuckled. 'I became two people. A raving, loony, left-winger in Belfast and a normal human being when I went home. Which wasn't very often.'

'Were you with Andrea then?'

'Just. She knew I did something dangerous in the Army. I only managed twelve days with her that year. Surprised she stuck with me. Mind you, I got some good information out. Surprising what you pick up when you're in a pub, acting pissed.'

'What happened?'

'Oh, things got too dangerous. My cover was ragged. I lived in squats and out of dustbins. The Army was hassling me in the streets as much as the Prods and

Catholics. Then we got a report that someone had been asking questions in the Coroner's Office in Pennsylvania. So they pulled me out.'

'Just that easy?'

'Yes. Just came and told me to get out.' He remembered when they'd come, remembered the boy soldier's face. 'Yes. Just that easy.'

They left the coast at Balbriggan and followed the road inland to Drogheda, where it met the coastline again, and then continued up to Dundalk.

'We're only three miles south of the border,' said Richardson as they passed through the town, then turned west and took the N53 towards Monaghan, some thirty-five miles inland.

There was a sudden increase in security vehicles and Gardaí police cars. For all the Irish greenery and beauty, Duggan sensed the increase in tension. The road, a two-lane highway, ran alongside the border all the way until it joined up with the N2, the Dublin to Monaghan expressway at Castleblaney. Duggan had already looked at a map before they left Dublin. He was surprised they weren't taking the N2; it was a more direct route. But he decided not to say anything; this wasn't his playground. He watched a British Army Lynx helicopter scouting to the north.

'Welcome to Northern Ireland,' said Richardson.

'But I haven't seen a border post.'

'You won't on this route. This road is in Eire, except for about four miles, where it becomes the A37 and runs through the southern tip of County Armagh. That's why it's known as the Concession Road.'

'So we're in bandit country?'

'Yes. This area's called the Casacom. That's Gaelic for "Place of Rocks". It's a favourite spot for illegal vehicle checks by PIRA gangs. There's more PIRA here than anywhere. They like to think they run this patch. See the blue van about two cars behind?' He waited until

152

Duggan had identified it in the vanity mirror on his sun visor. 'They've been after us for nearly ten miles. I think that's a Republican escort, checking up on us. And if they're not, someone else will be. We've probably been covertly photographed by both British and PIRA watchers. The Brits will also be feeding this car number into a computer to see if there's anything suspicious about us.' Richardson drove through a small village, Cullaville, then announced, 'We're back in Eire.'

In his mirror, Duggan saw that the blue van was still doggedly following them, keeping its exact distance as they moved along. They soon joined the N2 and continued their journey north-westwards.

They entered the market town of Monaghan forty minutes later. 'This town was bombed by Ulster paramilitaries in 1974,' recalled Richardson. 'The Republicans want to make sure that doesn't happen again.'

'Can't blame them.'

'Don't disagree.'

The traffic was heavy and they stopped at the Four Seasons for lunch, leaving the car in the rear car-park. 'I'll leave you to do most of the talking,' said Richardson as they entered the restaurant. 'This town is infested with Provisionals. Play the tourist. Go heavy on the American accent.'

They sat by the window and passed the time talking about the beautiful countryside and the friendly people. To the waitress who served them, they were a couple of tourists; that's what she told the man in the kitchen who always asked about strangers.

They walked around the town after they had eaten. Richardson nodded towards the large masonry cross in the centre of the town. There was a group of men sitting round the cross. 'Most of those guys are well-known fugitives,' said Richardson. 'It's their way of rubbing our faces in it. Even the Gardaí won't interfere. They'd never make it across the square.'

153

After a short stroll, they returned to the car and started back towards Dublin.

'Van's still there,' said Richardson.

'I never saw anyone following us.'

'You never do. There's plenty of illegal crossing points all along the border. Hundreds of roads and tracks were blasted by the Army in order to channel traffic along a few controllable routes. Local people resented that, can't say I blame them, and they opened the roads again. Not obviously, but enough so that local traffic can dodge its way round the craters.'

They turned left at Castleblaney and once more drove along the N53. They were a mile into the Northern Ireland section when the cars in front slowed down. There was only the blue van behind them. The rest of the traffic had continued along the N2.

'Shit. Didn't expect this,' said Richardson, easing the car to a stop. He pulled the 9mm Browning from his jacket, cocked it and put it between the seats, its handle towards him so that he could reach it quickly.

The blue van eased itself up to Richardson's rear bumper.

Duggan saw the first paramilitary guard walk round two cars in front. It was a shock, seeing the man instead of the picture in the newspaper he was used to. This was real. The Balaclava over his head, the grey parka, the dirty jeans over the black walking shoes; all real. Just like the Belgian FNC assault rifle he carried. Two further PIRA members appeared behind him, both dressed as their companion, both armed with German G-3s. The leader leant over to the driver's window and spoke to the occupants in the first car.

The men in the blue van stayed in their vehicle.

'Illegal border check-point,' said Richardson. 'Just remember, play the Yank. We're on holiday and I'm your English wife's brother. Carmella, right?'

'Yeah.'

154

'Two kids and you live in Washington. Adams Morgan.'

'You boys do your homework.'

'Supplied by your people. I don't know much else.'

The car being searched was waved on and the queue edged forward.

The van followed them, keeping its bonnet right up to the Escort's rear bumper.

'Provos behind us,' said Richardson.

'You sure?'

'Yes. They've blocked us in so that we can't reverse out. Standard stuff.'

'Are we in deep shit?'

Richardson hooted. 'Could be.' He was grateful that Duggan hadn't noticed how nervous he was. 'They run these illegal VCPs all round here.'

'VCP?'

'Vehicle check-point. These clowns do it all the time. All over the north, not just at the border. Shit. This area should be clear with us coming through.'

The terrorist in front stood up, waved the other car on and beckoned Richardson forward.

As the Escort crept towards the gunman, the blue van moved with it, its front bumper no more than six inches behind Richardson's exhaust.

The gunman leant down and tapped his gun-barrel on the driver's window. 'Open up,' he ordered. 'Get this window down.'

Richardson wound the glass down.

'Papers,' said the gunman. His two cohorts moved alongside him, their guns resting easily on their arms.

'Hey, what the hell's going on here?' Duggan leant over and asked. 'We're on vacation.'

'Yanks, are you?'

The van nudged itself up to the Escort, bumping it forward gently.

'Yeah. Who're you guys?'

'Just give me your passports. Come on, we haven't got all day.' The gunman was getting irritated now.

'Hurry up, will you?' shouted one of his companions.

'Your passports.' The questioner pushed the muzzle of the gun into Richardson's shoulder.

Behind them the two occupants of the blue van climbed out. Both of them carried hand-guns. 'Get a move on,' one of them yelled. 'Or the fucking patrol will get here.'

'Hold it, hold it,' said a frightened Duggan. He reached into his pocket and took out his American passport. He held it towards the gunman.

'Give us yours,' the terrorist bellowed at Richardson, ramming the gun harder into his shoulder.

Before the terrorist had the chance to grab the passports, the khaki-coloured Lynx helicopter came over the hill and raced towards them, chattering noisily and with soldiers and guns hanging out. The gunmen heard the sound first, and ran towards a red 1979 Cortina parked on the opposite side of the road. The men behind jumped into the blue van and reversed away, zigzagging down the road. The red Cortina pulled out, swung round and headed east. The van, as it backed down the road, nearly crashed into a military Land-Rover that came round the corner. The van did a 180-degree turn, then drove off towards the N2 junction.

The helicopter swooped lower over the Escort and landed in front of it. Behind them, the Land-Rover turned and gave chase to the blue van.

An army lieutenant, in full combat gear and armed with an Enfield SA-80 machine-gun, approached the Escort as Richardson climbed out.

'You're late!' snapped Richardson. Duggan joined him at the front of the car.

'I was told to make it as authentic as possible,' replied the equally irritated lieutenant.

'Did you know there was an illegal VCP?'

'Most unexpected that. That's why we decided to wait. Makes it more authentic, don't you think?' The lieutenant smiled through his sarcasm.

'Fuck off, Rupert,' said Richardson quietly, turning away. He took off his jacket as two ordinary soldiers approached the group. He turned to Duggan. 'Take your clothes off and put on the army uniform. Take your wallet and personal belongings with you. Just leave your passport behind. You'll get it back later.' As he spoke he took his shirt off and then his trousers. The two soldiers also undressed; they had been deliberately chosen for their similar builds to Richardson and Duggan. The four men exchanged clothes, then the two soldiers, now in civvies and with Duggan's passport, climbed into the Escort and drove off eastwards towards Dundalk.

The Land-Rover returned after its unsuccessful chase as Duggan and Richardson completed dressing. They were now, to all intents and purposes, soldiers in the British army, out on patrol in South Armagh. Two of the three soldiers in the Land-Rover got out and crossed over to the Lynx and boarded. The helicopter lifted off as Richardson and Duggan clambered into the Land-Rover. They were both handed an SA-80 by the driver, a sergeant.

'Keep an eye out for bandits,' he warned them. 'I want to make sure you get back in one piece.'

They turned north at Cullaville and followed the narrow twisting lane past the Army border-post where they were waved through, and then went towards Newry. Overhead the helicopter kept a watch on their progress, flying low so that it could react quickly to an ambush. But the run through the small hills and winding hedgerows was clear and they came into the outskirts of Newry thirty-five minutes later. Two more Land-Rovers joined them and escorted them up the A1 to Belfast. The helicopter returned to duty along the border.

To watchers, Duggan and Richardson were two soldiers coming back from patrol. Three had gone out in that specific Land-Rover and three now returned.

On the road between Dundalk and Drogheda, a green Lada with Eire plates overtook the Escort and flagged it down.

The occupants of the Escort weren't too worried; it was a busy road with traffic bustling along in both directions.

A man got out of the Lada and approached the two men. 'Are you both OK?' he asked when the driver wound the window down.

'Yes, why?' asked the driver in an English accent.

'I was behind you back near Monaghan,' came the reply. 'There was a terrorist check-point, then the Army arrived. I saw you get away. Just wanted to make sure you were fine.'

'No problem,' said the passenger in what appeared to be an American accent. 'Mind you, they nearly got my passport.' He pulled his passport out from his pocket and waved it. 'Lucky, hey?'

'You were that,' said the man who had stopped them. He knew an American passport when he saw one. 'Have a good trip,' he said. 'I'm glad you're both well.' He went back to his car, drove to the nearest call-box and rang his PIRA commander. 'They're tourists,' he reported. 'One was an American, I saw his passport. Just having a wee holiday, that's all.'

The two out-of-uniform soldiers who had replaced Richardson and Duggan continued on to Dublin, returned the Escort to the car-hire firm and caught the evening flight to London.

The Victoria Embankment
London

The Irishman leant against the stone wall and read the *Evening Standard* under the lamplight.

He was on his break and always enjoyed getting some fresh air after the mugginess of the bar at the *Tattersall Castle*. The headline story was still about the assassination of the PIRA gunman and the two Dutch supporters in Amsterdam. The whole affair, the deaths of Flaherty, Darcy and now the Dutch group filled him with a perverse joy. The Catholics deserved it. For what they'd done to Belfast. For what they'd done to his Ma. The tension had killed her, had caused her to have a stroke from which she never recovered. He'd been young then, a freedom fighter against the Catholics. But the fear of what might happen to him had killed her; she couldn't take the knowledge that he was out there, always in danger, always waiting for the Catholic assassin's bullet.

He felt the rush of emotion and fought to hold it back. He concentrated on the newspaper.

Angels. *What a fucking hoot!*

Who were they? They were either Orangemen or the British authorities. And he couldn't see the Government being involved.

Angels. *They were that all right. Avenging ange—*

Then he remembered his handler.

Remembered his code-name.

Remembered his expertise with a sniper's rifle.

He put the paper down and stared out across the Thames. A party steamer went past, its decks packed with heaving bodies, the music blaring as they faced the cold. It was strange the things people did to enjoy themselves.

He thought of Hampstead Heath and decided to go there later.

Sean tossed the paper into the Thames, watched it separate, sheet by sheet, and flutter into the water. He turned and walked back to the *Tattersall Castle*. An older couple looked at him reproachfully. *Litter lout*. He grinned and blew them a kiss.

As he crossed the gangplank he thought about the news item he had read.

He realized he knew an Angel.

Girdwood Park
Belfast

The three Land-Rovers entered Belfast on the M1.

Duggan kept his eyes open for snipers as he had been told to, the SA-80 straddled across his knees, ready for action. As they drove through the city, Richardson acted like a tour guide. Only this tour was based on tales of horror, of torture, of burnt homes, of exploded bodies. As he looked at the passers-by, he saw hate in their eyes. It was not a sensation he had experienced before. This was how invading armies must have felt; the expressions he saw were the same the Parisians must have had for the Nazis or the Muscovites for Napoleon. He'd never seen Belfast like this before. His uniform made him an object of hate. Children swore; one even threw a stone at the Land-Rover. A group of women, still with their prams and shopping bags, rushed over when they stopped at a traffic light and shrieked abuse at them. Richardson and the sergeant ignored it, dismissed it as if it wasn't happening in front of their eyes. Richardson warned him to ignore all passers-by, to avert his look otherwise they believed they had your attention and that increased their fury. So he looked away, a blank, haven't-seen-you sort of stare. He didn't know if it worked, but from that moment on, as he sat there in this strange army uniform, he decided to ignore what was going on round him. He gripped the gun tighter and looked warily round for snipers. He suddenly realized he hadn't thought about Carmella and the kids ever since they'd left Dublin. He wondered where she'd taken them. It was all so crazy. Some guy was giving his kids a good time, God knows where, and he was stuck in a four-wheel drive with a gun across his knees, looking for snipers. He cursed under his breath. It was a helluva way to get on with your life.

The jet-lag resurfaced and made him yawn. They turned towards the Antrim Road, and passed the notorious Unity Flats. He recognized them from his own research pictures in Langley; they had been the site of many violent disorders in the early seventies.

The barracks of Girdwood Park, where they were to meet Morrison, lay behind the Crumlin Road prison. Often, when the boom of an exploding bomb was heard in the city, a roar of triumphant approval from the prison inmates greeted its dying echoes. It was just one of the aspects of Belfast life that the soldiers of Girdwood Park had come to tolerate. Richardson pointed out the prison, the law courts and the barracks. 'There's an underground tunnel connecting the Crum to the law courts,' he said. 'That's where all the IRA trials are held.'

The Land-Rover turned towards the barracks. It was an olive-green building, fortress-like in appearance, made ready to defend itself against the mortar attacks that the Provos had been known to launch. Duggan relaxed and leant back as the three Land-Rovers crossed the staggered entrance and concrete sleeping-policemen, past the sentry point and into the safety of the mortar-proof protective walls. He swung his leg over the side and followed Richardson.

'I'll take those, please,' said the sergeant holding out his hand. The two men handed over their SA-80s, then Richardson led the way into the barracks. He knew his way round and walked briskly down the dingy, cream-painted corridor. He reached a door near the end, marked OC. GIRDWOOD and knocked.

'Come in,' said a man's voice. Richardson opened it and beckoned Duggan into the spartan but neat office.

There were two men in there. The OC, thirty-seven-year-old Major Dennis Farquharson, sat behind his black-topped mahogany desk that had grey plastic trays for documents on each side. His big leather chair, a trophy from some bombed-out store, looked as though it had belonged to Robert Maxwell before he jumped in the Atlantic without his water wings. Farquharson was a big, red-faced man. But, for all his bonhomie and being a Sloane Ranger born and bred, he was a tough professional, used to the pressure of Belfast.

Next to him sat Mick Dancer. An MI5 operative, Dancer was responsible for collating the raw information that came in through the various intelligence sources throughout the province. He co-ordinated this data and computer-fed it to Gower Street where analysts sifted through the information. A small, wiry man with a rat-like profile, he spent much of his time in the Intelligence Cell, a room near by which housed a colour-sergeant and two corporals to collate. Unlike the silver-spooned Farquharson, Dancer was a middle-class grammar school boy from Dulwich who had worked his way through school and college with distinction before being approached to join Five as an analyst in European politics. Now twenty-nine, he had been promoted to the Northern Ireland desk two years earlier. It was a responsibility he revelled in; he had never liked just sitting behind a desk when the intelligence game was really won or lost in the field.

'Richardson?' Farquharson asked, and the two men recognized the voice that had instructed them to come in.

'Yes,' replied Richardson. 'This is Francis Duggan.

CIA. Over here on the Flaherty investigation.'

Farquharson stood up and held out his hand. 'Major Dennis Farquharson. Officer Commanding.' He nodded at his colleague. 'Mick Dancer. MI5,' he continued as he shook hands. He waved the two men to seats round the small coffee-table.

Duggan peered at the map behind Farquharson. It was a tribal map of Belfast, coloured green for the Republican areas and orange for the Protestant. It was impaled with a mass of pins with different coloured-plastic heads. To the side of the map there was a montage of black and white photographs, all of faces, sullen faces like those staring out of prison records. The legend above read, PIRA TOP 30. Some of the faces had been crossed with a thick red fibre-tip pen. The names under them were, 'Thomas McMahon, Peter Murphy, Anthony Armstrong, Dominic McGlinchey'. Duggan knew, from his own files in Langley, that they were captured or killed terrorists. His eyes, tired with jet-lag, became blurred as he stared at the map.

'I keep that for old times' sake,' said Farquharson. 'If you're patient, they all come home to roost in the end.'

'Why do you want to see Captain Morrison?' Dancer asked Duggan.

'I've already explained—'

'Only to Mr Richardson. Not to me. Belfast comes under my jurisdiction. MI5.'

'I'm aware of that.' Duggan tried to wake up; he hadn't expected to be mauled by Dancer.

'So please tell me why you want to see Captain Morrison,' repeated Dancer.

'Because he was on a plane to Heathrow that took off just after Raphael called the *Washington Post*.'

'That's a thin connection.'

'It's the only connection. I mean, you people haven't come up with much more, have you?'

'It was agreed that—' Richardson tried to come to Duggan's aid.

'Please,' Dancer said pointedly, his look warning Richardson not to get involved. He turned back to Duggan. 'If we're to allow you to see Morrison, we want to be—'

'I thought you'd already agreed to that,' snapped Duggan.

'As I was saying. If you want to—'

'Then it was a waste of time me coming here,' interrupted Duggan again. 'I came here on the understanding that I would see—'

'As long as we're sure you've told us everything.'

'Why shouldn't I?'

'You tell me.'

There was a silence for a while. Then Duggan said, 'I'm a CIA analyst. My job is to sift through information, sometimes the most minor and insignificant clues, to find an opening. In my view, Morrison is a clue worth pursuing.'

'He is an active member of our armed forces. In Belfast.'

'So?'

'If you're trying to implicate him, then you could be trying to implicate the British authorities.'

'We're not accusing your government of anything.'

'But your actions are aimed at an active member—'

'Tell him, Francis,' cut in Richardson.

Duggan considered for a moment. He was being forced into a corner, but felt he had no choice other than to tell Dancer his reason for being there. He was so close to Morrison now, it would be stupid to lose the chance of interviewing the soldier. The risk was that Dancer would warn Morrison of the potential contents of the interview before Duggan got to him. He decided he had no alternative. 'The call to the *Washington Post* was made from a public phone in the British Airways terminal. Just before the flight to Heathrow. A passenger was late getting on board. The person who made that call would have been one of the last to board. That's why I want to question Morrison.'

'You suspect him?' asked Dancer.

'No. I don't think so, anyway. But I've got to check. Hell, he might've seen someone on that flight that he recognized. Something that could help us.'

'Or hang him. Did your people confirm who was the last person to board?'

'Yes. Well, it was the FBI, not us.'

'And it was Morrison?'

'Yes.'

Dancer thought for a moment. It was as Five had suspected. They knew Duggan had to have more information than he was letting on. 'OK,' he said eventually. 'But one of us, either Richardson or myself, must be present at any interview. And we have the right to stop it at any time. As does Morrison. He is attending voluntarily.'

'Of course.'

'And we'll tape it as well.'

'Audio or video?'

'Video.' Dancer stood up. 'Tomorrow. Eleven-thirty a.m. In one of the interrogation rooms. The video's already set up.' He smiled suddenly, his first show of emotion since they had entered the room. 'If you'd like to join me for a meal later in the mess, I'd be glad to treat you. About eight. See you all then.' He exited from the office.

'Well, there you go,' said the jovial Farquharson. 'And a free meal to boot.'

'He's a touchy sod,' commented Richardson.

'Goes with the job. Not like you and me. We can always go back to the Regiment. These chaps are out there on their own.' Farquharson stood up. 'I'll get you shown to your billet. We're a bit short on space, so I'm afraid you're sharing with each other.'

'What about my passport and some clothes?' enquired Duggan.

'They'll be here by the morning. As soon as the decoy team from Dublin gets to London, they'll be packed and sent here. That includes your suitcases.' The OC slid a thin paper file across the desk. 'This is a brief breakdown of Morrison's career. I presume you'll want to read it before you see him.'

'Does Dancer know about this?' asked Richardson as he picked up the folder.

'Oh, yes. It was his idea that you see it.'

'University type?' asked Richardson.

'Yes.'

'What's that mean?' said Duggan.

'There's two sorts of Box men over here. Ex-army and those straight from university,' Farquharson replied.

'That's why very few of us go into Five,' added Richardson. 'The eggheads run it, treat the service men like tea-boys. That's what happened at my interview when I considered joining them. There was an ex-colonel with three other varsity types on my selection panel. They had him making the tea and handing out the biscuits. Not for me, that.'

Farquharson laughed. 'Bit like Dancer that. Thinks we're all here to serve him. But tread carefully. He's top dog. And, to give him his due, he does know what he's doing.'

Five minutes later they were escorted by a corporal to their small room, olive-green in colour with no windows and two narrow iron-framed beds.

'Welcome to the British army,' said Richardson as he flopped down on his bed.

But it was lost on Duggan. His jet-lag had once more caught up with him and he was asleep as soon as his head hit the single Dunlopillo. Richardson rested for an hour, not sleeping, his mind going over the events that had led him back to Belfast. He wondered if the answer lay here, the answer to all those assassinations in distant countries. He blanked out on his own fears and was pleasantly surprised that his return to Ulster had not released his most terrifying nightmares, his reason for leaving the Army and joining Six.

After he'd rested, he unpacked his bag and hung his clothes up tidily in the small wardrobe. He was thrilled to find boot polish in the bottom of the chest of drawers and he spent the next ten minutes lovingly cleaning his shoes.

His restless mind forced him up and he walked round the garrison. Part of 39 Infantry Brigade, Girdwood housed a subordinate unit of infantry. Little had changed; it was still a dark place designed to shield men from their enemies outside. There were one or two efforts at brightening the place up and providing some creature comforts to the infantry company who were housed at the camp on their six-month tour. He watched the BBC news in a bright room which had a television set and a dartboard. After a few words with some of the squaddies there to determine that the laundry room was still where it used to be so that he could get his shirts cleaned, he continued his tour. There was a multi-gym with gleaming bars and weights, not something that had been there when he had lived in Girdwood. The whole effect was lightened by bizarre trophies that had been stolen from memorable bombing incidents, a reminder that humour was necessary to survive in an atmosphere where death was as normal as getting out of bed each day.

Eight o'clock arrived and Richardson went back to the small bedroom. Duggan was snoring deeply and he decided not to wake him. He joined Farquharson and Dancer in the small officers' mess for dinner. The food wasn't great, but he could remember how much he used to enjoy it when he'd come in from patrol. Unlike most army posts, soldiers didn't pay for their meals in Belfast which was officially termed a combat zone.

He reminisced with the two men for the rest of the meal, then went to bed and had another restless night. He was awake when Duggan stirred at four, but didn't say anything and the American drifted back to sleep half an hour later.

He still managed to block out the nightmare. He finally went to sleep at five, a smile on his face, Andrea on his mind.

A lance-corporal delivered Duggan's passport at seven the next morning.

They breakfasted in the cook-house, Duggan's stomach having trouble digesting British army food, and then read the report on Morrison before going to see him. Around them, soldiers rushed through their meal before going out on patrol. It was something Duggan had never known, the clank and clatter of military life.

Stamped RESTRICTED SPECIAL HANDLING, the file was sparse in content. Richardson explained this was normal in Ulster; one never knew into whose hands the information might fall. There were no personal details, no home addresses or telephone numbers, nothing that could be traced.

As they went through the report, it dawned on them that this was no ordinary soldier, that Morrison was the stuff heroes are made of. He had an enviable reputation that made him one of the key players in the Ulster story, a soldier who had risen rapidly through the ranks because of his outstanding professional ability.

Captain Daniel Morrison, GM, MBE, RAOC, had commanded the 3 Infantry Brigade Weapons Intelligence Section for the last two years. Based at Brigade Headquarters, his task was to visit the scene of all bomb and explosive attacks and all major shooting incidents or finds. During his tenure he had investigated almost every major incident in the Brigade area, often in circumstances of extreme danger. His experience from previous tours in the province as an Ammunition Technical Officer meant that he commanded complete respect from those he supported; here was an officer who had worked his way through the ranks and knew what he was talking about. The dangers they faced, he had faced. He was the acknowledged authority on terrorist techniques, weapons, methods of operation, explosives re-supply and Security Force counter-measures. He had also carried out very many close covert reconnaissance missions on suspect explosive devices, particularly in the border areas of South Armagh.

The report listed, in detail, three individual incidents he had been involved in, then went on to praise his exceptional skill and courage. The last incident concerned a land-mine which resulted in the death of five soldiers in a sophisticated 'come-on' trap. Morrison had recognized a similar device three weeks later and successfully defused the trap without injury to any personnel.

'Quite a guy,' commented Duggan when they had finished the three-page report. 'I understand why Dancer's nervous about me interviewing him. If he's involved, then it cuts to the core of the military establishment.'

'Well, let's not be judge and jury before we see him,' warned Richardson. 'Push too hard and he'll claim his rights and walk out.'

Where Duggan had expected a tough, battle-weary soldier, he met a smiling, round-faced, personable individual.

After the introductions, Duggan opened the proceedings. 'As you know we're here to—'

Morrison smiled and cut across him. 'Do you mind if I smoke?' he said.

'Of course not,' said Duggan. He waited while the

officer took out a packet of Silk Cut, offered them around, smiled when Richardson took one, then lit up and settled back. He beamed at Duggan.

'Like I said—'

Morrison spoke again. 'I hope it's understood that I'm here under my own steam.'

'Yes.'

'And that I can terminate the interview at any time.' His smile got wider as he spoke.

'Of course.'

'I want to be of help. Unless you cross into areas which could compromise me, my men, my responsibilities or any secrets which I may be privy to or which I consider would threaten the security of others.'

'I'd go along with that.'

'Fine,' Morrison beamed again. 'When you're ready.'

'You were in America when Tim Flaherty, the IRA gunman fighting extradition, was shot and killed in New York?'

'Yes.'

'You came back to England, to London, on a British Airways flight the night Flaherty was killed?'

'Yes.'

'Did you know he'd been shot?'

'No.'

'When did you find out?'

'Back in Heathrow.'

'How?'

'Newspaper headline.'

'You were the last to board the plane?'

'Probably.'

'Why?'

'I'm usually late.'

'Why?'

'Clock the other passengers. Make sure there isn't someone I don't want to see.'

'Like who?'

'Terrorists. Bad men.' The smile still remained on his face, half mocking.

'Did you see anybody you knew?'

'No.'

Duggan sensed he lied; there was a flicker in the man's eyes. He wished he could give him a polygraph. He decided to push harder. 'Did you make a phone call just before you boarded?'

'Yes.'

'May I ask who to?'

'Yes.'

Duggan waited; Morrison went on smiling. 'Who to?' asked Duggan patiently.

'My wife.'

'Why?'

'To tell her what time to expect me.'

'Is that normal?'

'Yes.'

'But she must have known the time of the flight.'

'They're often delayed. Funny, isn't it? Trains and people are late. Aircraft are always delayed.'

'That was the only call you made?'

'Yes.'

'How did you check on passengers getting on the aircraft if you were making the call?'

'You can see the boarding gate from the phones.'

'Why were you in America?'

'Holiday.'

'Without your family?'

'Yes.'

'Unusual, isn't it?'

'No.'

Duggan was getting exasperated with the officer's Gary Cooper monosyllabic answers. He decided not to show his frustration. 'Why not?'

'I sometimes holiday alone.'

'Why?'

'Because I live under extreme pressure here. I need my own space, my own time.'

'Doing what?'

'That's my business.'

'Did you know Martyn Darcy?' asked Richardson from behind Duggan.

'I only agreed to be interviewed by him.' Morrison smiled and pointed at Duggan. 'You're here as an observer.'

'Did you know Martyn Darcy?' repeated Duggan.

'Yes.'

'Did you spend any time recently in Dublin?'

'You mean when that bastard got killed and his girl-friend got blown up?'

'Yes.'

'No.'

'Where were you?'

'South Armagh.'

'On patrol?'

'Yes.'

'That's easy to check up on.'

'Why should I lie? This thing's being videoed anyway.'

'How did you know Darcy?'

'We were in the same business.'

'But you knew him personally?'

'Yes.'

'How?'

'I just knew him.'

'Did you know he was a supergrass?' asked Richardson.

'Did you know he was a supergrass?' repeated Duggan.

Morrison paused. 'Yes.'

'Did you handle him?' asked Richardson.

'Did you handle him?' copied Duggan.

'Yes.'

'On your own?' asked Richardson.

172

'On your own?' asked Duggan.

'No. He went through about three handlers.'

'But he reverted to the PIRA?' Duggan was on track again.

'His information dried up.'

'Didn't that worry you?'

'We had enough on him to always pull him back in line. If we were after something big.'

'And you didn't see him just before he died?'

'No.'

'How long had it been since you last had contact with him?'

'Years. Before this stint of duty.'

'Can I have the names of those who handled him?'

'You must be joking.'

'Did you handle Flaherty?' Duggan didn't know why he asked that question; it came from nowhere.

'No.'

'Did you know Flaherty?'

'Once.'

'When?'

'When he was arrested for shooting at a Protestant. Years ago.'

'But you remembered him?'

'I was part of an interrogating team. I always keep notes and have a good memory for names and faces.'

'Do you agree with what the Angels are doing?' asked Richardson.

'Don't you?' Morrison answered Richardson directly this time.

'Should I?'

Morrison shook his head. 'You've lost friends here. Like the rest of us.'

'Do you agree with what they're doing?'

'Yes. I think all those bastards should be taken out.'

'You'd do that?'

'If ordered to, yes. Soon put an end to this mess.'

'What about the Catholics?'

'What about them? Listen, it's only fear that makes them support the IRA. It's up to us to allow them to live as they choose as part of the UK.'

'What about the Ulster Defence boys?'

'They're as bad as the PIRA. All gangsters. Take them out as well. Leave the place for normal Catholics and Protestants to learn to get on with each other. That's your only solution. Take away the fear and teach them to trust each other.'

'Very simple,' said Duggan.

The warmth dropped for a moment and the hardness of the man came through. 'Listen, I've seen children out there, blown up, bits of prams scattered all over the road. I've seen families destroyed, fatherless kids, passers-by crippled for life. That's the horror of this place. Just because I defuse bombs and shoot the odd terrorist, doesn't mean I don't feel for these people. Catholic or Protestant. I live with it. Every day. It matters to me what happens in this province. Those gunmen don't give a shit. It's a way of life to them. They laugh at us, because we follow the normal rules of engagement, because we're accountable to a parliament, to a democracy, which they're not. Yes, we could end it. Take all the bastards out and then they'd soon stop shooting at each other. So yes, if you want to know do I support the Angels, yes. But if you're asking would I put my responsibilities and duties of a soldier aside to support them, then the answer is no.'

'Did you know about the Plan?' asked Richardson.

'What plan?'

'The Plan. For the Cabinet. To take out any terrorists.'

Dancer's voice blared over the small speaker above the video camera. 'All right, chaps,' he said. 'Let's not start breaching any possible official secrets.'

Richardson leant back, crossed his legs and looked down at the floor.

'Let's get back to Kennedy Airport,' said Duggan.

'Fine,' smiled Morrison, once more under control.

'When you were on vacation in New York, did you—'

'It wasn't just New York.'

'Where else?'

'I toured. Down to Florida and back.'

'Where?'

'Just Florida.'

'Miami Beach?' Duggan presumed that Morrison didn't know about the call between Dublin and Miami Beach.

'No.' Morrison seemed genuinely surprised by the question.

'Where?'

'Fort Lauderdale.'

Duggan sensed Richardson stiffen behind him.

'Why there?'

'Good place. Good fishing. Rented a boat for a week.'

'And then went back to New York?'

'Yes.'

'Were you alone?'

'That's my affair.'

'Does the name Mary Squires mean anything?'

'Why?'

'If I remember, she was booked into the next seat to you.'

'She was.'

'A friend?'

'Just leave it at that.'

'What? As a friend?'

'Yes,' replied Morrison softly. Then he grinned. 'You have to admit, I'm being straight with you.'

'And was she already on board when you went to ring your wife?'

'Yes.'

'That's why you rang your wife? To make sure she didn't come to the airport to meet you?'

'Something like that.'

'And you saw no-one else?'

Morrison considered for a moment. 'I lied. I saw one person.'

'Who?'

'Someone I'd served with.'

'In Belfast?'

'Yes.'

'Recently?'

'Quite some time ago.'

'Would you tell us who he is? I presume it's a "he".'

'Yes. And I need to think about it.'

'Why?'

'Because he's an old mate. And I can't see him being involved.'

'Was he getting on the plane?'

'No. He had another flight.'

'Where to?'

'I didn't ask and he didn't say.'

'Would you please give us his name?'

'Not now. Not until I've thought it out.'

'He's part of your Circle, isn't he?' said Richardson.

There was a knock on the door and a soldier in combat gear came in. He handed Morrison a note. 'Just came in, sir,' he said.

Morrison read the short note, then stood up. 'Sorry, gentlemen. But there's been a serious incident near Silverbridge in South Armagh. We've stopped a truck full of mortars and I need to get down there and link with the ATO team as soon as possible.' He smiled. 'Thank you. I hope I've been of some assistance.'

The two men sat there after Morrison had gone. Dancer came in and joined them.

'It would be difficult for us to order him to give any names,' said Dancer.

'Why? It's part of the investigation into the Angel case,' responded Duggan, hoping that the note for

Morrison had been genuine and not sent through to get Morrison off the hook.

'Not necessarily. You wanted to know why Captain Morrison was on that plane. And why he made a phone call just before boarding. I think he answered both questions satisfactorily.'

Duggan rose from his seat. 'Do you mind if I stayed on in Belfast for a while longer?' he asked Dancer.

'Why?'

'Just like to. Does that cause a problem?'

'Depends on what you want to do?'

'Don't know yet. Except I'll keep you fully briefed.'

'If you think it's any use.' Dancer shrugged off the offer.

'Can I ring Langley?'

'I'll make a line available.' He looked at Richardson. 'I'd like a word.'

'I'll catch you up,' Richardson said to Duggan. 'Won't be long.'

Duggan took the hint and left the interrogation room. Richardson stretched back in his chair, almost indolent in his manner to Dancer. The Five man sat on the edge of the table. 'Bit silly, that. Mentioning the Plan.'

'This whole thing always seems to come back to our people.'

'That's between us. Nothing to do with the Yank.'

'He already knew about the Plan.'

'You told him?' Dancer had been playing with a pencil on the table and he looked up sharply.

'No. The CIA already knew. They have their own contacts. Probably in Dublin,' Richardson lied. He didn't want to get Monaghan into trouble with his Gardaí bosses. 'They just don't know how far we went.'

'Do you think he's satisfied?' Dancer went on.

'As you said, he got the answers to the questions he came with,' replied Richardson.

'You don't like me, do you?'

'Not particularly.'

'Why?'

'It doesn't matter.' In truth, Richardson had not liked the way Dancer had treated Duggan at their first meeting; there had been no need for such brusque behaviour.

'We're on the same side.'

'Unless you're hiding something.'

'Like what?'

'I have no idea. You came in very quick when I mentioned the Plan.'

'I wouldn't like our American cousins to know we'd actually formulated a night of the long knives.'

'So it was considered?'

Dancer smiled patronizingly. 'Everything's considered.'

'Was Morrison part of that consideration?'

'He was one of the architects. That's for your ears only.'

'Is he based at Girdwood?'

'No. He's with 3 Infantry. At Gough Barracks.'

Richardson stood up. 'Was there anything else?'

'What're you after, Richardson?'

'The truth. That's what I was sent out to find.'

'No. You were sent out to baby-sit the Yank. To make sure nothing got out that could embarrass HMG. You could do well to remember that.'

Richardson walked out of the room. A bemused Dancer stood up, threw down the pencil, looked round at the video recorder and decided to wipe the last section off. He left the room to its weary shabbiness in this place he was forced to call home.

Gabriel had driven south from Mannheim to Switzerland as instructed.

The call had come into his hotel during the night, twelve hours after he had arrived in Mannheim. There were no key words the satellites would pick up. The message was simple. 'One hundred thousand. Use the stamp. Ring you back in Cologne in forty-eight hours.'

He'd slept for a few hours, bought a small briefcase in the hotel lobby, then driven his rental car south. He crossed the border at Schaffhausen and drove on to Zürich. He followed the signs to the airport, parked the car and went up to the Union Banque Suisse special counters on the second floor. He instructed the first cashier to call Monsieur DeLage, then went to the far counter and waited.

DeLage came out a minute later. Gabriel introduced himself, opened his wallet, took out a clear plastic envelope which contained one half of a rare and valuable Black Honduras stamp. He told DeLage he wished to make a large withdrawal. He informed him of the account number and said he would wait while DeLage confirmed the transaction.

Gabriel waited for five minutes before DeLage returned, apologizing profusely for taking so much time. He also carried a small clear plastic envelope. He opened it, took out the other half of the valuable stamp and paired it up with Gabriel's. The two halves formed together into a perfect whole. He gave Gabriel back his half, then resealed his own and passed a checking slip across the counter. Gabriel filled it in; the amount was US$100,000.

Ten minutes later, carrying the money in the small briefcase, Gabriel left the bank and drove back across the border into Germany. He continued northwards until he reached Cologne. He stopped overnight and waited for the next call.

'You've got to be joking.' Richardson couldn't believe what Duggan was asking for. They were back in the bedroom after a late lunch.

'I want to do it.'

'Why? You're a fucking analyst.' Richardson pulled his Browning from his coat pocket, crossed over to the American and held the muzzle against his temple. 'Out here, *bang bang* isn't something spelt out in a comic. It's a real sound. Usually the last thing you hear before you don't hear any more.' He pocketed the automatic and went back to his bed.

'I may be an analyst, but that doesn't stop me getting into the field.'

'Not in Belfast, Francis. This is not like the rest of the world. Christ, even Hizbollah tried to come here for training.'

'I want you to ask Dancer.'

'Have you cleared it with your own people?'

'Not yet. But they'll go along with me.'

'How do you know?'

'Because there's nowhere else for Langley to go. And they want a solution as much as anyone else.'

'You don't see this as some romantic escapade, do you?'

'Come on, Sam.'

'Because it isn't. I've had friends die here. I've seen the victims up close. On both sides. And the squaddies who're trashed in the middle.'

'I want to do it because we haven't exhausted our efforts here. The IRA may be the victims, but that could also mean they know who's gunning for them. Maybe I could find that out. And by doing that I could stop it happening again. Not just here, but also in my own country.' Duggan's tone had grown angry. 'I just want to spend a few days in the Catholic community. With my relatives. I could just pull something off. All I want you to do is ask him.'

'OK. But I can guess the answer.'

Richardson guessed wrong. He rang Dancer at Stormont, where Five were headquartered, and told him of Duggan's request. He heard Dancer chuckle, then tell him to keep the American busy until he got there. He had a few calls to make to confirm his decision, but didn't expect any difficulty with the idea in principle.

'Show him the mushrooms,' Dancer said sarcastically. 'That'll interest him, seeing that he's their expert on European terrorism.'

Richardson returned to the bedroom and told him about Dancer's response.

'Makes sense,' said Duggan. 'Anything to get more intelligence on the Provos.'

Richardson took Duggan to eat in the officers' mess, then, as the MI5 man had suggested, to the Operations Room. The ops room was the nerve-centre of company headquarters offices. The small seventeen feet by twelve feet room was manned twenty-four hours a day. The duty watchkeeper, a young lieutenant, sat at a console of radio and telephone instruments monitoring all communications. He turned as they let themselves into the darkened room, saw their Special Clearance passes pinned to their lapels, and went back to concentrate on a swell of dialogue that was coming over the loudspeaker. It was an army patrol, out in the streets of Belfast, checking a house where there had been reports of terrorist activity. From the radio chatter, it appeared that the patrol had been sent out on a false alarm.

The watchkeeper's responsibility was to take and give messages whilst keeping a careful log of all events. There were two television monitors on the wall, both switched off. They were connected to the two video systems that radioed pictures from army helicopters. Under one monitor was the sign HELI-TELI. This was the normal video, a long-range, high-density camera that was used on normal helicopter patrols, similar to the one by which Richardson and Duggan had been escorted while crossing the border. The second monitor had a sign SUPER SNOOPER. This was the special, all-weather, day-or-night camera with image intensifier that could deliver pictures in the worst of conditions and from the narrowest of angles. Both monitors were linked to video recorders.

'Did they cover us when we crossed the border?' asked Duggan quietly, so as not to disturb the duty officer.

'No. This just covers Belfast. We came under 3 Infantry Brigade. Their ops room is in Armagh. Anyway, this is a special unit room. Normally all the 39 Brigade stuff goes to an ops room at Brigade HQ. We would've been watched by another mushroom.'

'Mushroom?'

'Yes,' said the monitor-watcher, swinging round. 'Like me. Kept in the dark and fed on shit.'

Duggan laughed. 'Hi.'

'Busy out there?' asked Richardson.

'Not too bad this afternoon.' The mushroom swung back and monitored his console. It was important that he continuously monitored the information that was relayed through the room. His OC and Brigade staff depended on it. As they did on his ability to remain cool, efficient and sympathetic when an emergency blew up so that he could advise where necessary, whilst also appreciating the situation so his information could help the support troops who were sent in.

'No contact with 55 Sierra,' came a voice on one of the loudspeakers.

'How late is he?' said the mushroom.

'Twenty minutes.'

'Are you secure?'

'At the moment.'

'Keep an eye out. I'll be back.' The mushroom leant over and picked up the handset. He spoke into it. 'Ops room. One of our patrols is out to pick up 55 Sierra. Intelligence reported that he had been uncovered and we passed a message through to him via an informer. We gave him a time and place for a meeting. He's not turned up— Yes, sir, I'll do that.' He slammed the receiver down then went back to his microphone and flicked a switch. 'Stay where you are, in case he's been held up. Don't call me unless you see him.' The mushroom flicked another switch and spoke to a patrol near the Falls Road. He gave them 55 Sierra's address and told them to go there immediately and to pull him out. Then he called the Royal Ulster Constabulary and gave them 55 Sierra's car registration and told them to stop the car and escort the driver to Girdwood. As he finished, the door opened and Major Farquharson came in.

'They're on their way,' said the mushroom.

Farquharson turned to Richardson and Duggan. The concern in his eyes was obvious. 'Bring back memories?' he said to Richardson.

'Who's out there?'

'Robert Collett. Lieutenant. Liaison officer between Brigade and the RUC. He's been working covertly for nearly three weeks surveying Seán Martin's Drinking Club in Short Strand.'

'I've been there,' said Duggan. 'With my relatives last time I was over.'

'It's a veritable nest crawling with IRA. Collett's of Irish background. Catholic. Likes going in where others would be more careful. Bit like you were, from what I hear,' he remarked to Richardson.

'Hasn't he got a radio?' asked Richardson.

'Yes. But we're getting nothing. Rumour from one of our informers was that he'd been blown. That the boyos were out looking for him.' Farquharson directed his next statement at Duggan. 'Dancer tells me you want to go out there.'

'I thought I might see if—'

'You're a damned fool. I've got enough problems looking after my own men without having to worry about you.' Farquharson went over and sat next to the mushroom.

'Do you want me to increase the patrols or get the Super Snooper up?' asked the mushroom.

'No. We've got enough people looking for him. What car's he driving?'

'A Rover 200.'

'We've just got to sit it out. Maybe he went into hiding. Maybe he knew he'd been rumbled.'

The phone rang and Farquharson picked it up. 'Hello – yes, I'll send them along. Use my office – no, no news on Collett yet.' He put down the phone and eased himself round to the two standing men. 'Dancer's just arrived. I suggest you see him in my office.'

Dancer was dwarfed in the OC's vast leather chair when they walked in. 'We're prepared to give it a try,' he said. 'On certain conditions.' When Duggan didn't reply, he continued. 'First, you must clear it with your own people.'

'I've already suggested it. They have no real objection.'

Dancer nodded. He'd already picked that information up from the switchboard operator who'd linked Duggan to Langley, then switched the tap through to Stormont. 'The responsibility for this exercise lies with you. It's not a joint operation, although I reserve the right to recall you at any stage if I feel you're in danger or you're compromising British troops, the intelligence services or the Government. That doesn't mean we won't try and pull you out of a jam if we find things get . . .' he smiled at his own pun, '. . . sticky. As far as I'm concerned you wanted to go and visit your family and friends in Belfast after you'd come here on an investigation.'

'That's fine. My cover will be that I'm a journalist for the White House. I write PR reports for the White House staff about incidents that may cause the President some embarrassment. Because of Flaherty's shooting in New York, I'm over here to see what I can pick up which the President can then use in his speeches about the potential of terrorist situations exploding on American streets.'

'Sounds OK. Finally, we want you to wear a transmitter.'

'No.'

'It goes with the deal.'

'No. If I'm caught with a bug, they'll know I'm reporting back to you guys. And, if I'm out there on my own, then I don't want anything to consolidate that link.'

'OK. But we'll expect a full intelligence debriefing when you come back.'

'Fine. On the matter concerning the Angels.'

'We'll expect more.'

'Only if I feel whatever I've learnt is unlawful and could cause danger to someone else. I'm not going out to spy for you guys.'

'Will you need a weapon?'

'No.'

Dancer stood up. 'The ops room will be monitoring you. Not just from intelligence reports, but also from the various secret observation posts we have scattered around the city.'

'This should be a secret operation. I don't want

my description bandied around. Careless talk, and all that.'

'We're smarter than that. As you enter each observation post's area, we ask them to give us a complete report on what they're seeing. That way, they have no idea of what's going on, but they are ready to respond if something happens to you.'

'Where are these posts?'

'You'll see some, others are hidden in the eaves of roofs, that sort of thing. You'll be covered most of the time. Now, before you go I want the addresses of your family and friends.' He held up his hand as Duggan started to complain. 'There's no discussion about that. If things go wrong, I want to know where to come after you. I'll get you a hire-car. With Dublin plates. We'll make it appear that you've driven across the border from there. That's just being safe. You never know who might have seen you in Dublin. I'll also give you a list of numbers to be committed to memory. That's so that if you're in trouble, call us and we'll come and get you. You'll also be given some addresses. Safe areas for you to hide in if you're discovered. I want you to go through a Belfast map with Richardson. Absorb it. It'll show you where all the RUC police stations are as well as any army installations. Once again, head for them if you think you're in danger. I've already got our Dublin contacts to change the register at the Gresham. It'll appear that you spent the last few nights there and left early tomorrow morning for Belfast.' He walked to the door and opened it. 'I'll arrange for you to use one of the interrogation rooms. We'll get the maps and lists of numbers and addresses down to you. I'll catch up with you in about twenty minutes.'

'Well, you've talked yourself into the big one,' said Richardson when Dancer closed the door.

Duggan suddenly realized what he was unleashing on himself. He thought of the young soldier, Collett, out there, being hunted by the IRA, even possibly captured, tortured or killed. That was the world he was entering. It wasn't one he took for normal, not like Richardson or Dancer or any of the others he had come across since this crazy episode started on the streets of New York. 'It should be safe,' he heard himself say. 'I'm an American. I'm no threat to them.'

'You Yanks are a threat to everyone. Macho bloody cowboys. You really have no idea what you're letting yourself in for.'

'It'll be OK, Sam.' Duggan tried to convince himself more than Richardson. 'It'll be OK because I won't take any unnecessary risks. I'm no threat. Just a regular guy visiting his family.'

'I bet that's what the Japs said just before they bombed Pearl Harbor.'

As Duggan passed the eleven-mile marker to Belfast he saw the western hills covered with a fringe of morning light.

The splendour of the breaking morning sky and the bright green hills hit him with a start; it was the first time he had realized the beauty that surrounded him since he left Washington at the start of this crazy journey. He relaxed and tried to enjoy the picture-book version of Ireland which he had been brought up to expect; very Pat O'Brien and Squire Daniger and Hollywood visions of Maureen O'Hara running through the surf-wave grass.

Dancer had pulled him out of Girdwood in the same way they'd been brought in. This time Richardson had not gone with him. In soldier's uniform, sitting hunched against the back of a Land-Rover to the border, then an exchange of clothes and a transfer into a blue Granada rental car with Dublin plates. His suitcase was thrown in the boot and the troops vanished as quickly as they had come. It was six in the morning and still dark. He suddenly felt very vulnerable, imagined unseen eyes watching his every move, and he drove quickly back to the N1 then turned north towards Newry and the army border crossing.

Before he reached the border, he stopped the car in a lay-by and quickly searched the interior for any bugs or listening devices. He had already checked his suitcase and its contents before he left Girdwood. He didn't trust Dancer, but then it was what he would have expected of any good intelligence chief. He didn't check under the bonnet or in the boot. If they had a bug on the car, it would have been so that they could monitor him if he hit trouble. He also preferred to stay in the vehicle and not take the chance of stepping out into the dark and running into some nervous terrorist.

Twenty minutes later, having checked the interior thoroughly, he had satisfied himself there was no obvious bug and drove on to the border, past the Irish customs post and on to the British. The contrasts were startling. Beyond the Gardaí post, he saw the remains of a border post that had been blown up so many times that the army had given up and moved the observation post to just outside Newry. He drove past the burnt-out remains and kept on the road until he came to the new fortified border check-point complete with observation posts, blast walls, anti-rocket screens, traffic lights, Caltrop vehicle barriers which rose out of the road to stop charging cars, and a search point.

The traffic was building up, although it wasn't yet seven-thirty. He waited in line until an armed, cobalt-uniformed British soldier waved him forward. He took out his passport as he wound the window down. Behind the soldier, officers of the RUC grouped, automatic weapons slung across their chests, hat-brims pulled menacingly over their foreheads, watching the cars in the line.

'Where're you going?' asked the soldier; Duggan identified the London accent as he passed over his passport.

'American,' he replied. 'Been visiting Dublin and I'm

driving up to Belfast to see some family before I go home.'

The soldier flicked through the passport, then handed it back. 'Leave your engine running, hand-brake on, and open your boot, please,' he ordered.

'Boot?' asked Duggan, immediately regretting over-playing the American tourist. All he wanted to do was pass through. 'Sorry, you mean the trunk.'

He climbed out, walked round and opened the boot. He noticed the soldier stood back while he unfastened it, no doubt in case it was booby-trapped. The lid swung open and the soldier came forward and inspected it. While he waited, Duggan looked at the small building and saw a man at the window punching data into a computer. He knew, from what Richardson had told him, that his number would be fed into a data-bank to check its registration. The progress of his car would then be checked by covert unmarked vehicles on his drive into Belfast. It was standard procedure. The soldier slammed the boot-lid shut, then signalled Duggan back into the car.

As Duggan climbed in, the soldier pushed the door shut. 'Thank you,' said the American.

'You one of those bleeding hearts thinking all Irish are saints and John Wayne?' said the soldier, his eyes impassive. 'Think Gerry Adams is a fucking hero?'

'What do you mean?'

A sergeant came forward. 'We get all sorts here,' he said with a smile to Duggan.

'There's no need for that rudeness.'

'He doesn't mean anything,' continued the sergeant affably. 'The other day an old farmer drove up and we asked to look in his boot. Damn fool took off his wellingtons.' He laughed, then realized the American didn't understand his joke. 'Rubber shoes . . . ', he started to explain, then stopped. 'English joke. You'd better move on, sir.'

'I want to know what he meant,' persisted Duggan, hanging out of the car window.

'Run along, sir. We're rather busy right now.' The sergeant dismissed him, then turned and walked away towards the next car.

Duggan looked back at the impassive soldier.

The soldier shook his head and stepped back, then waved Duggan through. As Duggan drove off, he saw, in his rear-view mirror, the soldier move on to search the next car. *Another dollar, another day*. He suddenly regretted his sharpness with the soldier; they were out there at the sharp end and every car was a potential booby-trap. He turned his attention to the drive in. Belfast. City of Terror and Death. Only this time he wasn't safe behind the garrison walls of Girdwood Park. This time he was entering the portals of hell on his own.

He rang Maggie Maguire from a phone box at Lisburn. As he put the 10p coin in, he saw the car that had tailed him for the last two miles pull in to a parked line of traffic. He guessed it was a covert car, tracking him, following him to see if his story at the border crossing had been true.

'Hello,' he heard the familiar Northern Irish twang.

'Maggie,' he said.

'Aye.'

'Francis. Francis Duggan. From America.'

'Francis! What're you doing calling me this early in the morning?'

'I'm in Belfast.'

'Belfast!'

'Actually, Lisburn. I was in Dublin on some business and I finished early, so I decided to drive up and see you all.'

'Well, fancy that. What a surprise. Where're you staying, Francis?'

'I'll find a hotel.'

'You will not. You find your way here and stay with us.'

'I don't want to impose.'

'You'll not be imposing. You're my cousin. You are on your own, aren't you?'

'Yes.'

'Then get yourself over. I'll have you a room ready by the time you arrive.'

He told her he remembered how to get there, put the phone down and went back to his car. As he drove off, he saw the unmarked car swing out and follow him. Duggan opened the Collins Road Atlas and spread it out on the passenger seat. Using this as a guide, he drove into Belfast, crossed the Lagan River on the Queen Elizabeth Bridge, cut under the Bridge End flyover and turned down into Mountpottinger Road. The map showed he could have turned right into Bryson Street, but he knew it was divided by a high brick wall with the red iron guards at the top; he remembered that the houses on the left were Protestant and those on the right Catholic.

The area to the right, known as Short Strand, was the most remote of all Catholic areas in Belfast. On the Protestant-packed east side of the Lagan, Short Strand was a small island of green amongst the orange banners of Unionism. During the major uprisings of the seventies, even the IRA on the west side of the city, in the Falls Road and the Ardoyne and Andersonstown, knew they would have to leave Short Strand to fend for itself if its residents were besieged by Unionists. But, partly because of the Catholic vigilantes who patrolled the streets, and partly because there were old friendships going back over the years that bridged the religious divide, the area had escaped serious attack. In the end, however, even the friendships had not been enough and the dividing 'Peace Wall' was put up to segregate the areas.

The single houses and maisonette buildings, small in design, were of a modern, light-brown brick. The old terraced homes had long since been pulled down and these new blocks put up as a gesture to modernity. To all intents and purposes, it looked like a modern prison, divided by the wall that symbolized the crack that runs through Belfast.

Duggan turned into Madrid Street, past the few small shops, and came to rest at the house he remembered. As he climbed out, he knew he was being watched. Nothing went unnoticed here. By the time he got to the front door, a radio would be crackling or a phone ringing to tell someone higher up that there was a stranger in their midst. He opened the boot, took out his small suitcase, and walked towards the front door. It opened before he got there and Maggie came out of the three-bedroomed house. The daughter of his father's brother, Maggie was forty years old, stout and comfortable in build, with a plump face and, like Duggan, an uncontrollable shock of red hair. She put her arms round him and hugged him; he grinned shyly as she led him into the house.

'He's a stranger, but Maggie Maguire knows him,' reported the voice across the road. 'He's gone in with a suitcase.' The watcher then gave a description of Duggan and of his car. When he hung up, he settled down to wait for any further developments.

Further up, on the corner of Madrid Street and Mountpottinger Road, there was a big, fortified, RUC police station. An army watcher at the observation post noted the same scene and reported it on his radio. It was picked up in the OPS ROOM of Girdwood Park. Dancer and Richardson sat behind the mushroom.

'Step one complete,' said Dancer.

'If he hits problems, can I go in after him?' asked Richardson.

'No,' came the acid reply. 'Only if he can be picked

up by a passing patrol. Otherwise Mister Duggan's on his own.'

The border town of Clones
County Monaghan

The Army Council's orders had been specific. Concentrate all efforts along the Fermanagh border. That's why there had been few watchers on the loose around South Armagh when Duggan had crossed over.

The yellow 1976 Cortina 2000 GXL with five occupants, four PIRA gunmen and Lieutenant Robert Collett jammed between two of them in the back, had crept its way around the bomb craters of a side-road and crossed into Eire. The car took a winding road, between high hedgerows, to Cootehill, then left to Sherecock.

In the back, Collett feigned unconsciousness. He knew he had to wait for his chance, for that one moment when there was an opportunity to escape. It was how he had been trained, to wait for that one lucky break to save his life.

It had started the evening before. He'd followed Jim McCann to Seán Martin's Drinking Club in Short Strand and parked across the street. His next reported call sign, '55 Sierra', was due in to the ops room at 8.30 p.m.; he had an hour before he called-in on his radio. As he checked his watch, he didn't notice a man walking down towards him on the pavement. He looked up as there was a knock on the driver's window. He grinned. It was one of the drinkers, a suspected sympathizer, that he had been cultivating in a pub off Castle Street. He wound down the window. 'Eamonn,' he welcomed.

'I was on my way for a drink. Could you give me a lift?'

'Aye,' he replied. He had developed a Belfast accent over his various tours in the province. An Ulsterman by birth, and a Catholic, he had been educated at

Ampleforth, the top Catholic public school. He went on to Cambridge, then to Sandhurst. After that he served numerous tours in Belfast, never becoming a member of the SAS but liaising between the various forces including the RUC. This latest surveillance was one in a long career of covert actions. Maybe that's why he was unprepared, maybe he had been in the field too long and believed he was impervious to being discovered. He knew his target, McCann, always spent at least two hours in Seán Martin's, which is why he made his report each evening during that period. That gave him ample time to drop Eamonn off at Castle Street, no more than five minutes away, and return to watch the drinking club.

He leant over and unlocked the passenger door. Eamonn got in, his overcoat over his arm. As Eamonn closed the door, someone else knocked on the driver's window. Collett swung round and saw McCann. *What the—?* He was meant to be in Seán Martin's.

'Sorry, pal,' Eamonn said as he pushed the long barrel of the Uzi pistol into his side. The gun was a shortened and lightened semi-automatic version of the Uzi sub-machine-gun and, although larger than most hand-guns, was easy to fire one-handed. 'Let's get out,' continued Eamonn. 'Out of the driver's side. And nothing silly, my old drinking mate.'

McCann opened the door and Collett climbed out. Two men appeared behind McCann. Collett recognized one of them: Tommy Farrell, the PIRA's East Belfast Brigade Commander. The fourth man, whom Collett had never seen before, opened the back door and waved the soldier in. He had an old, six-shell army revolver in his hand.

'What the fuck's going on?' asked Collett indignantly.

'Get in, SAS man,' ordered Farrell. He didn't want to be seen in the street by any passing soldiers or police. Farrell's men had been searching for Collett for three hours now and the Brigade Commander knew that the information could well have got back to British watchers at Brigade Headquarters or any of the specialist units. 'Come on, move yourself.'

'I'm no fucking SAS man,' defended Collett.

'Fuck you,' swore Farrell and punched Collett in the side of his head, knocking him against the car. As he struggled to get up, McCann lashed out with his foot, crashing it into Collett's stomach. It winded the soldier and he rolled onto the pavement, but Farrell grabbed him by his coat collar and dragged him into the rear of the car. Collett cracked his head against the door frame and felt the first blood of the encounter run down his forehead and sting his right eye. Then he felt two men crash in on top of him, forcing him down on the floor. He tried to struggle up but was met by a rain of blows and kicks to his head and back. He lay still and felt the car engine come to life and surge away from the pavement.

They crossed the Lagan, cut through the back alleys to Divis Street and drove up the Falls Road. Halfway up, once safely in the Republican heartland, they turned into Clonagh Road and stopped near the safe house they had prepared. A group of men waited near the house and, on seeing the car pull up, they walked down in a group to give cover to those who were emerging from the vehicle.

The soldiers in the nearby observation post saw nothing, only a bunch of high-spirited youngsters on their way to the pub, jostling some men who climbed out of a parked car. What they didn't see was Collett being dragged out and bundled down a side alley to the next street where the safe house was located. They took Collett through the backyard, into a two-storey brownstone house and upstairs to the first floor. The fourth man, whom Collett had not recognized, returned to the car and drove to Aldergrove Airport, where he left the car in the long-term car-park. By good chance, no patrol car or RUC vehicle recognized it.

It was a long painful night for Collett. They stuck black insulation tape over his mouth and round the back of his head, then tied him to a leg of a thick wooden table.

'One nod for yes. One shake for no,' said Farrell. 'Simple conversation, eh, SAS man?' He nodded at McCann who hit Collett across his cheek with his elbow, then swung his arm back and snapped Collett's head the other way. 'Are you an SAS man?' asked Farrell again. Collett shook his head and McCann drew his fist back and slammed it into Collett's chest, winding him once again. The soldier tried to catch his breath, but it was impossible with the tape over his mouth. He started to choke, then inhaled through his nostrils. McCann slammed him again and Collett's eyes showed the panic he felt as he fought for air, almost like a drowning man being held under water as his lungs filled up.

McCann hit him in the chest again.

'Are you an SAS man?'

Collett shook his head frantically.

McCann hit him harder, pushing what little air he had out of his lungs. Then he elbowed him hard in the stomach.

'Are you an SAS man?'

Collett continued his negative report.

He got hit again. He fought to inhale through his nostrils and felt some freshness in his lungs. He saw McCann lunge again and wind him; his chest felt as if it was on fire. He fought for air.

'Are you an SAS man?'

He shook his head, felt the sharp pain from the chest-blow once again and then, mercifully, he passed out. As he lay there, tied to the table with his head slumped forward, he didn't know that they kicked and lashed at him. Later on, it would be discovered that they had broken seven of his ribs in this first attack.

196

'Take that fucking tape off,' ordered Farrell. 'Orders are that he stays alive. We keep him like that until we know he's an SAS man.'

'What if he's not?' asked Eamonn.

'He's a fucking soldier. That's all we need.'

They continued the beatings through the night, always taking Collett to the limit, never brutal enough to kill him. Each time he came round, they worked on another part of his body: his legs, his arms, his testicles, his back. They finally stopped at four a.m.; Collett had passed into unconsciousness eleven times during that period. To keep him quiet, they had taped his mouth for each beating, only ripping the tape off when he passed out so they ensured he didn't suffocate. The reason they stopped the torture was because they ran out of insulation tape. They left Collett's mouth taped up, untied him from the table and laid him on it, his feet dangling over the end. Then they dragged two mattresses from the second bedroom, laid them on the floor and took turns watching Collett and sleeping.

They had taken Collett out of the safe house at nine the next morning in McCann's yellow Cortina which was parked in the garage next to the house. The soldier was wedged between Eamonn and the fourth man who had now returned from Aldergrove Airport. Although the tape was removed from his mouth, they had wrapped him in a parka with the hood over his head. His body ached (one of the PIRA men had laughingly offered him an aspirin) and he sat quietly between the two men; the pair of guns nuzzled in his sides ensured his silence as they drove out of Belfast towards Dungannon and Fivemiletown.

With a variety of diversionary tactics created by other PIRA men to keep the army patrols busy, they had finally crossed the border by a back narrow road at Clones, and headed now for Sherecock. Farrell left them and was picked up by a van which returned him

197

to Belfast. He had already instructed the men as to what to do. It was just like the Army Council had ordered.

Now Collett kept still and waited for his moment of escape. He didn't know what they wanted with him, except they needed him alive. That was his ace. He accepted the pain for that, knowing that their eagerness to keep him alive would give him the chance to escape. To occupy his mind he thought of his mother and his two sisters, both younger than him. He suddenly regretted not having a woman, a girlfriend, a fiancée. He'd never bothered. That would've been nice, to have someone outside the family to love and miss you. Then he tried to imagine the type of girl he would like to have married.

Simple thoughts, simple pleasures. He calmed his mind with things that he would do when he escaped from this awful place.

Madrid Street
Belfast

Duggan had forgotten they drank fizzy white lemonade with everything.

He'd also forgotten how early the Irish started drinking.

Maggie had welcomed him with a cup of hot tea, then taken him upstairs to the small front bedroom and let him unpack. He opened the small, DIY-built wardrobe and saw the teenage girl's clothes. Those would be Tina's, the Maguires' nineteen-year-old daughter. As during his last visits, they would have moved her in with her brother, eighteen-year-old Danny. He hung his coat in the wardrobe next to the three shirts which were still clean, then finished unpacking and went down to join Maggie.

The first neighbour, a small, thin woman in her

sixties, had already arrived by the time he entered the kitchen.

'Do you remember Margaret O'Casey?' said Maggie, pushing another tea in front of him. 'She was an old friend of your Da's. You met her at the wake.' When Duggan, who vaguely remembered the woman, had re-made her acquaintance, Maggie continued. 'Harry's on his way back from work. I rang and told him you'd arrived.'

'There's no need for that,' he replied. Harry was Maggie's husband and worked at the local hospital as an orderly; he was a hard-working, God-fearing man of the old school, where values and tradition mattered.

'He'll go sick,' she said. 'He'll be wanting to see you, now that you're only here for a short time.'

By the time Harry arrived forty minutes later, five other neighbours, all women ranging in age from thirty to seventy, had joined the tea-party. Harry soon turned that into an alcohol party. White lemonade with Bacardi, white lemonade with Pernod, white lemonade with brandy; the drinks were handed out and the atmosphere got livelier.

Duggan stuck to a local supermarket-brand cola. It was sweeter than the Coke he was used to, but apart from the lemonade, it was the only soda in the house. Maggie made him a ham sandwich at three; he was unused to the thin slice of ham that was wedged between two door-step slices of white bread smeared with margarine. By then the house had become a party zone with nearly thirty people crammed into the kitchen and front room.

Danny Maguire came home from the Job Centre at four-thirty. Now eighteen, he had never yet held a job since he'd left school at fifteen. Duggan immediately recognized the frustration and anger in the boy's eyes, a sullenness that comes from inner torment and solitary brooding. It wasn't that he didn't like the American;

199

Danny didn't like anybody. Duggan remembered him as a happy-go-lucky youth, always smiling, always pleasant, always prepared to play a practical joke. That had been three years earlier and the American wondered what had happened to change the boy so dramatically. He was even more annoyed when Maggie told him Tina would be sleeping in his room for the next few nights and he sloped off sulkily up the stairs.

Tina arrived half an hour later; she worked as a junior in the front office of a local electrical contractor. Her temperament was totally opposite to her brother's. She had a fine spirit and was forthright in her views. Whereas Danny was red-haired and given to plumpness like his mother, Tina was petite, dark-skinned and straight-haired like Harry. Her eyes, hazel like Maggie's, were alive and enquiring; she clung to Duggan's arm and urged him to tell her about America, about its fashions, its people, its way of life.

He asked her about Danny, said he had noticed how unhappy the boy was.

'It's 'cos he's on the dole,' she replied, a note of sadness creeping into her voice. 'He's no job, no prospects.'

'What's he do all day?'

'No point looking for work. There isn't any. So he hangs round with that crowd.'

'What crowd?'

'You know. Bloody Republicans. They're a bad lot, but what can you do? I mean, if you've no work, then you go and mix with the rest of the boys. There's nothing for them to do but cause mischief.'

At eight o'clock the house was still heaving and Harry decided to continue the party at a local drinking club.

Duggan, with Tina on one arm and Maggie on the other, entered Seán Martin's Drinking Club at eight-thirty. He recognized the name above the door; he had last heard of it in the Girdwood ops room when

200

the soldier, Collett, had gone missing. He wondered if they'd found him yet. Many of the revellers from the Maguires' home, now that they were forced to buy drinks, had left the party and gone to their own homes. But there were still fifteen people left and the number soon swelled once they were inside the club. Harry, proud of his wife's cousin, introduced him to everyone. Some remembered his parents, some even remembered him from his last two visits. Tina brought a girl friend over, an older, voluptuous, dark-haired beauty called Simone. The woman, in her late thirties, was wearing a tight woollen mini-skirt and extremely high heels and attached herself to the American and soon made him aware of her interest.

'She likes you,' said Tina, pleased with herself for bringing the two of them together.

'She's nice,' said Duggan, trying to disentangle himself from Simone who had wrapped herself round him as he sat at the corner table. Embarrassed or not, he was beginning to get aroused as she continued to press against him. Tina gave him a knowing look, winked and went to get another round at her father's request.

At the other end of the club, Duggan saw Danny huddled over, now with youths of his own age, conspiratorial in their discussion.

'This is an old friend of mine.' Harry introduced a thirty-year-old man in working overalls. 'Tommy Farrell. Wanted to say hello to you.'

Duggan grinned, held out his hand and tried to stand up.

'Don't bother,' said Farrell. 'I can see you're otherwise engaged.'

Farrell and Harry laughed; Simone was almost sitting on Duggan's knee. Then Farrell slid round the table next to Duggan.

'And what're you doing over in Belfast?' asked Farrell, a beaming smile on his face, a Guinness in his hand.

Tommy Farrell. East Belfast Brigade Commander. The man in front of Duggan fitted the description and photograph Dancer had given him, one of many records he had been shown in case he ran into trouble. Duggan realized he was now being checked out by the IRA. 'I love this part of the world,' he gushed.

'There's a lot here who'd rather they were on your side of the Atlantic.'

'I don't know. We've got as much mugging and shooting as goes on here. Maybe more. And that's just in one city, like Washington.'

'From Washington, are you?'

'Yeah. I work there.'

'Doing what?'

'PR. Journalist. For the President's Office.'

'You know the President?'

'He's spoken to me. Once,' Duggan laughed. 'He caught me taking a short cut down a corridor that was reserved for him.'

'What'd he say?'

'"Don't do it again."'

Both men laughed; Simone joined in.

'Harry says you drove straight up from Dublin.'

'I did. Great scenery. Awesome.'

Farrell remembered the report he had read of an American in Monaghan, with an Englishman, the day before. He decided to check up on it. He didn't expect any problems with Duggan, but he was a thorough man, meticulous in his application. He said goodbye to Duggan, wished him well and went over to Danny's crowd.

Duggan watched him lean over and say a few words to Danny. The teenager turned round to look at Francis, but he buried himself in Simone's thick dark hair. He knew they'd spoken about him, guessed that Farrell had told the young man to keep his eyes open and monitor Duggan.

The party continued; by now Duggan was drinking Guinness. He wasn't particularly partial to it, but sipped the thick syrupy fluid so as not to offend his hosts whilst still retaining all his faculties. Next to him Simone and Tina drank everything that was put down on the table, but neither seemed to grow inebriated. The talk amongst the family was of 'Do you remember . . . ?' and 'When Tina was six she . . .', similar conversations to those carried on all over the world when distant relatives and friends meet, only different accents, different phrases. Duggan realized that, just like many other Catholic families, their Republican views had hardened since he last visited. He found out that both Danny and his father had been arrested several times, although never kept in custody. Maggie had once been hit in the arm by a plastic bullet; she had only been passing an area where a riot was suspected to be starting. Tina and Simone were often stopped by the Army or police and their handbags searched when on their way home from the dances. It was a life of a family under siege, no different from any other Catholic, or Protestant, family in the centre of Belfast.

The UDA and other Protestant organizations were, apart from being objects of hate, little more than idiots to be scorned. Harry told him of members of the UDA, at their base at the Newtownards Road, who had got 'caleyed' one night and decided to play Russian roulette. 'Bloody wankers,' he bantered. 'Instead of leaving one bullet in the chamber, they took one out and left five. First bloke was lucky. Second one topped himself.' He burst into a fit of laughter. Then he explained how they had dragged the body out and dumped it in a dustbin. 'Ended up blaming the Provos for knocking off the poor sod.'

At one stage he thought of Carmella. Adams Morgan seemed so far from here; another planet. She'd laugh if she could see him now, with Simone wrapped around him, reeking of cheap perfume and wearing cheap clothes. He suddenly felt very protective towards the Irish girl; it wasn't her fault she lived in Belfast and didn't have the opportunities Carmella did. *Why do I always have to defend myself?* he railed silently. He imagined his children with the gorilla. Then he imagined Carmella with the gorilla. He was suddenly jealous for her, seeing her in bed with the hairy male rubbing her all over. He hated himself for it, being jealous of the gorilla when he didn't love Carmella any more. It was the rejection that got to him. That hurt more than anything else. Simone snuggled up closer to him and he realized he had been unconsciously stroking her thighs as he thought of Carmella. He withdrew his hand but she grabbed it and placed it back on her thigh, under the table and out of sight of the other revellers.

At ten-thirty, Farrell came back and joined Duggan. Their conversation was of a general nature, dealing mostly with America. Farrell had never been there and was, like many Irishmen, eager to learn what life across the water was really like. Duggan felt the Irishman trusted him, but he never let his guard down. At one point, Farrell asked him what he thought about the British 'occupation' of Ireland. Duggan said, like most Irish-Americans, that he would like to see them out of the north. He added that there was little sympathy with the violent terrorist techniques used by the IRA, and if they eased up, the British might go some way towards finding a peaceful solution. With pressure from America, Duggan added. This immediately created uproar amongst the Republican sympathizers, including Farrell, who gave every argument as to why the British had to be defeated by any means possible.

'You don't understand', Farrell said, wagging his finger in the air to make his point, 'that the British have committed, and are committing, atrocities that are never reported.' He then launched into a run-down of several incidents where Catholics had been mistreated by the Army; even Maggie's affair of the plastic bullet was repeated several times. Duggan felt Farrell's outburst was as much for the crowd who had gathered round as it was for him. As he listened, his expression one of sympathetic concern, Simone snuggled up closer.

Duggan then broached the subject of the Angels. That created an even bigger outburst, with Farrell insisting the whole thing was a British government plot to cover their actions as they wiped out the IRA 'freedom fighters'. The others joined in, but no-one seemed to have anything new to add that caught Duggan's interest. 'At least they're sending Darcy's body home,' said one of the crowd. 'I heard that on the news earlier.'

Twenty minutes later, a man called Farrell over to the phone. Duggan watched the commander listen to whoever spoke, then start to joke to the caller. He seemed very pleased with the conversation and, when he had hung up, returned to the table. 'We'll see about them fucking Angels now,' he said, a triumphant gloating in his eyes. He wouldn't be drawn any further, except to remind people it was now eleven-fifteen and that he had been at Seán Martin's all evening.

Farrell left and the Maguires' party broke up soon after that.

'The Yank's leaving now,' said the voice over the speaker in the ops room.

Richardson had spent the evening listening to the latest movements in Madrid Street. Dancer was also in the room, but he had a headset on and was concentrating on some confidential messages which were being relayed from another source.

'He's got a tart on his arm,' continued the electronic voice. 'Bloody great tits and a walk I'd kill for.'

The mushroom turned and grinned at Richardson.

'Handy being a Yank, isn't it? All those dollars to spend.'

Richardson grinned back but was cut short by Dancer who tore the headset off and stood up sharply.

'What's the matter?' asked Richardson.

'They just found Collett. Fucking bastards.'

Dancer stormed from the room and Richardson stayed where he was.

'They're going back to the Maguires',' said the voice from the observation post in Madrid Street. 'And the bird with the tits is going in with him.'

The woods of Sherecock
County Cavan
Eire

The three men had dragged Lieutenant Collett from the car and bundled him into a small, disused barn in a field far away from prying eyes. The farmer, aware that the barn was being used by the IRA, ensured his workers kept well away from it. He wasn't a keen Republican supporter. In fact, he preferred a segregated Ireland within the European Community; that way he got higher subsidies. But he was frightened of what the IRA would do to him if he didn't support them. So the barn became a safe house, to be used when they wanted.

They tied Collett's arms behind his back and left him wedged between two damp bales of straw in the far, dark corner of the barn. McCann and Eamonn sat by the entrance and talked while the third man watched over the injured soldier.

Two hours after they arrived, in the early afternoon, as they had been ordered, they started to beat Collett once again. There seemed little purpose this time, apart from inflicting as much pain as possible. It was an animal instinct to hurt the uniform he represented; the man himself meant nothing to them. They kicked him and punched him wildly, half their blows simply skidding off his body and head.

Then they untied his hands and took all his clothes off. He could hardly stand and they had to prop him up to undress him. The third man put his revolver on one of the collapsed walls so that he could help support the soldier.

It was the moment Collett had waited for, that precise moment when he had the one chance to break from his captors.

He steeled himself, appeared to be helping them undress him. 'Come on, nancy boy,' he heard one of them say, then he was slapped on his naked buttock. The others joined in the merriment. He summoned up whatever strength he had left, and lunged past them towards the revolver on the wall. The sudden movement surprised the three men and it took a moment for them to react.

It was all the time Collett needed.

He grabbed the gun and swung round, pointing it at them.

He cocked it, and saw the shock in their eyes turn to anger.

All he had to do was hold them at bay, get to the car and drive away. He knew he could make it, weak as he felt.

And if they tried to resist, he would shoot them. It was what he was trained to do.

Then the men started to laugh.

The bastards were mocking him.

The tears filled his eyes; they were stripping away his dignity. After all they had put him through.

Bastards.

Shit to them. He pulled the trigger.

Click! click! click!

The energy drained out of him as he realized the revolver was empty.

Then Eamonn, the man he had bought so many drinks for, picked up a slab of paving stone and, still with that cheap taunting smirk on his face, smashed it against Collett's head.

'Fuck you, SAS man,' he heard Eamonn scream. Then he felt the pounding of the slab against his skull; it soon went beyond pain, was like a drumming that you heard through a long funnel. But he kept his pride; he was going to die a soldier.

'I want to confess,' he said. 'I want a priest.'

'What's he say?' shouted McCann.

Eamonn dropped the slab and knelt beside Collett. He listened carefully as the soldier burbled on, not aware that his mouth was covered in blood, all his teeth broken. Eamonn knelt closer. 'He wants a priest,' he said eventually.

'He's not Catholic, is he?'

'I don't—'

McCann pushed Eamonn aside and knelt beside Collett. He took his hand. 'Are you Catholic, son?' he shouted.

Through the funnel Collett heard the question. 'Yes, yes,' he shouted, not knowing it was only a whisper. Then there was peace for a long time; he held on to life so he might die with dignity and meaning. After an eternity, another man held his hand; it was a softer grip, almost gentle, and he heard the words, 'What is it, my son?'

At last. 'Father, give me absolution.'

'I'm here, my son. For final forgiveness,' said the priest.

'I have sinned.'

'What sins?'

'Absolve me, Father. For I have done wrong.'

'I absolve you in the name of the Father, the Son and the Holy Ghost. Amen.'

Collett, with one final effort, pulled himself up on

his elbows to see the face of the man who had absolved him from the sins of his life.

'Go in peace, SAS man.' The mocking face of Eamonn looked down at him.

It didn't matter after that. Robert Collett just lay down and died in the hopelessness of it all.

McCann took a knife and cut across the dead soldier's chest.

Then the three men dragged him to the tree they had chosen at the end of the Sherecock woods and tied him to it.

McCann rang the Gardaí station just before they crossed back into Northern Ireland at Clones.

When the Gardaí arrived, they found Collett tied to a tree, his arms broken and folded back like an angel trying to fly. He was naked and on his chest, cut deep into the skin, was inscribed, WE FUCK ANGELS. They only deciphered that when they had taken him to the morgue and washed the dry, caked blood from his body.

McCann, once he was back in Belfast, had called Tommy Farrell at Seán Martin's and told him what they had achieved. McCann didn't mention any names; they both knew the phone might be tapped.

'Did he admit anything?' was all Farrell asked when McCann finished.

'No,' came the reply. 'Not a bloody thing. Whatever the fuck else he was, he was a brave bugger.'

Madrid Street
Belfast

Duggan knew she would be coming into his room once the others had gone to bed.

Simone had returned to the house with the Maguires and, because she said she wasn't feeling well and didn't want to catch a taxi back to Andersonstown, asked if she could spend the night on the front-room couch. Maggie agreed; after all, wasn't she Tina's best friend who often spent the night there? After a knowing look between herself and Harry, she accepted that Simone and Francis were old enough to do whatever they wanted without the family cluck-clucking.

Where once Duggan would have resisted the obviousness of it, the Guinness he had sipped his way through had had some effect on him. His morals were hazy, his sensitivity dulled by the excess of unusual alcohol.

After forty minutes, when silence had pervaded the rest of the house, he decided she had either fallen asleep or changed her mind. The memory of her ample yet firm body crushed up against him lingered in his mind and he slid his hand down between his legs and started to stroke himself. It didn't take long for him to reach his climax and as he was about to ejaculate, the door opened quietly and Simone came in. He couldn't hold himself. He squeezed the end as tightly as he could, but it was too late, he lost control. He tried to regulate his harsh breathing and turned away from her, wiping the dampness on his hands over his body so as not to stain the sheets.

She slipped into bed next to him. She was naked apart from a T-shirt she had borrowed from Tina, and she put her arm round him.

'You've been a naughty boy,' she said, as she stroked him and discovered his secret.

'I didn't think you were coming,' he replied sheepishly.

'I won't be now, will I?' she giggled. Then she pulled her hand away from him and put her fingers noisily in her mouth, hoping the sounds would start to turn him on again. She then wrapped herself round him with both arms and started to stroke his nipples. 'I had to wait until everyone was asleep,' she said.

He felt his nipples harden, but he refused to turn

over; he was embarrassed to be found in such a state. *Big CIA agent, my arse.*

'Come on,' she urged him. 'You've only done what's natural.'

How different from Carmella. She would be laughing at him now, tormenting him. Recollections flashed across his mind: Carmella refusing to make love to him so that he snuck off to the bathroom, locked the door and masturbated, always with the air purifier on so that she couldn't hear his breathing. He believed she used to follow him sometimes and listen outside the door, but she never acknowledged it. Deep down he knew she was aware of his behaviour, but felt it gave her a sense of power over him. He hated her, even though his stomach turned at the thought of her with her smooth body under the hairy gorilla.

'Well, if you won't take charge, I will,' said Simone, pulling herself on to her knees and pulling him on to his back. 'We'll soon have you upright again, like a bloody ladder.' She took off the T-shirt then leant over and started to lick the dampness around his thighs; he felt himself stirring. By the time she slipped him into her mouth, he was big.

Carmella had stopped doing that once they were married.

He wondered if the gorilla had hair all over his penis; he imagined it like that in Carmella's mouth.

That thought, and the stab of jealousy that followed, excited him and he pushed harder into Simone's mouth.

She pulled back and smiled at him. 'Well, that didn't take long.'

She climbed on top of him and pushed down; she was wet and ready for him as he plunged upwards. She leant over, her breasts falling against his chest as she gasped at the ferocity of him, then she hooked her arms under his shoulders and buried her face in his neck. He wrapped his arms round her, squashing her down, feeling her

211

breasts spread out over his chest. In his mind it was Carmella; he pumped away with hatred as he saw the hairy one enter her, the blackness covering her like a waterfall as the gorilla came inside her. Duggan hated them both and forced himself harder and faster into Simone who bit the inside of her mouth so she wouldn't yelp as she enjoyed the energy of his frantic movements.

He came within three minutes.

She, sensing he was losing control, followed him a few seconds later.

They collapsed side by side, trying to ease their breathing, hoping no-one had heard.

She said she would stay till dawn, then return downstairs. 'You're some lover,' she said. She'd had better, but she enjoyed the ferocity of his passion. And it was nice to go with a Yank instead of all those local boys she and Tina knew so well.

He muttered something about how good it had been.

Then he shut his eyes and wished she hadn't stayed. It was the first time he had spent the whole night with a woman since Carmella left home.

Richardson lay on the bed, fully clothed, and thought about Lieutenant Robert Collett.

Dancer had told him what the Gardaí had found in the Sherecock woods. He'd come back half an hour after leaving the ops room and taken Richardson to Farquharson's office. Dancer took both men through the Gardaí report. When he'd finished, neither man spoke. They were both used to violence, but still had the capacity to be shocked by it when it occurred.

'He was an only son,' said Farquharson eventually.

'His parents still alive?' asked Dancer.

'Mother is. Father died a few years ago. TB, of all things.'

'You knew them?'

'Yes. We shared a command once. When we were

younger. She lives in Hastings.'

'Usual method of informing her, I suppose.' Dancer knew that an officer would make a personal visit to the mother and that any stress support would be provided by Army welfare and a chaplain. It was a common feature in the lives of those who served in Ulster.

'Terrible that. Losing both men in your life.' Farquharson laughed ruefully. 'Last time I saw him, I told him he was a smelly bugger.'

'Why?' asked Richardson.

'Took his job too seriously. Wanted to be like the rest of the animals he was trying to infiltrate. He looked and smelt the part.' Farquharson swore again. 'Shit! Dammit, he was one of the best.'

'Should we pull Duggan out?'

Dancer turned to Richardson. 'No. Why?'

'WE FUCK ANGELS. They think Collett was part of it. That puts Duggan under possible suspicion. He's in danger.'

'No. I don't think they thought Collett was an Angel. I think they killed him and dragged him over the border into a foreign country to show they don't give a shit. Otherwise they would've dumped him here. They took too much of a risk crossing the border with an army hostage.'

'They took Nairac across the border when they killed him.' Captain Robert Nairac, a liaison officer who was suspected of being an SAS covert operator, was brutally killed by the PIRA after being abducted and interrogated in South Armagh in May 1977.

'Only just across the border. And not all the way from Belfast. They took Collett a long way into Eire to prove their point.'

'What point?' asked Farquharson.

'That the Provos will now retaliate against any soldier, that they will continue the torture and vicious brutality that they exerted on Nairac and now Collett.'

His next statement was for Farquharson's benefit. 'I think Brigade should make sure no-one goes out as a single, whether it's a squaddie in a pub or a covert operator. I know it's Brigade's decision, but I'd recommend that.'

'I'll pass it on.'

'And you still want to leave Duggan out there?' asked Richardson.

'It's his choice,' Dancer shrugged. 'He's not one of ours.'

'But you're still keeping him under surveillance?'

'Of course.'

Dancer came back too matter-of-factly for Richardson. He didn't push it, but the look between Dancer and Farquharson told him what they had done. He didn't want to know any more, so he excused himself and went back to the bedroom.

Word about Collett had already got around the barracks. There was a sense of bewilderment and sorrow about the place. By tomorrow it would have turned to anger and the soldiers would be out there, being more zealous in the pursuit of their duty. It was a rotten place; very few of them wanted to be in Belfast, piggies-in-the-middle, separating the two factions and getting most of the shit themselves.

Richardson rang Andrea. He was glad she was still awake and she knew when to listen. He remembered that the call, like all radio-telephonic calls, was being monitored by GCHQ, so he was careful with what he said. He told her about Collett, sparing the worst of the details from her. He knew he wasn't breaching any security there; the news would be in the morning papers anyway. He said that Duggan was visiting some relatives in the city and they would probably return in a few days. And no, he didn't think the American would be staying over for long.

'You sound like you're brooding,' she said eventually.

'A bit'

'Being back there, it's getting you down.'

'Yes.' He sighed. 'Why the hell wasn't my dad a plumber, or something?'

'He was a good man.'

'I know. And I've been fighting it all my life. To be as good as—'

'You are as good.'

'He wouldn't have panicked that night. When I went crazy.'

'It's in the past.'

'He wouldn't have panicked.'

'You don't know that. All you know is what you've been told.' She suddenly fought for him, tried to become his strength. 'You don't know what went through your Dad's mind. But you're his son. And, if he was alive today, he'd be proud of you.'

When he put the phone down, his mind wandered back to Collett. He tried to imagine the horrors the young soldier must have endured. It was always the same in the barracks. Most of the squaddies would be thinking about that, wondering how he endured the pain, whether they could face the same terrors as he did without going crazy in the process. That's what made this place different from any other war zone. Men came from civilized homes, from crackling fires and *Coronation Street* and Dave Allen joking on the box, to this place of fear; here, where the thin crust of civilization you believed in, because of the comforts of home, was stripped away and replaced by an animal cunning and cruelty that became part of the daily characteristic of survival. Yet you looked through the windows of the streets you patrolled and you still saw the crackling fires and Dave Allen leaning against his mike-stand. It was like turning a well-fed, well-groomed dog out of the house to fend for itself. Within weeks, that friendly, soft-eyed pet would have turned into a ferocious hunter because of its survival instinct. Man was no different, in Richardson's eyes. All were animals, all with the same need for survival. All based on fear; the fear of not understanding what other people's intentions really were. If you didn't understand them, they were enemy. And you took enemy out before they took you.

His depression grew so he turned back to the operation at hand. It focused his mind away from Collett and Belfast.

The Plan.

Everyone knew about it, including Monaghan, Morrison, Carter and Dancer. *Like Santa's reindeer. Or a firm of bent solicitors*. He grinned. At least he could still crack a joke, however weak it was.

The Plan. It had never been discussed before he came on the mission. But it was there, buried in some dusty filing cabinet, waiting to be triggered off. They all knew about it, probably even the Prime Minister. It just hadn't been executed, or approved. All it needed was someone to authorize it.

Maybe it had already been authorized, was already in play.

Where did that leave him?

And what the hell did Carter mean when he had said, back there in the Special Forces Club, 'Sever the lead. By whatever means available. You're not out there just to help the Yanks, you're also there to protect us.'?

The thing was closing in on him, and the shame of it was he didn't know why.

'What the hell does he expect to find out by going into Belfast?' asked Mickleton.

The meeting had been hurriedly called late evening after the British reported Robert Collett's death. Mickleton was angry because he had been interrupted at an important dinner at the State Department. He was in black tie, as was Lacelle, also at the same function.

Mickleton's outburst was in response to the NSA's enquiry about Duggan which had resulted in McNabb stating that the analyst had gone walkabout in Belfast, amongst his friends and family.

'He's a Catholic,' upheld McNabb. 'He felt he might pick something up while he's in a Republican area.'

'You're asking for trouble, Cliff,' said Mickleton. He and McNabb were rivals but also friends. He didn't want the CIA man to end up with egg on his face. 'He's not experienced. You've got to pull him out.'

'Why?' asked the NSA. 'We're short on any other leads. Let's leave him there.'

'Because this latest killing puts a new slant on it. It's not about retaliation against those who support the PIRA any more. Now they, the Angels, will have to attack direct Republican targets. Maybe even in Belfast. Maybe even political parties like Sinn Féin or the Ulster Socialist groups.'

'Why?'

Mickleton tried not to show his impatience. Out of the corner of his eye he saw McNabb nodding in agreement. 'Because the PIRA have thrown down the gauntlet. They've done this to challenge the Angels to go after them in Belfast. Otherwise they're just going to increase the attacks on British servicemen and British sympathizers. In Ulster. That's really opening the door on genocide. And not something we want to get compromised on because we've got an agent in the field there.'

'Did you learn anything new from the Morrison transcript?'

'No. Except, if he was involved, it points straight at the British authorities.'

'You think that's possible?' the NSA asked McNabb.

'Looked at that way, yes,' replied the CIA Director. 'It also takes the heat off us.'

'Apart from the phone calls that have been made to the States.'

'We'll still continue our investigations on US soil,' added Mickleton. 'I think we should pull Duggan out and see what the Angels do next. I don't believe there'll be any further attacks in North America. Hell, NORAID's almost wiped out and there's no-one awaiting extradition. We can't be on the target list any longer. If we get Duggan out, then we've removed the only possibility of us being compromised. It's a British problem. Let them bury themselves.'

The NSA considered, then turned to McNabb. 'Pull him out, Cliff. Let's go the FBI route for now.'

'Except that all the calls were made back to Florida,' McNabb said calmly. 'It still traces back here. And the Brits know that.'

'Not a problem,' smiled Mickleton. 'We'll still investigate that. But at least that's on our own soil. All I'm asking is that we pull your man out before he embarrasses us.'

Hotel Kosmos
Cologne
Germany

The call came earlier than expected, but Gabriel wasn't surprised. He'd watched the news on CNN and knew the Angels would have to react.

'Heard the news?' asked Lucifer.

'An hour ago,' replied Gabriel. 'Poor bugger.'

'No time for sentiment. Only quick action.'

'They're inviting us into their parlour.'

'There's more than one way of skinning a cat. I want you to go to London. Usual place. Michael will contact you.'

'Am I working alone?'

'No. Michael will join you. But we may need some extra help.'

'What sort?' Gabriel was concerned; it was policy that they never went outside their own circle.

'Someone who has no love for the opposition. But someone who knows his way around the London scene. Someone you trust because he fears you.' Lucifer decided to end the conversation. 'Get there and wait. Take the cash with you. Michael will explain tomorrow night.'

Lucifer put down the phone in Worth Avenue, Palm Beach, and walked across to the car-park. He left the exclusive shopping area and drove back to his base.

Gabriel packed and drove north towards the Dutch border. In case the phone call was picked up, he didn't want to catch a local plane. He headed for an hotel near Schipol Airport; there were regular flights to London from there. He knew Michael wouldn't be arriving in the UK until tomorrow. That meant Gabriel could spend an interesting evening in Amsterdam in the company of some new friends.

He grinned. That was what he liked about Amsterdam. It was a city that catered to all tastes.

Madrid Street
Belfast

If Harry Maguire thought that Duggan and Simone had spent the night together, he made no reference to it.

The two men, after a breakfast of bacon, mashed potatoes and fried eggs, had decided to walk around the neighbourhood and clear their hangovers in the cold morning air. Harry wasn't on duty at the hospital until twelve and he enjoyed showing off his American to the rest of the street.

Simone had gone by the time Duggan awoke, and he had stumbled into the bathroom, washed at the basin, cursing the fact there was no shower, then dressed and hurried down to where the family was already at breakfast. The television, that great escape for Belfast housewives and those on the dole, was blasting away in the corner as he dug into his breakfast. It was one of those morning shows the British had copied from American TV, only taken it further. As Duggan ate he watched a blonde woman interview a well-known film star; they both sat, half-undressed, on a bed instead of a couch. It was a ridiculous interview, but the Maguires laughed unashamedly at the sly innuendoes between the two. Then Tina went to work and Danny returned to his room.

'More than half the folk here are on the dole,' Harry remarked as he and Duggan turned the corner into Lisbon Street. 'It's become a way of life, you know. The dole, drinking, watching your back for some stupid Prod who's out to get you.'

'Ever thought of moving away?'

'Where would we go?'

220

'There must be places better than the middle of Belfast.'

Harry laughed. 'Two families moved out of here about fifteen years ago. Bought houses right next door to each other. They went up-market, to a nice residential area to the east. Professional types, you know. Lawyers and accountants and doctors for their neighbours. Protestants, mind you, but educated people who didn't want any truck with the IRA or the UVF. Five weeks later, one of the men opened his front door on his way to work and a gunman shot him dead. He had his nine-year-old daughter with him. He was going to drop her off at school. His neighbour packed up and moved straight back here the same day. Sold the house.' He pointed at a street running off Lisbon Street. 'The family still live down there. Where can they move to?'

'England. Or America.'

'Why? Our friends are here. This place we're walking on, that's our roots. Some of us don't want to go anywhere else. Just 'cos we watch *Dynasty* and *Dallas*, doesn't mean we want to live like that.'

Across the road a British armoured personnel carrier pulled up and the road was suddenly full of armed soldiers. The speed with which it happened stunned Duggan and Harry laughed at his shocked response. The soldiers, seven of them, pushed past the people in the street, and took up positions so that they covered each other from an attack by possible snipers.

'Shouldn't we get out of here?' asked Duggan.

'No. They'll only be harassing some poor bugger.'

One of the soldiers had taken cover in a house doorway and the front door suddenly opened and an old woman in curlers came out, swore at him and told him to get off her property. The soldier ignored her and she continued to berate him. It was a game, no more, no less, however deadly its potential. It was at that moment Duggan realized how these people lived;

horror to them was just the normality of the day. Then he looked at the soldier, no more than twenty years old. He was just doing his job, earning his wage. He didn't want to be here any more than the woman wanted him. Yet these were their lives, inexplicably entwined in the gutter of Belfast.

The soldier, on a signal, moved out of the doorway and entered a house three doors down with two other soldiers. The remaining ones kept watch on the street. A young boy, no more than eight, started to swear and throw stones at one of them. The soldiers, as they had done with the older woman, ignored the child. It was just another irritation in the normal process of being on patrol.

'They'll be hounding the family,' informed Harry. 'It used to happen to us. Just come in and search the house when they want.'

Duggan remembered their conversation from the night before. 'They were after Danny, weren't they?' he ventured cautiously.

'Aye. He was always in trouble. Like that young kid there.' Harry pointed at the eight-year-old who was still venting abuse at the soldiers. 'It's just the way it is. They grow up hating the uniform. There's no logic to it, it just happens.'

'Was Danny involved with the IRA?' Even more cautious this time.

Harry looked at him warily. It wasn't the sort of question people asked round here. 'No. Sympathized, maybe. But not an active member. Trouble is, when we had to form our own vigilante groups to protect us from the Prods – I'm talking about when the recent troubles started – I was out every night guarding the street. We didn't have guns, just a few kitchen knives and big oak sticks. Anyway, the police used to run me in regular. Danny was only a kid then, but he grew up hating the boys in blue and khaki for what they were doing to his

222

dad. Twisted him against them. But then, that's how it is for all of us. And it would be for you, corralled in here, behind that bloody great "Peace Wall".'

They walked back to the corner of Madrid Street, past the ugly, mortar-proof fortress of the RUC police station.

'They'll be watching us,' commented Harry. 'From one of those observation posts. I'm surprised they haven't been out to question you. They always pick up a new face on the street.'

Duggan didn't look up to see if he could spot a watcher. He knew, from what Dancer had said, that he would be monitored.

He decided not to push any further with Harry; he didn't want to alienate the head of the house.

The two men returned to the Maguires' home on Madrid Street.

The soldiers came after Duggan thirty minutes later.

He was in the front room with Harry, cup of tea in hand, watching BBC1's *Morning Show*, when there was a loud banging on the front door.

'What the fuck do the buggers want here?' shouted Harry, getting up quickly. Duggan followed him into the hall. Harry opened the front door and two soldiers came in, their SA-80s levelled at Harry's overflowing gut. At the same time there was a banging in the kitchen, then Maggie yelled an obscenity. Two more soldiers came into the narrow hallway from the kitchen. The army had surrounded the house.

A captain, according to the insignia on his collar, shoved past Harry and signalled Duggan into the front room. Harry started to follow and the officer swung round and ordered the men to hold Harry where he was. 'I've a warrant from the RUC,' the officer said, holding up a sheet of officially typed paper. He closed the door and turned to Duggan. 'Who're you?'

'Francis Duggan,' came the reply as Duggan reached into his pocket.

'Hold it there!' the officer barked, pushing his gun-barrel straight into Duggan's stomach.

'I'm just getting my passport,' answered Duggan. 'I'm an American.'

'Bring it out slowly,' warned the captain, his gun still pointed at Duggan.

The American slowly pulled out his passport and handed it over. The officer examined it, then handed it back to Duggan. 'What're you doing here?'

'Visiting. Mr Maguire's wife is my cousin.'

'Strange place to come for a holiday. Like going to Beirut.'

'I was in Dublin. On business. And I decided to come here for a couple of days. To see old friends and relatives.' Duggan didn't know if the officer knew who he was and decided to play it the way it appeared. 'My parents are buried in Milltown and I want to visit their grave before I go home.'

'You know this is a Republican house?'

'No.'

'Their son. Danny Maguire. Was dragged in a couple of times for throwing petrol-bombs during riots. He's a dangerous customer.'

'I didn't know that,' Duggan replied honestly.

'I suppose you're an IRA sympathizer. Back in America. Something to brag about during happy hour, I suppose.'

Duggan decided not to get involved in an argument that could lead to him being taken in for questioning. 'All I'm doing is visiting family.'

'I hope that's all?'

'Of course. I'm an American citizen on vacation. Is that unlawful?'

The officer swung round and went back into the hall. A soldier was coming down the stairs.

'Anything?' the captain asked him.

'No, sir.'

'All right. Let's go.'

The soldiers left the house as quickly and noisily as they had entered. Harry slammed the front door shut as Danny came down the stairs.

'You all right, son?' the father asked Danny.

'Fucking bastards!' came the vicious reply. 'Fucking bastards!' he repeated.

Duggan saw the frustration and violence in the teenager's eyes. He was nearly out of control, so intense that he couldn't handle himself.

'Fucking fucking shithead bloody bastards!' he exploded once again, then slammed his fist into the wall and ran back upstairs.

Harry looked at Duggan, shrugged, then went into the front room. Maggie smiled from the kitchen door and told him she'd make a fresh brew.

Duggan followed Harry into the front room. The Irishman was back in his chair, laughing at a comedian who was being interviewed on the TV. The whole episode had shaken Francis, but he realized it was routine here. He felt as sorry for the soldiers as he did for the family. They were all trapped. He slid into a chair beside Harry.

Life in Belfast had returned to normal.

Richardson was in the officers' mess eating lunch when Dancer found him.

'Like it in here, do you?' smirked Dancer.

'Meaning?'

'You were an NCO, weren't you? Thought you'd prefer it in their mess.'

Richardson ignored the little man. It was his instinct to try and get under your skin; he'd met plenty of ferrets like Dancer in Five and Six. 'Is this social or are you after something?'

Dancer grinned and sat down. 'Nice of Farquharson

to give you use of the officers' quarters.'

'OK. Your position on the class war is noted. What're you? University type out of a middle-class family. Eh? Must be nice with Mummy and Daddy slaving away to provide you with an education just so you can get sarky with those who didn't have it so lucky.' He saw Dancer grimace; he'd hit home and reminded the little yoik about his middle-class life and values.

'They want your pal out of Belfast.'

'They?'

'The Americans.'

'Why?'

'Didn't ask.'

'Then you'd better run along and organize it.' Richardson dismissed the Five man.

'Not quite so simple. I explained that if we simply went in and yanked him out, the Provos would realize he was a plant. That could place his life in danger, if not here, then possibly in America. After all, his family knows where he lives.'

'Thought you didn't give a damn about him.'

Dancer chuckled. 'I'd rather he stayed where he was.'

'Why?'

'He might just stumble onto something.'

'I know what you've set up.'

'Oh? Farquharson been talking?'

'No. I'm not stupid. I know why you want him to stay in Short Strand.'

'Well, we all have our points of view. Anyway, I got them to agree to let us pull him out in our own time. When we feel he's safe.'

'And when's that?'

'Oh, tomorrow or the following day. I'll get a warning to him.' Dancer stood up. 'Just thought I'd keep you in touch.'

Richardson watched the intelligence man walk away. He opened his pack of cigarettes. Andrea would be pleased with him. So far he'd stuck to his quota. He saw there were seven left. He took one out and lit it.

He knew Duggan would never trust him when he found out what Dancer had done.

He grinned ruefully. *That's why you never trusted anyone in this game. That's why you were best working on your own.*

**Army Council
Dublin**

'It went like a dream,' said Baxter, the intelligence chief, to the six other men. 'The Brits have no idea how we pulled it off, where we crossed the border, even how we rumbled Collett in the first place.'

'Well, Séamus,' added Michael Griffin as he turned to McAteer, the director of operations, 'looks like you finally got it right. Well done.'

'Let's not be patting ourselves on the back too much,' warned Father O'Malley. 'We don't know what their response will be.'

'We've got Belfast sewn up. Nothing'll move without us knowing,' said Baxter.

'And you still going away on holiday,' rebuked Griffin.

'It'll run like clockwork while I'm away. And I'm not changing my plans. I can ring every day from America. We've worked out all the codes so nobody'll pick up our conversation. Anyway, I've got to go otherwise she'll be leaving me.'

'The Army Council's getting like the Civil Service,' rejoined Griffin.

'I'm not saying any more. All I know is that I've got more agents on the ground looking for anything unusual than we've ever had. Nobody'll fart in Belfast, or on the borders, without us knowing.' He pulled a photograph out of his top pocket. 'Like this. It's an

American who's staying with a Republican family in Short Strand.' He waited while the others looked at the picture. It showed Duggan and Richardson walking towards the stone cross in Monaghan. 'The Yank's a cousin. Francis Duggan. Born in America, but his Ma and Da came from Belfast. He buried them in Milltown five years ago. That's him on the left. With the hair. Said he was in Dublin on business and he drove up to Belfast 'cos he had some spare time.'

'This picture's not taken in Short Strand. It's in Monaghan,' said Father O'Malley, recognizing the monument.

'Aye. That was taken before he arrived in Belfast. By one of our people who watches the border for anything unusual.'

'Who's the man with him?'

'Sam Richardson.' He waited for a moment before continuing. 'He's an ex-SAS man.' He got the desired effect. He went on when their surprised comments had subsided. 'Not been seen in the province for more than five years. As far as we know, he left the Army. Anyway, they were in Dublin together. They drove up to Monaghan, then back to Dublin. By chance, they were stopped by one of our road-blocks near the Armagh border.'

'Where exactly?'

'At the Casacom. Unfortunately, before they could be thoroughly quizzed, an army helicopter patrol came along and sent our men running for cover. We picked them up again near Drogheda. One of our covert cars stopped them. The driver said he saw the Yank's passport and that the driver was an Englishman. So it looks like they went back to Dublin.'

'What's he doing with an ex-SAS man?' asked McAteer.

'We'll find that out tonight. Tommy Farrell's already spoken to him. He says the Yank is some sort of public relations journalist in the President's Office.'

'President?' enquired Griffin.

'Aye. Of the United States.'

'Bloody hell.'

'If that's true, we'll not be wanting to harm him,' counselled Father O'Malley. 'Not if we're to keep American public opinion on our side.'

'I just wanted to point out that we've everything under control,' finished Baxter. 'Duggan's staying with the Maguires. Harry Maguire was a strong supporter of ours in the seventies, in charge of the Short Strand vigilantes.'

'I remember him,' said Father O'Malley. 'He was a good man.'

'He's not so active now, but he's still a Republican through and through. His boy, Danny, is one of us. On the fringes, but always ready to help.' Baxter was pleased with himself; he felt he had shown the others that he was still very much in control. 'Anyway, because I'm away, which is not for long, it won't make much difference for a few days.'

'What about the funeral arrangements?' Griffin asked.

'All set,' replied McAteer. 'They'll be buried with full military honours.'

'We've checked the coffins. And the bodies,' added Baxter. 'There's no listening devices.'

'They don't need them. They're recording and filming everything from the bloody helicopter. They're probably even taking pictures from the space satellites.'

'At least we've none of you lot there,' confirmed Father O'Malley. 'If they came in and caught me, there'd be nothing to hold me on. Unlike you lot.' He turned to Baxter. 'What name are you going to America under?'

'It's a fake passport and ID,' replied the intelligence chief.

'Good. Make sure the kids remember they're under different names.'

'And the police and the Army at the funeral?' asked Griffin.

'As far as we know, they still take the view that they observe at a distance. Especially this one. It's going to be one of the biggest.'

'What if they try and break through?' Father O'Malley queried.

'Do you mean the police, Army or the Angels?' asked Griffin.

'It doesn't matter who tries,' said McAteer. 'We're surrounding the cortège and the cemetery with black cabs. No-one will get through, and if they did, by the time they were through, we'd all have broken up and they wouldn't find anything. Not even a black armband or a black beret.'

Madrid Street
Belfast

Duggan spent the afternoon doing the rounds with Maggie.

They called in at a number of friends in the Short Strand area. At one stage, she took him up to the Peace Wall which separated the Catholics and Protestants at Bryson Street. She chattered on incessantly, occasionally pausing to apologize for her non-stop gossip, before continuing on in exactly the same vein. She let little out about the family's Republican ties, except to admit she was worried about Danny 'mixing with bad company'.

At five they got back to the house where they found a coy Simone waiting on the front step. She went in with them and Maggie made the customary cup of tea. They moved into the front room and Duggan was subjected to his first viewing of the Australian soap, *Neighbours*. He was amazed by their fascination with the antics of the small televised community, then realized that the Maguires, like most Northern Irish people, were of working-class origin. The whole Catholic–Protestant war was a working-class war, just as the quality of their leaders was. Their leaders and generals were plumbers and shopkeepers, not professional soldiers or politicians brought up on university degrees. The whole struggle was based on fear and a class system that was Victorian in its ethic. Until they could bring themselves out into the modern world, they would always continue in this struggle with no meaning and no end. It was a tribal reaction, no different from those seen in the genocidal wars of Africa or Asia. For all his Americanization, Duggan suddenly felt a great warmth for his cousin, not in a patriotic way, but out of sympathy for her predicament. He suddenly wanted to reach out and hold her.

The soap finished; Tina came home, they called the sullen Danny and settled down to their evening meal. Afterwards Maggie put Harry's food in the oven and the girls went upstairs to prepare themselves for another night out. Simone came down first and joined Duggan in the front room. She had changed into a short black skirt and low-cut bright-green sweater; her cleavage invited him to join in.

'Will you be wanting me to spend another night with you?' she asked nervously.

He was embarrassed and didn't want that, but neither did he want to hurt her feelings. 'Fine,' he said.

That perked her up and she snuggled into him. 'Let's have a little cuddle before the others come down.'

His resistance was low and his expectation high after she had worked on him for twenty minutes before they heard the front door open and Harry yell out that he was home. By the time he entered the front room, Duggan and Simone were sitting apart, although Duggan had his legs crossed to hide his obvious embarrassment.

'Are you ready for another wild night?' Harry asked Duggan.

'Yeah. Where we going?'

'Seán Martin's. They've got a ceilidh on.'

Simone wiggled and giggled; the ceilidh was an evening of music and dance and she would make sure she had Duggan to herself on the dance floor.

They left the house at seven-thirty to walk to Seán Martin's. Danny was with them this time, having been cajoled by Maggie to join in the celebrations while Duggan was their guest.

'You'll be OK,' she yelled up the stairs at him just before they left. 'It'll be after seven as far as the others are concerned.'

'What was that about *after seven*?' Duggan asked Simone as they walked down the street.

She leant towards him conspiratorially. 'You mustn't say I said, but the IRA Green Book – you've heard of that, haven't you?'

'Yeah. Their army rules, isn't it?' He knew what the Green Book was, knew it intimately. He had studied it as part of his research into European terrorism. The Book was the Bible of the IRA, laying out its rules and methods for tactical warfare, long-term objectives and the procedure to deal with capture and interrogation.

'Yes,' she whispered, keeping very close to him. 'Well, one of the rules is that an IRA man shouldn't get drunk. Shouldn't even be in a pub, unless it's in the line of duty. Otherwise it loosens your tongue. Now, everyone knows you can't separate an Irishman from his booze. So the Army Council – they're like the generals – well, they compromised and said that IRA men can go in the pubs as long as it's after seven in the evening.'

'Is Danny IRA?'

A look of consternation flashed across her face. 'That's not for you to ask, nor me to admit,' she replied. 'But I'd be careful of saying things like that around here.'

232

The personnel carrier came round the corner and pulled up alongside the group. As the soldiers poured out, Danny turned to run towards the house.

'Stay, boy!' Harry yelled. 'Stay!'

Danny stopped where he was. The soldiers, as they had done earlier that day, took shelter in the doorways and set up a covering pattern.

The officer, the same captain who had been on duty that morning, approached Danny. 'Against the wall, lad,' he ordered.

'He's done nothing,' said Harry, stepping towards Danny.

'Stay where you are,' said a sergeant, bringing his gun to bear on Harry. Harry stopped. 'Just take it easy,' the soldier continued. 'Just checking for weapons.'

Danny assumed the search position against the brick wall, his arms and feet spread indolently. Duggan could tell the teenager had faced this situation many times before. He watched the officer search Danny then step away.

'All right, lad,' the captain said. 'You're lucky this time.' He turned towards Duggan, then walked over to him. Simone clung closer. 'You're not – how do you Americans put it – carrying, are you?'

'If you mean a weapon, no.'

'Let's have a look, then. Against the wall.'

'Leave him alone,' shrieked Simone. 'He's no—'

'Against the wall,' the officer ordered. 'Without the girlfriend hanging on to you.'

'You can't lea—'

'It's OK,' said Duggan, gently taking her arm from his. He turned and leant against the wall. He felt the officer frisk him, run his arms up Duggan's legs, then across his shoulders.

'They want you out by tomorrow,' the captain whispered.

Duggan didn't respond, wanted desperately to ask if his cover had been blown.

The captain continued, 'That's from Washington. Dancer says he wants you back at Girdwood by tomorrow night.' He stepped back from Duggan. 'So you're not carrying a gat, then,' he said loudly in a fake American accent.

'Very funny. Can we go now?'

'Yes. Why don't you report back to one of those Kennedy boys in the Senate? Tell them what bastards we are.' He walked away from Duggan and signalled the sergeant to call the men back into the APC. The small group stood and watched the soldiers clamber into the vehicle and drive away.

'Are you OK?' asked Harry, coming up to Duggan.

'No problem. Just like being picked up for speeding back home.' Duggan was shaken. The whole thing had jolted him, even when he was passed Dancer's message. He looked at Danny; the teenager was smiling at him. Duggan grinned back.

'Now you're an Irishman,' Danny said, coming over to him. Then he turned to Tina and held out his hand. She opened her handbag and took out an old revolver and passed it over to him. He tucked it into the waistband. 'Just for safety,' he told Duggan. 'In case we need defending from any Prods.'

The eyes Duggan looked into were wild, the eyes of a fanatic. He continued to grin at Danny, there was no point in alienating him now, not when he had less than twenty-four hours left in the Republican camp.

Seán Martin's was crowded; the music blasted from the group on the small stage. They found a table and Harry and Danny went off to buy the drinks. Before they came back, Tommy Farrell came over to the table.

'How're you doing, Francis my boy?' he asked.

'Having a great time.'

'Good. Let me drag you away from these lovely

girls and introduce you to some friends of mine.'

'Ah, no,' complained Simone.

'You can't keep him all to yourself, Simone,' smiled Farrell. 'Come on, Francis, we won't be long.'

Duggan told Simone he'd be back soon and followed Farrell across to the other side where four men sat. There was a distinct atmosphere about the men; although they were part of the crowd, they were somehow above it, somehow in charge. Theirs was not a space to be intruded on. As Duggan approached the group he realized there were no women on the tables adjacent to them. These were bodyguards; it showed in their stance. He was at the heart of the terrorist power.

'This is the Maguires' American cousin,' Farrell introduced Duggan. 'Francis Duggan.' Then he introduced the four men. Duggan already knew who they were. He recognized them from Dancer's files. Two were military deputies from Farrell's Belfast Brigade, the third was the commander of the Derry Brigade and the fourth – he recognized the grizzled bearded features immediately from his own files in Langley – was Father John O'Malley from the IRA Army Council. There was no attempt at disguising their identities. Then Farrell pulled up a chair for Duggan to join them. 'Will you have a drink?' he asked.

'No, thanks,' said Duggan. 'There's one waiting for me over there,' he waved towards the Maguires' table.

'So what do you think of Belfast?' asked Father O'Malley.

'Different.'

'I bet it is.' The group followed Father O'Malley's example and laughed. 'I hear you were stopped by a patrol on the way here.'

'They don't waste time, those boys, do they?'

'They say practice makes perfect. What do you do, Francis? For a living.'

'I'm with the President's Office.'

'So I hear. The President himself?'

'He has a big office. And a big staff.'

'You're still one of his men. Now, what was that film called?'

'All the President's Men,' interrupted Farrell.

'That was it. Are you one of his men, Francis?'

'You could say that,' replied Duggan.

'Not Deep Throat, are you?'

Duggan realized he was being checked out. 'They never found Deep Throat.'

'That's right. I forgot that. Tell me, what were you doing in Dublin?'

'That's confidential.'

The men laughed. This was their territory; nothing was confidential here. 'I think you should tell us, Francis,' went on Father O'Malley when their amusement subsided. 'It would help your position.'

'What position?' Duggan tried not to show how nervous he had become; his forehead suddenly felt very damp. It was the moment he realized he was under more than suspicion. *How? How could they know?*

'There are those who feel you might be a plant. So just tell us the truth and we can go about our business.'

'We know you're not wired,' added Farrell. 'Simone and Danny already went through your clothes. Simone a bit closer than Danny.' He grinned as the men laughed again.

'What were you doing in Dublin, Francis?' Father O'Malley repeated the question.

'I was on special assignment. The . . .' Duggan faltered; he tried to play the frightened man which he realized was unnecessary – he was genuinely scared. '. . . you know about the shooting in New York. Tim Flaherty. Well, I was sent to Dublin after their bomb explosion there, to see if there was any link. We don't like people shooting . . .', he carefully avoided the word 'terrorist', '. . . those whom the courts have released as innocent. That's vigilante stuff and it makes the President look bad. That's why I was in Dublin.' He took out his wallet, pulled out the special visiting card that had been prepared for him with the presidential seal, and showed it to Father O'Malley. The priest inspected it and nodded, then Duggan slid it back in his wallet.

'Did the British know you were there?'

Duggan recognized a sixty-four-thousand-dollar question when he heard it. 'Yes.' *What the hell did they know?*

'Who's this man?' Father O'Malley took a photo from his pocket and pushed it across the table to Duggan. It was Richardson and him in Monaghan.

'Sam Richardson.' He stuck to the truth; it was the safest way.

'Who's he?'

'Our State Department wanted me to have someone along who knew the Irish scene. That was the man the British nominated.'

'Was he a soldier?'

'He said he was Foreign Office.'

'Did he tell you he was ex-SAS?'

'No.' Duggan played it cool, although his insides were churning and he desperately wanted to go to the toilet. 'He gave the appearance he was ex-military. But we never discussed his past. Well, let's say he never volunteered it.'

'Why did you visit Monaghan?'

'I wanted to see the border. I was over here and I thought it would be interesting. Once a journalist, always a . . .' he paused. 'He said he was an expert on Northern Ireland. I picked his brains.'

'Did you find out anything about who shot Tim Flaherty?' questioned Farrell.

'No. The trip was a waste of time. That's why it finished early and I decided to visit here and see the Maguires.'

'When're you returning to America?'

'I think I'll be going back tomorrow. To our embassy in London first. Then back home.'

'I think that's a good idea,' said Father O'Malley, raising his glass and drinking from it. 'That way there'll be no misunderstandings. Tell me, do you think these Angels will strike again?'

'I don't know.'

'They're cranks, you know. Probably supported by the British government. You should tell your President that. Mind you, after what happened to Lieutenant Collett, they may not be so keen to continue.'

'What's that mean?'

Farrell tapped his nose. 'That's not for you to know. Except, I can tell you, for every attack on our freedom fighters, one of their men could get hurt. Maybe Collett was only the beginning.'

'Leave it,' snapped Father O'Malley. 'Ignore what he said. Tommy gets a bit carried away. Well, Francis Duggan,' he smiled, 'it's been nice meeting you. I hope you have a safe trip home. You'd better get back to your friends now.'

Duggan realized he was being dismissed. He stood up and smiled, then headed straight for the men's room. Later, when he had relieved his anxiety, he rejoined the Maguires. This time he kept some distance between himself and Simone, but she insisted he dance with her and pulled him onto the dance floor.

'I hear you've been through my clothes,' he said as she clung to him.

'Only 'cos I was ordered to,' she replied innocently. 'I mean, I don't want trouble with that lot. And you were clean, anyway.' She reached up and put her arms round his neck. 'I was with you 'cos I wanted to be with you. That had nothing to do with them. I swear that to you.'

He danced with her, but decided to be watchful.

He didn't want her reporting back that he had suddenly grown wary of her; they would be looking for any suspicious actions. As he danced, he wondered why the CTC was pulling him out of Belfast. McNabb had been supportive of his idea and they had agreed Duggan would try and spend at least four days in the Republican area. Yet his orders were clear; get out by the next evening. Maybe there was more to the Republicans than they were letting on. The photo of him and Richardson; that had shaken him. Could it be that the Provos knew more, maybe they had informants of their own? Or had the British intelligence teams found out that he was in danger? He dismissed that; if he had been in real peril, the army patrol would have bundled him into the personnel carrier and immediately returned him to Girdwood Park. He decided to carry on, and ensure he didn't raise any further suspicions. He had until the following evening and something might come up in that time. As he gyrated to the wild Irish jig, he went over the meeting with Farrell and Father O'Malley in his mind. Apart from acknowledging that they had been responsible for Collett's death, there was little else of interest.

When Duggan and Simone returned to the table, he stuck with a Coke. Someone had bought a Guinness for him and he occasionally sipped from it so as to appear to be following the pattern he had established the night before.

The Maguire party left Seán Martin's at eleven. For Duggan, there had been no further developments, apart from Father O'Malley leaving with Farrell and some men who Duggan presumed were bodyguards. It wasn't the authorities they were concerned about, more the Loyalist paramilitaries who may have discovered Father O'Malley was back in Belfast. The priest had smiled and waved goodbye to the American, who had returned the gesture.

Once in bed, even after Simone had fallen asleep, he stayed awake most of the night, just in case the Provos came after him. Simone had excited him sufficiently to make love and, like the night before, it had all been over within a few minutes.

He lay on his back with his eyes open, Simone snoring gently as she slept with her back to him.

Once again he went through the events of the last two days.

He had learnt nothing.

As he listened and watched for any movement that would warn him of possible danger, he realized the CTC were right. It was time to go home. He was no nearer the truth about the Angels. All he had done was compromise himself and the Agency. If he ever wanted to return to Belfast in the future, however innocent his reasons, it would always be under a cloud of suspicion. He didn't even know if the woman lying next to him was there out of choice or because she had been ordered.

He sighed and accepted his own vulnerability. At the end of the day, he was no James Bond, just a Langley third-floor analyst. Coming to Ulster had been a waste of time.

Richardson watched the house in Madrid Street from the observation post of a burnt-out building on the opposite side.

He had come there after the speaker in the ops room blasted out that Duggan had returned from Seán Martin's to the Maguire home. 'Got the bird with him again,' the watcher had reported.

Richardson waited; his instincts told him Duggan was in mortal danger.

It seemed for ever before he saw movement in the empty, midnight street. There were no street lamps ablaze, no house lights illuminated behind drawn curtains. The only illumination was the red glow in the sky from the distant city and a few flecks like white laser-beams spilling out from the RUC police fortress at the end of the street.

It was all very still and very black.

He still noticed the movement; sensed it rather than saw it.

As he peered into the darkness, he made out a man, crouched low, running along under cover of the house walls, hugging them so as not to be seen by the observation post at the RUC station. Richardson realized the man didn't know he could be seen from the ruined house across the road. Richardson leant over and picked up the Stinger surface-to-air missile launcher. He slipped it over his shoulder; he would use the image-intensifier night-scope to pick out his target. Before he looked, though, he searched for the soldiers who were meant to be in the observation post with him. They'd gone and he cursed silently. Probably on a bloody tea-break; that's what happened when democracy ruled the armed services. He balanced the launcher, nestled against the eye-piece, saw the world through a greenish-yellow haze and picked out the crouching man.

He had stopped running now and the semi-automatic Browning 9mm in his hand was clearly visible. It was probably from some soldier the gunman had once taken out.

Richardson tightened his finger on the trigger-button which would release the missile and blast across the road at speeds just below Mach-2.

He was about to release it when he saw the second figure. Then the third. Then some more.

The street was crawling with gunmen, all running low towards the Maguires, all armed. Some had machine-guns, most had revolvers. They all, like the first man he had seen, wore Balaclavas so as not to be recognized.

Within minutes Madrid Street was swarming with masked terrorists.

He looked round the observation post once again, but there was no help there. He couldn't shout without alerting those on the street.

The gunmen by now had surrounded the front of the Maguire house and one of the men banged loudly on the front door. 'Open up,' he yelled. 'We've come for the party.'

Then the street exploded in light, with bunting draped across from lamp-post to lamp-post, with tables set and laid for a street-party, with music from an Irish band booming out. But there was no-one else in the street, only the gunman waiting at the Maguires' door.

He saw the gunman knock again and then the door start to open.

It was Duggan who stood there.

Richardson knew the music and the street-party were just a trap.

He pulled the trigger, activated the missile and watched it, in slow motion, leave the launcher and float across the street, a long fire-tail coming out of its rocket exhaust.

The gunmen were all pointing their weapons at Duggan; nobody heard the rocket.

It sliced through the crowd, exploding as it did, cutting through fragile bodies and blowing the side of the Maguires' house down. Then there was only Duggan, watching him with a quizzical expression. 'Why'd you do that?' he heard Duggan say, shaking his head in disbelief, a big hole next to him where the wall had been, debris still falling across the street. 'It was only a party. Just some fun.'

Then there was blackness again but Richardson's dreams weren't over.

There was the face of the soldier, running towards him, warning him.

He was back in South Armagh, deep in bandit country, waiting to take out a gunman he had arranged to meet.

Richardson lay under a hedge, his self-loading, 7.62mm, FN FAL rifle tucked in the crook of his arm. The man he was to meet, Gerry McCann, Quartermaster for the Armagh Brigade, believed he was coming to arrange a shipment of explosives from France to Northern Ireland. Richardson had worked undercover for months gaining the trust of sympathizers who had finally agreed to pass on details to McCann and fix a meeting. The quartermaster had contacts with the PLO and other terrorist organizations second to none. He also had extensive agreements with people in America and Europe. Take him out and it would slow down the supply of weapons and explosives into the province quite substantially.

The trouble was that Richardson's cover had been blown. Which is why McCann agreed to the assignation.

In truth, the IRA were there to take out Richardson.

The Englishman hadn't known this as he sat waiting under the hedge. But intelligence at Brigade had been informed at the last moment that the Englishman was in danger. They sent patrols out to find Richardson. One of the patrols parked in a nearby lane and set out on foot to alert him.

Richardson heard the whistle that told him McCann was near. He cupped his hands and hooted back, a bad imitation of an owl. The whistle repeated and he knew he had made contact. He eased himself out from under the hedge and moved towards the hedge on the other side, hunched low as he ran across the field.

The young soldier saw him outlined against the night light on the slope of the hill. He turned round and saw he was spread out from his colleagues, so he started to run towards Richardson, his rifle cocked and ready for instant use. He knew there were bandits in the hedge opposite Richardson, probably four or five of them. When he was about a hundred yards from Richardson he shouted a warning. He saw Richardson hit the ground, taking immediate cover. He knew he'd be all right; knew Richardson would give him covering fire. He raced towards the fallen figure, yelling for cover.

He heard the gun-fire from the hedge across the field; he didn't need to see the flames from the muzzles to know they were aimed at him.

'Cover me, cover me,' he yelled as he ran towards Richardson, now no more than twenty yards away.

Richardson had frozen. He was cowering in the soft, recently ploughed earth, lying in a furrow. He turned his head as he heard the soldier yell for assistance. He saw the boy's face, a youngster, probably on his first tour in Northern Ireland. He saw the panic as their eyes met, then the soldier's eyes were lifeless and he rolled over into the soft earth, landing in a heap no more than five yards from Richardson.

Across the field, more soldiers had opened fire and were shooting towards the hedge. Richardson picked up his FN FAL and opened up in the same direction. He knew it was only for effect, to show the others he was returning fire. All he could think of was that he had let the boy die when he could have saved him. And all the young soldier had done was warn him and save his own miserable life.

The boy, his helmet looking like a plastic toy on a child's head, suddenly stood up and started to yell again at Richardson. 'Cover me, cover me.' Then the boy's faced changed into Duggan's and the American mocked him for his cowardice.

Then someone came and put a gun to Richardson's head and pulled the trigger.

Click, click, click.

The man was Collett and all three of them laughed at him.

Then Dancer came and took them away and Richardson started to cry.

Great big tears. Relief. At last they all knew what a shit he had been.

That's how he awoke, sobbing, with tears running down his cheeks. He sat up in his bed and looked across at the empty one opposite. As he calmed down he hoped Duggan would be all right.

Then he thought back to that awful time in South Armagh.

They had killed two terrorists; no more soldiers were hit.

On the way back, Richardson had sat apart from the rest of the troops. He hadn't asked what the dead soldier's name was; he didn't want to know any details about the boy. When the patrol returned to Bessbrook, Richardson had given a simple report detailing that he had returned covering fire but that had not been sufficient to protect the soldier. Nobody questioned his account because the rest of the troops had been too far away. In the end it was decided the young soldier, due to his inexperience, had acted hastily and should have remained with his patrol while they ambushed the terrorists from behind.

Somebody told Richardson the boy's name, but he chose to forget it instantly.

He never attended the funeral and returned to Manchester now that his cover had been broken.

He knew he couldn't sleep now. He stayed awake, his mind wandering over a thousand details as he waited for morning to break.

Schipol Airport
Amsterdam

Gabriel watched dawn break over the flat Dutch countryside as he pulled into the car-rental return centre at Schipol.

He was tired, but satisfied. The long night in the company of various young men had been all he expected. He would miss it when he returned to the base; Amsterdam hookers had a style of their own.

He walked into the airport with his suitcase, bought a ticket to Heathrow and went into the self-service restaurant for a quick breakfast before he caught his flight.

He recognized the face before he could put a name to it.

The man was standing in a food line waiting to be served. He was in his mid-thirties and he waved across at one of the tables where his wife and two children sat. The children, a boy and a girl, were about nine or ten, boisterous youngsters, obviously excited by their surroundings.

The realization of who it was chilled him.

It was the hair. It should have been long and black. It was now cropped short and dyed blond.

Fergal Baxter.

The Army Council's director of intelligence.

Gabriel concentrated on his croissant; he didn't want to attract Baxter's attention. He had already noted that the Irishman was constantly checking to see if he had been recognized. He munched through his croissant, watched Baxter pay at the till, then take the tray full of food over to the table where his family waited. Gabriel heard the first call for his flight and decided to ignore it. He could always buy another ticket, but the chance of seeing what Baxter was up to would never present itself again. He toyed with the idea of taking the Irishman out. That would make them all sit up. He chuckled. *Now that's what you call retaliation*. He wondered what Lucifer would say. Probably reproach him for not following orders. *Information is power*. That's what he needed. Information.

His chance came when the two children spoke to their parents and then ran out of the restaurant. He finished his coffee, picked up his hand-luggage and sauntered out after them.

'You and your sister are very excited,' he said when he walked into the men's toilet. The boy was standing against the child's latrine and was intently watching the stream of urine shoot out between his legs. 'You nearly ran me over coming out of the restaurant,' Gabriel continued when the boy looked up.

'Sorry, Mister,' came the cheeky reply.

'Irish, are you?' said Gabriel, adopting a slight Irish accent himself. 'On holiday?'

'Aye. We're off to Disney World.'

'Good for you. In Florida?'

'Orlando.' The child had trouble forming the word.

'You'll love that. Have fun, son. Hey, what's your name?' He knew Baxter would be travelling under an assumed name.

'Jimmy.'

He decided not to push in case the child told his father and Baxter changed his plans. 'Well, like I said, have fun in Orlando, Jimmy. Say hello to Mickey.'

The boy finished, zipped himself up and rushed out. Gabriel followed a minute later and went to the information desk. He determined which flights were going to Orlando, then found a phone booth and made an international call.

'Imperative speak in next thirty minutes.'

'Call Flamingo Drive,' came the answer.

Gabriel went back to the ticket counter and changed his ticket for a later flight to Heathrow, saying he was waiting for a colleague to deliver something important from Amsterdam and it hadn't yet arrived. Then he returned to the phones and called one of the numbers he had memorized, this time in Flamingo Drive.

'Sorry to break cover,' Gabriel said. 'But you've got a visitor.'

'What sort?'

'Enemy. Going to Orlando. With his family. Wife and son and daughter. Kids're about ten; wife's about thirty-five. They're going on to Disney World.'

'Is this codespeak?' Lucifer was perplexed.

'No.' Gabriel then gave the timetable of the next two flights to Orlando. They were both leaving in another hour, and he added that he couldn't guarantee which flight they would be on. 'The boy's name is Jimmy.' He then gave a description of Baxter, what he was wearing, and his wife and children.

'You want us to intercept them?'

'Yes. Imperative.'

'Can you say why?'

Now it was getting difficult. There would be over a thousand people going into Orlando on those two flights. Mixed with travellers from other flights, there would be many passengers looking similar to Baxter. He didn't want to breach confidence on the phone, but he knew they had to find Baxter. It was their ideal opportunity to redress the balance with the IRA. 'Fergal Baxter.'

'Say again.'

Gabriel realized he had spoken too softly. 'Fergal Baxter. Spymaster. With his family.'

'Jesus.' It was softly spoken at the other end. 'Are we talking about the same man?'

'Yes.'

'Thought he was in Dublin?'

'No. Kid said they were going on holiday.'

'We'll meet the plane.'

'Do I still go to my next destination?'

'Yes. Michael is on his way there.'

Gabriel put down the phone and went back to the restaurant. The Baxters had left, so he wandered down to the gate where the American flights were boarded. He caught sight of Baxter's wife and Jimmy disappearing through the boarding gate.

Then he went and caught his plane to Heathrow.

Madrid Street
Belfast

The day started quietly in the Maguire house.

'I'll be heading home today,' Duggan informed them as he dug into soda-bread and margarine at breakfast.

'Aah,' complained Maggie. 'We'll miss you, Francis.'

'We will,' added Harry. But it was said without emotion and Duggan knew the IRA had warned him to monitor the American. 'When will that be?'

'Later on. Probably this afternoon. I need to get back to London first. Call in at the Embassy before I go back Stateside.'

'Good. Fancy a walk before then?'

'I'd like that.'

When Harry left the room, Duggan told Maggie he would also be visiting his parents' graves in Milltown cemetery. 'What's the best way up there?' he asked. 'I don't want to take the car.'

'Use the black cabs in Castle Street. You'll find them across the bridge, no more than a mile from here.'

It was what Duggan wanted, to ride in one of the infamous black cabs. He excused himself, went upstairs and packed. He heard Harry calling him and he slipped on his coat before joining him for his short constitutional.

At one point they went into a small newsagent's near Mountford Road. Duggan recognized the owner from the night before; he had been sitting with Farrell and Father O'Malley. Harry introduced him as Liam Quigley. Once again, Duggan remembered the name from his Langley records. Quigley was the quartermaster for the Belfast Brigade, one of Farrell's right-hand men. The shop was quiet so Quigley had time to talk to them.

'Did you hear I was done over last week,' Quigley enquired of Harry. He continued when Harry shook his head. 'Aye, two lads; the oldest was seventeen, came in here with masks on their heads and clubs in their hands.

One had a gun, an old thing, all rusted, I wouldn't be surprised.'

'Protestants, were they?'

'That's what I thought. But they were Catholics. From across the river in the Ardoyne.'

'Did you find them?'

'Aye. They took four hundred pounds out of my till. Then my money belt. I had over three thousand in that. Funds for the boys.'

Duggan realized Quigley had been holding money for the IRA.

'The money turned up an hour later,' Quigley continued. 'With a commander in Ballymurphy. These two lads had gone out to get funds. Not for themselves, but for the boys.' He laughed. 'They thought this was a Prod street. I wish I'd been a fly on the wall when they were told who they nicked the money from.'

Harry joined in the laughter. 'Did they have to bring it back?'

'Themselves. Very sheepish when they walked in.'

They had continued the walk, then Harry had returned home to collect his sandwiches and leave for work. He and Duggan had said a fond farewell with the usual pleasantries and 'See you when you come to America.' Then after a quick bite for lunch and a relaxed conversation with Maggie, Duggan put his suitcase in the car boot and walked across Queen's Bridge, following Maggie's directions, and arrived at Castle Street. He enjoyed stretching his legs, this time striding out instead of the more gentle stroll he had shared with Harry.

There was a line of black cabs waiting there.

He approached them warily; he knew what they represented.

Ever since the seventies, when Belfast buses were regularly blown up or attacked by gunmen, both the Protestants and Catholics had devised their own transport system within their own sectarian areas. They imported second-hand black cabs from London and ran these vehicles from the city centre into their respective areas. The Catholic cabs started at Castle Street, and cruised up Divis Street to the Falls Road and Andersonstown Road, stopping as people flagged them down, running very much as a scheduled bus service would. The fare was cheap, usually no more than 10p. It suited the IRA well, as they used the black cabs as an intelligence network to warn them if any strangers were loose in the Republican areas.

'Are you sure you want one of these cabs?' asked the driver when Duggan approached him.

'I want to go to Milltown cemetery.'

'Why?'

'My parents are buried there. I've been staying with relatives in Madrid Street. They said I should take one of the cabs.'

'What're your relatives called?'

'Maguire.' Duggan gave him the rest of the Madrid Street address. 'Getting a ride with you is more difficult than applying for an American Express card,' he joked. 'Do you need any more references?'

The taxi-driver grinned. 'You can never be too careful. Specially on a day like today. Come on, jump in.'

In the ops room the watcher's voice from the observation post in College Crescent told the mushroom that Duggan had taken a Republican black cab.

The mushroom picked up his phone and called Dancer. 'Our man's on the move. Into Republican territory in a black cab.'

Dancer came into the ops room with Richardson as the soldiers on top of the Divis Flats reported the cab crossing Westlink into Divis Street and turning up towards the Falls Road.

'Where's the Q car?' asked Dancer.

'Got him in his sights. Only they'll all know the

Yank's being followed. They'll be extra watchful today.'

'Tell the Q car to follow him until he gets out. Then keep going. I don't want any extra risks today.' Dancer turned to Richardson. 'What the fuck's he up to? Doesn't he know?'

Duggan was unaware that he was being followed by an unmarked army patrol. But the taxi-driver had already noticed the Q car behind. It didn't surprise him; they were used to being followed. Having made a mental note that it was there, he decided to keep an eye on it in case it did something suspicious. He picked up his radio and warned the other cabs that there was 'a sheep loose on the Falls Road, going south'.

Duggan was interested in his route, past the Divis Flats and into the Falls Road, the centre of the Republican area. The shops were small, many still boarded up, the road narrower than he expected. It was busy and he passed at least five groups of men in green uniforms with berets, some carrying musical instruments, others with banners draped over their shoulders. He wondered what the celebration was. To the left he saw glimpses of the main Peace Wall, put up to separate the Falls area from the Shankhill Road Loyalists. To him it was worse than the Berlin Wall; at least the Berliners hadn't spent their time shooting and bombing each other as the Irish did. The area looked run-down; it was, after all, a war zone. Yet there was an air of normality, people shopping, children in push-chairs, traders arguing with housewives. A contradiction in living, where death was as common a currency as a pound coin or a pound of potatoes.

They passed the shopping area, then drove past the houses and schools near Donegal Road. Milltown cemetery was on the left, opposite the fortified RUC station on the corner of Glen Road and the Falls Road. The cab pulled up at the pavement.

*　　*　　*

'He's getting out at Milltown cemetery,' said the mushroom.

'Is he crazy, or what?' Dancer asked Richardson.

'Pull him out,' urged Richardson.

'How? If we stop the Q car and pick him up, we endanger him as well as the surveillance team.'

'Let me go in.'

'No. Not enough time. What the hell's he doing there?'

'Visiting his parents' graves.'

'Today?' he asked incredulously. 'Why today?'

'The Q car's asking what they should do?' interrupted the mushroom.

'Keep going. Leave him. It's his bloody mess,' snapped Dancer. He waited until the message had been relayed. 'Have we got any operatives up that way?' he asked when the mushroom finished.

'One. But he's on his way out of the Falls Road. Brigade wanted the area cleared.'

Dancer swore again, then looked at Richardson. 'He's still our responsibility.' He swung round to the mushroom. 'Get me Brigade. And ask the OC to come down here.'

Duggan walked into the large sprawling Catholic cemetery that is Milltown.

He strolled along the paths between the gravestones, thousands of them stretching from the Falls Road to the motorway. It was an untidy place, overgrown and lacking in the precise and neat order of most large city cemeteries. He enjoyed the tranquillity of the place; it was somewhere to reflect and stand at a distance from the hurly-burly of everyday life. He wondered if there were spirits, if his parents were around him as he walked towards them. His father would have berated him for allowing the cab-driver to charge him £3 for such a short trip. He'd always said that Duggan never stood

253

up enough for himself. *Well, Dad, if you're there, what do you think of Belfast now? Did you do the right thing in being laid to rest back here? I bet it's nothing like you remember it.*

He found the graves easily. They were well tended as Maggie had said they were; Duggan sent money every month to an organization that looked after the graves. He knelt in front of them, his mother on the left, his father on the right, and prayed for them. Then he sat on his haunches and just stared at the graves. His mind went blank; he tried to remember his youth and the happy times he had had with them. No worries, no pressures. A time of youth and joy and not giving a damn about anything. He explained to them the split with Carmella and how beautiful their two grandchildren were; told them of things the family had done before the divorce.

He stayed there for half an hour, wishing he had brought some flowers, something to remember them by, to leave something solid behind as a memory of his visit. In the distance he heard the thump-thump of a big bass drum, then a trumpet. *The parade must be warming up*, he thought as he turned northwards to listen to the sounds coming from the Falls Road.

Knowing it was time to go, he kissed both headstones, the tears welling in his eyes as he realized how much he missed them, said a final prayer and slowly walked away. He didn't want to leave this place; it was the first time he had felt any peace since he'd left America. *Not true, no peace even before that.*

He strolled back, in no rush, towards the Falls Road. He was surprised at how many people there were in the cemetery.

'Mr Duggan?' a voice behind him asked. 'Are you Mr Duggan?'

He turned round, surprised. He hadn't expected an English accent out here. 'Yes.'

The man was tall with long, blond hair and thickened

254

features. In his late twenties, he wore an old duffel coat with the hood down. The appearance was shabby, the eyes bright and aware. 'Mr Dancer's sent me in, sir. You need to leave this place. Now.' He spoke with quiet authority; Duggan knew he was British Army. 'If you'd follow me, sir?'

The man turned and walked towards the entrance, Duggan following. He hoped it wasn't a trap set up by the PIRA to see if he was a plant. 'Who're you?' he asked as they strode towards the entrance. The banging of the bass drum suddenly appeared much closer.

'Lance-Corporal Vaughn. I was on my way out of the area when they called me. Told me you were here.'

'How did they know where I was?'

'They know where everyone is. That's their job.'

They walked on, not too fast so as not to attract obvious attention. A helicopter came into view from the east, from over the city. 'Vaughn. That's a Welsh name, isn't it?' commented Duggan, trying to keep a semblance of normality going.

'Yes. Only we're not short and dark like the other Welsh. All Vaughns are descended from the Vikings. That's the name. Vaughn. Welsh for Viking.'

They reached the entrance. Duggan was surprised there was such a crowd there. He looked down the road and saw the procession coming towards them. There were thousands of people. 'What is it?' he asked Vaughn.

'IRA funeral. Darcy and Flaherty. They're burying them with full military honours.'

'Christ!' Duggan realized why he was in danger, especially with a British soldier next to him.

Across the street the crowd had blocked off the side-roads. 'Can't get to my car,' said Vaughn. 'We're stuck here.' There was a sudden tension in his voice.

'I was OK on my own.' Duggan regretted the words as he said them. The man was risking his life coming after him. 'Let's make sure you're not identified.'

Vaughn pulled up the hood of his duffel coat. They moved backwards into the crowd. Duggan looked at the oncoming funeral cortège and saw the two coffins, side by side, being carried towards the entrance. Behind them walked some members of the family, then Father John O'Malley, Tommy Farrell and Gerry Adams, the bearded politician whom many regarded as the leader of the whole PIRA movement. To the front and rear came the black cabs, outriders in this bizarre procession. Across the road, behind the crowd, stood a heavy presence of armed RUC officers.

'I forgot to tell you this was on today,' said Harry Maguire, appearing behind Duggan.

'I only came up here to see the graves,' replied Duggan, looking round for Vaughn. The Welshman had quickly disappeared into the crowd when Harry came up.

'Maggie said. She should've warned you.'

'I don't mind.'

'You may not, but others might. There're those who like these things to be private affairs.' Harry laughed and pointed at the helicopter hovering at the far end of the cemetery. 'Fat chance, mind you, with that thing buzzing around.'

The funeral procession turned into Milltown gates and the crowd formed round the close mourners. Duggan reckoned there must have been seven or eight thousand people there; the brass had insisted the turn-out be good. Across the street, the police officers, now strengthened by the arrival of soldiers, kept their position. That meant they would not be entering the cemetery unless trouble erupted.

As Farrell passed he looked up and saw Duggan. He frowned, then beckoned one of his attendants to him and gave him instructions. As the man left and pushed into the crowd, Farrell turned and informed Father O'Malley of Duggan's presence. The two men stared at the American, who could do nothing better than smile back.

'Shit,' Harry said behind him, now aware of their predicament.

The band played on, the crowd swelled and someone raised the Republican tricolour.

On the other side of the street the RUC and military decided not to interrupt the proceedings, even if the tricolour had now been raised. The orders from Brigade were simple. 'We've got people in there. Observe and be ready to take action if needed. Otherwise don't exacerbate the situation.'

The black cabs had now pulled up and blocked off the entrance. Any attempt to swarm the cemetery by the troops would have been delayed by the vehicle presence and formation.

The man Farrell had sent over reached Duggan. 'What're you doing here?' he asked.

'He came up to pay his respects at his parents' graves,' interjected Harry. 'No-one told him we had a funeral today.'

'You must be bloody joking,' the man turned on Harry. 'Letting him this close to us.'

'I told you!' snapped back Harry. 'He never asked and I didn't know.'

Duggan saw how frightened Harry was, for all his bravado. 'He's right,' he said. 'I didn't tell him I was coming here.'

'Stick with him,' the man ordered Harry. 'Make sure he doesn't do anything you'll regret.'

The man went back to report to Farrell. Duggan and Harry were swept along in the crowd. In the distance the helicopter kept an overhead eye on the proceedings. Duggan searched the crowd for Vaughn but couldn't see him. He presumed the army man had crossed the road into the protection of the RUC.

The graves were side by side. The pallbearers lowered

the two coffins onto the supporting poles that criss-crossed the freshly dug graves. When they had completed their task, the families of the men moved next to the coffins, the IRA leaders behind them. Darcy had a wife and two children he hadn't seen for three years. His wife, even though she had long since given up on her errant husband, enjoyed the emotion of the moment and broke down, falling to the earth and sobbing, as the priest came forward to start the burial ceremony.

Duggan had been pushed by the crowd until he found himself just behind Father O'Malley and Farrell. He tried to avoid them and buried himself in the crowd, and they didn't know he was there.

'Silly bitch,' he heard Farrell say. 'She couldn't wait for Martyn to get himself blown up. She'll have the insurance now.'

'It's all in a good cause,' replied the ex-priest. 'It'll look good on the television news. Heart-broken wife and suffering kids.' He looked at his watch. 'Old Fergal will be somewhere over the Atlantic now.'

'Bloody Disney World! I could do with going there.'

'It's a shame the whole Army Council couldn't be here. It would've put some backbone into the troops.'

'Whose decision was it to stop them coming?'

'All of us. No point. With a funeral this big, the Army's just waiting to move in.'

'I thought they would have. Once we got the tricolour up.'

'Aye. Funny that.' Father O'Malley watched the young priest come towards the grave, a container of holy water swinging in his hand. Father O'Malley turned to Farrell. 'Get some of the men to have a look round. It's all a bit too calm.'

'You don't think they've got something on the Collett thing, do you?'

'No. Is McCann here?'

'No.'

'Then keep him away. Make sure you and Eamonn and McCann aren't seen together. We've lost enough good men. I don't mind them getting our weapons, we can always buy plenty more of them. But people. Dedicated soldiers. They're not so easy to replace.'

The young priest started his graveside blessings and the crowd quietened.

Duggan tried to move away from the two men, but suddenly felt pressure in his back. He turned round and saw the man Farrell had sent over. 'Just stay there, Yank,' the man said, 'till this thing's over.'

The priest continued, splashed holy water over the coffins, then threw some earth on them when they were lowered down. The crowd and the watchers above watched.

In the ops room, Richardson and Dancer looked at the Super Snooper pictures being transmitted from the helicopter.

'You sure he said Disney World?' Dancer asked the mushroom.

'Sounded like it.'

'And Fergal?'

'Yes, sir.'

'Fergal Baxter. That's the only Fergal O'Malley would talk about.'

'What's he doing in Disney World?'

'Whatever he's doing, he's still halfway over the Atlantic.' Dancer crossed over to a phone and dialled hurriedly. 'Jason, I want you to send whatever pictures we have of Fergal Baxter . . . the same one, over to the FBI's counter-terrorist department in Washington. Inform them that we believe he's on his way to Disney World . . . I think in Florida; it might be California, but it was Disney World, not Disneyland. Tell them he's supposedly halfway over the Atlantic at this time. I suggest they put whatever they can into operation and try to

259

catch the bugger . . . I'll come back to them if I hear any more . . . I suggest you pass that over to GCHQ. It's up to them whether or not they tell the Yanks. Ask them to use Disney World, Fergal and Baxter, in addition to the usual catchwords; that way they might pick up a phone signal in the last few days that could help . . . No, I have no idea where he's flying from.' Dancer put down the phone and returned to watch the monitor.

On the screen they saw Duggan standing stiffly behind O'Malley and Farrell.

The second monitor was connected to the camera which was slowly scanning the crowd in a search-pattern.

There was no sign of Vaughn on either screen.

The priest finished and stepped back.

Six armed gunmen, in paramilitary uniforms, black berets and gloves, all wearing Balaclavas so as not to be recognized, stepped out of the crowd, their rifles aimed upwards. On a command, the men fired a series of volleys in the air in recognition and honour of their dead comrades, then melted back into the crowd as quickly as they had appeared. Duggan watched the men hand their weapons to other people, watched them quickly dismantle the rifles and pass the smaller components amongst the crowd, no doubt to take them away safely, then hand them to the quartermaster at some later stage for reassembly. The gunmen undressed out of their paramilitary uniforms, then washed and scrubbed down out of buckets so that no ballistic examination would discover that they had handled the weapons. The uniforms were passed into the crowd and the men put on normal clothes. Duggan recognized Liam Quigley, the newsagent from Short Strand, as one of the guard of honour. Then the men disappeared into the crowd, no doubt towards the black taxis which would whisk them away in separate directions. If the police or Army had tried to arrest the guard of honour, they would have found nothing. All the Army and RUC could do was try to identify then arrest those who produced guns at the graveside.

The sound of the shots had echoed across the hillside as the grave-diggers moved in. Darcy's wife had another attack of hysteria and tried to throw herself onto his coffin, only to be manhandled away by one of Farrell's men.

'Should've let her bloody drop in,' said Father O'Malley, then turned and saw Duggan behind him. 'Hello, Mr Duggan,' he said, a cruel smile forming on his lips. 'I wanted a word with you.'

'I didn't realize all this was—'

'Ach,' Father O'Malley waved his hands in irritation. 'That's not important. No, what I want to know is what you and Richardson were doing with Chief Inspector Monaghan of the Gardaí Síochána in Dublin?' He watched Duggan closely. 'Don't look so surprised. We've had good reports and a description of you three visiting Darcy's place of residence. Now why would you be wanting to go there?'

'I told you. I'm preparing a document for the President.'

'You're not CIA or FBI, are you?'

'I work in the President's Office. The report deals with Flaherty's death. Darcy's death in Dublin was obviously linked. I just wanted to get as much research as I could so the President could answer any necessary questions in the future.'

'The CIA and FBI also report to the President,' interjected Farrell.

'I'm no threat to you.'

Someone started shouting in the distance, from the gravestones to the south, about a hundred yards away from the funeral service. The mourners turned their attention away from the burial and towards the commotion. Then, in the confusion, someone ran up to Farrell. 'We've found an Englishman. SAS man. Over by the graves there.' The man pointed to where the uproar was coming from.

'Don't do anything till I get there,' yelled Farrell. He turned to the man behind Duggan. 'Bring him with you,' he ordered, then pushed his way through the crowd. Duggan followed; he now knew the pressure in his back was from a revolver. Father O'Malley brought up the rear. The crowd, sensing something was up, followed, pushing and straining to see what was going on.

It was Vaughn they had found.

Duggan saw men were kicking him on the ground; his face and lips were already badly bruised, one eye was cut and bled heavily and his right arm was in such a strange position that Duggan was convinced it was broken.

'Stand the bugger up,' screamed Farrell as he reached the group.

They dragged Vaughn to his feet. He stood there swaying. For a moment his eyes met with Duggan's, but he showed no sign of recognition.

'What're you doing here, SAS man?' bellowed Farrell, punching Vaughn in the stomach.

'Cover your head, for God's sake,' warned Father O'Malley. 'Otherwise the helicopter'll recognize you.'

Farrell grabbed a Balaclava from another man, slipped it over his head, then moved in on Vaughn. The crowd closed in as Farrell viciously kicked the Welshman in the groin, then on his shins. Vaughn howled in pain, but didn't break.

'Finish it,' ordered Father O'Malley.

Farrell turned to one of the minders and demanded his weapon. Duggan recognized Danny Maguire's eyes behind the Balaclava. The eighteen-year-old handed over an old service revolver.

'Hurry up, will you?' urged Father O'Malley.

Vaughn's eyes, half-closed from the beatings, looked at Duggan, but by now he was nearly unconscious.

Duggan never did find out what made him do it.

It was as if he was suddenly someone else.

He pushed forward and stood in front of Vaughn as Farrell raised the heavy revolver.

Duggan held up both his arms as a warning to the IRA men. 'Shoot me on television,' he shouted, 'and you'll never get anything out of America again. Not one fucking dollar. Not even enough lead to make one fucking bullet.'

One of the men behind Vaughn leant over and slammed his fist into the back of Duggan's head, sending him sprawling to the mud. As he scrambled to get up again, ignoring the pain at the base of his neck, he saw Farrell cock the revolver.

'No!' he screamed.

'No!' The second shout came from Father O'Malley.

Farrell paused, then, with the gun still pointing at Vaughn, turned to the ex-priest. 'He's an SAS man.'

'I don't care. The Yank's right. Not here. Not with him around,' he indicated Duggan. 'Take the soldier somewhere else and do it.'

Farrell ordered his men to grab Vaughn, but Duggan pushed them aside and threw his arms round the soldier. He couldn't believe he was doing it; he was surprised that he felt no fear, only a belligerent anger against those who would harm the soldier. Vaughn yelled in pain as the pressure built against his broken arm.

'Whatever you do now,' Duggan said to Father O'Malley, 'it'll all be seen. Drag me off him and then cold-bloodedly murder him – whatever – it'll all go against you in America. Even in Boston and New York. They won't stomach that. What're you going to do? Slap me round until I let go?'

'You're a dead man,' shouted Farrell, raising his gun again.

Duggan's anger was slowly turning to fear as he saw the black hole of the gun pointing at his head. But he clung tighter to Vaughn, drawing some small comfort from their closeness. He was frightened now, but surprisingly felt no regrets.

'I said leave him,' came Father O'Malley's warning. He turned to Duggan. 'Walk away, Yank. This isn't your fight.'

'It is now. I only walk out of here with him.' His words had a life of their own; Duggan clung to Vaughn in desperation, his mind blank of logic and reason as the fear gripped him.

'We'll find you,' growled Farrell. 'Wherever you bloody hide.' He moved closer to Duggan. 'Remember what happened to that bastard Collett. That was my orders, you little shit. And that's what you can look forward to.'

The helicopter was suddenly overhead, the down-draught from the big blades ramming a gale into the crowd. Father O'Malley looked up and saw the cameras pointing down. He pulled his collar up and walked away into the crowd. Farrell passed the gun to Danny then also melted into the throng. The men with the Balaclavas broke and ran off in all directions. But the crowd stayed, watching Duggan and Vaughn.

Duggan, with his arm round Vaughn's shoulders, led him slowly and painfully towards the cemetery entrance. The crowd surrounded them, making their progress difficult. Duggan half expected someone to step in front of them and shoot them. But no-one did. Nothing happened until they reached the gate.

It was Danny.

His father stood behind him.

'You're no Duggan,' the boy screamed, then spat in the American's face. 'You're fuck-all.'

Duggan reached out towards the Maguires; he wanted them to know he hadn't betrayed them. But Danny and

Harry disappeared into the crowd as the soldiers and police finally reached Duggan and Vaughn.

The Welshman smiled as he looked into Duggan's eyes. 'Not sodding bad,' he quipped, 'for a fucking colonial.' Then he passed out.

They took him away in an armoured ambulance and drove Duggan back to Girdwood. On the way he gave his car keys to one of the policemen and asked that his car be picked up and brought to the barracks. Then he looked out of the armoured vehicle for his last memory of the Falls Road and the place that had once been his family's home. He was shaking uncontrollably now; the fear chilled him and he asked someone for a blanket to keep warm. A soldier took off his flak-jacket and wrapped it round the American's shoulders. It had little effect; he shivered all the way back to Girdwood.

When they picked up Duggan's car twenty minutes later, they found it was already booby-trapped with Semtex. The army bomb disposal squad rendered it safe, took Duggan's suitcase from the boot and returned the car to its rental company.

The BBC television documentary crew in the helicopter, who had been filming for a religious programme about burial rites throughout the world, rushed their video tape to their Belfast studios and transmitted it to London. By the time the six o'clock news went out, it had been finely edited and had shown, without dialogue, all that had happened at Milltown cemetery.

It was the lead story.

The American, Francis Duggan, reported as a tourist in Belfast visiting his parents' graves, became an overnight hero for his tremendous bravery in protecting the soldier who had stumbled into the cemetery by mistake.

*   *   *

Dancer was waiting in Farquharson's office when Duggan walked in with Richardson and the OC.

'Exciting days,' he commented to the American.

'It was Farrell who ordered Collett's murder,' advised Duggan. 'Only it's my word against his. That's all you've got.'

Dancer grinned, then crossed over to Duggan and held out his hand. 'Can I have your coat, please?'

A bemused Duggan took off his jacket and passed it to Dancer. The Five man took a Stanley knife from his pocket, removed the cover from its sharp blade, then carefully slit the collar open. He put the knife back in his pocket, the blade once more protected by the plastic cover, then put his finger inside the collar. He fiddled around inside, then slowly brought out a miniature transmitter, its aerial a thin sliver of wire tucked into the fold of the collar. He held it up, then handed the coat back to a stunned Duggan.

'Sorry about the coat,' apologized Dancer. 'Cute little thing, isn't it? Picked up by one of our mobile trackers at a range of half a mile.'

'You bastard.'

Dancer shrugged. 'Let's say it saved your life. And hung Mr Farrell.'

Dancer left the room without another word.

'I only found out after you'd left Girdwood,' explained Richardson.

'They checked me for bugs,' said Duggan. 'Jesus, what if they'd found it?'

'Well, let's be pleased they didn't.' Farquharson changed the subject. 'How about a wash and scrub up? I'm sure you'll want to speak to Washington after that.'

Richardson and Duggan went to their quarters. Duggan stalked ahead, not saying a word. When they entered, the American swung round and slammed the door shut.

'Did you really not know I was rigged up?' he asked.

'I honestly didn't know. Not until you were out there.'

'Then they told you?'

'I guessed. From what they were saying.'

Duggan looked round the room. 'This place isn't bugged as well, is it?'

'I doubt it.'

'Fuck them. It could've got me killed.'

'It also saved your life. That's why they sent Vaughn in after you.'

'Is he going to be OK?'

'Yes. Just a good kicking, that's all.'

Duggan slumped onto the bed and started to laugh. 'I just don't—' He stopped, the laughter increasing.

'You handled that well. For a desk jockey.'

'Yeah. For a damn analyst. Shit, I was scared. I just don't know what made me . . . and Dancer had wired me all along. He's a dick. I feel like that crazy joke.'

Richardson knew that Duggan was suffering from an adverse reaction to the danger he'd been in; it was a situation the American had never experienced before. 'What joke?' he asked in an attempt to normalize the situation. 'Tell me.'

Duggan looked up, surprised. Then he shook his head in disbelief. The English really were crazy; in the middle of all this Richardson wanted to hear a joke. He started to laugh again. Then, with a sigh, said, 'This small-town cop pulls up a stranger for speeding. Gets him out of his car and draws a circle in the dust. He tells the stranger to stand in the circle, not to move out of it until he's finished searching the car, otherwise he's going to shoot him. Then, because the cop doesn't like strangers – he thinks they're all big-city drug dealers – he starts to rip the car apart. He tears the upholstery, rips out the dashboard, smashes the lights, cuts the tyres, just destroys the car. Takes him twenty minutes. Then he notices the stranger's laughing his head off. "What's so funny?" he asks. "While you've been doing that, you haven't seen me jumping in and out of the circle," replies the stranger.'

Richardson laughed. 'I presume you're the fool in the circle?'

'Damn right.'

'Dancer was only doing what he thought was right.'

'Fuck him!' The anger was starting to come through again. 'I told him I wasn't prepared to be wired.'

Richardson tried to keep Duggan's mind off Dancer's treachery. 'It'll be forgotten. What will be remembered is how you protected Vaughn. They would've slotted him, have no doubt about that.'

'Slotted?'

'Killed. Old army expression.'

'Then it was worth it.' Duggan sensed the admiration in Richardson's voice. He suddenly felt some pride at what he had done.

There was a knock on the door and a squaddie came in. 'The OC would like to see you both in the Intelligence Cell,' the soldier said.

The two men went down the corridor into the small room. There was a sergeant present, in addition to Dancer and Farquharson. A small video system was set up.

'Thought you'd like to see the movie of the book of the video,' Dancer smiled; the joke got the flat reception it deserved. He turned to the sergeant. 'Let's see it.' As the colour images moved on the screen, Dancer said, 'This was taken by the Super Snooper. You can see the quality's good; we can pick up good pictures from the most oblique of angles.' He turned to Duggan. 'Sound quality's down to you.'

Duggan ignored the comment. He watched the screen as the movements unfolded.

The camera concentrated on him; it wasn't close up,

there were usually at least half a dozen people around him. The Super Snooper had picked him up near the gate, just before the procession turned in. He saw Vaughn's duffel-hooded shape disappear out of frame; the cameraman hadn't known who it was. The sound was scratchy, although dialogue could be clearly identified. He watched the procession pass, then saw Harry Maguire come next to him, then the man sent by Father O'Malley come over and warn him. Duggan saw himself being pushed along by the crowd, then ending up next to the grave, right behind Father O'Malley.

'Did you plan that?' asked Dancer.

Duggan shrugged as if to say, 'Of course I did.'

Then the crowd surged towards where Vaughn had been hiding. Duggan watched the Welshman being beaten, then saw himself stand in front of him as Farrell raised the revolver.

The video moved on to where Farrell said, as loud as if he were in the room with them, 'Remember what happened to that bastard Collett. That was my orders, you little shit.'

'Freeze it there,' Dancer ordered the sergeant. He turned triumphantly to the others. 'We've got the bastard. By his own words.'

'If it'll hold up in court,' warned Farquharson.

'We can sync-match the words on the tape with the movement of the suspect's lips on the video,' confirmed the sergeant. 'That's no problem.'

'I want Farrell brought in, anyway,' said Dancer. 'Even if we give him seven days of hell over this.' The Five man grinned, referring to the fact that, since the end of internment, suspects could be held for questioning for up to seven days. 'That goes for the good Father O'Malley, too.'

'You haven't enough on him,' concluded Farquharson. Then he snorted with laughter. 'But it'll take a lot of

269

sweating on their part before they work that out.' He went to the door. 'I'll get them picked up,' he said as he went out of the room.

'Have you contacted Washington yet?' Dancer asked Duggan.

'No.'

'I suggest you do. They want you to return to London.'

Duggan just wanted to go home. But the old feeling of dread flared up again. *So much for being a hero*. It didn't take the fear away. 'Why?'

'Well, the old BBC got a film of you and they're running it on the six o'clock news. Government tried to stop it, but they've no just cause. Makes you into a sort of hero.' Dancer chuckled. 'They want you back as soon as possible so that Grosvenor Square can brief you.'

'This is not my scene,' Duggan appealed to Dancer.

'It could also put him in more danger,' added Richardson.

'Not my decision,' shrugged Dancer. 'You'll need to sort that out in London. Anyway, let's not forget we haven't got the Angels yet. I think that's why your people want you to be high profile. It shows they're getting on with things.'

'When do I go?' asked Duggan.

'Tonight. By special transport out of Harbour Airport. We're sending Richardson back with you.'

'To hold my hand?' Duggan knew they didn't completely trust him and that Richardson would be his bodyguard. *That's what comes of being a Catholic*.

Dancer ignored him. 'We may also have some news on the Disney thing. That was a good lead. Both GCHQ and your National Security Agency are scanning the calls over the last few days between Europe and the States. We think Fergal Baxter, the IRA's head of intelligence, could well be arriving there –' he looked at his watch, '– about now. We despatched photos of Baxter to the

270

FBI and they're putting surveillance teams into Orlando Airport as well as any other airports that have connecting flights to Florida. It may have nothing to do with the Angels, but it could help us close down another supply route out of North America.'

Duggan and Richardson watched the news while they ate in the officers' mess. The small canteen was crowded and the American was embarrassed as he watched himself square up against the masked Farrell in front of Vaughn. The newscaster said little was known about Francis Jack Duggan, except that he was on holiday in Ireland and was an American citizen who had been visiting his parents' graves when the trouble erupted. He smiled at the mischievous comments of the other officers; in his view they were out in the front line at all times doing what he had accidentally stumbled on and received plaudits for.

After dinner they were once again summoned to an interview room by Dancer.

On a television monitor they watched a sullen Farrell being interrogated; the interview room was connected by close-circuit television. There were two army officers in the room with the Irishman.

'I thought you weren't allowed to interrogate IRA men?' Duggan commented. 'Surely only the RUC can do that?'

'Know your rules, don't you?' snapped Dancer. 'Do you want to watch or not?'

'I'll watch.'

'For your interest, we're allowed to screen a suspect when we pick him up.'

'Screen?'

'That's the official word,' responded Richardson. 'That means we can ask certain questions until such time as the RUC get here and re-arrest him. Then they whip him round to the police station and interrogation centre at Castlereagh. That's when they have their turn.'

Farrell's behaviour was the classic IRA response to any form of questioning.

'Are you Tommy Farrell of Lisbon Street, Belfast?' asked one of the two interrogators.

Silence.

'Are you Commander of the Belfast Brigade of the Provisional IRA?'

Silence.

Farrell was then asked where he was on the night that Collett disappeared.

Silence.

'On that evening Lieutenant Robert Collett was murdered by members of the Provisional IRA. Were you present when Lieutenant Collett was killed?'

Silence.

'We have on record that you were responsible for the death of Lieutenant Collett.'

Silence. Followed by a sneer.

'In your own words.'

Silence.

'To a reliable witness.'

Silence.

'We've got all the time in the world, Farrell.'

'Then I'd like a Guinness and a bag of chips, mate,' came the cheeky answer.

'Bang to rights, Farrell.'

Silence.

'We know about McCann.' The interrogator tried one of the names mentioned at the graveside.

Silence.

'And about Eamonn. It's all recorded. All in your dulcet tones.'

Silence. A long sigh, a look of hatred, a crossing of the arms and another bored sigh. Then silence and a blank stare.

The interrogator suddenly laughed. 'You're not thinking of going away, are you? To Disney World?'

Farrell was surprised by the question. He shook his head in bewilderment and went back to his morose pose.

The questioning continued like that for more than half an hour before Dancer took Richardson and Duggan out of the viewing room. In all that time Farrell had only spoken twice, once to ask for the Guinness and chips, and the second time to ask if the drink was on its way.

'Is it always like that?' asked Duggan.

'Yes. Unless we've got something that really frightens them. And that isn't very often. They're more frightened of their own people thinking they've grassed, anyway.' Dancer held out his hand. 'Sorry it didn't work out.' He shook hands with Duggan. 'And about that miniature transmitter . . .' he paused.

'Yes?' Duggan warmed, expecting an apology.

'American. Damn good equipment. You should be proud of it.' He grinned and shrugged his shoulders. 'I'd do it again if I had to.' He turned to Richardson. 'See you, Sam. Take care of the media star.'

Dancer went back into the viewing room with a final acknowledgement in the form of a salute.

'You could really learn to dislike him,' said Duggan. 'If he wasn't here doing such a shit job.'

The two men went and packed their bags and headed back to London.

As they flew out of Belfast's Harbour Airport in a Royal Air Force HS 125 jet, Duggan looked back at the brightly lit city.

It was night and from the air there was no sign of the turmoil he had lived in and the terror that stalked the streets he left behind.

It was another impossible meeting.

Impossible because the men in the SitRoom had no direct control over what was going on across the Atlantic. For all their power, for all their resources, all they could do was sit on their hands and hope something broke which would give them the opportunity to release the vast capability that they possessed.

And now the matter was exacerbated by the fact that one of their own, a junior operative, had stolen the limelight and shown their collective impotency.

'His wife's been on, demanding to be put through to him,' said McNabb from the CIA.

'I thought his report said they were divorced?' commented the NSA.

'They are. I think she's trying to get into the publicity. Said she wanted to prepare the children once the media got on to her.'

'Why should the media . . . shit, she's probably ringing them right now to make sure they know where she is. Nothing like instant fucking fame, is there?'

'Do we admit to the Press he's one of our men?'

'No. Tell him to keep his cover going. Journalist. From the President's staff.'

'They'll guess he's intelligence. That's how they'll report it.'

'The Brits shafted us,' cursed Mickleton.

'Why?'

'Think about it. We asked them to pull him out. They said they needed time. Next thing we know is that our boy's got his picture on the front page. To anyone, that involves us in their mess.'

'What're the chances of them coming against us?' enquired Lacelle.

'Who? The IRA?'

'Yeah.'

'Who knows? They're crazy people. There's no logic in anything they do.'

'I don't think they will,' butted in McNabb. 'That's why they pulled back from shooting the Brit. They will not want to alienate the Americans. Even if they think our intelligence services are involved.'

'You're asking us to take a big risk by accepting that view,' said the NSA.

'Maybe. I'm not saying we don't tighten up on airport and immigration security.'

'More queues at airports. Great for public morale.'

'I just don't think they'll hit back at us.'

'The Angels might,' Mickleton added quietly. 'To embarrass the IRA further. Do something nasty and blame it on the Provos.'

'Has the Puzzle Palace got anywhere with the information GCHQ provided?' the NSA asked McNabb. He referred to the dialogue that had passed between Farrell and Father O'Malley at the graveside.

'Not yet. They're tracing key words like Baxter, Fergal, Disney World, Ireland, Orlando – that sort of thing. It'll take a while. They're scanning thousands of telephone calls over the last three days. If they don't find anything, then they'll go back even further.' McNabb turned to Mickleton. 'It's down to you, Hank. Let's hope you pick him up at the airport.'

'Don't count on it,' came the defensive reply. 'All we've got to go on is a couple of old pictures. We don't know what airport he's arriving at, or which airline he's on. I'm warning you, it's a real needle-in-a-haystack situation. And I don't want my balls on the line just because we don't find him.'

BOOK THREE

ANGELS WITH DIRTY FACES

Elgin Place
Hammersmith
London W6

Sam Richardson was annoyed that Andrea wasn't home.

He had missed her while in Belfast and he wanted to spend time with her before Duggan, who had been driven directly to the American Embassy from RAF Northolt, returned to the flat.

The note Blu-tacked on the lounge door read 'Emergency at work. Back about twelve. Love you, A.'

He had two hours to kill. He went through and unpacked, made himself a cheese sandwich and settled down to watch *Newsnight*. The main story was about Duggan and his antics in Milltown cemetery. He watched the action again, then saw Duggan at a news conference which, according to the caption on the screen, was being transmitted live. The American stuck to his cover. White House journalist on Presidential mission about the Angels goes to visit his family in

Belfast, and while attending his parents' graves, gets caught up in IRA funeral and all that follows. *Very John Wayne*. He watched Duggan modestly explain how he had no choice but to help Vaughn. 'I believed they wouldn't shoot an American,' Duggan said naïvely. *Give them a chance, pal. Just give the bastards a chance*.

The phone rang when Duggan had finished. It was Carter.

'Try and be in early, will you?' he said. 'About seven. Just to tidy things up.'

Then Richardson fell asleep on the sofa. Andrea wakened him with a kiss at twelve-thirty. They didn't say a lot; they were both overjoyed at being together. They went to bed and wrapped themselves around each other.

They had been making love for fifteen minutes, in a slow, warming-up, all-the-time-in-the-world manner, when the doorbell rang. Richardson swore, put a towel round his waist and went to the front door.

'I'm sorry it's so late,' apologized Duggan, his suitcase in his hand.

'The prodigal son. Couldn't the CIA afford a hotel?'

'You said to come . . .' Duggan started to turn away. 'I'll catch you tomor—'

'Come on in,' said Richardson. 'Come on.'

Duggan pulled a face in apology, then entered the flat.

'You know where the bedroom is,' said Richardson, following him into the lounge. 'There's food in the fridge if you're hungry. I'll see you in the morning.' He went to the door, then turned round. 'I rang about Vaughn. No broken ribs, nothing internal, no concussion. Just his arm and a few bruises. He sends his regards. Goodnight, Francis.'

Richardson climbed into bed with Andrea and embraced her with his whole body.

But the moment had passed.

Instead they kissed each other goodnight in a companionable sort of way and went to sleep.

Carter met Maxwell Claris, a deputy director of SIS and head of the Terrorist counter-intelligence section, at six-thirty, forty-five minutes before he was due to see Richardson. Claris, a Grade 3 civil servant, had a comfortable, modern, well-equipped office looking out over the Thames in MI6's new Headquarters on the Embankment. Carter never enjoyed coming over from his own offices in Curzon Street. The old MI6 building, known as the Cinema because of the canopies that ran round the building at street level, was austere, and the inside resembled an abandoned tenement building in the sleazier parts of London. Coming here was never good for the morale of those left behind at the Cinema.

'Our friends at Five advise me that Richardson was aware of the Plan before he met with Captain Morrison at Girdwood,' remarked Claris.

'So I believe.' He didn't need to add that Dancer had faxed him a complete transcript of the Morrison interview.

'Should we be concerned about that?'

'I don't think so. Sam's a good man, and used to obeying orders.'

Claris pondered for a moment, then sighed and reached for the cup of tea in front of him. 'I'll leave it with you. Just don't let him get too enthusiastic. Some things are best left unattended.' He drank from the cup, then reflected as he held the cup to his lips. 'He seems to get on well with this CIA chap?'

'Seems to.'

Claris clinked the cup back in the saucer. 'He might need reminding that his first duty is to us, not to some misguided loyalty based on friendship.'

'Unlikely. He's a professional. Nothing gets in the way of that.'

'It did once.'

'Apart from that incident, he was an exceptional covert operator.'

'His . . . refusal to act cost the life of a soldier. He's not been in a real spot of bother since then. How do we know he won't freeze again?'

Carter shrugged. His instincts told him Richardson was a good man to have next to you when your back was against the wall. But there was little point in contradicting Claris. 'I'll watch him closely. Just in case.'

Claris waited until Carter left the room before picking up the phone and calling Downing Street. 'Sir Walter Inger, please,' he asked when the line connected. 'Maxwell Claris for him. Foreign Office.'

'Yes, Claris,' came Inger's brusque words. Rudeness was Inger's manner; he used it on everyone, especially on cabinet ministers who were about to be or had been sacked. As Cabinet Secretary he was directly responsible to the Prime Minister, and was the most senior civil servant in Government. He was used to being obeyed. He could be like that; after all, he could break any man in the civil service with a single phone call.

'Things seem to be under control, sir. Our man is aware of the Plan, but—'

'What plan?' Inger interrupted rudely.

Claris backtracked immediately. 'No plan, sir. Just that we are monitoring the situation with the American and giving every assistance we can.'

'Can our chap cope with that?'

'Yes. He's aware of the predicament regarding former officers in Ulster and is under orders to safeguard our position.' Claris felt that explained that Richardson was aware of the Plan and would protect those who could be compromised by it.

'If necessary?'

'If necessary.'

'Excellent news, that. About the American protecting our man in Belfast. Good for morale. And should get considerable support for the British point of view in Northern Ireland. Keep in touch.'

The phone went dead. Claris rose from the table and walked to the window. The Thames, dirty and muddy after a recent rain-storm, swelled its banks. He watched it, almost in a trance, then remembered Reggie Flowers. It had all been such a long time ago; all seemed so innocent and necessary at the time.

He closed his eyes and recalled Flowers's retirement party. The old chap, just fifty-five, had taken him through the whole sordid tale as they sat in the corner of the pub after all the others had gone. He'd needed to know the whole truth. After all, Flowers was passing on the baton to him then. The whole affair had become his responsibility.

He smelt Africa as he remembered, smelt the earth and the continent that was so different to anywhere else. And he thought back to the story Flowers had told him, all those years ago.

As the old man had said, 'It really was a dirty game.'

The child plunged the bayonet into the man tied to the tree. Flowers couldn't stand any more and turned away. He thought of Edgbaston and wondered what the latest Test Match score was. 1976 was a bad year for English cricket.

A splash of rain fell from the leaves and ran down Reg Flowers's neck. He shivered at the surprise of it. He'd forgotten how wet it could be at this time of the year; it was a long time since he'd last been in Africa. He suddenly pondered what madness had made him decide to make this trip, to find himself thirty miles east of Jamba in south-eastern Angola. He was an office-wallah now, not some ambitious young field agent out to make a name for himself. He was also a very senior office-wallah. He chuckled. *Ego. That's all it was. So close to retirement and all he wanted to do was show the others he could still run a field operation. Bloody ego. Vanity wasn't something readily admitted in the c.v. of a senior intelligence officer. But then, he was only months away from turning fifty-five, the SIS's compulsory retirement age. Only a handful lasted beyond that, those who were promoted to the most senior echelons of MI6. After a lifetime of intelligence service, Flowers wanted to go out with a bang, not just fade away from everything he had ever known.*

That's why this first trip was the most important. If the project was to succeed, it was up to him to iron out the bugs.

After all, the whole thing had been his idea.

To raise funds for the UNITA rebels in Angola, at a time when there was no money available from official funds, even the secret sources normally accessible to Britain's Secret Intelligence Service.

As he listened to the sounds of murder from behind, he thought back to that first meeting, some three months earlier. It had started at the weekly planning meeting between the Requirements and Production sections. It was how MI6 worked in those days. Requirements analysed what information each government department required, then Production went out and got it, by whatever means possible. It was a different system to that used by the American CIA. The Americans collected, analysed and acted on their own information. MI6 concentrated on the collection of information, then passed it on to whichever government agency it concerned. What they did with it after that was up to them.

Flowers had been packing his papers away after the meeting when MacReadie, the Deputy Assistant Head of Production, signalled him to stay in his seat. Flowers pushed his papers away and leant back in his chair. He hated this room. It was a cheerless place, sanitized, its centre-piece a wooden-slabbed table with thin green iron legs. Very British, very MoD. When the room had emptied, there were three of them left. Flowers, MacReadie and the Head of Requirements.

'There's been a decision to further our involvement in Angola,' started Requirements. Flowers now understood why he had been asked to remain behind. South Central Africa was his domain; Zambia, Zaire, Tanzania, Malawi and Angola his areas of operation. 'At arm's length, of course,' warned Requirements.

'From now on anything relating to this matter is just between the three of us,' added MacReadie. 'You report directly to me.'

'Absolutely,' confirmed Requirements. He had all the dry, academic arrogance that Flowers scorned; university men who played at intelligence whilst the professional soldiers made it work out in the field. The intelligentsia who had let Philby and his friends run loose through the SIS. 'We've heard, on the grapevine, that the Americans are considering introducing new legislation, something called the Clarke Amendment, to prohibit all military and financial support for UNITA.' He watched Flowers closely for a reaction, then continued when he got none. 'Both the CIA and our own people agree that any such action would be highly dangerous and succeed only in handing Angola over to the Russians.'

Flowers nodded. 'Not just Angola. The rest of Africa.'

Ever since the Portuguese had finally pulled out of Angola in 1975, this richest of colonies, the USSR had concentrated on using Angola to spearhead Soviet influence throughout Africa. Whilst the KGB pumped funds and manpower into the Marxist Popular Movement for the Liberation of Angola, including bringing in 80,000 Cuban troops in 1975, Britain and America supported the rival Union for the Total Liberation of Angola. The bitter Angolan Civil War that followed, eventually costing nearly 100,000 lives, between the MPLA and UNITA became a central platform for the battle of the hearts and minds of the African people. It was a defence against the new imperialistic ambitions of the USSR, fought mostly by the British and South Africans, both emblems of the old imperialistic powers. The British government had refused to supply money to support UNITA, but had a sizeable intelligence operation throughout the region. The Americans supplied money and weapons in an attempt to hold the MPLA and its Soviet masters at bay. The withdrawal of these funds by the American administration would have disastrous results.

MacReadie went on. 'The latest report we have is that MPLA officers are being sent to Moscow for a one-year training course at the KGB's Andropov Institute. It's just another sign that the Russians are turning up the heat. We think they've sent out General Konstantin Shagnovich. He's a 3-star man. Highest ranker ever posted outside the Warsaw Pact. It's an indication of Soviet determination to control the region.'

'Another reason why we've got to be successful in funding UNITA,' sniffed Requirements.

'It's going to require a vast source of money.' Flowers stated the obvious. 'What about our own secret funds?'

'The Government doesn't want to be seen openly supporting the rebels. After all, the MPLA is the recognized government of Angola.'

'We use SIS funds for equally dangerous—'

'The answer is a firm no. It's not even open for discussion. We have to find alternative sources of income.'

'Even for weapons?'

'Yes. And don't count on anything falling off the back of a Royal Ordnance lorry. Not even one grenade. All I want you to do is raise the money. Then they can buy everything they need.'

Including arms from the British government, *thought* Flowers.

'It really has to be a stand-alone operation,' interjected

284

MacReadie. 'We need something fast that we can put into effect immediately. Our American friends tell us this Clarke Amendment should be through in a couple of months.'

'I want some ideas by next week,' said Requirements, standing up and collecting his papers. 'Workable ideas. Nothing too fancy. But a plan I can submit to the Foreign Office.'

'For their approval and secret blessing, I suppose,' said Flowers, immediately regretting his words.

Requirements ignored the comment and walked to the door. He swung round to MacReadie. 'We'll hold the meeting in my office. Three copies of the paper only. One for each of us. Call me when you've got something.'

The two men waited until Requirements had left the room. 'That wasn't very bright,' said MacReadie. 'You know these chaps in Requirements like to think they're independent of the FO.'

'Bloody politicians. Everyone knows we're covertly supporting the MPLA because of our interests in Angolan oils and other resources. We all know about Soviet officers and their Luger pistols, don't we? Two-faced bast—' Flowers stopped himself; emotion wasn't appreciated in Six. The Luger he referred to had been presented to the training-team leader of a British security company, Defence Systems Ltd, by a senior Soviet officer responsible for the tactics and professional soldiering standards of the MPLA forces. The Luger had been captured by the officer's father on the Eastern Front in World War Two. It was a gift which acknowledged that the British team had succeeded where the Soviets had failed. 'How do they expect us to safeguard security if they keep turning the tap off?'

'That's the way it is,' MacReadie sighed. 'Let's not forget, because of that very fact, there are increasing UNITA antipathetic factions both in the SIS and the Government. I don't want any plan to be picked over by

*them, then stalled before it gets off the ground. We have
to accept that, whatever we do, UNITA will continue as
a guerrilla force. Even if, as seems to be happening, they
have difficulty in maintaining support from Zambia and
Western Europe. Whatever we put into place must have
a chance of continuing even if we pull out.' He rose from
the table. 'Any first shots?'*

'The usual route, I suppose. Trade the money in.'

'What's strong in commodities over there?'

*'Gold. In Huila. Emeralds from Cuango and Cubango.
And vast aquamarine deposits south-east of Serpa Pinto.
There's also alluvial diamonds.'*

*MacReadie's eyebrows shot up. 'Would we need com-
mando raids or any other military support?'*

*'No. The faithful amongst the UNITA rebels would
simply collect them for us.'*

*'Gold and diamonds would be easiest to sell on the
foreign markets.'*

*'Gold's too bulky to transport. After all, we're going
to be moving it out of Africa. We don't want shooting
squabbles with MPLA troops.'*

'How rich is Angola in diamonds?'

*'Rich enough for our needs. And they're easy to
transport.' Flowers laughed. 'Wouldn't that be something? Destabilize the Soviets by flooding the market
with diamonds.' Flowers didn't need to add that the
USSR was one of the world's largest suppliers of
diamonds. 'Knock the bottom right out of their economy.'*

*'Leave that little caper for the future. This year, just
make sure that we keep UNITA in the style to which
they've become accustomed.'*

*The plan, when Flowers presented it five days later,
was simple. Get UNITA to collect the alluvial diamonds,
transport them through special couriers to Switzerland,
sell them secretly, and then use the money, through an
undisclosed numbered account, to finance arms sales and
training for UNITA.*

'What about the CSO?' asked Requirements, referring to the Central Selling Organization the South Africans, and indirectly, the Russians, used to control this most flagrant of cartels.

'No problem. The CSO knows it can't police the whole diamond market. They expect a 20 per cent seepage rate of uncontrolled gems. Brazil's a big threat to them. Yet the CSO seem to accept Angolan diamonds. It's a yellow-tinged stone, good quality, but it's on their doorstep and they feel if things get out of hand the South Africans could always shell Angola, then invade it. I mean, it wouldn't be the first time they sent troops into the country through Namibia. I think they're more worried about the Russians breaking ranks with the cartel.'

'Who pays for setting this little scheme up?'

'We can get some modest financing from Tanganyika Holdings, who own the Benguela Railway. They want a settled territory. This civil war is playing havoc with their railway tracks. They already pay UNITA a blackmail levy to avoid being blown up.'

Requirements read through the four-page report that Flowers had prepared for the meeting. 'Sounds good,' he said eventually. 'How long?'

'Three months before we make the first shipment.'

'Got to be done sooner.'

'Impossible.'

'Not a word I'm familiar with.'

'We have to train people. The diamond-graders for a start. They've got to be fairly intelligent, as well as being trusted UNITA members. I expect we'll have to send them to Antwerp for a rudimentary course in diamonds. We can't have these sooties scampering round, sending brightly coloured pebbles to Zürich. Not if we want to raise some real money.'

'I want it speeded up.'

'Certainly. As long as you're prepared to take the risk that haste could breach our security. The sort of accident

287

*that the Press love to see happen. They'd soon trace it
back to the SIS and Britain. That's what could happen.
If we rushed things.'*

*Requirements sighed. 'No more than two months,
then.'*

'I'll have to involve my man in Zambia.'

'All right. Remember, eight weeks. No longer.'

*Ten weeks later Flowers put the plan into operation.
The whole project had taken longer than he imagined;
the tight security surrounding the exercise had limited the
amount of support he could expect.*

*Flowers had left his Zambian agent in Lusaka to
deal with the UNITA rebels and their leader, Savimbi,
and concentrated on the European money route and the
Antwerp diamond merchants.*

*It had been his first trip to Antwerp, although he had
visited Brussels many times at the end of the war. He had
never liked the Belgians. They were a complaining race;
after they had been liberated from German occupation
in 1945, they soon turned against the British. They saw
Brussels as the centre of the new Common Market, and
they turned on all those who opposed it. To Flowers, they
were takers, and history supported his view. He also
found them an ugly race; beauty was not something that
came naturally to them. But those were his private
thoughts; he was well used to charming all those he dealt
with.*

*Leopold Voerens, a gnarled and stocky man, had not
been aware of his visitor's distaste as he welcomed him
across the desk in his Antwerp office.*

*'What can I do for you?' asked Voerens after the
customary formalities had been exchanged and a cup of
coffee was placed in front of Flowers. 'Your consulate
in Brussels said I should offer you every assistance.'*

*'It's not a difficult matter,' replied Flowers. 'But
one that should be profitable to both of us.'*

Voerens smirked. 'Profit has a different meaning to

everybody. Mine can be counted in the simplest of terms. Swiss francs or dollars – even sterling.'

Flowers smiled back at the cheap jibe. It was something the British had got used to in the days of currency devaluations and economic crises. *'Swiss francs, in this case.'*

'And how will you take your profit, Mr Fielden?' Voerens used Flowers's alias.

Flowers's smile grew wider as his dislike for the Belgian increased. Voerens would be used to agents creaming off a little bit for themselves. *'My business, Mr Voerens.'*

'You are Secret Service?' came the patronizing response.

'I represent the Foreign Office.'

'Whatever you wish. Tell me how I can help.'

'I should point out that we will require the tightest security on this matter.'

'Everything I do, Mr Fielden, requires the tightest security. That is second nature in the diamond trade.'

'We're dealing with an IDB situation.' There was no reaction from the Belgian at the mention of illegal diamond buying. *'From a country where IDB activity already takes place. We would simply be moving the goods through another route.'*

'I don't need to remind you that any diamonds can immediately be traced to their source. A Brazilian diamond is as easy to identify as a South African or Russian gem.'

'We know the CSO mops up all IDB operations where possible. By going through you, we would expect the CSO to buy the stones.'

Voerens was relieved; he didn't like duping the Central Selling Organization who dealt with all world diamonds, including illegal diamonds, that came on the market. It was their way of controlling supplies and prices. *'How many carats are we talking about?'*

'Between ten and twenty thousand carats a trip.'

'And the quality?'

'Mostly top grade. Anywhere between twenty and fifty US dollars per carat. Could you handle that?'

'Of course.' Voerens immediately calculated that each trip would produce between US$100,000 and US$1 million. 'How many trips?'

'At least one a month.'

'For how long?'

Flowers shrugged. That was up to his political masters. 'As long as necessary.'

'Where do these stones come from?'

'Will you handle it?'

'Yes. Your consulate will vouch for my co-operation in the past. I presume you will already have cleared me on a security basis.'

Flowers had indeed done that. The contents of Voerens's seedy life and requirements were well known to those in the consulate. 'Angola.'

'I thought as much.'

'Any problems with that?'

'No. What else do you need?'

'Experienced men to teach the Africans how to grade the diamonds before they're shipped over.'

'That can be arranged.'

'And a bank in Switzerland where we can deposit the stones and be paid for them.'

'We have good banks here, in Belgium.'

'No. I'll only deal through the Swiss.' Belgium, like Switzerland, Luxemburg and Liechtenstein, had the facility of allowing unlimited amounts of money to pass through unnoticed. They were as discreet as the more publicized banking methods of the other countries, but Flowers didn't want all his eggs in one basket in this matter. There was always the chance that Voerens would recommend someone he was close to and that was not a risk Flowers could take.

'The Union Banque Suisse are fully geared up for such transactions.'

'I'll open an account for my African friends with the UBS as soon as possible. I'll wire you the account number.'

Voerens nodded. 'There is the question of my commission.' He paused for a while. 'Five per cent.'

Greedy bastard. 'Too much.'

'Those are my terms.'

'The consulate also gave me other names.'

The Belgian shrugged. Getting on the wrong side of intelligence forces in the current world climate was not to his taste. 'Three.'

'Two.'

'Three.' This time he knew he was on firm ground. This sort of transaction was always good for a rate between 2 and 3 per cent. It was worth holding out.

'All right.' Flowers wanted to force him down, but he was working to a strict deadline. 'Three per cent. But you pay the graders to train our people.'

'As long as you pay for their transport and accommodation.'

'Yes.'

'And whatever equipment they need.'

'All right.' The small amounts were not worth arguing over.

'Who will be acting as courier?'

'We're not sure yet.'

'They will also require three per cent.'

'I'm aware of that.'

'We could arrange it – for a reduced rate of an extra two per cent.'

'Thank you, but no.' Flowers despised Voerens and his greed, but he kept the smile on his face. 'It is our policy to keep all sections of an operation separate from each other.'

'You live in a twisted and untrusting world, Mr Fielden.'

'Don't we all?'

'Not like yours. By supplying the CSO, you help keep the price of diamonds high. That's good for the Russians. High prices means they earn more foreign exchange. And find it cheaper to supply bullets to the Cubans in Angola.'

Flowers laughed. 'Yes. And, because they want to keep the prices high, they become part of the CSO and buy our diamonds – which gives us the money to provide bullets which will be fired at their Cuban bully boys. You're right, Mr Voerens. It is a twisted world. Whichever way you look at it.'

He had left for Zürich the next day, arranged the secret numbered account with the UBS, then returned to London. It was while he was over the English Channel that the idea had come to him. Why not? It would be his swan song.

'I don't think it's a good idea,' MacReadie had argued.

'I've no other projects on the go,' Flowers replied. 'And, in view of the security aspect on this one, I'm the logical person to ensure it works the first time without a hitch.'

'I think you should follow this from your desk.'

'If I'm spending my time recruiting people then training them whilst I'm still setting the scheme up, there's little chance of us hitting the deadline. We're already two weeks into the schedule.'

'Will you complete in eight weeks?'

Flowers remembered his assurances to set the operation up in eight weeks. He had simply agreed to that for convenience. 'That was always impractical. On something this size. And with a total security blanket around it. I estimate twelve weeks.'

'From now?' MacReadie was alarmed.

'From kick off. Another ten weeks should be ample.'

'All right. But make sure you have someone ready to take over once you've completed the dummy run.'

Flowers felt the flush of pleasure. 'Don't worry. Once

I've run it, it'll go like clockwork.'

'And don't take any unnecessary risks. There's a war going on out there. And you're on the wrong side – if you get caught.'

'I have every intention of collecting my pension at the end of the year.'

'It's not your pension I'm worried about. It's mine.'

It had taken another seven weeks for the Zambian agent to set up the Angolan organization. Voerens, by then, had organized two experienced diamond-graders who were sent to Lusaka under cover of setting up a small office for the Antwerp firm. Under this guise, the two men trained eight Angolans in the art of diamond selection; not a difficult task when the only purpose was to differentiate between an actual rough diamond and an ordinary stone. The final selection of quality would be made in Zürich, before the funds were passed over to the UNITA bank account. The Angolan graders soon returned to Jamba, their grease-boards and other equipment safely packed in their cases, once their training was complete. The next stage was for the UNITA supporters to collect the alluvial gems.

On the tenth week, a fortnight ahead of his dead-line, Flowers flew out on a British Airways flight to Lusaka, his passport listing him as an auditor from the Foreign Office. As he stepped from the VC10 jet, he realized what he had missed most about Africa. The heat. Blinding, blistering-your-brain heat. The surprise of it after London and the air-conditioned plane stopped him at the top of the wheeled-staircase that led down to the tarmac. A female passenger, surprised by his sudden halt, collided into him from behind. He turned and apologized before continuing. How he loved the heat, felt it sink into his flesh and his bones. He took his time walking towards the recently built terminal, a modern flat-roofed double-storey building that would sit comfortably in any European airport. The other passengers, eager to get to the comfort of the arrivals lounge, scurried past him. The stiffness he felt in his bones started to evaporate; he grinned. The arthritis brought on by the damp and cold of endless British winters was already easing.

Maxwell Claris, then a junior-associate from the Embassy, was waiting for him when he came through Passport Control. In his mid-thirties, Claris, an old Harrovian, had joined the SIS after Cambridge and a short, boring stint in the Foreign Office. Like Flowers a gifted linguist, Claris was relishing his first overseas posting. But he missed the social life he had left behind in London and he bombarded Flowers with questions as they walked to the black 1972 Vauxhall Cresta that was parked in the diplomatic bay.

'No point in drawing attention to ourselves,' said Claris, as he climbed into the car, wound down the windows to let out the stifling heat and switched on the engine. 'Lusaka's crawling with every intelligence service in the world. If I'd parked in the general car-park, the Russians would be doubly suspicious.'

'Have you put the word around that I was coming over?'

'Yes. Routine visit from Head Office. We were due one, anyway. The KGB are creatures of habit in that sort of thing. Expect the rest of us to be the same.'

'Everything set up?'

'Just about. We expect the first delivery to the diamond-graders in Jamba tomorrow. There were a couple of hiccups, nothing major. Just the blacks falling all over each other.'

They drove along the newly tarmaced road into the city centre. The car windows stayed fully wound down to combat the lack of air-conditioning, and Flowers sniffed the air, enjoyed the tangle of smells that is Africa. 'I presume I've got a room at the Pamodzi.' He liked the older hotels.

'No. The InterContinental.'

'I prefer the Pamodzi.'

'It's too open. If anyone decides to tail us, that'll make it too easy for them. The InterContinental is in the city centre. We'll have a clear view if someone comes after us.'

'Anybody following us now?'

Claris chuckled. 'Why? They'll already know you're booked into the InterContinental.'

Thirty minutes later they arrived at the newly built hotel. Flowers registered and the two men took the lift to the fourth floor and entered the modern, air-conditioned room. Claris poured them both a beer which he had bought in the bar downstairs while his superior unpacked. When he'd finished, Flowers took his plastic cup of Heineken and went to the window.

'Air-conditioning and Africa don't go together,' he commented as he sipped the beer, then held it away with distaste. 'Neither does semi-chilled beer. This is a lager, isn't it?'

'It's all they have.'

'No African swill?'

'None.'

'I swear the whole world's designed for American tourists and nothing else.' He watched the traffic and pedestrians moving down Haille Selassie Avenue. He doubted the room was bugged, but the two men had decided not to discuss business in any area where security wasn't guaranteed. 'So what've you got planned for me?' He watched Claris's surprised reaction. 'I suppose it's the usual tour of the High Commission with everything running smoothly.' He grinned as Claris relaxed. 'I'd like to go out on the road this time.'

'You're expected at the High Commission first thing tomorrow.'

'All right. But I'd like to see more of Zambia this time.'

The next morning, Flowers was picked up in the Cresta and driven to the High Commission. Once in the privacy of Claris's office, they went through the plan. Flowers was *pleased with Claris; it seemed that he had covered every point.*

'When do you want to start?' Claris asked after the briefing.

'Tomorrow.'

'Everything will be ready.'

'Good. Let's get some lunch and a drink. I'd like to walk round Lusaka.'

'And be seen?'

'Why not? They know I'm here.'

That night Flowers, after his customary large Scotch and water, dozed off. It was a fitful night's sleep; the air-conditioning fan kept waking him up and he switched it off. But it got too hot, and after discovering the windows were sealed shut, he had no choice but to switch the fan on again. When the operator rang the next morning with his seven o'clock alarm call, he was already up, shaved and ready for the day. Claris joined him for breakfast – they both had a beer with their meal – and then drove him to the airport.

'The old KGB chap's seen us,' said Claris as they went through the gate where the private planes were parked.

'Too late now,' replied Flowers. 'All they can do is guess. As long as I'm not spotted at my destination.'

The plane, a 1957 Cessna 180, single-engined and with four cramped seats, had its propeller turning as they walked towards it. The pilot, Jamie Rae, leant over and pushed the passenger door open for Flowers, who threw his overnight bag into the back and clambered into the seat. The rear seats had been replaced with two metal ten-gallon petrol containers.

'Remember. I've gone into the deep country for a camera safari,' he shouted above the roar of the engine.

Claris laughed. 'That should confuse them. They'll know I'm lying.'

The plane, cleared on a VFR flight to the north,

taxied out to the runway and was airborne within three minutes. Thirty minutes later, when Rae knew they were clear of all radar and could not be seen from any road, the plane turned west. Rae kept clear of the main roads that ran across Zambia and followed the plains and forests where there was little population. Five hours later, after having landed once in the bush and refuelled from the fuel-containers, he saw the grass strip on the edge of the forest and swung down to land the Cessna.

There was an old, grey Land-Rover waiting for the plane as it jolted to a stop on the bush airstrip. An Ovambo tribesman, Louis Entada, waited for them. He was dressed in combat gear and wore the insignia of a colonel. Around his neck were a variety of gold chains, all of different thickness and design, some carrying large gold medallions. His watch was a solid gold DayDate Rolex supported by an even thicker gold bracelet. The reflective sunglasses under his black beret topped off this ludicrous, yet fearsome, image. The Sten gun lying across the front seat of the Land-Rover was a final testimony to the power of Entada amongst his own people.

'Welcome back to Angola, Mr Flowers,' he said as Flowers and Rae came towards him.

'Hello, Louis,' replied Flowers, holding out his hand. 'It feels good to be here.'

As they shook hands, Flowers reflected on Entada's history. A chieftain of the Ovambo tribe, he had been educated in Portugal, then travelled round Europe before returning to Angola. A dedicated anti-Marxist, Entada had soon joined his tribesmen in the struggle for power and become one of their most feared leaders. Entada's reputation grew as he weeded out MPLA supporters from the UNITA ranks; he was ruthless in his commitment and personally enjoyed handling the public execution of these spies using the most hideous of methods. To his people he became known as the Avenging Angel; his nickname amongst the mercenaries was the Black Angel. Flowers knew that Entada was a renegade amongst the UNITA forces, a maverick leader who thought himself beyond the control of Jonas Savimbi and UNITA's government. In truth, UNITA forces had a reputation for treating prisoners with every consideration. Nuns, Cuban pilots, diamond mine-workers and even a group of British SAS captured by UNITA had all reported fair treatment and been released at neutral borders. Flowers remembered reading a recent report about three captured nuns who had been given the chance to be freed after a UNITA raid, but decided to stay with the rebels whom they found to be good and kind-hearted people.

Flowers decided to keep his eye on Entada. He sensed that if the colonel didn't change his ways, one of Savimbi's men might just decide to change them for him.

After pulling the plane into a small, camouflaged tin hangar, Entada drove the men towards Jamba. The town, which had grown into the capital of the UNITA forces, was a ramshackle, sprawling shanty town that troops and Savimbi's political allies made their centre.

'We will not be staying in Jamba,' said Entada. 'A small bivouac has been built in the forest. The less people who see you the better.'

'Good. How're things going?'

'In the war, or with the diamonds?'

'The diamonds. I read about the war in the papers.'

'Everything is on schedule. The first batch of diamonds has arrived. There are some more en route to us, and I hope to have a full shipment for you by tomorrow.'

'Good.'

'Are you sure you want to return to Lusaka by land?'

'Yes. I want to make sure there are no problems with the route.'

'I'll accompany you. Just to make sure you're protected. What about the plane?'

'Jamie'll fly that back in three days' time. I want to arrive back before he does.'

'The Russians will be watching for you in Lusaka, and possibly Switzerland.'

'They will. But they won't see me.'

'We have uncovered one traitor who is reporting to the MPLA.'

Flowers tried not to show the rush of alarm that engulfed him. 'How much does he know of the operation?'

'Only that something is up. He doesn't know all the details.'

'Are you dealing with it?'

'Of course. He will never report back to the Marxists again.'

Flowers remained quiet for the rest of the drive. He tried not to think about what Entada would do to the traitor. The Black Angel's fearsome reputation went before him.

They camped that night in the small area of tents that UNITA had provided. The three of them, with four sentries guarding the outskirts of the camp, settled down for an evening of beer-drinking and reminiscing. When Flowers eventually went to his bed, he was ready for the deep sleep he knew he was going to enjoy. No air-conditioning, just the emptiness of an African night sky under which he laid his head and dreamed of schooldays long past. He had hated the sixties, and the present-day seventies were a restless period. Form and order. That was the way Flowers liked it, but those were the old days; it would never be like that again.

Entada woke him at five. 'It's a six-hour journey. We'll keep to the forest, otherwise the communist air patrols might see us.'

They left Rae behind; there was nothing for him to do except while away time until he flew the Cessna back to Lusaka. He would have liked to go into Jamba to pull one of the bar girls, but Flowers had forbidden it. He curled up and went back to sleep; hanging around was *an essential part of any pilot's life.*

Entada drove the Land-Rover to the outskirts of Jamba, picked up one of the diamond-graders and headed east towards the Zambian border. They were safe from any surprise attack; this was UNITA country and the communist MPLA troops kept clear of the zone.

They followed an overgrown track through the forest, occasionally darting across the plain before camouflaging under the trees. At last they came to one of the old diamond areas and Entada showed Flowers how they found the diamonds, buried amongst the rocks and debris of the river bank, washed down from the mountains. The diamond-grader produced his grease-board and demonstrated how the selection was made. It was an easy task; the board, about eighteen inches square, was covered in grease. The grader simply rolled the diamonds and stones over it. The diamonds were the only objects that stuck to the grease. Then, having been lucky enough to find one extra-valuable stone, they drove eastwards for another two hours before meeting the small group of UNITA supporters, local villagers, who had collected the first shipment to go to Zürich. Flowers waited while Entada talked to the tribesmen, a mixture of men, women and children, building their confidence and listening to their problems. Some of them were armed; simple old-fashioned rifles with bayonets attached. They looked like a cast of battered toy soldiers, but Flowers knew the weaponry would improve once the diamonds worked their way into Europe.

While Entada spoke, the diamond-grader worked his way through the pile of dull rocks. When he had separated the good stones from the waste, he spread them on a raffia mat and signalled Flowers to inspect them.

The diamond-grader appeared impatient as he waited in the rain.

He was suspicious of the big white man who knelt on one knee, the diamonds spread out in front of him. He

300

watched him poke at them with his finger and spread the dull, uncut stones around the mat.

'How many bottles?' asked Flowers, looking up at the diamond-grader.

'Three. It will take three.'

Flowers grunted. The rule was never take more than two. But then he couldn't leave these diamonds behind, not on this first run. He would have to take the chance. 'OK,' he said, standing up. 'You pack them.'

He watched the Ovambo tribesman squat down, lay the three empty bottles, two beer and a Coca-Cola, next to the diamonds. The African started to pack the diamonds expertly into the bottles, wedging them in tight before sealing the tops with a leather cover that was held down by a strand of wire wrapped round the bottle neck.

Entada finished his pep-talk with the Ovambo tribesmen and came over. 'Are you happy with this first load?' he asked the Englishman.

'There's too much. In future, you need to keep the extra diamonds safe until the next courier. Three bottles are too bulky to conceal in a small case.'

'Are you going to take three this time?'

'Yes. It's easier than worrying about what to do with the additional diamonds.'

'All right. You must put some in an account for me.' Entada met Flowers's surprised look with a mocking smile. 'For my risks, I expect a small commission.'

Flowers agreed. 'I'll arrange that. But nobody else must know.'

Entada nodded, then went over to the Land-Rover, opened the rear door and pulled out a .303 rifle with a bayonet attached to it. He came back and stood next to Flowers and watched the diamond-grader finish filling the bottles. As the two men waited, some of the other tribesmen circled the diamond-grader. Flowers, his mind already on the next stage of the operation, was unaware of the sudden increase in tension.

The diamond-grader finished sealing the last bottle and looked up. His mouth opened as he realized a circle of armed tribesmen had formed round him, were all staring expressionlessly at him. He gasped and stood up sharply; the sudden movement startled Flowers out of his thoughts.

'What the hell's going on?' he asked Entada as the diamond-grader tried to back out of the circle, but was pushed back into the centre. The man suddenly collapsed on his knees and started to sob, his hands held upwards, imploring mercy.

'I told you. We had a security leak.' Entada shouted a command at the tribesmen who grabbed the sobbing man and dragged him towards a tree. 'It seems our diamond-grader prefers MPLA blood-money to the loyalty of his tribe.' He watched the man being tied to the tree. 'Some of my people are like children. It's important for them to understand why they should remain faithful to UNITA.' Behind him a woman, young and very beautiful, was screaming and Flowers realized it was the diamond-grader's wife. She was surrounded by other tribeswomen who restrained her.

Entada walked towards the bound man, his rifle held loosely in his right hand. He waved the other tribesmen away, then stood in front of the frantic diamond-grader. They stood like that for nearly a minute before Entada turned away and signalled a small group of children over, half-naked urchins no older than ten. He knelt in front of them, then faced the diamond-grader and calmly pushed his rifle bayonet into the man's groin.

The diamond-grader screamed, but it had no effect on the watching crowd. They all knew he would die; violent loss of life was nothing new to any of them. His wife, realizing the inevitability of it all, stopped crying and turned away. The last thing she wanted to do was draw attention to herself.

Entada placed the rifle into the hand of the nearest

young boy, then held him close to his chest, and helped him push the bayonet into the man's leg. The child giggled as the victim twisted uselessly, trying to free himself from the ropes that held him. Entada patted the child on the back, then handed the rifle to a girl. She, eager to take part in this new game, closed her eyes, turned her head away from the victim, and pushed the bayonet towards him. The rifle was too heavy and the bayonet sliced into the man's left foot, spearing it to the ground. She dropped the weapon in alarm and ran to her mother. Entada laughed, then handed the rifle to the largest boy there. Then he stood up, faced the diamond-grader and pointed at his stomach. As he turned away, the boy ran and lunged, and buried the steel blade into the point Entada had marked. The bayonet slipped easily through the thin African and penetrated the bark. The gun was stuck in the tree with the force of the blow and the boy stepped back, his hands off the gun that wobbled helplessly, pinning the diamond-grader to the tree.

Entada pulled the weapon out, twisting it slowly as he did, then put it over the man's heart and rammed it back in. There was a final scream, then the diamond-grader slumped dead.

Entada pulled out the rifle for the last time, then wiped the blood off the bayonet in the long grass. The dead man's wife started to sob again and he shouted out an order. The woman was led away from the clearing.

'What's going to happen to her?' asked Flowers now. He had tried to keep his head averted from the wretched death of the diamond-grader.

'I have given her to the men. To do with as they want.'

'They'll kill her when they've finished with her.'

Entada shrugged. 'She's of no use to anyone else. A traitor's wife. It's a pity she's so beautiful.' He laughed harshly. 'But, in the end, I can't risk her going back to the MPLA.'

'Why didn't you just shoot him?'

'You English – too soft. Anyway, why waste bullets? We need them for the communists.'

Flowers didn't believe Entada. Maybe the diamond-grader had been an informant. But it was more likely that he was a witness to the extra quantity of valuable stones, some of which Entada wanted in his own private numbered account. There would never be any rumours about the colonel stealing from UNITA now. It was the way these Africans were. No thought for life; it was an everyday commodity. Then he laughed at his own arrogance. The whites were no better; he remembered the Russian gulags and Hitler's concentration camps. We're all the same. Just animals in different-coloured skin.

The next morning Entada drove Flowers into Zambia at the border town of Shambongo. They followed a small dirt road through the forest, climbing towards the high Zambian plains. It was a long, bumpy ride, taking nearly a full day to cover the seventy miles. Flowers tried to doze in the passenger seat, but found it impossible as the Land-Rover slithered and bounced along the track. He offered to drive to relieve his discomfort, but Entada shook his head and pressed on. When they reached the Zambian border, they simply drove across it: there were no border patrols in this remote part of the continent.

A blue Hillman Hunter waited for them. The driver, an Angolan who worked in Lusaka, recognized the Land-Rover and stepped out from the car.

'Look after our cargo, my friend,' said Entada. 'Angola's future lies in your hands.'

And your bank account. Flowers smiled. 'Of course. The first trip of many.'

Flowers sat in the back with the window open as the Hillman worked its way east towards Senanga, then turned north on the red laterite road which ran across the plain to Mongu. The driver, on Claris's instructions, had placed a crate of African beer in the back and Flowers settled back to take what enjoyment he could on the lonely

road back home. By the time they reached the main east–
west highway that was four hundred miles west of Lusaka,
the car was covered in a red dust from the gravel road
surface. The main road, single-lane tarmaced, was light
on traffic and the driver kept the speed up to sixty
kilometres per hour for most of the journey. They arrived
at Lusaka in the early evening and went straight to the
airport.

Claris was waiting as the red-dusted blue Hillman
pulled up outside the terminal. 'Get the car out of here
and wash it,' he instructed the driver as Flowers climbed
out, a green Barbour jacket over his arm. 'If anyone
sees it, they'll know you've come from the west.' As the
Hillman pulled away he took Flowers's arm and led him
into the terminal. 'Your bag's all ready to be checked in.
Any problems?'

'Went like a dream. I've got the bottles in my coat.'

They went through customs; the officer's sole interest
was in whether they were taking any kwacha, the Zambian
currency, out of the country. With Claris's help, Flowers
loaded his bag, shook hands with his subordinate, and
crossed the tarmac to board the South African Airways
flight to Zürich. He was seen by a KGB watcher, but it
was too late to determine where Flowers had come from.
In the end, the senior KGB officer at the Soviet Embassy
in Diplomatic Triangle would file away the watcher's
report and simply state that Flowers had been on a
routine Head Office visit. To cover his back, he contacted
Moscow and told them that Flowers was on a plane for
Zürich, although he didn't see anything suspicious in the
Englishman's behaviour.

The SAA Boeing 737 touched down in Zürich nine
hours later. The effect of the sleepless car journeys and
the beer from the Hillman helped Flowers sleep for most
of the trip. He used the green Barbour as a pillow;
no-one could take that from him even though he was in
a deep sleep. He dreamt of the Black Angel and children

305

charging with bayonets. Only they weren't running at the diamond-grader, they were running at him. But he slept through his nightmare and was only wakened by the stewardess twenty minutes before landing.

Having hurriedly wet-shaved before landing, Flowers entered the main terminal, his Barbour now slung over his arm, and walked with some of the other passengers towards the Transit Lounge where he would connect with his London Heathrow flight in an hour's time.

He slowed down and let the other passengers get ahead.

When he was sure that he wasn't being observed, he slipped through an unmarked door next to the entrance to the Transit Lounge. He closed the door and climbed the stairs to the next level. He passed through another door and entered a large open area; a banking area with a counter at one end and cashiers in their booths. The sign, Union Banque Suisse, hung over them. Flowers knew this was no ordinary bank, although it fronted as a Bureau de Change. *It was specifically designed for the easy movement of money and other valuable objects into numbered bank accounts without crossing customs.*

'Monsieur Fouquet, s'il vous plait?' *Flowers asked the first cashier.*

She nodded and waved Flowers to the end booth. He watched her leave the counter and enter the back of the bank. A minute later a thin, elderly man came through to where Flowers waited.

'Vous cherchez Monsieur Fouquet? Lui même,' *the old man introduced himself.* 'Monsieur?'

'Fielden,' *Flowers replied, using the alias he had given Voerens. He held up the Barbour and took the three bottles out, placing them on the counter.*

'Is this all, Mr Fielden?' *said Fouquet in perfect English.*

'Yes. My plane leaves in an hour.'

Fouquet nodded. 'Would you like a coffee? Or a tea, perhaps?'

306

'Tea would be ideal.'

'Please take a seat. It shouldn't take long.' Fouquet took the bottles and left the counter.

Flowers took a seat, was served a pot of tea in beautiful bone china, and waited for the banker.

Half an hour later Fouquet returned to the counter. He handed a typed sheet to the Englishman. 'Fifteen thousand carats. We only expected ten thousand.'

'I know. Our suppliers were over-enthusiastic on this first trip. Does it cause a problem?'

'No. Only that we may have to hold the extra five thousand carats longer than we expected. We would not want to pay for them until we had disposed of the other merchandise.'

'All right. Let's capitalize ten thousand and we'll hold the extra in a separate account.'

'As you wish.' Fouquet leant forward and pointed at the typed sheet. 'Our surveyor is impressed with the quality. He suggests $40 per carat. That's—'

'$400,000.' Flowers decided not to bargain. It was slightly more than he had expected.

'Would you like it all deposited in the special numbered account?'

'I need a second account. Also numbered. There is a commission of five per cent to be paid after each transaction.' He didn't know why he increased the figure that Entada had asked for, but it was too late to retract now. 'I'd like the extra five thousand carats deposited in that account. When you can change it to cash, put the money, all of it, into the second account.' He knew why he was doing it now. It was insurance for the future. He felt himself sweating; he had never been dishonest like this before. He heard his voice continue on; another being within him was speaking the words with calmness and authority. 'That'll be $200,000, when it's cleared. All future transactions will include the five per cent commission to be paid into the second account. And *any additional diamonds that are above the ten thousand carat limit. Is that all clear, Mr Fouquet?'*

It wasn't up to Fouquet to argue. He did as he was told by his clients, and Flowers was his client. 'Certainly. That means we will be depositing $380,000 in the first account, in the name of Mr A. Unit. The second account will be opened and hold the diamonds, until they are cashed, which will then be a sum of $200,000. In addition to that a commission of $20,000 will be paid into that account, and in future any additional diamonds and a guaranteed five per cent commission.'

'Perfect,' replied Flowers. 'There will, of course, be interest accumulating on both amounts. All the interest is to be paid into the second account.'

'What name would you like that account in?'

'Engel. Louis Engel,' came the reply. He liked that one. Angel for Engel. 'Thank you, Mr Fouquet. The tea was excellent.'

'Will we see you again?'

'I think not. I will contact you, by phone, monthly, to get a report on the account. During our conversations, make no mention of the second account. Unless I ask you to.' There was no way Flowers wanted London asking who Engel was. Even members of the SIS weren't immune from having their phones tapped. 'In future, the only people you will discuss our affairs with are those who give the secret numbers of each account.' He knew UNITA would use their own people to take money from the Mr A. Unit account for arms purchases. The second account number would be his alone, as well as any future colleagues he may wish to involve. He took out his wallet, extracted a stamp from it and placed it on the counter. 'A rare Black Honduras,' he explained. Then he tore the stamp in half and passed one section over to Fouquet. 'Anyone who comes to you with my half should be allowed access to the account,' he said, putting the remains of the Black Honduras back into his wallet. The

*Swiss Banker picked up the other half and slid it into
an envelope.*

*The business concluded, Flowers returned to the Transit
Lounge entrance via the secret stairs. He waited for fifteen
minutes before his flight was called. Officially, Flowers
had never set foot in Switzerland; as far as the authorities
and customs were concerned he was simply a transit
passenger waiting for a connection. The KGB watcher,
who had been alerted by Lusaka, never saw Flowers and
reported back that his man had simply changed planes for
London.*

*Flowers was back in his London flat three hours later;
it was a wet, humid day and the rain beat against the
window as he looked out on the dreary city street below.
Oh for the dry heat. Oh for Africa.*

*Six days later he received a telex from Claris in Lusaka.
The Americans, who were based in Zaïre, had reported
that Colonel Louis Entada, a UNITA officer, had been
killed when he drove his Land-Rover over a land-mine
near the Benguela railway, the natural boundary between
the UNITA and MPLA forces. He had a woman companion with him; there was nothing else except the fact
that she had been the wife of a diamond-grader who had
recently died near Jamba. She was also killed by the blast.
Claris suggested that possibly the diamond-grader had not
been an informer, simply the husband of a woman Entada
had coveted.*

*It didn't matter to Flowers. He was already winding
down in preparation for his retirement. He recognized the
UNITA action against the black colonel for what it was.
Savimbi and his men didn't believe in unnecessary cruelty.
Entada's actions against the unfortunate diamond-grader
in the jungle, as well as their belief that he was skimming
some of the diamonds for himself, had forced their hand.*

Flowers knew his death was no accident.

*But then it wasn't his problem any more. In his years
with the SIS he had served loyally and honourably; never*

put himself before duty; never let the side down.

All Flowers was worried about now was making sure he received the pension he was entitled to.

And now it was Claris's turn to start worrying about his pension. The rain hammered against his window, broke his recollection and was a reminder that he had started what only he could finish.

He cursed Sir Walter Inger, sitting up in his ivory tower, shielded from the flak, and went back to his desk.

The game was running now; there was nothing he could do to stop it.

He hadn't started it anyway.

That was the tragedy of it for him.

Someone else's game, someone else's ball. He was just standing on the sidelines.

But if it went wrong, he'd be the loser who had to shoulder the blame.

The Cinema
Curzon Street
London W1

Carter wore a big 'I ate the canary' smile and chuckled his way through Richardson's debriefing.

'Poor old Langley,' Carter remarked when Richardson had finished. They were both in Carter's office, a simple, square, white-painted room with a worn desk that had seen service since the Korean War, and metal filing cabinets along one wall. Carter was kneeling on the floor, waiting for the electric kettle plugged in beside him to boil. Two cups, already milked and with instant coffee in, waited to be filled. 'Teach them to send someone without field experience. I bet the old FBI will be laughing their socks off.'

'Looked at objectively, we've done rather well out of it,' Richardson defended Duggan.

'Of course we have. I just find it amusing. I do enjoy the politics of the security services,' he said mischievously.

'At least we've got Farrell.'

'For the moment. There is, of course, the argument that we release him after seven days. He'll be concerned about how we picked up McCann and Eamonn's names, linking them to Collett's death. As soon as he's out, he'll be searching high and low for an informer. That could cause the old Provos a few headaches. Witch-hunts always do. Terrible for morale.'

'Unless they believe Duggan was wired.'

Carter shook his head. 'No. Duggan said they searched his clothes. Dancer used the latest technology, almost impossible to detect. Mr Tommy Farrell will definitely be looking for a grass once he's out of custody.'

'Anything from GCHQ?'

'Still scanning phone calls, not just from here, but from all over the Continent. As will the Americans. If they've dug anything up yet, they've not informed us.' The kettle started to boil, and Carter switched it off. 'Five mentioned you'd asked Morrison about some sort of – Plan,' he dragged the word out, 'in Belfast.'

'Yes.'

'Not very clever, that, Sam. Not in front of the American.'

'Except he already knew about it.'

'Where from?'

Richardson decided there was little point in getting Chief Inspector Monaghan into trouble. 'It seemed to be common knowledge.'

'He mentioned it to you earlier, then?' As he spoke, Carter poured the hot water into the cups.

'Yes. In Dublin. While we were comparing notes. Over a drink.'

'And you said you knew about the Plan?'

'I would've looked foolish if I said I didn't.'

'So you let him presume you knew.'

'Something like that. And I wanted to find out how much he knew.' Richardson had no choice but to brazen it out.

'So the CIA was aware of it?'

'Just that there was a plan to take out top IRA men in one fell swoop. That's all that Duggan told me.' He paused and stared back at a silent Carter. 'Was there?' he asked eventually.

Carter stood up and put the cups on the table. He sat down in his chair and pulled his cup towards him and blew on it to cool it down. 'For your ears only. Not for the American's.' He spoke while he continued to cool the coffee. 'It was quite a few years ago, five or six. A captain, no need for names, a G3 Int B, Catholic intelligence based at 3 Infantry Brigade was asked by Whitehall to prepare a plan which resulted in the execution or capture of known Provos. The Plan was produced, but to the best of my knowledge, never presented to the Cabinet or the Prime Minister. I believe it went from Brigade HQ to HQ Northern Ireland. Whether it went from there to the Northern Ireland Office at Stormont, then on to the Secretary of State for NI, I don't know. It was a pretty detailed plan and covered all suspected Provos both in the Republic and overseas.'

'Like NORAID and the Ierland Komitee Nederland?'

'Possibly.'

'But not in Ulster?'

'Ulster was included.'

'There've been other plans to take on the paramilitaries.'

'Not like this. This only involved the Republican supporters. The Protestant organizations weren't in the scheme of things. The idea was, that if you took out the Catholics, then the Orangemen wouldn't have any grounds for continuing.'

'Very naïve.'

'Agreed. But, the Government, so muddled about the Maastricht Treaty and all the other confusion over Europe, didn't want Brussels getting involved in Ulster. You can imagine what those idiot bureaucrats would do. Tie up the whole province in red tape. God, we have enough trouble now keeping up with the gunmen. With Brussels involved, we'd have our hands tied behind our backs.'

'The agreement with the EC is that member states look after their own security.'

'Yes. Except we uncovered a plot by the PIRA to hit British targets in the EC. You can imagine the damage that would do. We'd have trouble keeping Brussels out then.'

'Why wasn't the Plan presented to the Cabinet?'

'Because it could rebound against us politically, even drag the UN into the Irish problem. There were some fears that it could unleash a full-blown civil war, based on the religious divide. That wouldn't go down well in Europe, and certainly wouldn't be appreciated by Her Majesty as Head of the English Church. We don't mind the Yugoslavs blowing each other up, but it's not something we want to see outside Tesco's on a Saturday morning. Finally, if it was to be a covert operation, not linked to HMG, then funding it without being discovered would be almost impossible.'

'Can I see a copy of this Plan?'

'No need.'

'Can I see a list of people involved in drawing up the Plan?'

'No need.'

The frustration built up in Richardson; he hated facing the unemotional wall of officialdom. 'Do you

313

want me off this thing? Back to what I was doing?'

'No. Stick with Duggan.'

'Why? To help him find the Angels – or to stop him finding them?'

'They're not an authorized organization.'

'But we're supporting them?'

'Of course not.'

'Maybe not the SIS. But someone else is. Like Five.'

'There is absolutely no support for them from any section of HMG.' Carter picked up his cup and sipped from it. It was still too hot and he put it down. 'Never could take hot liquids.'

'Then why can't I see documents that could help me discover who the Angels are?'

'Not as long as the American's around. I think we should clean up our own mess.'

'So it is our mess?'

'*If*,' Carter emphasized the word, 'it is our mess.'

'Mick Dancer told me that Morrison was one of the men working on the Plan.'

'Did he?' Carter seemed genuinely surprised. 'Does Duggan know that?'

'Not from me. Wasn't Morrison an intelligence officer? Based at 3 Infantry Brigade?'

Carter didn't answer him directly. Instead, 'I wonder why Dancer should admit that to you?'

'Maybe he wanted to see what sort of reaction he'd get.' Richardson decided to keep pushing. 'Were any of those involved in the Plan specialists in bomb work, or close-quarter killing? Or sniper use?'

'I'm quite sure we had a variety of experts like that on call.'

'Named?'

'Even if they were, it didn't matter. It was only a plan. They wouldn't have known their names were on the list until they were asked to go out on specialist duties. And that never happened because the Plan was never sanctioned.'

'I'd still like to see the Plan. And any related material.'

Carter puffed his cheeks up, then slowly blew the air out through squeezed lips. 'OK,' he finally decided. 'But for your eyes only.' He suddenly terminated the meeting. 'Go and find your Yank, Sam. I'll get you the brief.'

Richardson stood up. 'You do want these Angels found, don't you?'

'Of course. I really do have no idea who they are. But, my original instruction holds. If it leads back to HMG, make sure you sever the lead.'

Richardson nodded. It was something he had understood all along. He was expected to do whatever was necessary to protect the Government from any embarrassment.

Whatever necessary. He didn't need anyone explaining to him what that meant.

Orlando Airport
Florida

Penuel was quick to notice that the airport was swarming with surveillance teams.

He bought a *Fortune* magazine at the news-stand and headed back to the car-park. Lucifer and Raphael were standing by the rental car, a Lincoln Town Car, and Lucifer was halfway through a Marlboro.

'Probably FBI, with a few local cops to help out,' said Lucifer when Penuel told him. Lucifer was a broad man, in his early fifties, a soft, smooth-skinned face crowned by a bald dome. The eyes didn't match the baby face; they were slit and hard and discouraged people from approaching him. He pulled a blond wig out of his pocket, looked round to make sure he wasn't seen, and slid the hair-piece onto his head. Then he took

315

out a pair of reflector Serengetti sunglasses and slipped them on. 'What about the flight?'

'On schedule. Should be touching down about now.'

'OK. Let's get to our stations. And remember, just follow him for now.'

Raphael got in the car and drove out of the car-park to the arrivals pick-up zone. Lucifer and Penuel walked into the big modern terminal separately, Lucifer taking a good vantage point in the Quick Service Restaurant while Penuel lined up with the other welcomers at the international barrier.

The FBI surveillance teams had an old picture of Baxter, in which he was younger and dark-haired. They expected him to be in disguise and they had fanned out across the arrivals hall so as not to miss him. There were further agents in the customs hall, both with the immigration officers and customs officials.

They didn't expect him to be travelling with a wife and two young children.

Baxter picked up on a surveillance man as soon as he joined the line for Immigration. He was travelling on an Eire passport, under the name of Peter Donnelly. He nudged his wife and warned her. Then Baxter tripped his son. The child fell to the floor and started to cry in pain. Baxter bent down and picked him up, hugged the boy to comfort him. People near by looked at him sympathetically and he saw two of those he took to be FBI men look in his direction. Once they were satisfied, they looked away, their eyes still searching through the crowds. Baxter knew they didn't recognize him; his ploy with his son had worked. When the family reached the immigration desk, the official asked him why he was over.

'On holiday,' Baxter replied. 'To get away from the miserable rain and get some sun.'

The immigration officer grinned and checked through the passports. Behind him, the FBI man had glanced across at Baxter, dismissed him and gone back to watching the people still in line.

The immigration officer gave the passports back and wished the Donnellys a good vacation in Florida.

Baxter and the family walked through, wheeling their luggage on a trolley, and headed for the car-rental desks.

The FBI missed them completely; no-one would have thought the IRA intelligence chief was only on holiday.

Lucifer picked him up first, slid out from the table where he had been drinking an iced tea, and signalled Penuel.

The two men, still keeping apart, followed the Baxters to the car-rental counters. Penuel joined the line and heard Baxter's conversation with the clerk. He asked the way to the Sheraton Sea World Hotel in International Drive. Then, as Lucifer tailed Baxter out of the building, Penuel pretended to arrange to hire a car, before saying he had left his wallet behind and would return when he had recovered it from his case.

Lucifer went straight to Raphael and the two men watched the Baxters climb into a Hertz air-conditioned bus that would take them to the main car-rental offices. Penuel came out, joined his colleagues, and they followed the bus. Penuel told the other two where Baxter was staying and they decided to tail the Irishman to the hotel, just in case he had deliberately given the rental official the wrong destination.

Being economical with the truth was something that came naturally to those in the intelligence game.

SIGINT City beat GCHQ in tracing the transatlantic call.

The operator in the TCOM room at SIGINT City, in addition to the normal key words, fed in Orlando, Disney World, Army Council, Collett, Fergal and Baxter to his individual work station. The first two words brought up endless conversations and it became necessary to call in further operators to monitor them. Army Council and Collett brought up several phone calls, mostly between the offices of newspapers and television stations. The mother-lode came with Fergal Baxter. In a world of codespeak, it was unbelievable that the Angels had carried out such an open conversation.

'Must've been in one helluva hurry,' said the operator. 'There was no need to rush an open message like that. If Baxter was about to take a ten-hour trip to Orlando, that was enough time to set up a procedure call using proper codes.'

'What's that tell you?' asked his superior, pulling up a chair and joining him as they ran through the transcript on the monitor.

'That the guy making the call was in a rush. If it was Schipol Airport – we haven't confirmed that yet – then he was rushing to catch a plane. Once we get the time of the call, we'll work out which planes left soon afterwards. I guess the second reason could be that whoever he was calling was more than ten hours away.'

The two men looked at each other. 'No way,' said the supervisor. 'Hell, you can charter a private jet anywhere in the States and get to Orlando in six hours max. That's door to door, including time to stop off at Wendy's.'

A transcript of the tape was immediately faxed to the CTC room in Langley, then passed to Mickleton who alerted his agents in Orlando. By the time the new description of Baxter had been released, the planes from Amsterdam had long since been cleared and were on their return trips across the Atlantic.

An immigration officer recalled the man with his wife and two children. The officer, like all his colleagues, was trained to recall those who passed his counter. 'Donnelly,' he said. 'With his kids for a vacation. One of them was called Jimmy.' He pulled out a copy of his

318

entry data, then checked the number on the passport. The State Department called the Passport Office in Dublin and it was confirmed that there was a Peter Donnelly whose passport number coincided with that of the man who had landed in Orlando. No, there was no record of him being married, and there certainly were no children. Anyway, Peter Donnelly had been dead for eleven years, having died in a car crash in Belfast.

The FBI then checked the car-rental companies. Nobody remembered Mr Donnelly, although one clerk at the Hertz desk found something vaguely similar about another client. A Mr Jed Biltmore from Ireland. Yes, he had seen the man's driving licence. No, he hadn't inspected his passport; it wasn't something they were meant to do. He remembered giving directions to a hotel, but couldn't remember which hotel. Everyone, simply everyone, asked for directions to a hotel. That was Orlando. Fun City, USA.

By the time GCHQ had dug up the transcript on their system, the NSA had traced the first call to Flamingo Drive, east of Fort Lauderdale. The operator had then searched for the words Flamingo and Flamingo Drive amongst the transatlantic phone calls prior to the one made by Gabriel from Amsterdam.

There was one call logged. It consisted of just two sentences. It had also been made from Amsterdam.

'Imperative speak in next thirty minutes,' said the voice they now identified as Gabriel.

'Call Flamingo Drive,' was the answer they matched with the voice that had spoken to both Raphael and Penuel.

FBI agents were despatched to Flamingo Drive where they found the number was a phone booth in the hallway of a shopping mall.

'What about the phone the call was made to, the one asking him to ring Flamingo Drive?' asked the supervisor.

'It was a mobile,' said the operator. He yawned and stretched back. He'd gone as far as possible with this thing for now. 'We checked with Cellular One, the local mobile operators. They run the franchise from Miami up to Palm Beach. This particular phone was stolen nine months ago from a car. It was a portable. They cut the service off, but these days a good electronics guy can fit chips which connect the mobile into the network without anybody being billed. They're using an illegal set.'

'At least we know he was half an hour away from Flamingo Drive.'

'Two million people must live half an hour from Flamingo Drive.'

The operator laughed. 'Yeah. Well, that's the Feds' problem. Until we narrowed it down to two mill, they had nearly three hundred million suspects.'

Lucifer left Penuel to watch over Baxter.

Penuel booked into the hotel, traced the Baxters' room, then asked to be transferred to the same floor. Baxter had booked in under the name McCarthy; Penuel was convinced that wasn't the name Baxter had crossed the Atlantic under. Penuel hated hanging round Orlando; holidays, kids and Mickey Mouse were not things he was fond of. Lucifer instructed him to observe Baxter, but not to be so over-zealous that he might be discovered.

Lucifer returned to base with Raphael to await word from London.

There was a tension again between the American and the Englishman.

Richardson had returned from his meeting with Carter to find the American out, a note on the mantelpiece informing anyone who read it that Duggan had decided to visit the local shops. Richardson knew that meant phoning the American Embassy. He rang Carter and told him to warn GCHQ. Twenty minutes later Carter rang back and gave him a breakdown of Duggan's conversation with the legal attaché. It was a run-down of all that the NSA had picked up, including the information that Michael was on his way to meet one of the Angels in London. Carter told Richardson that GCHQ were now scanning all the phone calls at the time stated by SIGINT City and would have a complete transcript of the conversations as soon as possible. Unless, that was, the CIA or FBI decided to release the information sooner.

'That puts it back in our court,' said Carter. 'If they're in London, they mean trouble.'

'They'll be retaliating over Collett.'

'Yes. That's my view. By the way, the PIRA have claimed Collett's death. That came through about half an hour ago.'

'Michael is another Angel's name.'

'That's what Duggan said when he phoned the Embassy.'

'Any luck with the file on the Plan?'

'Probably this afternoon. Should be ready for you about two. I wish we'd officially trace this call, or that the Americans would give us the information they've got. All this fumbling around in the dark is going to slow us down. In the meantime we've alerted Five and Special Branch.'

When Duggan returned he was just as silent as his colleagues in Langley.

They both hedged around, each knowing more than they were prepared to admit. To pass the time, Richardson pulled out a pad of lined A4 paper, put it on the dining-room table, and the two men went over all the details of what had happened up to that point. In an attempt to open up Duggan, Richardson told him that the IRA had officially claimed they were responsible for Robert Collett's death. It had no effect on the American, apart from his comment that it was what they had both expected. The two men listed all the incidents that led up to their present predicament. Richardson once again mentioned all the Archangels' names, hoping that the mention of Michael's name might spur Duggan to admit he knew the Angel was on his way to London. But it had no effect. The whole exercise took over two hours, then Richardson said he had to return to Six to put in a report.

Richardson took the Bentley into the city. He enjoyed the admiring glances it drew and he drove her sedately along the frustrated, slow-moving streets, never in a hurry to jump lights or close the gap in front immediately. These actions attracted the odd honk or gesture of damnation from his fellow-travellers, but he enjoyed their frustration as he glided along the road.

'There's not much,' said Carter, when Richardson reported to him. There was a slim file on the desk, A4 size. 'There never is on these types of operation. But you know that anyway.' He rose from his desk and walked to the door. 'Use my room. No more than fifteen minutes. Don't take it out of here. And, as far as anyone else is concerned, I'm not aware that this report was made available to you.'

Richardson pulled up a chair when Carter had left the room and opened the file.

It wasn't the Doomsday Plan, as Monaghan had told

him, but headed OPERATION CARTEL.

He flipped to the last of the nine typed pages. The document was signed by two men. The first was Captain Daniel Morrison, G3 Int B (Armagh). That meant Morrison had been in charge of 3 Infantry Brigade Intelligence dealing specifically with Catholics, the PIRA, the Official IRA and the INLA, the Irish National Liberation Army terrorists. He recalled that Morrison was now OC Wpns Int. It was a definite promotion, no doubt partly aided by his contribution to this plan.

The second signature was Captain Ray Nathaniel, G3 Int L (Lisburn). That put him with 39 Infantry Brigade in charge of liaison for special intelligence operations. Richardson had heard of Nathaniel; a committed intelligence officer who had made a name for himself by bringing Protestant paramilitaries to justice in the 1980s. His efforts had been regarded by some as too zealous and he was eventually moved into a desk-bound post. Richardson couldn't remember what became of Nathaniel and decided that he would attempt to trace him.

Back on the front page, under the title OPERATION CARTEL, the names of those the report was intended for were listed in order of importance. The first two names were whitened out. Richardson held the page up to the light, but the typist's white paint was too thick and he couldn't decipher the names. He presumed they were senior politicians; on something this important probably the Minister for Northern Ireland and the Prime Minister. The next name was the then-chairman of the Permanent Secretaries Committee on the Intelligence Services, a committee consisting of the highest-ranking civil servants in the Foreign Office, Defence, Home Office and Treasury. The other names included a senior civil servant in the Northern Ireland Office at Stormont, a Deputy Director at MI5, two officers at Headquarters Northern Ireland, a colonel GS Intelligence – Military, and an Assistant Sec. Political – a recognized MI5 officer. It was a short list, no doubt reflecting the importance of such a sensitive document. He was surprised that no copy had been sent to the Joint Intelligence Committee. This group met every week and included the heads of all the intelligence organizations and senior members of the main customer departments. There was also no mention of the SIS. Richardson grinned and wondered how it had come into Six's hands. No wonder Carter didn't want anyone to know they had it.

'You and Sam seem to have a great relationship,' Duggan said in the Crown and Anchor as he put the two drinks on the table and sat down.

'We get along well,' replied Andrea. She picked up her glass of white wine and sipped from it. 'Cheers.'

'To you and Sam,' toasted Duggan, holding up his beer. He was pleased to be alone with her; she'd returned from work and gladly accepted his offer of a drink.

'I needed that,' she said as she put the glass down.

'Tough day?'

She nodded. 'Sometimes people forget that nurses don't like the sight of blood and gore any more than anyone else.'

'Then why do it?'

'It fulfils me. Until it goes wrong. You spend hours in the operating-theatre, working like hell to save someone's life, and then, sometimes, it just doesn't work out. Seems a waste of all that effort.'

'Tell me about it.'

'Why? I'd only depress myself further.' She took another sip. 'What've you two action men been up to?'

'Just going over the facts, analysing them.'

'And?'

Duggan sighed. 'Everything's come to a full stop.'

'What did your people think of you becoming a television celebrity?' she teased him.

He smiled, felt a deep warmth as she baited him. She was so different from Carmella. She was real; there were no games, no prizes to be won. 'They weren't pleased.'

'Sam was impressed. That you should do that for a soldier. Not a lot of people would've stepped forward to protect him.'

'I couldn't see them harming me. Not an American.'

'Don't tell me you thought all that through as you leapt forward,' she giggled, 'into the teeth of danger.'

He shrugged. 'Not right away. It was instinct, I guess.'

'It was a brave thing to do.'

'Why? Because Sam says so?'

'Don't be silly. Because I say so.' She watched him closely. 'I'm not sure if you approve of Sam.'

'He's OK.'

'You're both very different.'

'He's more into the action thing than I am.' He realized how pompous and demeaning he sounded as he spoke.

'Just because he was a soldier doesn't mean he's thick,' she snapped defensively.

'Thick?'

'Brain dead.'

'I didn't say he was.' Duggan regretted crossing the line; it spoilt the closeness they were building. He rapidly tried to repair the damage. 'Listen, I respect people in the field. Really, I mean that. It's easy for guys like me to sit at desks and plan actions. Only we don't have to do it. I know how difficult that is. Especially after Milltown. Hell, I know what they go through. I have nothing but admiration for people like Sam. Particularly when our plans go wrong and the guys in the field have to fix it.' His words seemed to mollify her. He leant forward and laid his hand on her arm. 'Really. I have a lot of time for Sam. Maybe it's myself I'm criticizing.'

She looked at him, doleful eyes that made his stomach flip into an empty hole. 'I'm sorry.'

'Don't be.' He kept his hand on her arm. She started to smile and he returned it. Then her smile turned into an uncontrollable giggle. 'Something I said?'

'Not important. Sorry.' She tried to hold back the mirth, but to no avail.

'You'd better tell me what's so funny,' he said defensively. But he kept his hand on her arm.

'You won't like it,' she replied through her laughter.

'Try me.'

'Sam says you've . . . had a . . . ', the giggles overtook her again. Then, '. . . charisma bypass.'

'Everyone's entitled to his own view,' Duggan replied huffily, then withdrew his hand.

'I'm sorry – I shouldn't have.' She reached over and took his hand in hers. 'I shouldn't have. It was during the first day you were here. You just didn't get on, did you?' Andrea tried to justify Richardson's jibe, but somehow made it all so much worse. 'I didn't mean to hurt you.' She squeezed his hand.

'What the hell!' Duggan shrugged. 'He's pretty much on the mark.' He sighed. 'There is a jealousy in me. Against people like Sam. Because they achieve things. I guess I'm also jealous over you. He's a lucky man. As soon as I saw you—' he paused, then slowly withdrew his hand. 'I'm getting too heavy. Sorry.'

'You hardly know me.'

'In the passage of time, maybe not. But I felt I'd always known you as soon as you walked through the door.'

She went back to her wine, sipping it thoughtfully. He couldn't tell what she was thinking. 'You mustn't say any more,' she said eventually.

'I didn't mean to go so far.'

'Then you shouldn't have.'

'It's how I feel.'

'It's—'

'One more thing. I don't mean to do anything behind Sam's back. I appreciate his hospitality. But – you've just got through. I'm sorry. I won't bring it up again.'

'I love Sam.'

'I understand that. Like I said, it won't ever be brought up again.'

She finally looked directly at him. 'Friends?'

He grinned, then shrugged. 'No choice.'

'You said—'

He held up his hands. 'I know. Friends. Best of.' He held out his right hand. 'Shake on it.'

'No. You've done enough touching for one day, Mr TV hero.'

'Am I ever going to live that down?'

'Never. Once a star—'

'Always a star.' But he couldn't let go. 'What do you see in him, Andrea? What makes him get a beautiful person like you?'

'Because he isn't chasing a dream. That's what you see. A dream. Of being with someone very beautiful. An infatuation.'

'Not true.'

'I've seen it before. I'm not being conceited, but I have that effect on a lot of men. When I was a working model, out on the catwalk, that's what I was paid for. To sell a dream. And men believed it. I was being chased all the time, tremendous pressure with offers of jewellery and holidays. All the time. And it wasn't true. None of it.' She laughed. 'All the hunks a girl could dream of. A friend of mine summed it up once, after her millionth love affair with one of them ended in tears. She said, "They looked good from far, but were far from good."' She paused, reflecting on her own thoughts before continuing. 'Child abuse is

327

a very popular theme right now. For the fashionable do-gooders. But, it's a fact. It does happen. Happened to me. When I was nine. A neighbour. He did it to me for two years. And I never said anything. I didn't know how to. I'm not asking for sympathy. Just telling you. Until I met Sam, I believed I was naturally promiscuous. Because I always felt different. Even when I was nine. You see, when you're that age, and some old bastard's taking your clothes off, you don't think the other person's doing wrong. You just feel it's all your own fault.'

'And Sam changed that?'

She nodded. 'Because he's solid and nothing fancy. That's what makes him different. With Sam, you get what you see. He's square and solid and he polishes his boots with the same intensity that men used to chase me. I love him because he polishes his boots. Because he hangs his clothes up neatly, for his inability to give up smoking. Because he's as honest with me, and about me, as any man could be. He doesn't threaten me, doesn't make me feel vulnerable. He just makes me feel good and I don't want anything else.'

Duggan took it all in and understood that he, to her, was like the others. It didn't stop him feeling strongly about her, but she had pricked his dream. He suddenly thought of Carmella and the gorilla and his two babies and cursed that she hadn't been like Andrea. *Damn you Carmella, damn you for damning me.*

He held up his beer. 'How about something to eat and a movie if he's going to be late?'

The smile wiped him out. 'We'll see,' she said. 'We'll see.'

Richardson took his time over the report. Although it was only nine pages, it was packed with explosive information.

The first page carried a short summary of the Plan and its objectives.

The second page went on with a description of the various brigades and their intelligence support staff and resources. That section had obviously been detailed for the politicians and civil servants in London and was simple in its presentation.

There were three brigades active in Northern Ireland: 39 Infantry at Lisburn, 3 Infantry at Armagh and 8 Infantry in Londonderry. Each brigade had a TAOR; the appendage explained this for the politicians as a tactical area of responsibility. The intelligence staff within each brigade was broken down to include:

Grade 2 intelligence staff officer. A major. Richardson recognized names from his own tour of duty.

Grade 3 Int A. A captain responsible for Protestant and Loyalist groups.

Grade 3 Int B. Morrison was one of the captains listed dealing with Catholic, PIRA and INLA members.

Grade 3 Int L. The three names, including Captain Nathaniel, the co-author of the document.

Captain OC Intelligence and Security. Each captain was responsible to his own brigade for Command intelligence, collation staff, the organization of source handling and control of field intelligence NCOs.

Captain OC Weapons. These officers investigated all bombings and shootings in their TAOR with a team of plain-clothes Regimental Military Police. Richardson recalled that each OC Weapons was an experienced RAOC bomb disposal officer.

In addition to these officers, each brigade had a Military Intelligence Officer who sat with the local heads of Special Branch. The MIO's task was to ensure SB information was suitably sanitized to protect SB sources. Each MIO was responsible to a Special Military Intelligence Unit which, in turn, co-ordinated its efforts with the police at RUC HQ in Knock.

The final list dealt with the independent, all-arms unit of very carefully selected and trained men and women who were part of the 14 Independent Intelligence Company. Long-term surveillance was dangerous but boring with rare moments of action or reward. That meant that 14 Int members were highly motivated and required tremendous discipline. It was something Richardson had sympathy with; he remembered his own lonely tour and how a moment's lack of thought or concentration could destroy months of work, often, as in his case, with tragic results.

The third and fourth sheets dealt with the PIRA and how its organization worked on both sides of the border. It gave a profile of the PIRA, its objectives, number and disposition of activists, current target strategy, tactics, logistics and long-term objectives. It stated that over 400 were directly involved in terrorist operations, the majority of them under PIRA Northern Command. Another 400 undertook support activities such as hiding weapons, ferrying explosives, scouting and keeping safe houses. The report stated that the most dangerous terrorists were those who planned and executed each operation; these principal operators numbering a hard core of a mere 40 people. Many of them lived in the Republic and were on the run from the security forces for crimes committed in the North. There was a list of all the towns where the terrorists could be found, from Letterkenny and Burnfoot in County Donegal to Belturbot in County Cavan. There was also a list of men in Dublin, including all the members of the Army Council, who were well 'carded', but were careful not to expose themselves too often on operations in the North. They orchestrated the violence from the safe haven of the Republic. The final paragraph, printed in capitals stated that: REMOVING KEY MEN FROM THIS FINAL GROUP, AND ALSO THOSE WHO WERE KEY OPERATIONAL PERSONNEL IN TERRORIST ACTIVITIES, WOULD LEAVE THE

The fifth page dealt with sources of information. There were case histories ranging from a top member of the Provisional Army Council to a miserable snout of a traffic warden in Newry. These sources were motivated by idealism, greed, revenge and fear often brought about by the British security agencies using suitable leverage against the informant. Finally, the page listed sources belonging to official agencies such as the Gardaí and other Eire establishment forces. This information was particularly sensitive so real names had not been included. Code-names were used. A1 sources headed the list, with A2, B1, B2, B3, then F1, F2, F3, F4, etc., listed below. An A1 source was utterly reliable and always 100 per cent correct in his or her information. A1 sources were extremely rare and Richardson saw Trojan listed as one of them. He recognized Monaghan's code-name immediately.

The sixth page identified the targets.

The Army Council came top of the list, followed by the Brigade Commanders.

Tommy Farrell headed that list.

There were fifty names on the page, typed closely together, double column, with their last known addresses, their positions in the organization and descriptions. A note at the bottom stated that the number next to the name was a file reference for an identifying photograph. Most of the names had a number. Nearly a hundred lived in the Republic. It included Tim Flaherty and Martyn Darcy, identified as gunman and bomber respectively. He was surprised Darcy was on it; after all he had been one of their best informants.

A small panel listed the MOST WANTED TOP 30 on-the-run PIRA terrorists. Darcy made number six.

The statement at the bottom read, 'If the PIRA is to be hurt, then it is their trained personnel who are the most important and vulnerable targets. New sources for weapons and explosives can always be found. There is also a growing fund of sympathizers within Northern Ireland and the Irish Republic. But trained, dedicated, motivated and experienced soldiers are the most difficult to replace. If the PIRA were to find themselves with a short supply of experienced terrorists, they would be hard pushed to carry out their actions as efficiently and regularly as they do at present. The loss of "heroes" to the movement would also result in a decline of morale amongst both active members and supporters of the PIRA. Any successful action as proposed in this document would mean that the Republican movement would be set back many years and, if the security forces were to keep a tighter grip on the ensuing situation, may never become a strong terrorist force again.' *Too right. Too bloody right*. Then Richardson went on to the next sheet.

The seventh page gave a breakdown of the areas which were to be hardest hit.

County Monaghan's PIRA controlled terrorist operations in East Tyrone, Fermanagh and Armagh. Dundalk took care of South Armagh and was heavily underlined as the main target area. Londonderry, Strabane, Castlederg and Londonderry County were the responsibility of County Donegal PIRA. All these targets were within a few minutes driving time of the border.

The lower half of page seven listed members of the Gardaí and Irish Special Branch who could be counted on to be supportive of any covert action by British forces in southern Ireland. Once again, Monaghan was named. There was an additional column with the names of Protestant paramilitary groups who could also be enlisted. Sean Coyle's name stood out. Richardson realized he wasn't the only one who had dealings with Coyle. He decided to go and see the barman as soon as possible.

The eighth and ninth pages were the most illuminating. It showed how Operation Cartel was to be carried out.

It opened by saying that if the action was to be official, no more than one PIRA terrorist should disappear every six months. That was as far as anyone could dare go without drawing suspicion to the authorities. But such an operation wasn't feasible as it could run to twenty-five years, too long by anyone's standards. To speed up the timetable, Protestant paramilitaries would have to be used and the blame laid squarely on their organizations. This would also include a couple of bombings at clubs and drinking houses frequented by the PIRA, although the report specified that any such attacks must be planned to avoid injury to innocent victims. Richardson knew that was an impossible remit. The buildings would first be raided in the daytime by the Army, which would include a bomb specialist amongst its ranks. The specialist, unknown to the others in the troop, would leave behind a hidden bomb of enormous destructive potential. That evening, when the club was full, the bomb would be detonated by remote control. There would be non-combative victims, but it should be remembered that all the inhabitants of these Republican clubs were IRA sympathizers. No organization would claim responsibility for the operation and, with the use of selective disinformation, the blame could be attached to the INLA, other discontented sections of the PIRA and also the Protestant paramilitaries. At the same time, SAS men would take out a number of PIRA gunmen and bombers at the known addresses, with the blame once again being distributed amongst the other illegal organizations, including the INLA and the IPLO.

This previous section had a red line drawn through it and the words: NO ACTION TO BE TAKEN WHERE INNOCENT CIVILIANS ARE AT RISK OR WHERE LOYALIST PARAMILITARIES BE USED AS SURROGATE FORCES OR

WHERE BOMBS ARE HIDDEN BY SOLDIERS. Richardson was relieved; at least it showed the army hierarchy preserved its strategy of fighting within the rules of civilized combat, however enthusiastic the motives of those who had prepared the document.

The second section related to a document that was not included in the file. It referred to a series of named targets and the access to each target, with a clear routing to where the hit could be made and an escape plan from it. The missing document also included up-to-the-minute details on targets' houses, local pubs, girlfriends, car numbers and other information on their day-to-day lives. The information had been provided by individuals in the south of Ireland who could be counted on to assist in the Plan. He couldn't identify any of them as their code-names were used, although he did recognise Trojan once again. The targets they pin-pointed were in Dublin, Dundalk, Castleblaney, Monaghan, Belturbot, Letterkenny, Belfast and Londonderry. Richardson understood why this document was missing. It was probably never even received by Six; was either destroyed or buried in some filing cabinet in Brigade HQ. It didn't matter; after all this time the targets would have changed address or moved on to other duties. It also pointed out that committed and sympathetic contacts would be prepared to kidnap terrorists on their side of the border and transport them to out-of-the-way border crossings where British Forces would take charge of them, and make sure they were never seen again. This would save the problem of British specialists having to cross the frontier lines where they might be captured.

Next came the methods of killing. The only choice, apart from bombs, was guns or knives. There was a list of specialists next to each weapon, people who would be expected to take part in such action. Richardson noted his own under knife and close-quarters. It went on to say that all guns must either be non-attributable or

334

attributable to a Loyalist group. That meant the gun would have to be stolen from the UVF or UFF. Richardson pulled his small diary out of his pocket and made a list of the names. The Angels could well be amongst them.

Body disposal was covered next. The ideal operation was a covert one where the victim was never seen again. It was imperative that no clues were left once a PIRA operative had been killed. The body must be totally destroyed and the most effective way was disposal in a furnace. There was a list of the furnaces, two of them in steel foundries, where such action could be safely carried out.

The final item dealt with security and intelligence. It reflected the highly dangerous content of Operation Cartel. Everyone involved would have to be totally committed and trustworthy. Clean transportation and clean weaponry would be needed on both sides of the border. There would also have to be a full monitoring of troop movements and operations in Northern Ireland and Eire so as not to conflict with Cartel's actions or put the whole plan into jeopardy.

The last paragraph concluded that many of the targets lived in the Republic, most of them within thirty minutes of the border, beyond British jurisdiction. The sanctity and sovereignty of Irish soil was paramount. British operations across the border would never be tolerated by the Irish government. If an official act was discovered, the British government would be forever damned and find itself in an irredeemable hostile situation with the Republic. Therefore a decision to take out the terrorists would have to be official at the highest level.

Or unofficial and known only to a small dedicated group prepared to risk all for an effective blow to the opposition.

Or a renegade group which, if discovered, might just save the politicians' faces. The key to this type of operation would be funding by monies that couldn't be traced. All purchases and resources would have to be left to this outfit so that they would appear to be a solo operation with absolutely no official ties.

Richardson scanned through the nine pages once again, making notes in his diary of things he had missed. He realized why the SIS had never been on the original distribution list. They always worked to the principle of no possible compromise on assassination, or wet jobs as they were known. Just as he read through the last page again, Carter walked in. Richardson slipped his diary into his pocket, then collected the sheets and slid them back into the folder.

'I hope you haven't been making notes,' commented Carter.

'No, sir,' Richardson lied. He knew that Carter had seen the diary, but he wouldn't have been shown the document unless he was expected to remember all the contents.

Carter sat at his desk, took the folder and slipped it into his top left-hand drawer, then locked it with a key from his key-chain, which he pocketed in his jacket. 'Any questions?'

'Captain Ray Nathaniel. What happened to him?'

'Aggressive sort of chap. Difficult to control. When Operation Cartel was turned down, he blew a fuse, demanded that the matter be taken higher. In the end, they moved him back to the mainland, to some office job. He wanted more excitement, so he applied to us.'

'And?' queried Richardson when Carter suddenly stopped.

'He was with us for a while. In your position, actually. It was just after the Berlin Wall came down and we were looking for a new role in the security system. Thought we'd be more involved on the Northern Ireland front. Five outfoxed us on that. Anyway, he left after about six months. Went into private service, some sort of bodyguard to an Arab prince. You know the type.'

'Did he take this report with him?'

Carter smiled benignly; the uncle patronizing his favourite nephew. 'I leave you to draw your own conclusion.'

'Inspector Tack Monaghan of the Gardaí gets a lot of mention. Both he and Morrison were bomb disposal officers. I know Monaghan. He joined the Gardaí Special Branch after he left the Irish Army where he was a Commandant. I presume that's where the link was forged.' Carter gave no response. 'Or was he close to Nathaniel?' Still no response. 'What about the funds? Presuming the Angels are a renegade outfit.'

'I don't think you can presume anything in this matter.'

'What if I find that all this is official?'

'Then protect the authorities.'

'Why?'

'Because that's what you're paid to do.'

'I'm expected to go further on this, aren't I?'

'That's up to you.'

'That's why I was shown the report.'

'What report? I mean, SIS were never privy to the Plan in the first place.'

Richardson grinned. The game with Carter wasn't worth pursuing. 'I'd like more information on Nathaniel.'

'I'm sure that can be arranged.'

'Through whom?'

'Leave a handwritten list, in pencil, of what you want with Marlene.' Carter named his secretary, a bright cockney sparrow with peroxide hair who was now in her fifties and had been with Carter for years. 'If we find anything that could be helpful, I'll get her to dead-letter you.'

That meant Richardson really was on his own; that the SIS wanted nothing traced back to them. 'Fine,' he said, standing up.

'Be careful,' warned Carter.

'Of what?'

'Things are not always as obvious as they seem.' He opened another drawer and took out another file, opened it and spread the papers in front of him. 'Work to do. Thank you, Sam,' Carter dismissed Richardson.

Richardson went to his small office, checked through his diary again, then wrote a short list for Carter. He used a pencil as requested; it would later be rubbed out by Marlene once Carter had read it, then disposed of in the shredder. Then he left the note, sealed in a buff MoD envelope in Marlene's office and drove the Bentley home.

All he thought was why had Carter shown him the Plan? What was the role they wanted him to play? Which strings were the bastards pulling to make him sing for his supper?

There was another note waiting for him, this time pinned to the fridge door by a magnetic 'Scotland the Brave' sticker, a reminder of a pleasant week he and Andrea had spent touring the mountains in Aberdeenshire. He recognized her rushed scribble. 'Gone for meal and out to pictures. Love you. See you about ten. Will cook then, if you're hungry.' He cursed, presumed she'd gone with Duggan, then smoked one of his three remaining cigarettes for the day, the taste of which he washed down with a mug of coffee. Then he took the Bentley out again and made his way to the Victoria Embankment.

He saw Coyle coming down the gangplank of the *Tattersall Castle*. Richardson double-parked the Bentley, much to the annoyance of the cars following in his lane, and strode after him. It was just starting to rain and he wished he'd brought his raincoat, but it was imperative he talked to the Irishman.

'Sean,' he yelled as he approached Coyle.

The Irishman swung round; Richardson could see

he was jumpy. He was obviously surprised to see Richardson there. He smiled, a wary smile, his eyes darting around nervously. 'Hello, Mr Richardson. Didn't expect to see you here.'

Richardson noticed Coyle was in civvies, not wearing his barman's outfit. 'Finish early tonight?'

'Yeah. Wasn't feeling well. They gave me the night off.'

'Take more than a headache to get a tough sod like you to give up work.'

Coyle laughed, his confidence returning. 'Maybe I'm meeting someone worth giving up a night's wages for?'

'I hope you wear a condom, Sean. With all this AIDS going around,' was Richardson's sarcastic rejoinder.

'You know how it is. It always happens to someone else.'

'I need a few minutes before you go.'

'Make it quick, Mr Richardson. I'm late already.'

'Captain Ray Nathaniel mean anything to you?'

'He was an intelligence officer in Lisburn. Captain, or a major.'

'Did he handle you?'

'No, just knew his name. He had a bad reputation. Liked to wade in if he was interrogating you. One of the ones you tried to keep away from.'

'Who did handle you?'

'You did.'

'Don't get smart. Who else? I can find out through other sources.'

Coyle paused before answering. 'There was a Captain George Fleet.'

'From where?'

'Londonderry. He was intelligence, as well.'

Richardson remembered Fleet's name on the Cartel list. He'd been a G3 Int A from 8 Infantry Brigade. Coyle would have been his responsibility, as Int A dealt with Protestant and Loyalists. 'Seen him recently?'

'Not since I left home. Don't even know if he's serving any longer.'

Richardson disbelieved Coyle, but it was instinct rather than the manner in which Coyle replied. 'Was he one of your lot?'

'What? Gay? No chance.' He giggled, then looked at his watch. 'I'm late, Mr Richardson. And getting wet. Can we leave this till another time?'

'You working tomorrow?'

'Tomorrow night.'

'I'll catch you then.'

'Night, Mr Richardson.'

Richardson watched Coyle hurry away. As he turned back to his car, he saw a foot-policeman approaching the Bentley. The rain was heavy now and he ran back, apologized for double-parking and listened patiently to the inevitable lecture. Before he pulled away into the line of traffic, he searched the pavement for Coyle. There was no sign of the Irishman.

At home, Andrea wasn't back so he undressed and went to bed.

When she came in with Duggan at ten-thirty, Sam Richardson was asleep, his thumb in his mouth. She smiled and checked the packet of cigarettes on the bedside table. Two left. She hoped he was finally succeeding.

Then she joined Duggan for a nightcap. She'd enjoyed his company; listened to him purge himself about Carmella and his children. He was a lonely man, looking for something that was only a dream. But he was amusing and she realized she was attracted to him, not as a lover, but as one would be to a close friend, a brother. So she let him talk, and she listened, and nodded sympathetically, and Richardson snored softly and shared his sleep with the nightmares of dying soldiers.

*   *   *

Gabriel watched Richardson run towards his Bentley before opening the door of the Ford Sierra and waving Coyle in.

'Hello, ducky,' he said as Coyle clambered into the passenger seat. 'Who's your friend?'

'An old pal.'

'He doesn't look like one of the boys. More professional than that.'

'He was with your lot in Belfast.'

'What's his name?'

'Sam Richardson. He was a sergeant.'

'Thought you preferred officers?' Gabriel smiled, then leant over and kissed Coyle viciously on the lips, forcing his tongue down the Irishman's throat. Coyle gasped, unprepared for the sudden act, and fought for breath. Gabriel pulled back and laughed as the Irishman choked and started to cough. Out of the corner of his eye he saw Richardson's Bentley go past. He noted the registration number in case they needed it.

'Are you just going to fuck me or have you something planned?'

'Plenty of time for that, my old fruit,' replied Gabriel, putting the Sierra into gear and pulling out from the kerb. He slipped into the right-hand lane to go north. 'We're going to meet a friend of mine. Michael. We've a little job on. In Kilburn.'

'Tonight?' Coyle stiffened; this was the excitement he desperately missed. Kilburn meant they were going after the Republicans.

'In an hour or so. When the pubs are turning out.'

'How much?'

'A couple of grand. Should keep you in the style to which you've become accustomed.'

They drove on in silence for a while. Then Coyle said, 'Are we taking someone out?'

'Probably.'

'The asking price on the street's nearer five grand.'

Gabriel chuckled. 'Don't get greedy. Two's what you'll get. Think of the sport. I presume you still carry that little tool of yours?'

For an answer, a stiletto knife, some eight inches long topped with a white pearl handle, instantaneously appeared in Coyle's right hand. 'For the sport, then,' he said. 'I've been reading the papers.'

'And what do they tell you?'

'About these Angels.'

'And you remembered my code-name and put two and two together.'

'That's what I called you. Gabriel.'

'It was.'

'It's our secret.' Coyle put his hand on Gabriel's thigh and stroked it.

'Make sure you keep it like that.'

'If I'd wanted to turn you in, I'd've done it by now.'

'Then don't just stroke me. Show me how much you really care.' Gabriel took his left hand off the steering wheel and unzipped his trousers. He pulled his stiffening member out and stroked it, then put his arm over the back of Coyle's head and forced him down to his groin. Then he put his hand back on the wheel and drove sedately along, a curious pleasurable smile on his face, as the Irishman noisily worked him to his climax.

It was three in the morning when the bedside phone rang.

Andrea awoke instantly; she was used to emergency calls that resulted in her sometimes going in to the hospital. She had been lying with her arms around Richardson, his back pressed up against her stomach. As she swung round, she felt the first tremors of a hangover. She knew she'd drunk too much wine the night before; it always left her in this condition. She groaned as she picked up the phone, dreading the fact that she probably would have to go in to work. She gave the number to the caller.

'Mr Richardson, please,' a man's voice asked politely at the other end.

Andrea looked at the bedside clock then answered indignantly, 'Do you know what the time is?'

'It's a matter of some urgency, I'm afraid,' the polite voice continued.

'Hold on.' She turned over and gently shook Richardson. He always slept through these late calls; he'd become used to them over the years.

'What?' he grumbled drowsily.

'For you.' She held out the receiver.

He reached up and switched on the bedside light, then took the phone, a worried frown creasing his forehead. She giggled; he reminded her of a basset-hound.

'Yes?' he barked into the phone.

'Mr Richardson?'

Richardson didn't recognize the voice. His training demanded he knew who he was speaking to before he confirmed his own identity. 'Who is this?'

'Emmett. At the office, sir. Mr Carter asked me to call and said he would appreciate you coming in.'

'Now?'

'Yes, sir. Mr Carter's on his way here. According to the police, there's been a slight rumpus.'

'Where?'

'Kilburn, sir.'

'I'll be there in thirty minutes.'

Richardson hung up. 'I've got to go in,' he said. He kissed Andrea and climbed out of bed.

'You're not going away again, are you?' came the concerned response.

'I don't think so. Don't worry, I'll be back soon.'

'I don't suppose you want Francis in on this.'

'If I'm not back in the morning just tell him I

had to leave early for a meeting.'

He left the house quietly, started the Bentley and drove towards central London. He switched the radio on but all he picked up was music on all frequencies; he was between the half-hour news bulletins.

Carter was already there, at his desk, when Richardson arrived. 'Been some action in Kilburn. Did you listen to the news?'

'No. I didn't manage to get anything on the radio.'

'An ambush. Outside Biddy Mulligan's.'

Richardson knew Biddy Mulligan's, a pub on the junction of Kilburn High Road and Willesden Lane. It was one of the places known to be a meeting place for IRA sympathizers, and had been bombed some years earlier by Loyalists. 'Anybody killed?'

'Six. Four men and two women. Two of the men were American.'

'That's all we need.'

'I've spoken to Five and Special Branch. They're happy for you to go down there, in view of our involvement in the Joint Liaison group.'

'What happened?'

'It was near closing time. Two Americans, Boston Irish—'

'Sympathizers.'

'Probably. They came out with a small group. Two men and two women. All Irish.'

'Any known terrorists?'

'One of them was a known gunman. Jimmy Walls. The second man hasn't yet been identified. Neither has one of the women. The second female was Walls's girlfriend, Betty. We don't know her surname. It appears that the six of them had left the pub on their way back to Betty's flat. It wasn't far from Biddy Mulligan's. Special Branch had Walls under surveillance and knew he was staying with her. They hoped he would lead them to an ASU. Anyway, the six of them left the pub and were ambushed about a hundred feet from the building. There were witnesses, some said two men, some said three. There was gun-fire, semi-automatic stuff. Walls and his girl-friend were killed at close-quarters, stabbed.'

'What sort of knives?'

'The bodies have been taken to the pathologist. They should have a primary report soon,' Carter sighed. 'That's about it.'

'So why send me along? That's not usual, for an SIS man to get involved in domestic affairs.'

'I agree. Except this time there are American victims. Because of your man Duggan,' Carter made sure that Duggan was still seen as Richardson's responsibility, 'both Five and Special Branch agree you should remain involved in the case. That'll help mollify Langley and any other Americans who are going to get upset that their citizens are being knocked off on London streets.'

'By the Angels?'

'Probably.'

'Who do I contact?'

'First stop is Kilburn. Biddy Mulligan's. Box have brought Mick Dancer out for this one.'

'Why?'

'He's their best and most experienced counter-terrorist expert. They flew him straight over after the incident.'

'Not the easiest person to get on with.'

Carter was surprised. 'He asked specifically for you.'

Richardson left a few minutes later and drove to Kilburn. The main road running through the centre was cordoned off by police cars, fire-engines and other emergency vehicles.

'I wouldn't drive that beauty down there,' said the policeman, pointing at the Bentley. Richardson had presented his ID card when he was stopped and the policeman signalled him to park next to the barrier.

345

'There's bomb squads looking for devices all round the streets here.'

'Have they been warned of anything?' asked Richardson as he climbed out of the car.

'Don't think so. Just taking precautions.' The policeman swung the barrier open. 'Who're you looking for?'

'MI5 people. Or Special Branch.'

'There's plenty of them about. And if you see a parcel that shouldn't be there, for God's sake yell.'

Richardson walked down the wide deserted street towards the groups that had fanned out and were searching the shops and houses. The area had been evacuated and there was a ghostly, film-set sort of loneliness about the place. The searchers moved in a hushed pattern; it wasn't a time for shouts and excited action.

'Sam!'

Richardson heard his name being called from the group on the left. Mick Dancer emerged from the searchers and walked towards him. 'Hi,' he said when Dancer got closer.

Dancer stuck out his hand and gripped Richardson's in welcome. There was a rare smile on his face. 'Good to see you,' he said. He let go of Richardson's hand. 'Good to see a friendly face. I hate being back here.'

'In London?'

'Yes. Bloody concrete tinseltown.' Dancer led Richardson towards Biddy Mulligan's. 'Believe it or not, I love Northern Ireland. It's not all Belfast shit, you know.' He grinned. 'Of course you know. Nothing better than disappearing into the countryside there. The most beautiful God ever created.' He pushed through one of the bomb squads which was searching some dustbins. 'Waste of time,' he commented to Richardson. 'No bloody bombs here. But, it's what the politicians want. To be seen to be diligent in their duties.' The two men reached Biddy Mulligan's. 'What have they told you?'

'That two Americans were taken out.'

'Shot. Close range. 9mm hand-guns.'

'And four Irish. Two men and two women. One of them was a known gunman.'

'Jimmy Walls. The other Irishman was Damon Fitzpatrick. He was a runner, gophered for various ASUs. Both men were knifed.'

'And the women?'

'Irish again. Girlfriends and known supporters.'

'9mm?'

Dancer nodded, then reached an area where a small forensic group was working under high-intensity lights. Richardson saw the blood on the pavement and some of it splattered against the brick wall. He looked round; it was a good place for an ambush. There were four deep recesses in the brick-wall side of the building. The street lights left a patch of darkness in this section. He suddenly imagined the six victims coming along here, on their way out of the pub, when the assassins stepped out from the darkness and delivered their gruesome message.

'There were three operatives,' continued Dancer. 'Two hand-guns. We found spent shells in those two recesses.' He pointed at the last two. 'From the way we found the bodies, the two girls were leading the way, with the two Yanks behind them. The shooters would have taken care of them. The two PIRA men were behind. Neither of them was armed. I think the third man stepped out from behind as they passed, from that first recess, and knifed either Walls or Fitzpatrick. While he was doing his stuff, the two gunmen stepped out in front of the group and shot them in the head. They must have been good close-quarter men, because they only used eight bullets.'

'That's how we were trained in the SAS. Point-blank range and two bullets to the head for each target.'

'And – they had to make sure they didn't hit the knifeman. He probably shielded himself behind his first

347

victim, then took the second one out as soon as the shots stopped. Those eight shots, four for each gunman, would've taken three seconds at the most.'

'What about the knifeman?'

'He was good. Stiletto blade. Pushed upwards, through the back of the neck, and straight into the brain. Instant result.'

Richardson felt a cold shiver; he knew immediately who it was.

'Any ideas?' asked Dancer.

'No.' Richardson had no choice but to lie.

'We'll find him. I mean, doing it that way will be on someone's file.'

'The Red Hand gangs. Shankhill butchers. The Protestant paramilitaries used it, sort of trademark. What did they call their leader? Spence. A cunt in a cravat, wasn't it?'

'I wondered if you'd remember,' Dancer taunted him.

'I do now. Like you said, it'll all be in the files.' Richardson changed course. 'Didn't anyone hear anything?'

'They used silencers. There were quite a few people around. But it all happened too fast.' Dancer pointed to Messina Avenue. 'They were seen running down there. Nobody saw a getaway car. There could've been a fourth person, a driver waiting for them.'

'Or they used one of the flats round here as a bolt-hole.'

'Don't think so. This wasn't a Provo hit. Nobody can hide around this part of Kilburn who isn't known to Republicans.' Dancer waited while Richardson inspected the area where the killings had taken place. The forensic men looked up with irritation because he disturbed them but knew they couldn't object. Richardson came back to Dancer.

'I don't think Walls was a specific target,' Richardson said.

'Why not?'

'Because the killers couldn't have waited there for long without being seen by someone. I think they were waiting for the pubs to turn out, then walked down here and waited for the first potential victims. Probably recognized Walls. That was a bonus.'

'Unless one of the group deliberately brought him out at a precise time.'

'Except they were all killed.'

Dancer shrugged. 'It's one way of getting rid of someone who might talk.'

'Can't see it. There's no advantage in taking out the Americans. Probably didn't even know they were Yanks.'

'Yes. Really unlucky, that,' Dancer commented drily. 'They all think it's a bloody Mickey Rourke film. Serves them right, getting caught in the shit with the rest of us.'

'If it's the Angels, it's to show they can hit right at the heart of the IRA supporters. Right here in Kilburn. They're revenging Collett.' He looked up sharply at Dancer. 'What's the game? You've worked all this out, anyway.'

The Five man nodded. 'Nice to see you're as good as your reputation.'

'Meaning?'

'Have you and your CIA chap discussed the Florida and Schipol phone calls?'

'No.' Richardson had guessed that Dancer already knew about the transatlantic calls.

'The voice prints show it was Gabriel at Schipol. We matched the call with the one made after the Amsterdam killings. Absolutely no doubt. By the way, we've told Langley that we've traced the calls. No secrets between us now, are there?' He shook his head in disgust. 'We also checked if there was a flight leaving for London soon after the Schipol transatlantic. There was. To Heathrow.'

'So there's two of them loose over here.'

'If his friend Michael is up to the same game, yes.'

'But three people were used on this little caper.'

'Looks like they had local support.' He watched Richardson closely, but the SIS man gave nothing away. Dancer sensed he knew something which he wasn't sharing. 'You remember the Plan, the one you mentioned during your interview with Morrison?'

'Yes.'

'It was called Operation Cartel.'

'I know.' Richardson decided to get Dancer off his back, so he showed one of the cards he had up his sleeve.

Dancer was genuinely surprised. 'Have you read it?'

'No.' The lie came easily to Richardson.

'But you know it exists. As do, I presume, your masters at Six.'

'Of course.'

'Have they got a copy?'

'Probably.'

'And does your Mr Duggan have access to that information?'

'Of course not. But I'd like to know who Morrison saw in New York before he caught his plane.'

'I'll ask. But he may decline to tell me.'

Richardson started to walk towards his car and Dancer followed him. 'I suppose you're checking all these flats and shops for anything to do with the Provos.' Richardson gestured to the empty buildings around them.

'Too right,' Dancer chuckled. 'Having cleared the whole area because of a bomb threat, we're now searching for documents in offices, searching bed-sits, clothes in wardrobes, anything for clues regarding the IRA. Shit, it's like being allowed into Downing Street after the bobby on the front door's been sent away. We're even planting bugs as we go along.' He laughed loudly. 'I mean, they can't all move out of Kilburn, can they? It'll take them forever to find all the things we've been up to.'

Richardson said he would contact Dancer the next morning, then drove the Bentley home.

It was after six when he let himself in. Andrea had taken her hangover to work on the early shift and he made some toast and coffee. There was little point in going to bed, not when he knew who the knifeman in Kilburn was. He set out the lists he and Duggan had drawn up and he studied them again, trying to find that little clue that the two of them could have missed.

Duggan found him still there an hour later.

'Mind if I get some coffee?' the American asked.

'Help yourself.' Richardson watched Duggan make himself a cup of decaf; he was still in his pyjamas. 'Sleep well, did you?' he said with more than a hint of irritation.

'Didn't you?' came the bemused answer.

'Two IRA men, their girlfriends, and two visiting Yanks from Boston were killed in Kilburn last night. Shot and knifed. Very Mafia.'

'What were the Americans doing there?'

'No idea. As they can't tell us. But you can take it for granted they were sympathizers.'

'Or journalists.'

'Their passports said they were businessmen. Probably supplying arms to these bastards.' Richardson felt the irrational anger welling inside him. 'For a profit. Under the name of patriotism.'

Duggan slammed down his coffee. 'What is the matter with you? Is it just that you don't like us because we're—' He stopped.

'What? Better than us?'

'You're nuts.'

'That's what you think, though. That we're some second-rate nation. That we deserve what we get for enslaving those poor fucking Irish.'

'Let's forget all this.'

'No!' bellowed Richardson. 'Is that why you didn't tell me about the call between Schipol Airport and Flamingo Drive?' He saw Duggan look up sharply. 'Yeah. I know about it. Because we traced it, too. You fucking knew about it and you didn't bloody say.'

'Look who's talking. I'm the dickhead who was wired in Belfast. Don't tell me you didn't know about that.'

'I didn't. And, like I told you, by the time I found out it was too late.'

Duggan shook his head and sat down at the table. *Charisma bypass, indeed. Who did the bastard think he was, anyway?* He drank angrily from his cup. 'OK,' he said eventually. 'So we're both pissed off with each other. Let's start again.'

'You already said that.'

'This time let's do it. Tell me about Kilburn.'

Richardson went through the events of the night before. He included his meeting with Dancer. The only part he kept to himself was the details for Operation Cartel and the names involved. Those were state secrets; the sort he was paid to protect.

'Will Morrison give him the name?'

'I don't know.'

'My instinct always told me that was the key.'

Richardson dropped his bombshell. 'I know who the knifeman was.' He watched Duggan freeze, his cup halfway to his lips. He waited until the American turned to look at him. 'Sean Coyle.'

'Your barman friend?'

'That was his favourite way of disposing of the Catholics. It became a trademark; in the end most of the Prods used it. But Coyle was the first. Had a pearl-handled knife. Probably still using it.'

'Who else knows?'

'Just us. But I can't hold it for ever.'

'You going to see Coyle yourself?'

'I don't know how to play it yet. Why don't you get dressed, then we'll talk about it.'

Duggan finished his coffee and went to the door. 'Any other surprises?'

'I think I've got a good idea who Gabriel is.'

'Jesus,' came the soft reply.

'I want Coyle to confirm it. Until then, this thing's between us. OK?'

This time Richardson believed Duggan when he nodded assent. For now, they needed each other to find answers.

Burt and Jack's Restaurant
Port Everglades
Fort Lauderdale
Florida

Hank Mickleton waited alone in the famous restaurant's Oak Room. He had arrived early for the meeting; his plane from Washington National having touched down at Fort Lauderdale International less than an hour earlier. He took a cab straight to the restaurant for the luncheon meeting that he had called before leaving DC. The main FBI office was in Miami, but he decided not to visit the local centre and advertise his presence until the operation was under way.

The restaurant, owned and run by film actor Burt Reynolds and restaurateur Jack Jackson, was sited on the edge of the city's large port which had the distinction of being the world's largest cruise-ship harbour, serving the Bahamas and Caribbean. The restaurant, sitting on a small promontory, looked out on the port and the city beyond, an ideal site for one of the world's most romantic eateries. The Oak Room was a private dining-room in the centre of the restaurant, its wood-panelled walls hung with signed photographs of the many sporting and entertainment giants who always visited Burt and Jack's when they were in town.

The restaurant was always closed at lunch-time, but the Miami FBI office had rung and asked for it to be opened specially and a small staff laid on to feed the FBI men. They knew no passers-by drove down the dead end that led to the restaurant during the luncheon hour.

Mickleton looked at the photos that surrounded him. Baseball legend Mickey Mantle stared back at him. Next to him was Miami Dolphins quarter-back Dan Marino and another baseball star, Moose Skrowron. The names, known to millions of Americans, meant nothing to Mickleton. To him, his responsibilities to the Bureau were all that mattered. He was a man devoid of humour, of compassion, of understanding. In the true tradition of J. Edgar Hoover, Mickleton saw himself following in the tradition of the great man, except wearing skirts, high heels and suspender-belted stockings was not something Hank Mickleton had the imagination, or inclination, to do. Like most FBI men, Mickleton found it difficult to believe that Hoover was now portrayed as a notorious homosexual who regularly wore women's clothes and used his position to satisfy his sexual fantasies.

While he waited, a glass of iced water in front of him, he thought back to the CTC meeting in the SitRoom of the White House. The NSA had called it early; they had all sat down at seven in the morning, muffins and coffee in the middle of the table.

They were getting nowhere and they all knew it. For all the power they commanded, for all the terror and fear they could instil in others, the men who controlled the security services of the greatest nation on earth were fighting a losing battle.

Or as the NSA had painfully pointed out, 'We don't even know where the battlefield is.' He held up that morning's *Washington Post*. The lead story and covering picture dealt with the death of the two Americans in Kilburn. 'The President says we have to react.'

'Where?' asked a frustrated Lacelle. 'Where on earth do we go next?'

'We can't even trust the British any more,' added Mickleton, turning to the CIA's McNabb. 'My people in London say that Duggan was wired when he went walkabout in Belfast. Story is that's how they found out about Baxter going to Orlando.' He repeated the rumour the legal attaché had passed back about Fergal Baxter's holiday via Duggan's hidden microphone, no doubt passed on by MI5 or Special Branch colleagues.

'Duggan can't verify that,' came the defensive reply. McNabb had heard the same rumour. 'Where'd you get that from?'

'Sources.' Mickleton knew he was safe there; the unwritten rule amongst security heads was that they never revealed their informants.

'Well, let's get some facts before spreading rumours,' replied McNabb tetchily. 'It's a goddamned shame we missed Baxter at Orlando.'

Mickleton shrugged the barb off. 'If SIGINT City had got through to us earlier . . . Hell, do you know how many thousands of tourists pour through Orlando every day?'

The NSA took charge again. 'You're covering Disney World?' he asked Mickleton.

'Yeah. Orlando comes under our Tampa operation, but they've only got about a hundred and fifty agents. So we've drafted in extra help from Miami. We're covering the entrance gates in both the Magic Kingdom and Epcot. Disney World's security chief is an ex-bureau man, so he's in on the operation. That means we've got access to all their security staff as well as hotel receptionists, entrance and parking-lot personnel. There's operatives mixing with the crowds, riding the mono-rail system, checking through all the local hotels, both in Disney World and Orlando. The photo of Baxter has been restructured to include blond, cropped hair, similar to the description we got from Immigration at Orlando. We've run computer checks on Donnelly through the hotels, but nothing's come up that fits the family's profile. We're also checking under Baxter and McCarthy—'

'Why McCarthy?'

'His wife's name. Still drew a blank. That means he's either changed to another alias, or else he's moved out of the area.'

'There is also the tricky problem of what we do if we find him,' said Lacelle.

'We have no reason to arrest him. Other than for travelling on a false passport. I mean, even the Brits haven't anything on him. A big dossier, but nothing concrete, like most of these Army Council guys. Shit, we can't hold him for terrorizing Mickey Mouse.' Mickleton grimaced at the futility of it all. 'Even if we catch him going out of the country, all he'll yell is that he was travelling under an assumed name to protect his kids. So we deport him back to Ireland. That's where he'll want to go anyway.'

'Unless we trace him, put him under surveillance, then trap him with his contact over here,' said McNabb.

'We don't even know that. He could just be on vacation. Like the British said.'

McNabb snorted. 'Like hell. He'll be over arranging arms or something equally devious.'

The men round the table looked at each other; the discussion, like so many before, was going round in circles. Hard facts, that's what they needed, concrete information.

'I think you should head this thing yourself, Hank.' The NSA broke the silence. 'Get down to Miami and take charge.'

'I can run it equally well from here.'

356

'The President wants us to be seen reacting. The death of two more Americans makes that even more necessary. We'd like you down in Florida.'

Mickleton had looked round the table. The others stone-walled him back. He sighed; there was always a scapegoat and now they were choosing him to walk down towards the execution block alone.

'Hey, that's Mickey Mantle,' he heard a voice behind him now as the door opened in the Oak Room.

Mickleton swung round and stared at the intruder. It was one of the FBI Miami Desk assistant directors. The man froze when he saw Mickleton, and he smiled apologetically, then entered the room. There were eight men in total, all section heads of the various local FBI zones. When they were seated, Mickleton, without any welcoming statement, got straight to the point. 'Anything on the American victims in Kilburn?' he asked.

'No, sir,' replied the Special Agent in Charge of the Miami Field Office, Confessor Bonnilo. A forty-three-year-old of Cuban heritage, Bonnilo was used to dealing with the diverse tourist trade that flowed through South Florida. International affairs with the IRA in Europe were not part of his everyday brief. 'All we've got so far is that they're both from Boston, both Irish-American, both were happily married with kids. One was a plastic surgeon, the other a tile salesman.'

'Not a lot in common to be travelling together.'

'They were golf nuts. Went away on golfing trips, were playing partners at the same club. But, apart from a moral – well, more an emotional tie, to the Irish cause, it would appear that the doctor was over there on a convention and his friend went along for a short vacation and a game of golf.'

'Did they have their clubs with them?'

'No. But the hotel confirmed they had one game at somewhere called Wentworth. Just outside London.'

'Wow! That's a great—' The assistant director who

357

had commented on Mickey Mantle stopped sharply.

'Great what?' asked Mickleton.

'Golf-course.'

'If I need any more sporting information, I'll ask.' Mickleton signalled Bonnilo to continue.

'We contacted the club and they'd both played there, hired clubs for a game.' Bonnilo scratched his chin. 'To be honest with you, I think they just went out for a drink into the Irish area and got caught in the cross-fire.'

'Walking down the road with a known IRA gunman?' Mickleton asked incredulously.

Bonnilo held firm. 'For what it's worth, yes.' He was a man who stood his ground. 'I think that's what happened. These guys have absolutely no link to the IRA. Nothing. Maybe they got talking to this guy and he said he was IRA and they said they supported him so he thought he'd get something out of them. I don't know. But there is nothing to show they have ever had any connections with NORAID or any other IRA organization. Apart from supporting Irish-American organizations within the Boston community. You know, fund-raising dinners, that sort of stuff. More social than political.'

Another full stop. Mickleton's stomach churned. The execution block got closer. 'It's up to us to bring this to a quick and successful conclusion. The Press are jumping up and down on us, already blaming us for killings that were outside our jurisdiction. They say the USG should've warned any Americans abroad not to get involved in areas where they could be taken for IRA supporters.' He slammed his fist on the desk; the others reacted nervously. 'For Christ's sake, they can't blame us because some crazy Boston Irish decided to go drinking in Kilburn. And the British press are turning the screws on. Damn tabloid gutter shit; they're screaming about America supporting the terrorists. Shit, after Lockerbie and the World Trade Center bombing, that's the last thing we want. Especially after all the help we've given the Brits against the IRA.' He stopped, his face reddened with anger. He took some deep breaths and calmed down. There was no point in wasting his energy against his own men.

Then he became the professional once again and turned their attention to increasing the hunt for Baxter, alias Donnelly, alias anyone the Irishman had decided to become.

Cork
Eire

They met in a small park to the south of the city. The rain hammered down mercilessly.

The six council members had travelled separately south from Dublin, all surrounded by armed wingers. They knew this was to be their last meeting until the Angels were dealt with, otherwise they were putting themselves in unnecessary and extreme danger. The killings in Kilburn had proved that. This meeting had been hurriedly called.

They sat in a huddled circle and talked in the park, the wingers scattered around the perimeter and in the trees, ever watchful for any sign of danger. One of the wingers carried a ghetto-blaster and the sounds of a local radio station blared across the park. The men in the small circle spoke softly, keeping their lip movements to a minimum, speaking as though they were ventriloquists. In this way they ensured that no watcher with a long lens could lip-read their conversation and that no scanner could pick up their words across the ghetto-blaster's noise.

The conversation soon turned to their biggest concern: the effect the Angels were having on their funds and supplies. The PIRA needed a minimum of £4.5 million a year to function. The raids on their overseas contacts would soon have the effect of forcing their supporters to break contact with the IRA factions. Many of the Boston Irish had already cancelled trips to Ireland because they were afraid of reprisals against them. The death of the two Americans outside Biddy Mulligan's would certainly add to that. It wasn't so much the American funds that concerned them; those were minimal now anyway since the FBI clamped down. It was the support in the vociferous publicity against the British government that counted, as well as the American President's fear of losing the Irish-American vote as he neared an election. And the Irish-American ability to arrange arms and explosives shipments. Any further escalation by the Angels would have a damaging effect on the Americans and force the IRA to rely more on its links with the Eastern European countries. But that brought its own dangers. The British could bring economic muscle to bear on the former Soviet Bloc nations who, having supplied weapons and explosives, then gave confidential information to HMG on secret arms shipments for the Loyalist terrorists as well as the PIRA. What really hurt was that the goods had been paid for, even though British and Irish customs intercepted the shipments.

In the end, having reached no conclusion, the Army Council decided to continue their actions on the mainland as before. Only this time they were more subdued in their approach, less strident in their call for revenge. The sheer speed and savage reaction of the Angels made them uneasy and extremely vulnerable.

The meeting broke up half an hour later. They all went their separate ways, back into their own anonymity.

'It's all right for Fergal bloody Baxter,' was Griffin's parting shot at Father O'Malley. 'He's bloody soaking up the sun.'

The ex-priest turned his collar to the rain. Aye, it was all right for some. Bloody lucky bastard.

**Twenty miles south of Orlando
Florida**

Penuel sat by the swimming-pool and watched the Baxter family enjoy themselves.

He was impressed with Baxter's professionalism.

The man had dyed his hair red and absorbed as much sun-tan as possible. There was no hint of the fair-haired, pale-skinned man who had walked through Immigration at Orlando Airport. Baxter had also moved to a new hotel after the first night. This time he was registered as Michael Patton. When Penuel reported that back, Lucifer guessed that Baxter would do that every day, thereby making it almost impossible to be traced.

'I can move in now,' said Penuel. 'Slot him in a couple of seconds.'

'No,' ordered a thoughtful Lucifer. 'Maybe it's time to change tactics. With a little help from us, we could learn more about the PIRA. Now wouldn't that be something. All that information, straight from the horse's mouth.'

'Do you want me to progress things here?'

'Wait for the others to come back. Michael should be leaving any time now. Calling from Gatwick, to confuse any listeners in the sky. Then he's driving up to Manchester and catching a flight to Miami. He'll be here in the morning.'

'And Gabriel?'

'Tidying up. He'll be back soon.'

Elgin Place
Hammersmith
London W6

Sam Richardson was leaving the house with Duggan when the phone rang. It was twelve-thirty and they were on their way to the *Tattersall Castle*.

It was Carter, who read him the transcript of a call that had been made to *Today* newspaper. ' "The execution of the murderers Jimmy Walls and Damon Fitzpatrick, and their two supporters, was in accordance with the Rules of Engagement as laid down by the Irish Republican Army. In an attempt to fight fire with fire, as the only means now left open to resolve the question of Irish terrorism, Soldiers Michael and Gabriel, under orders of the Highest Command, carried out the execution of the criminals Jimmy Walls and Damon Fitzpatrick. Should the acts of violence by the Republicans continue, then the Highest Command will have no alternative but to order quick and terrible retribution against those who are the enemies to a peaceful and just solution for the Irish situation. The deaths of two Americans were not planned, but should serve as a warning to those who are prepared to help the IRA and other terrorist organizations in the future." '

'Surprise, surprise,' commented Richardson. 'That's two accounted for. Our Box man believes there were three.' Richardson knew that Carter understood he meant Dancer.

'Do you?'

'Yes. And if they've only admitted two, then the third will remain in the UK.'

'That's Dancer's view. They, and the boys in blue, are running checks on all the airports and ports. Running names through the computer.'

'I saw some names yesterday. In your office. We should run those names as well.' Richardson meant the

SAS and other covert operators who had been included as part of Operation Cartel.

'Already done. I don't suppose we need to run a check on you.' The joke was lost on Richardson. 'Are you coming in?'

'I was going back to Kilburn,' lied Richardson.

'Alone?'

'With the American. He asked to see the place.'

'All right. Call me if anything comes up.'

The traffic was heavy so, rather than drive, Richardson flagged down a taxi and instructed the driver to go to the Victoria Embankment. They got out half a mile from the *Tattersall Castle* and walked along the Embankment. Richardson wanted to ensure he wasn't being followed, or that the floating restaurant wasn't under surveillance.

He saw nothing.

Gabriel recognized Richardson from the evening before. The Angel sat in the front of one of the long lines of coaches that always parked along the Embankment. He had recognized one of the drivers as gay, made advances and now sat in the coach flirting outrageously. It was an ideal surveillance point. He saw Richardson and Duggan cross the gangplank and enter the ship.

Sean Coyle smiled at them from behind the bar but the look on Richardson's face told him this was no social visit. 'What can I get for you gentlemen?' Coyle asked, wiping the bar in front of them as they sat down.

There was a couple by one of the windows, lost in each other's emotions; apart from them there was no-one else in the saloon.

'You were busy last night, Sean.' Richardson got straight to the point.

The barman grinned. 'Only in what I always do, Mr Richardson. Having a good time, that is. Now, what would you like to drink?'

'A beer for me and . . .' Richardson turned to Duggan.

'Diet soda – uh, Coke.'

'Right away, sir,' acknowledged Coyle, turning away to open a bottle of beer.

Richardson watched him. 'Biddy Mulligan's,' he continued as Coyle poured the drinks. 'Messy job. But professional. Had your hallmark, Sean. Long stiletto in the base of the neck. Shoved upwards. Straight into the brain and the victim dies instantly. Not too much mess, no noise and bloody effective.'

'So that's how they were cut,' said Coyle, putting the glasses in front of the two men. As he spoke, he poured from both bottles, one in his left hand and one in his right. 'I read about it in the morning papers. That they'd been knifed.' He grinned at Duggan. 'Was my game, that. I suppose Mr Richardson's told you,' he finished chillingly.

'Who set it up, Sean?' asked Richardson.

'Not me. That was the old days.'

'Whoever it was knew you from the old days. That's why they involved you.'

Coyle put the bottles in a container behind the bar, then leant on the counter. 'That sort of talk could get me into trouble, Sergeant.'

'Of your own making.'

'No. Listen, I'm glad those Provos got stuffed. They deserve it. But it wasn't me. The last thing I want is trouble with the police. Things are good for me. I'm not going to risk that.'

'How much for the job? Three, four grand?'

'I hope you're not spreading rumours to the authorities, Mr Richardson. Getting me into trouble.'

'Your hallmark. And you left early last night.'

'That's just a coincidence. Me getting involved in that game is as unlikely as seeing Lord Lucan ride by on Shergar.'

Richardson grinned; the joke was lost on Duggan. Coyle had always been one of the coolest operators the Englishman knew. 'Rumour, according to Special Branch, is that you occasionally hire out for a job.' Richardson was lying now, but he wanted to see how far he could push the Irishman. 'They've never had the evidence, but that's what they believe.'

'Nah! If they did, they would've pulled me in for questioning. I'm a good boy.' Coyle smirked. 'As far as that's concerned, anyway.'

'What about George Fleet?'

'What about him?'

'Is he an Angel?' Richardson asked softly.

'You're off beam, Sergeant. Don't know what you're talking about.'

Richardson saw the almost imperceptible flicker somewhere deep in Coyle's eyes; the Irishman had been disconnected for a second. It wasn't much, just a recognition that Richardson had hit home. He stood up, his drink untouched. 'You know me, Sean. I go on pushing until something gives.'

'I know you better than most, Mr Richardson.'

'Remember me. As I was. Don't underestimate what I'm capable of.'

Richardson swung round and started to walk towards the door, Duggan hopping off his stool to follow.

'Mr Richardson,' appealed Coyle.

The couple by the window looked up, startled by his loudness. Richardson and Duggan came back to the counter.

'You're getting me into deep trouble.' There was no response from Richardson. Coyle realized the Englishman would probably walk out of the bar and straight to the authorities. He was convinced that Richardson hadn't said anything yet, otherwise Special Branch would be swarming all over the *Tattersall Castle*. 'If I know anything, then now's not the time to tell you,' he stalled.

'When?'

'When I've found something.'

'No.' Richardson was adamant.

'I've never let you down before.'

'You weren't this deeply involved before. Not since you left Belfast. It is Fleet, isn't it?'

Coyle made no pretence of denying it. 'I'll see what I can come up with. No promises. But you'll have to wait. I'm off tonight. I'll start then, try and have something for you tomorrow.'

'Tomorrow.' Richardson left the threat unsaid. He turned and walked out with Duggan behind him.

'He knows something, doesn't he?' said Duggan as they walked down the gangplank.

'I think so.' Richardson stopped on the pavement and looked around. No sign of anyone watching, but his instinct told him someone was out there, that he was in someone's sights. 'I need to go into the office,' he said.

'They want me to drop in at Grosvenor Square.'

'We'll get a cab. Then I'll meet you. I think we could be busy tonight.'

Duggan didn't ask why; after all, this was Richardson's territory. They hailed a passing taxi.

Gabriel watched them go and knew that Coyle needed talking to.

As soon as Richardson dropped Duggan, he rang Dancer on his portable.

'What can I do for you?' asked the Five man, surprised to hear from Richardson.

'I'd like to meet. And you need to bring along some information.'

'On what?'

'I need info on a Captain George Fleet. G3 Intelligence A—'

'I know him,' cut in Dancer. 'Remember this is an open line. Anyone else?'

'Ray Nathaniel.'

'I know him, too.'

'What don't you know?'

'Not enough. Sounds like you've been a busy boy. Hope you've got something to trade?'

'Of course.'

'OK. Let's meet for coffee. InterContinental. Park Lane. Give me an hour.'

Richardson returned to the office and followed the police reports on Biddy Mulligan's. There was nothing new, just a mass of eyewitness accounts of people saying they had seen nothing; shadows chased, sounds of imagined gun-fire and people screaming. It all amounted to nothing. The pathologist's report had been faxed over and he flipped through it. The killers were professional; it was a copy-book SAS close-quarters raid. He was surprised no-one had left behind any orange armbands. There was also an FBI document on the dead Americans. They were typical Irish-Americans, in love with a dream of a republic for a country they had long since abandoned. He chuckled; give the Yanks a chance to come back and live on the Emerald Isle without air-conditioning and fast-food stores, and they'd run a mile.

He arrived at the InterContinental at the same time as Dancer and followed him through the revolving door into the lobby. The two men found a corner table and ordered some coffee.

'So who's been a naughty boy and shown you the Cartel file?' asked Dancer.

'Cartel?'

'Better than you have tried to mess me about, sunshine. Fleet and Nathaniel. They're part of Cartel. And that ties in with what's going on.' Dancer looked round the lounge; coffee-tables full of high tea and businessmen trying to impress each other. 'Be something if a bomb went off here. Right now. They'd soon wonder why a Box man was having tea with someone from Six. Probably tie us in with Cartel as well.'

'Point taken. Yes, I know about Cartel.'

'You lied to me before. About not having seen it.' Dancer didn't wait for a response. 'At least I know Six had a copy.'

'I didn't say we did.'

'Yeah. Pull the other one. Seriously, I thought we'd junked all the spares. There was only one with us and one at the War Office. Under bloody lock and key. I suppose you feel the way I do. That someone's activated the Cartel Plan.' He waited while the waitress brought them cups and poured the coffee. After they had refused a plate of sandwiches and Richardson lit up his seventh cigarette of the day, much to Dancer's annoyance, they were finally on their own. 'Why does Fleet interest you?'

'Who is he?'

'Just a name on the Cartel list. Like Nathaniel. What makes you think they're involved?'

'Didn't say they were.'

'Don't piss me about, Sam.' Dancer leant back in his chair. 'I know all about you, about that little accident in South Armagh. Not so easy to live with—'

'There was no proof—'

'Come on, Sam. We all freeze sometimes. Everyone knows what happened.' Dancer crouched forward, intense in his posture. 'I'm no sadist, you know. I don't keep extending my tour of duty in Belfast because I enjoy it. No, it's fucking revenge. Nothing more than that. My wife and kid were over in Northern Ireland. I didn't want them there, but she said we should stick together. I was only posted as a stand-by replacement for six months. In 1990. My wife went round with the sprog to see a friend of hers; wife of an RUC officer who'd put herself out for us when we first came over. Bad luck, really. The Provos hit the family in their house when the officer came home. Boom. Took him out, his missus and

mine as well. Then, as they were leaving, they tossed a
grenade in for good measure. Another boom, and I was
the only one left in the Dancer family.' There was an
iciness to the man as he spoke, a cynical objectivity, as
though he were talking about just another case history.
Richardson realized the Five man had never allowed the
emotion of the experience to touch him. 'Nobody is as
dedicated as me to getting those Irish bastards killed.
But it's got to be done legally. Just because I lost my
family to terrorists, doesn't mean I'll break the law to
hit back at them. Otherwise we're no different, are we?'
Dancer eased the sudden tension out of his body with a
long sigh. 'So give me what you've got and we'll finish
this together.'

Richardson told the Five man about Sean Coyle
and his method of killing when he had been a member
of the Red Hand.

'You knew that last night, in Kilburn, didn't you?'
Dancer commented when Richardson had finished.

'Yes.'

'I thought you'd sussed something. Doesn't matter.
What's he got to do with George Fleet?'

'Fleet handled him.'

'So did you. And you're on the list.'

'Stuff you.' Richardson dismissed Dancer's cheap
jibe. 'Listen, the phone call this morning claiming
responsibility said two Angels were involved. Michael
and Gabriel. We both know that three people took part
in the killings. It has to be someone they can't mention,
someone who is vulnerable because he's out in the open.
A contract man. Last night Coyle left work early. The
method the knifeman used was one he perfected. It all
points to him.'

'And Nathaniel?'

'I don't know. I just wanted to know who else
planned the operation with Morrison.'

'Morrison and some other intelligence people had an

input, but the architects were Fleet and Nathaniel. Fleet was a bad one. Sadistic brat. And queer as a five-bob note.'

'How the hell did he keep his position? The Army and SAS are extra diligent about that.'

'Occasionally, someone gets through the checks.'

'Coyle's bent as well.'

'Is he? Anyway, the story was that Fleet worked with the Protestant gangs against the PIRA. I don't know how much truth there is in that, but as the intelligence officer responsible for the Loyalists, he would certainly have plenty of opportunities to warn them of any danger. He was almost court-martialled over an interrogation where he supposedly caught a PIRA man in some fields near Armagh, then stuck needles under his toe-nails. Long, four-inch needles. Then he slowly cut the man's tendons, one by one, like a bloody surgeon.'

'And we kept him on?'

'Couldn't prove anything. Moved him to the Rhine in the end. Vicious bastard. Not a lot on Nathaniel. Once again, too aggressive. Liked to go in and rough up the opposition. Moved him to a desk job in the end, out of the province. He had your desk at Six, didn't he? Didn't last long. Not really SIS's type. And no, he wasn't a poofter. There's nothing to link him to Fleet. Or Coyle.'

'Except they served at the same time. And had aggressive table manners.'

'As they say, you judge a man by the company he keeps. One more thing. Small, but suddenly noteworthy. Fleet's code-name was Avenger.'

'Avenger?'

'Avenging Angel?' Dancer raised his eyebrows. 'That was his signature. I think we need to find Coyle?'

'He's not working tonight. But I have a good idea where he's going to be.'

'It would help if we could talk to him.'

Richardson told Dancer about Duggan, that he had been present at the meeting with the Irishman.

'Was that wise?'

'I don't know. We're a bit thin on trust. Between us.'

'His masters in Washington think we're involved. Officially.'

'Are we?'

Dancer shrugged, a big mocking grin across his face. 'Wouldn't it be shit if we were? Now that would get everyone jumping.' Dancer paused, a frown flitting across his face before he continued. 'I've been at the sharp end for too long to trust anyone. I mean, the thing I can't get to grips with is who's funding it. This sort of operation needs excellent logistics and a ready supply of considerable cash. Well-laundered cash. Non-traceable cash. That's what I can't fathom.'

'Does that mean . . . ?'

'Just that. I don't trust anyone. Above me or below me. And I suggest you do the same. Just do your job as you see it. Do what you believe in. Leave the games to the experts.' Dancer snorted. 'They're good at it. That's all they do, from the Prime Minister down. Super bloody Nintendo freaks playing with real targets.' He paused, then said, 'You don't sympathize with the Angels, do you, Sam?'

'Don't you?'

Dancer was taken aback by the suddenness of the rejoinder. He grinned, to relax the tension. 'Sometimes. But, just enough to be human. Trouble is, Sam, you and me, we can't afford the luxury of seeing the other side.'

When Duggan returned to the flat, just after eight, Richardson was waiting for him.

'Have you eaten?' Richardson asked.

'Yes.' He had shared a quick meal with the legal attaché in the Embassy commissary.

'Good. Don't bother taking your coat off. We're going out.'

They drove in the Bentley towards Hampstead Heath. Richardson took the American through his meeting with Dancer. His concern over Coyle was genuine; Richardson was convinced that Coyle had been part of the Biddy Mulligan's group and that his old-handler, George Fleet, might well be deeply involved with the Angels. If that were so, then Coyle was in immediate danger, mostly because he knew too much. 'Have your people come up with anything yet?' he asked Duggan when he had finished.

'No.' Duggan ignored Richardson's quizzical look. This time he had nothing to hide. 'The FBI are stepping up their activity. Drafting more agents in.'

'What about Fergal Baxter?'

'No luck. Unless they're not telling me. Where are we going?'

'Hampstead Heath. To find Coyle.'

'You really are worried about him.'

'I'm convinced he was the third man.'

'And that Fleet's an Angel. Because his code-name was Avenger.'

'It's all we've got, Francis. Coyle's our only direct link to them. Let's just say we need to protect our assets. Our only fucking asset.'

FBI Miami Field Office
16320 NW 2nd Avenue
North Miami Beach
Florida

Confessor Bonnilo, Special Agent in Charge of the Miami office, passed responsibility for the operation to one of his Assistant SACs, Jerry Reilly. Reilly, a second-generation Irish-American, had no doubt as to where his loyalty lay; it was to protect the US government from any terrorist activity, Irish or otherwise. He had never supported the Republicans' view of a united Ireland; the only land he had any view on was the US of A.

Reilly put two squads together, each with its own supervisor. One was dedicated to liaising with the Tampa field office and helping track Fergal Baxter. The other, the larger of the two squads, concentrated its efforts in finding the possible whereabouts of the Angels between Miami, Fort Lauderdale and the West Coast of Florida.

'I need more resources,' said Solomon Jiggs, supervisor of the second squad.

'We're stretched already,' replied Bonnilo. 'I can authorize about twenty more agents. That's all. We're pulling them off the Caribbean end and white-collar crimes.'

'How can I cover the Everglades? That's over a million acres of wetlands. Not to forget all the conurbations.'

'The NSA have okayed any satellite surveillance you might need,' added Reilly.

'Great. If we know what we're looking for.' Jiggs knew there was no point in pushing for what wasn't there. 'We're concentrating our efforts on identifying all the British and Irish people and organizations over here. Everything, from financial companies to an old woman who owns a pet parlour. I tell you,' Jiggs shook his head, 'I didn't realize how many Brits have moved to Florida. I mean, they're into everything.' He decided to change the subject. His team was good, they just needed time, no hassle and a few breaks. 'Any luck on Baxter?'

His superiors looked at each other. 'No,' said Bonnilo, shaking his head. Things were not going as smoothly as he'd hoped. But at least Mickleton was off his back, having flown to Orlando to direct the search for the missing Irishman. The London legal attaché had wired

373

a more up-to-date picture of Baxter that he had received from MI5. 'They're intensifying their effort in Disney World. Anyway, let's concentrate on our end. Go on, Solomon,' he grinned at Jiggs. 'Get outta here and stop changing the subject when I'm talking about something else.'

Jiggs chuckled and left the room.

'He's the guy to find them – if they're in our neck of the woods,' supported Reilly.

'Yeah. If they're in our neck of the woods.'

While Hank Mickleton waited for the reports to come in from the hotels about Irish holiday-makers, Penuel watched Fergal Baxter and his family leave the small, off-road family hotel to the south of Lake Kissimmee.

Baxter was in an old-model, open-top Chrysler Le-Baron, his wife beside him and the kids in the back. The Irishman had rented the car from a Rent-A-Wreck company outside Kissimmee. It was a good move as the rental firm was not one of the large companies and therefore had no central computer that the FBI could monitor. But that also suited Penuel; the convertible made his task easier.

He turned over the Thunderbird and swung out after Baxter.

In his rear-view mirror he saw Raphael take up his position in the green Dodge pick-up. Lucifer had gone to pick up Michael at Fort Lauderdale International, where he was returning from England on an American Airlines flight from Manchester, changing at Chicago.

As Penuel followed the LeBaron, he realized that Baxter was getting confident, that he had almost returned to his normal self and had made little effort to disguise himself.

He followed the Irishman north, back towards Disney World, Raphael following behind.

The two Angels tailed Baxter to his next hotel,

alternating surveillance, thus making it difficult for the Irishman to realize they were behind him.

Baxter was finally winding down, but the Angels retained their vigilance as the three cars drove towards Orlando.

Hampstead Heath
London

They left the Bentley at Jack Straw's Castle and walked towards the west part of the Heath.

'I'm glad it's not the middle of summer,' said Richardson. 'There'd be hundreds of people here, some of them even run barbecues and picnics. Sex with the vegeburger, eh?'

'Can this end up violent?' Duggan asked nervously.

'No,' grinned Richardson. 'Not unless you join in some of their fun and games.' He stopped by an opening in the bushes. 'Well, this is as good as anywhere.'

'Aren't we chasing a needle in a haystack?'

'We'll find him.'

Gabriel, from behind a tree across the road, watched the two men go into the bushes and slither down the muddy embankment. It didn't matter now. There was nothing Coyle could tell them that they didn't already know. He walked slowly back towards Jack Straw's Castle. He would wait there for the two men to return; Coyle had already told him about Richardson.

As Gabriel waited in his car he went over the events of the last two hours. Half an hour after Richardson and Duggan left the *Tattersall Castle*, Coyle had come down the gangplank. Gabriel, after exchanging telephone numbers with the coach driver, crossed the road and joined Coyle. The two men had a drink at the Red Lion in Parliament Square, then decided to go out for a last night's excitement on Hampstead Heath before

Gabriel left the country. The Angel never mentioned seeing Richardson, and Coyle decided to let matters lie on that front.

They drove up to the Heath in Gabriel's rented car. The Irishman was preoccupied, but Gabriel ignored the real reason for his reticence, joking instead that Coyle was rusty after the action at Biddy Mulligan's.

'Not so,' replied Coyle. The truth was that his old handler terrified him, was one of the few men who ever had. But then, George Fleet, as he knew him, was a man to whom evil and cruelty came naturally, a sort of in-built revenge against the world for having made him gay and different from most of the army colleagues he had shared so much of his life with. His viciousness was second nature to him; it was part of his sex and his attitude to life, as Coyle knew to his own cost. The Irishman still bore scars from Gabriel's treatment of him years before. In truth, he knew that his life was now at risk and that there was little he could do to save himself. That was the power of Gabriel, and their sex from the night before bore testament to the fact that Gabriel's appetite for violent intercourse had increased since they last met.

They parked at Jack Straw's Castle and walked down onto the Heath, along the very route that Richardson and Sam would use later that evening. It was dark now and the Heath was starting to come to life in its deeper areas. A few men were already parading half-naked, their trousers off, their coat or shirt-tails flapping. Gabriel slipped his arm through Coyle's, gripping it tight as they walked down the narrow pathway. There were shouts from the bushes, some inviting, some cajoling, some teasing, one a shriek of pain. Along the path, men stared at each other, inviting the other to make the first move.

A young man, still in his bus-conductor's uniform and peaked hat, stepped in front of Gabriel and posed outrageously. Gabriel laughed harshly and swung his free arm at the man, hitting him across the bridge of his nose, cracking it as he snapped the cartilage. The man yelped in pain and staggered sideways, his hands going up to his nose as blood gushed out. Gabriel propelled Coyle further along the path, away from the injured bus-conductor.

'There was no need for that,' said Coyle.

'Didn't fancy him, dear. Can't have him thinking I did, can I? That was always their trouble.'

'What was?'

'The young ones. That stupidity they have. That you forgive them everything because they're young.'

They passed the pond and the Orgy Bush; there were three men there, one naked except for a T-shirt, the other two in track suits. The naked man was on his knees while the other two kicked and beat him with bamboo canes. The more they beat him, the more he wanted, screaming at them to increase his punishment. In truth, he probably didn't know the two men; it was like that on the Heath, a place with no shame and no guilt. Gabriel and Coyle watched the threesome as they continued further down the path. Twenty yards further on, when he felt they were clear of any onlookers, Gabriel guided the Irishman behind some bushes, then pushed him down on the damp ground.

'I thought we came here for some action, George,' said Coyle. 'If there's just you and me, we could've done it in comfort at my place.'

'Tell me about Richardson.'

'I already did.'

'He came to see you again.'

'Aye.'

'You didn't tell me that.'

Coyle shrugged. 'It wasn't that important.'

Gabriel knelt down closer to Coyle. 'That's for me to decide, dear. What did he want?'

'He wondered whether I'd been involved in Biddy Mulligan's.' Coyle knew there was little use in lying. The sounds of a couple only a few yards away, involved in their own promiscuity, didn't register. He knew he had to convince Gabriel. His knife was in his waistband, but he had little inclination to use it, not against Gabriel.

'Why?'

'Because of the way the knife was used.'

'Ah! Your trademark. I forgot, you said he handled you in Belfast.'

'I told him I wasn't involved.'

'Did he believe you?'

'Yes.'

Gabriel smiled gently. 'But then, maybe he didn't.'

'I'm not going to tell him anything, am I?'

'You're an easy man to read, Sean Coyle. Sometimes you don't have to say much.'

'I'm not going to hang myself by telling him anything.'

'Unless he threatened to run you in. Tell his police friends so that they'd come looking for you.'

'No chance, George. No chance.'

'Who's Richardson work for now?'

'Security Services.'

'Which one? Military?'

'Five. Or Six. He's not Army any more.'

'Which is it? Five or Six?'

'I don't know. Honest to God, George. He never said. Just that he was out of the Army and with a security service.'

'Did he mention the Angels to you?'

'No.' Coyle hoped he hadn't lied too quickly. The last thing he wanted Gabriel to know was that Richardson had mentioned Fleet by name.

'Then what did he want from you? Come on,' he hissed sharply, making Coyle jump. 'What did the bastard want? Not your fucking body, was it?'

'No. He was trying to find out if there was any activity against the Provos.'

'What sort of activity?'

'You know. Activity. From any old mates of mine.'

'Ulster boys?'

'Aye. That's what he was after. See if any of my old mates were involved.'

'What about his friend?'

'A Yank. Something to do with the FBI or something, I think. I presume he's over because of Tim Flaherty being taken out in New York. He was with Richardson when I was asked about our lads taking on the Provos.'

'And that's it?'

'That's it.'

Gabriel realized he wouldn't get any more out of Coyle. With a few omissions, that was probably all Coyle knew. Gabriel leant back against a tree and closed his eyes, letting out a long sigh.

'Are you going to kill me, George?'

Gabriel opened his eyes and laughed. 'Think you know me, don't you, Sean?'

'Nobody knows people like you.'

'And you think I'm going to kill you. So why did you come with me? Here, of all places?'

'No point running from you. I learnt that years ago. Maybe, by—'

'Talking, I'd change my mind. That is, if I was out to get you.'

'I've done you no wrong.'

'I believe you, Sean. It's a funny old time, isn't it?' Gabriel looked up at the night sky, his view broken by the overhanging tree. 'It's a different sky, wherever you are in the world. Same sky really, only it always looks different. Here, in America, even Belfast which isn't that far away. You know, Sean, all I ever wanted to be was a good soldier. What did you want? When you were young and before we got involved in all this shit?'

'To play for the Reds.'

'Manchester United. Catholic team.'

'Didn't matter. They were the best.'

'Well, I wanted to be the best. To save the world. To be a fucking hero. I remember going out on patrol. There was a camaraderie, the squaddies used to sing songs, like kids on the way to a football match. That's how it all started. All one fucking team. Then it got serious. No more boy soldiers. Just friends getting killed, stepping on mines, being taken out by snipers. And the worse it got, the more I turned into myself, the less I wanted to trust anyone else. I didn't know I was queer until I fell for a young lance-corporal on patrol. Felt for him like you feel for a woman. Wanted to protect him, make sure he didn't get hurt. Took some getting used to, feeling like that about a man.'

'Did I know him?' Coyle had known most of the gay soldiers.

'He wasn't gay. Never touched him. Just made sure he was OK. Until a sniper took off his head in Armagh when we were out on patrol. Lost it all, then, Sean. Lost any innocence I had left. After a week grieving over him, I decided no-one was ever going to fuck me up again. So I got hard. Made myself stuff them all. Knew I preferred men, so I just started to put myself about. Got chucked from the SAS for that. They don't like poofters. When this lot came along, I knew I could hit back for my little lance-corporal.' He leant towards Coyle. 'Come on, dear. Time for some fun. Don't see why we shouldn't be like the rest of the boys round here.' He leant over and stroked the back of Coyle's head. 'I feel gentle tonight, Sean. Nothing kinky. Just straight and fast, eh?' He took his hand away. 'Bend over. Now.'

Coyle didn't know if he was out of hot water. He stood up, lowered his trousers and underwear, and held the pearl-handled knife before it fell to the ground. The two men looked at each other. Then Coyle knelt forward. He waited, half anticipation, half fear. Nothing happened for a while; it all added to the excitement. Then he felt Gabriel's body next to his, the flesh against his bare buttock before Gabriel invaded him. The suddenness shocked him; he felt a spasm of pain at the harshness of it. Behind him, Gabriel's breathing became more urgent, then his voice took over as he urged Coyle to climax with him. The Irishman suddenly felt safe, knew that Gabriel wouldn't hurt him. He built to a crescendo with Gabriel. Within a minute he was ready to explode. He felt Gabriel reach the same point. That's when he screamed and let himself erupt.

Gabriel picked up the knife and slit Coyle's throat as he climaxed.

When the body, still quivering, fell to the ground, Gabriel rammed the knife into Coyle's anus.

Then he left the bushes, ignored the suggestive men roaming the Heath and went towards Jack Straw's Castle. That was when he saw Richardson and Duggan. He waited for them, knowing he would have to follow them.

The police car and ambulance sirens informed him that Coyle's body had been discovered. By then men were scattering from the Heath, some running towards the car-park where Gabriel sat waiting. He started the engine and slipped out of the car-park to reposition down the road. He knew he'd eventually see Richardson's Bentley. As he drove away from the Heath the first police car passed him, all blue and white lights and frantic alarms.

He regretted killing Coyle; they'd had good times together. But that was the rub of the green. Even though Gabriel wanted to get away from this place, he knew there was more to do. He parked down a side-street and waited for the Bentley.

*   *   *

Richardson and Duggan waited until Dancer arrived.

They hadn't found the body; that had been discovered by another couple looking for a private place.

After the police got there, Richardson had made himself known to the senior officer and asked that a message be sent to Dancer. When the Box man arrived, Richardson waited for him to view the body before retreating to a quieter part of the Heath. By now the place was alive with journalists, police and television lights, tracker dogs and half of London as onlookers. It was nearly two-thirty in the morning.

'Fleet,' stated Richardson.

'Why?'

'Because Coyle knew him.'

'That's only guesswork.'

'Coyle didn't deny Fleet was working him again.'

'Neither did he confirm it.'

'Trust me, Mick,' snapped Richardson. 'I handled Coyle for a long time. I knew him, knew when he was lying. I'm convinced it was Fleet.'

Dancer paused for a minute, then shrugged acquiescence. 'I'll get his picture circulated. See if any of these gay types saw him down here. And I'll pass it on to the FBI's legal attaché.'

'What about Nathaniel?'

'What about him?'

'I'd suggest you give them his picture, too.'

'That's ripe. It really implicates us.'

'Shit to that. Only an idiot would deny it was our guys causing all the trouble.' Richardson desperately wanted a cigarette; he had left his last unsmoked one in the car.

'Anything else?'

'No.'

'When's Duggan going back to Washington?'

'He hasn't said.'

'How'd he react to Coyle?'

'Gruesome. Retched all over the place when we saw him. He's not used to it.'

'Who is? They're over-the-top, these Angels. Lips round a cock in Dublin, now a knife stuck up an arse.' Dancer grinned. 'He certainly got the point on that one. Anyway, I'll catch you tomorrow.' Dancer watched Richardson walk away, then remembered his latest information and called after him. 'Sam.' Richardson swung round. 'I forgot to tell you. The guy Morrison saw at Kennedy Airport. Phil Rush. Ex-captain. Ex-SAS. Ex-Northern Ireland.'

'And?'

'Has a green card. Was married to an American, but it broke up. According to Morrison it totally messed up his life. Had two kids as well. Lives somewhere in Florida.'

'Where?'

'Didn't know.'

'What was his speciality?'

'Close-range work.'

'A la Tim Flaherty.'

'Yes. I suppose you want me to send the Feds a snapshot of him, too.'

As Richardson drove the Bentley home, the Ford Sierra followed at a discreet distance. Gabriel was surprised when Richardson swung across the road and pulled up next to an electric milk-float. He kept going, past the Bentley and round the next bend.

Richardson didn't notice the Sierra as he climbed out of the car. He greeted the milkman and bought two pints of milk, one skimmed for Duggan and a natural one for himself. The two men sat in the car and drank from the bottles.

'Do you have milkmen in Washington?' asked Richardson as he wiped his lips between swigs.

'Did. A long time ago. Now it's all in cartons in supermarkets.'

'We've got those, too. But there's something about coming home in the early hours and hearing the rattle of a milk-float. Reassuring, really. In a world of crap. Takes me back to when I was young and on my way back home from some bit of skulduggery, usually with a bird. Like when I used to come back from Northern Ireland. First thing I used to do was buy a pint of milk, some bacon, sausage and eggs, and a bit of black pudding, then fry myself a big, greasy nosh-up.'

'What's black pudding?'

Richardson grinned. 'I'm not even going to bother telling you. You'd be horrified after the sterile foods you people eat in the States.'

'We're not that purist.'

'Do you eat liver?'

'No. That's offal.'

'Or kidneys?'

'Do you know what kidneys do?'

'Of course. Then you definitely wouldn't eat black pudding.' Richardson finished his milk, slipped into gear and pulled across the road. 'Dancer wants to know when you're going home?'

'That's up to Washington. But I guess pretty soon. Why? Do you want to see the back of me?' Duggan chided.

Richardson smiled. 'Morrison came up with the name of the guy he saw at Kennedy.'

'Go on.'

'Ex-SAS man. Called Rush. Dancer's sending any information on to the FBI and your people. He's also got pictures of two others. Possible Angels.'

'Fleet and Nathaniel?'

Richardson nodded. 'To be honest, Francis, I think this thing points upstairs.'

'Why're you telling me?'

'Because that's just my instinct. It's not for your people. I'm telling you because – I really don't know

what's been going on. If it goes all the way to the top of
the British government, then it could well involve your
people, too.'

'I'd come to that conclusion already.'

'Anyway, at the end of the day we just do what our
masters bid us. I just want you to know it's nothing to
do with me.'

FBI Miami Field Office
16320 NW 2nd Avenue
North Miami Beach

Confessor Bonnilo threw the four photographs on the
table.

'The Brits are certainly coming up with the goods,'
he said. He waited until Reilly and Jiggs had examined
the four pictures. 'They're marked on the back. One
is the latest they have of Fergal Baxter. The picture's
not bad, considering it was taken with a thousand-mill
lens. Those boys don't usually stand around posing for
portraits. Let's get a bunch of copies out to Orlando,
including the Disney World security people.' The order
was for Reilly. Bonnilo pulled a chair up, straddled it,
sat and turned to Jiggs. 'Ray Nathaniel and George
Fleet. Those could be two of the boys you're looking
for, Solomon. Both served with the SAS in Northern
Ireland. You've got two pictures of each of them. An
army mug shot and a personal picture of them together
at a party.'

'These were taken a few years ago,' commented
Solomon Jiggs. 'I'll get the boys out with them in the
morning.' He looked at his watch; it was nearly nine
and he was hungry. 'Do we have any other information?'

'There's a further picture coming through tomorrow.
Another ex-SAS man. Philip Rush. I guess it'll be the
same sort of mug shot. All three were at the sharp end

in Northern Ireland. Between them they are experts in explosives and arms. Any of them could have carried out the attack on Tim Flaherty, or in Dublin, or on the six people in London.'

'Were these guys all in the Service at the same time?'

'I don't know. We have to presume that. I mean, the Brits are sending us these pictures, but not a lot more. They obviously feel they could be involved, only they're not saying why.'

'You want me to run these names through the computer and through Immigration?' asked Reilly.

'It's done.'

'These guys could still be in the Army,' Jiggs added.

'I'm informed they're not.'

'So why give us this information? Unless it's meant to take us down the wrong street.'

Bonnilo shrugged. 'Let's just watch our arses. But treat it like correct information.'

One of Jiggs's team opened the door and walked in. 'Got a fix on a security firm called Risk Asset Management Security. They work out of Pompano Beach.' Pompano Beach was forty miles north of Miami, the next city up from Fort Lauderdale. 'An American incorporated company, but run by British personnel. Supposedly all ex-Army.' He explained the lead had come from a business contact who had dealings with RAMS, as the company was known. 'They're consultants in security and also run a survival training camp for business executives. Weekend warrior types.'

'Let's get a run-down on the directors and the company.'

'Already did.' The agent held up a sheet of printed paper. 'RAMS is a private company. Last year took in less than three hundred thousand dollars. Not so big. It's been operating for five years as a Florida corporation. Started by a guy called Philip Rush.'

'Got 'em,' hissed Reilly.

'He's not the head honcho. Not according to the IRS returns. RAMS was started in his name. We ran it back through Immigration. Rush was given a green card because he had an American wife. Divorced now.'

'But he still works there?'

'Yeah. Still a director. But the Pres—'

'Is called George Fleet,' interrupted Bonnilo.

The agent looked up, surprised. 'No. But he's also a director. There are five of them.'

'What about Nathaniel?'

'Yeah. He's President.'

'Five,' said a triumphant Jiggs. 'Penuel, Gabriel, Raphael, Michael and Lucifer. The five Archangels.' He turned to Bonnilo. 'I'll get the place staked out. And run whatever we can on the rest of the directors' names.'

An hour later Confessor Bonnilo rang Hank Mickleton in Orlando and updated him. The SAC had a round-the-clock surveillance running on the RAMS office, a second-floor office suite of three small rooms in a small mall off North Federal Highway. The painted wooden sign, at the communal entrance at street level, simply stated, 'Risk & Asset Management – 2nd Floor'. The phone number, taken from the directory, had been tapped. Southern Bell had verified the phone had been ordered by RAMS five years earlier. The bills had been paid regularly and a list of numbers called was being prepared. The real tit-bit was that no-one had used the phone for over a year. Southern Bell would later confirm that very few calls had been made since installation. Bonnilo surmised that the phone was used for incoming calls only, a ready-to-use dead-letter drop. They had asked a few discreet questions of the local police and postman. There was nothing unusual to report; the postman confirmed that mail was delivered there, although deliveries were few and far between.

The two men decided to leave the stake-out team in

place and wait to see who turned up in the morning. If nothing happened, then they would probably force an entry into the offices.

Before Bonnilo hung up he confirmed he would investigate the contact who had first told them about RAMS.

Then Mickleton went back to the problem of Fergal Baxter in Orlando.

Neither man had mentioned the obvious, even though the telephone line was dedicated and couldn't be overheard.

How much did the British really know?

And was the Bureau being asked to clear up their mess?

The Wedding Cake
MI6
The Embankment
London

Maxwell Claris drummed his fingers on the desk and waited for his secretary to leave the room. It was seven in the morning and the Deputy Director had never been one for getting in to work before nine. This was for no other reason than that he would happily work through the night, but could never get all his senses clear first thing in the morning. It all went back to his days in Africa, when late nights and late mornings were the order of the day.

'Too much happening too fast,' he said when he and Carter were finally alone.

Carter picked up his cup and drank from it. It was too hot, but he didn't allow Claris to see his discomfort. He had cancelled an important meeting after being urgently summoned by Claris. 'I thought we were finally making solid progress,' he said eventually, his tongue momentarily swollen by the heat.

'It's out of control. Running away with itself. Dammit, it's looking more and more as if our security services have planned the whole thing.' Claris pushed the intercom button to his secretary. 'No calls until we're finished. Whoever it is.' He snapped the set off. 'From now on you report to me on everything. And whatever we discuss stays between us.' He waited until Carter had nodded his agreement. 'The Cabinet Secretary has had the chaps from Trevi on.' The Cabinet Secretary was Whitehall's most senior Civil Service mandarin, answerable directly to the Prime Minister and responsible for overseeing all of the intelligence community. His responsibilities included the Cabinet Office committees on Defence, Overseas Policy, Intelligence Services and Terrorism. This last committee was headed by the Home Secretary which included the Foreign, Defence and Northern Ireland Secretaries for State on its panel. Trevi, the European Community joint structure on international terrorism and violence, had contacted the Foreign Office with their queries about the Angels and it had been passed up to the Cabinet Secretary.

'Our *friends*,' Claris made the word sound indecent, 'in Europe feel we're in deeper than we'll admit. It's the bloody Spaniards, of course. Now that Vera and his lot have rid themselves of ETA, they think they can play holier-than-thou.'

Carter knew there was a great degree of truth in what Claris said. Rafael Vera, Spain's Minister for Security, had set about the destruction of the Basque separatist terrorist organization, ETA, in the late eighties and early nineties. ETA had been responsible for over eight hundred deaths in the eighties. The fight against ETA was a successful operation, although never traced directly back to the Spanish government. Because of the intense pressure from the national forces, most of the ETA High Command operated out of France, similar to the Army Council and other PIRA activists who lived

389

in southern Ireland. The French government treated the ETA men as political refugees and the terrorists moved freely across the border. That was until 2 August in 1985, when two motor-cycle gunmen assassinated a top ETA official near the town of St Pierre-de-Paul. In the next two years eighteen more ETA personnel were taken out and many others, including women and children, were wounded. The killers, a group known as GAL, Freedom from Terrorists, were a secret hit-squad based in Lisbon, mostly Angolan ex-mercenaries and veterans, who were recruited by senior Spanish police officers from Bilbao in northern Spain. There was little doubt that the control ran all the way back to Madrid. The French government finally got tough on ETA, mostly because they had now caused terrorism by GAL on French soil, and a Special Forces unit captured the last of the ETA extremists in a single raid. It was a triumph for cross-border co-operation and ETA was now regarded by the Spanish authorities as a spent force.

'There was an ETA bomb a few months ago,' said Carter. 'In Madrid. Killed seven soldiers and wounded some schoolchildren waiting for a bus. ETA still operate.'

Claris shrugged. 'The damage is done. It'll take a long time for them to build up their organization again. Resources, personnel, finance. It'll take generations. I have to say, much as I dislike the Spaniards, it was a successful operation. But, not the way we're expected to solve our problems.'

'Have Trevi offered any help?'

'No. But the tone of their communication was that they suspected we were involved and, if we were, then we couldn't count on their support. It has, to say the least, put the wind up the Cabinet Secretary and, no doubt, the Prime Minister. They don't want to be alienated on something like this. They were cut up enough by the shenanigans of the peace talks in '93. All that secret dialogue with Sinn Féin being thrown back in their face after they'd denied meeting them in the first place. It closed a road our politicians were not prepared to go down in the future. Silly of Sinn Féin, really. Going after short-term political points. Makes you wonder if they really want peace in the end.'

'Are we involved?'

'Not in any way that could trace back to the Prime Minister.'

'But it could trace back to us?'

'It's nothing we're actively involved in. But, with all these conspiracy theories gathering strength, I suggest we make sure it doesn't land on our doorstep.'

'I need to know what our connection with the Angels is.'

'There is no connection,' Claris insisted. 'Nothing direct. We just feel that we know how, and why, they're doing it.'

'We?'

'Those who need to know.'

'Does that include the Prime Minister? Or someone close to him? On one of the security committees?'

'That doesn't concern you.'

'Am I to be told?'

'No, Richard,' was Claris's firm reply. 'Your job is to monitor the situation closely. Now that we've unleashed the information on the Angels to our friends, we must ensure that it doesn't get out of hand. We had no choice but to release those pictures. The FBI were closing down on the Angels anyway, would've soon got there without our help. No point in appearing obstructive.'

'How can I help the situation?'

'Get Richardson over to Florida.'

'Officially?'

'Arrange for him to go back with Duggan.'

'Duggan'll be returning to Washington.'

'Then try and arrange it so that Richardson gets to

Florida. Just say, as they did about Duggan, that we want an observer over there. After all, the Angels do all appear to be British subjects. And ex-services. What could be better than having one of their own kind helping the authorities?'

'Is he just there to observe?' Carter's question was slow and weighted.

'Unless HMG needs protecting.'

'And then?'

'Don't play the innocent, Richard. You know exactly what could be needed. After all, that's what Richardson was trained for in the first place. Dammit, he knows about the Cartel Plan. Who better to deal with it if things go bad?' Claris snapped the intercom back on and spoke to his secretary. 'I'm through now. Any calls?'

'No, sir.'

'All right. Mr Carter's just leaving.' Claris shut off the intercom as Carter rose, his coffee virtually untouched, and walked to the door. Claris's voice stopped him as he was about to open it. 'It's a shame, Richard. How we train these fellows into specialists. Guns, explosives, survival techniques. A one-man walking army. Then some minister decides to cut his budget and we release a dozen well-trained killers back onto the streets. No rehabilitation. No training to help them become bank managers or anything worth while. All that they've got is some half-arsed pension and a place in a dole queue. In truth, I'm surprised we don't come across a bad-un more often.'

Elgin Place
Hammersmith
London W6

After a short sleep, Richardson took a taxi to the Cinema. He had been woken by Carter who asked him to go in immediately for a meeting. Andrea had gone back to sleep once she knew the call hadn't come from the hospital. He moved quietly, taking his clothes into the bathroom where he dressed so as not to wake her. On his way out he stopped and listened outside Duggan's door; the American was in a deep sleep as his snores testified.

He didn't see Gabriel watching him as he ran towards the taxi he flagged down.

The Angel watched Richardson round the corner. He decided not to follow him. The American Coyle had mentioned was still in the building. Gabriel sensed there was more mileage to be gained there.

He left his car and walked to the nearest phone box, which he had already determined was in the next street. He was uneasy about ringing America, but Lucifer had left him in no doubt that any further action had to be cleared by him. He dialled the illicit mobile telephone number.

'Still here,' he said when it was answered. 'Further developments after last night's action. Friend of the despatched Irishman has been run to earth. Suggest we close that door permanently.'

'Why?'

'His knowledge could be dangerous.'

'Are you sure?'

'Not certain. But likely.'

'He's one of ours.'

'The Yank's still with him.'

'Don't compromise any further. Unless you feel totally threatened. And I mean totally.'

'I'll do whatever's necessary.'

'Agreed. But no severe action. I don't want either of them slotted. They're not on the other side.'

Gabriel put the phone down and went back to his surveillance point in the car. He knew Duggan was still in there, probably asleep after the late night. He decided to investigate further, to find out if there were any clues as to how much Richardson knew. He got out of the car and circled the block, working out the best way to proceed further.

The Cinema
Curzon Street

Richardson watched Carter go through his ritual of making coffee with the kettle on the carpet. He remembered how it had shocked him the first time he came for an interview. It nearly made him turn down the job at Six; somehow its dignity was cheapened when you watched senior officers making a drink on the carpet. But that's how it was in the Cinema; that's how it would always be until they moved to new premises.

Carter put the cups on the table, then sat in the spare chair next to Richardson. 'Just you and me, Sam,' he said confidentially, sitting beside Richardson to elicit trust. 'Both being sucked deeper into this.'

'Then we are involved.'

'Probably. Only nobody will admit it.'

'I don't disagree with the Plan.'

'None of us do. Privately, that is,' Carter chuckled. 'Being brutally honest about it, nobody's against it. The public, even the Press. There is a grudging sort of respect and acquiescence there. Gives a whole new meaning to the word *privatization*. These boys are sorting out what the Government and the security forces should have dealt with a long time ago. That's the public view, anyway. I even read an article in one of our tabloids yesterday urging HMG to now follow the Angels' lead and intern, or *take any further necessary action against*, which is how they put it, the terrorists. They won't, of course. Can't be seen publicly to support or be involved.'

'And now the whole thing's about to hit the fan?'

'Yes. They want us to sort it out.'

'Us? Or me?'

Carter smiled. Richardson was making it easy for him. 'You must trust me, Sam. I don't know who is behind this. Except that it's got our people spooked. And it's not just Six. It goes a long way further.'

'Does Dancer know?'

'He probably suspects. Like the rest of us. But there is no official link to the Cabinet.'

'There never is.'

'In fact, I doubt even the Cabinet know. It's the way these things work. Someone has an idea, someone else progresses it, then everyone turns it down and walks away from it. Only, by then, someone has acted on it, made it happen.'

'How long've you known?'

'Since seven this morning.' Carter sighed. 'Not to say I didn't guess what was going on. Although, it may still be that our people are only involved on the periphery.'

'How?'

'Some help with finance. Secretly, of course. Maybe information. I doubt if they'd supply arms or anything like that. It sometimes helps for the left hand not to know what the right hand's doing.'

'Where do I fit in?'

'We're requesting that you go to Florida as an observer. Shouldn't be a problem; after all, that's why Duggan came over here.'

'Florida?'

'That's where the Angels are based. And they are, or appear to be, British subjects. I think the FBI would agree that an ex-SAS officer would be of help to them. I mean, they're not proven guilty yet. It is only a suspicion.'

'Damn good one.'

'Maybe. But nothing's proven. It could all be quite harmless, as far as they're concerned. Anyway, we suggested to the Americans that you may be able to talk to them when they're eventually in custody.'

Richardson laughed. 'Those boys won't allow themselves to be taken.'

'That was our consensus.'

'What do you want me to do? Talk them into surrendering?'

'On the contrary, Sam. Like all good soldiers, I want them to appreciate they're expendable.'

'Shit to that.'

'That's how it is.' Carter held his hands up. 'Not my decision.' *Damn*. He regretted it immediately; knew it showed his own weakness. He put down his hands.

'And – if they don't surrender – do I take them out?'

'I never said that,' rejected Carter. 'You must do whatever you feel is right and proper.'

'I knew this was a dirty game, but . . . shit.'

There was a knock on the door. 'Yes,' called Carter.

His secretary walked in and told him GCHQ were on the phone and it was urgent.

Elgin Place
Hammersmith
London W6

Duggan left nearly an hour after Richardson.

Gabriel watched him go and decided to wait and satisfy himself the American would not be returning. Twenty minutes later he left his car and walked towards the front door Duggan had come through. He confirmed that Richardson's flat was on the first floor. The door, a communal entrance, had a rim-latch lock. He pulled a Y-shaped leather pouch from his pocket and took out two rim-latch master-keys. He inserted one in the lock, then slipped the second one over the top of it and gently manipulated it until the tumblers fell into place. When

396

he heard them click, he turned the keys and pushed the door open. The whole operation had taken no more than forty seconds and, as he looked back into the street as he closed the door, he confirmed that no passers-by had grown suspicious. He put the pouch back in his pocket. The pouch was a standard lock-pick set supplied to the armed forces, the police and all the security services. He grinned as he quickly climbed the stairs to the first floor. He recalled how the SAS men had always sneered at the pick-lock sets they were taught to use; the sledge-hammer technique had always proved quicker.

He found two flats on the first floor. He already knew 2A was Richardson's. The door was protected by another rim-latch lock and a mortise underneath it. He climbed the next two floors, checked there was no-one about to disturb him, then pulled out the pouch once again, extricated some of the dozen mortise-lock key forms and worked his way through them until he finally cracked the tumblers. He then opened the rim-latch in the same manner as he had the one at the entrance and quietly slipped into flat 2A. This time it had taken five minutes to gain entrance.

Gabriel eased the door shut behind him, flicking the latch into the lock position. He walked quickly into the lounge and started his search in the small bureau by the window. The drawers were unlocked and he leafed through the papers in each compartment. Nothing important, just household bills and receipts. Richardson was obviously a neat man; that pleased Gabriel for he knew anything hidden would be easier to find. When he was satisfied there was nothing in the lounge, he went into the first bedroom. The single bed was unmade. The suitcase, open by the window, told him this was a guest-room, probably the American's. He went through the drawers, found nothing, then examined the contents of the suitcase. There were some clothes that Duggan still hadn't unpacked; he was obviously an untidy type.

Between two sweatshirts Gabriel found a jotting-pad. He pulled it out and flicked through it. It was the breakdown that Duggan and Richardson had worked on when they first came together, before the identity of the Angels, or even the name of the organization, had been discovered.

The last pages of the pad gave a rudimentary report on the Cartel Plan.

So they knew it existed. Even the Yanks knew.

But they didn't know who operated it.

Gabriel returned the pad to its hiding-place. There was nothing else to do but get out of this place, get back to his comrades. Richardson and Duggan were only doing their job. At least they were all on the same side. And if he took them out, more would follow. It wasn't what this whole thing was about, anyway.

He stepped back into the hall and closed the guest-room door.

'Francis,' he heard a woman's voice call from behind him as he went towards the front door.

Shit. There was someone still in the flat. He swung round and saw Andrea; to him she was a black woman in a pair of silk pyjamas. 'Who the hell—?' he heard her shout. His instinct took over. He stepped towards her and hit her, the palm of his right hand forward, karate-style across her neck. He heard the crack and saw her jerk across the hall and into the wall before she crumpled to the floor. She lay there; no sound, no obvious movement. He didn't think he'd killed her; there was no need, not if she was an ex-comrade's woman. The surprise and speed of it all would have meant she probably wouldn't be able to identify him. Gabriel went back into the lounge, opened drawers and scattered papers across the floor. He would make it look like a burglar who had been interrupted. He went over to the TV set and pulled the video recorder from underneath. It was what he always took, the modern-day thief. He moved quickly to the front door and unlocked the latch.

As he turned the knob, the door swung hard against him, opening into him. He stepped back as Duggan came in.

'Jesus!' gasped the surprised American. Over Gabriel's shoulder he saw Andrea lying on the floor. He tried to pull backwards, out of the flat, but Gabriel had him by the neck and dragged him through the door. Duggan wrapped his arms round Gabriel; it was the only thing he could think of doing, to somehow pin his attacker down. The video recorder was jammed between them.

Gabriel head-butted Duggan, who yelped in pain, released his grip and staggered back. Gabriel swung hard, following up his advantage, and hit Duggan across the jaw with a clenched fist. The American shot backwards, trying to keep his balance. He was unsuccessful and collapsed against his bedroom door. Gabriel decided to get out, it would take a few moments for Duggan to collect himself and give chase. He ran from the flat, the recorder still under his arm.

Richardson was late getting back.

He didn't see the police officers from the Specialist Armed Response Unit, SO-19, taking up their positions. Seven of them, scattered across Elgin Place, taking cover behind parked cars and their own black, unmarked Range Rovers. Seven men, armed with Browning automatic pistols with Pachmeyer grips and Heckler & Koch sub-machine-guns, wearing baseball caps with black-and-white chequered bands and body armour.

The urgent call from GCHQ to Carter had stated that a voice-print and tone-recognition computer had immediately matched Gabriel's call to Lucifer with one made earlier by the Angel when he rang to warn his comrades in Florida that Fergal Baxter was going to Orlando. The tape was played back to Carter and Richardson over the phone. They realized immediately that one of the Angels had discovered Richardson's home. Carter called SO-13, the police anti-terrorist branch, who in turn pulled in the Blue Berries, as SO-19 were known.

The SO-19 team arrived as Duggan was entering the front door. They were still taking up position when Gabriel came out of the entrance, the video recorder still under his arm, and down the five steps that led to the pavement. He stopped sharply on the bottom step when he saw the armed policemen.

The police officers didn't move; they weren't aware who they were looking for. The photographs of Fleet, Nathaniel and Rush hadn't reached them yet. All they had been told to do was take up immediate positions and be ready for trouble.

Gabriel didn't know that.

He flung the recorder down and started to run down the street, away from the black Range Rovers.

'Stop where you are,' a senior officer shouted. 'Police.' He had a megaphone in his hand but was reluctant to use it in case the man running away wasn't who they had come after, was just an innocent resident who had been startled by the armed police. Using the megaphone might well warn whoever was inside Richardson's flat. He turned to one of his men. 'Get after him. Stop him for fuck's sake.'

The second officer raced after Gabriel. Another policeman provided back-up and followed him. Gabriel stopped on the corner as the two men charged towards him. He didn't realize that they didn't know who he was. He reached in his pocket and took out the gun Coyle had got for him for the Biddy Mulligan's job. He knew he wouldn't use it. He knew that wasn't part of the Plan, to take out his own people.

The first police officer shouted a warning to the others and dived behind a car, reaching for his Browning.

His back-up dived to the pavement, bringing his SMG up to bear on Gabriel.

The Angel smiled; there was nowhere for him to go; it was time for George Fleet to pay for all he had done wrong in his life. It was how the five of them imagined it would end, in some lonely place and without a happy ending. His one life against the three he had taken out in Amsterdam and the two men at Biddy Mulligan's. Five for one. That levelled the odds for the friends he had lost in Northern Ireland.

He turned the gun to his temple and pulled the trigger.

It was all over when Richardson and Carter arrived six minutes later. The road was cordoned off and the police had already entered the flat. Richardson ran past the ambulance next to where Gabriel had fallen, pushed past a policeman at the building entrance and ran up the stairs to flat 2A. The first paramedic team had arrived only seconds earlier and were tending to Andrea. Duggan sat on the floor, leaning against the wall, his face bloody from the gash on his forehead where Gabriel had head-butted him. He tried to stand up when Richardson came in, but was too weak and slid down again. Richardson acknowledged him and went over to where Andrea lay.

She was still, her eyes closed, unconscious. He couldn't see any blood. He stayed where he was, not wanting to impede the paramedics. One of them was finishing applying a cervical collar to her neck. Richardson sensed her vulnerability; nobody needed to tell him she was near death. He stood there, watching her, urging her on silently, willing his strength into her.

A second paramedic team came into the hallway, carrying a special, hard-based stretcher.

Richardson watched as they gently manoeuvred Andrea onto the stretcher, then strapped her to it, making sure there was as little movement as possible.

'Husband?' one of the paramedics asked him. Richardson nodded; now was not the time to differentiate between husband and live-in lover. 'We're taking her in to hospital now. I'll need some details when we get there.'

'Her neck, is it?'

'Looks like it.'

'What are—?'

'Let's get her somewhere safe, son. Where we can do more good, eh? Save the questions till then.' The paramedic put his arm out and squeezed Richardson's elbow. Then they took Andrea out.

Another paramedic was cleaning Duggan's face. 'More bruising than a deep cut,' he told the American. 'Doesn't even need a stitch.'

Duggan looked up at Richardson. 'I went out. I got hit when I came back. He was standing inside the door. He was already in here, Sam.'

'Don't. I'll see you later,' replied Richardson as he followed Andrea's stretcher out onto the road.

Dancer had arrived and he came up to Richardson as the stretcher party came down the front steps. 'Sorry,' he said. He followed Richardson to the ambulance. Richardson was about to get in the back after Andrea when Dancer grabbed his arm. 'Can you go on later?'

'Bugger that.'

'Just a couple of minutes. Then I'll take you there myself.'

Richardson sighed and stepped back as the paramedics closed the door and the ambulance, siren blaring, shot off down the road.

'Come and look at this,' said Dancer as he led Richardson to where Gabriel lay. A policeman pulled back the blanket that had been placed over his face. The top half of his head was blown away. The rest of his features were untouched; there was almost a peaceful look on his face.

Richardson couldn't control himself and he lashed out with his foot, kicking the corpse as it lay there. The policeman put himself between Richardson and Gabriel while Dancer pulled him away. 'Come on, knock it off,' warned Dancer.

'OK, I'm OK,' growled Richardson, backing away.

'That's better. Just tell me if you recognize him. That's all.'

Richardson stepped up and looked at Gabriel's face. He recognized it from the photographs but was convinced he hadn't seen him the night before on Hampstead Heath. 'I know it's Fleet. But I've never seen him before. Who slotted the bastard?'

'He did. Topped himself.'

The two men looked at each other. That wasn't normal behaviour for an SAS officer. 'What now? Fucking suicide squads?' asked Richardson.

'Who knows?' Dancer pulled four wads of banknotes from his pocket. 'These were on him.' He held them out for Richardson to examine. They were US dollars, brand-new $100 bills, some fifty in each wad. Each one had a wrapper around it, a brand-new Union Banque Suisse band. 'Mean anything?'

Richardson shook his head. 'Unless that's how they get their funds. Through Swiss banks.'

'Makes you wonder, doesn't it?'

Dancer drove Richardson to the hospital.

By then, Carter had called Claris on his mobile phone and told him of the fresh dollar bills wrapped in UBS bands. The sudden concern in Claris's voice didn't escape him; he realized things were now getting too close to home for some people's comfort.

The Entrance to Disney World
Orlando

Fergal Baxter and his brood were no different from any other family out to enjoy themselves in the Florida warmth and fantasy of Disney World.

The rented car they were in cruised west on the BeeLine Expressway at a steady fifty-five, past Orlando Airport and the signs to SeaWorld, then cut south on

Interstate 4 towards Tampa. Six miles further they swung off on the Disney World Expressway and pulled up amongst the hundreds of cars that were queuing to drive through the wide span of the Disney World ticket-booths. It was going to be a busy day at the theme-park; Baxter knew the queues for the attractions would be endless. He didn't mind; all the easier to hide in.

The sharp-eyed gateman recognized Baxter from the photo-kit he had Sellotaped to the desk in front of him. The man wore sunglasses and had darker hair, but there was no doubt in the gateman's mind. He was a student from Florida State, working through the vacation period, majoring in medicine from which he hoped to graduate to the rich pickings of plastic surgery. Facial structure and form were his speciality, and the man sitting in the car in front was definitely the man in the photograph.

He gave Baxter his change and his tickets. 'Have a good one in Disney World,' he shouted through the glass booth. 'And you kids just keep your eyes open for Mickey. He's waiting on Main Street just for you.' He waved them through, then noted the car registration number and dialled his supervisor.

The car-park supervisor missed the car; the call to alert him from the ticket-booth supervisor had come across too late. By then FBI men were scurrying towards the car-park and the transportation centre. The car-park man, a portly, out-of-trim fifty-year-old, ran along the line of cars waiting to be allocated parking spaces by the attendants. There was no sign of Baxter's car so he lumbered along the row of recently parked vehicles. By the time he found it, already two rows deep after only a few minutes, the Baxter family had locked up and left the park. He called the Disney World security chief on his mobile and told him where the car was. Then he waited for the FBI and others to arrive.

Goofy sat next to Baxter's children on the tram that ran to the transportation centre. He made the children laugh; the Baxter parents smiled at each other. This was what it was all about. Sun, children, happiness.

In the frenzied rush, one of the agents remembered to call Hank Mickleton.

'Don't take him,' reminded the FBI chief. 'Monitor and await instructions.' He then went to the transportation centre in an electric golf cart with Disney World's security chief.

The Baxters, thanks to Disney World's exceptional efficiency in moving large crowds, passed quickly through the transportation centre. It was a modern, Grand-Central-Station sort of place, with queues running in all directions, but moving rapidly towards their destinations. Some people waited for the mono-rail that ran from the transportation centre to the Resort hotels, the science and technology Epcot Center park, and the Magic Kingdom, home of Mickey Mouse, Snow White and all the rest that made up Walt Disney's creations. The Baxters decided to take the ferry, a steamboat affair, across the large lake and into the Magic Kingdom.

The boat pulled out across the lake, its steamboat-whistle shrilling across the water, as Hank Mickleton joined the security staff and his own men at the transportation centre. They scanned the queues, trying not to be too obvious and alert Baxter. By now the gateman who had first identified the Irishman had been brought over to join the search and was questioned by Mickleton. The FBI man couldn't get him to change his mind; he was convinced he had seen Baxter. When he explained why he had recognized him, because of his medical training and his interest in facial structures, Mickleton believed he had seen the Irishman. The order went out to intensify the search, this time accompanied by a complete description of the missing family. Searchers entered each carriage of the mono-rail. But, with the multitude of families swarming over Disney World, Mickleton soon accepted that 'finding a needle in a haystack was a damn sight easier than digging out a vacationing Irishman in the crush of Disney World'.

The order went out to concentrate efforts in the Magic Kingdom. It's where parents with young children would go. The start of their Disney World adventure. Mickleton headed back to the security building where he could monitor the screens from the remote-control cameras all round the park.

The ferry-boat docked next to Main Street and Baxter led his family down the gangplank. He was elated to have got here, to finally bring his family on the holiday of a lifetime. His guard was down; there could be no possible danger amongst these crowds.

Raphael and Penuel walked down the gangplank after the Baxters. Their guard had not dropped; they had already seen the squads of security men searching through the crowds. Penuel had looked over the shoulder of one of them at the transportation centre and glimpsed Baxter's photograph. As the two Angels followed the Irishman, Penuel informed Raphael that the searchers, probably FBI, were on the look-out for Baxter.

Lucifer enjoyed the scorching dry heat on his back. He was wearing an Epcot T-shirt, blue Bermudas, a Los Angeles Raiders hat and reflective sun-glasses. It was why he enjoyed Florida, had never been a great fan of England's damp grey climes. Michael, in a Hard-Rock Orlando T-shirt waited next to him, slurping a pistachio ice-cream as he watched the ferry-boat passengers walk up to Main Street. He and Lucifer had gone on ahead from the car-park and taken the mono-rail.

Michael nudged Lucifer, who was searching through postcards, when he picked up Baxter in the crowd. They watched Raphael hurry past the Baxters and enter the souvenir shop.

'FBI all over the place,' he reported to Lucifer. 'Looking for Baxter. They've got a photo of him.'

'Just means we've got to be more careful when

we hit him,' came the calm reply. 'Scatter-surveillance mode and nobody move until I say so.'

The Baxters entered the souvenir shop and spent the next ten minutes buying; two Goofy hats, a Dumbo basketball, some T-shirts and a guide to Disney World. They left the shop and joined the vast throng that surged, like giant waves, down Main Street USA towards Cinderella's Castle.

In the TV control-room the light popped in Mickleton's head. 'Nathaniel,' he shouted. 'That's who—' He swung round on the Disney security chief. 'Do you record all this stuff?' Mickleton asked.

'No. Not unless we specify.'

'That camera, there.' Mickleton pointed at one on the top row of the monitors. 'That one – where is it?' He moved in front of the screens and touched the set he referred to.

'Jason?' The security chief asked one of the operators.

'Souvenir shop. Top of Main Street. Just up from where the ferry docks,' replied Jason.

'You been recording that?'

'No, sir.'

'Not even on random record?'

Jason shook his head. Recordings were often taken in a random, unselected mode.

Mickleton spoke into his radio. 'Angels are on the loose. Probably looking for our man. Double your vigilance out on Main Street. Looks like that's where he could be.' He turned to the security chief. 'One of the men, in that shop, wearing a Raiders cap and T-shirt. Had shades on. Thought he was familiar. I'm sure that's Ray Nathaniel. If he's here, then so are the others. And they've got to be after Baxter.' He reached into his coat pocket and took out a photograph of Nathaniel. It was a copy of one sent from London. 'I need that copied fast and then distributed.'

The Disney chief handed the photo to his assistant

with instructions to rush the copies through. 'Record every camera we've got on Main Street,' he instructed Jason, then turned back to Mickleton. 'The Baxters must've come across on the ferry. That's the only way we could've missed them. And that's how they got into the souvenir shop.'

'At least we know where they are. Unless that wasn't Nathaniel. Dammit,' he cursed. 'Even if it wasn't, Baxter's got to be taking his kids into the Magic Kingdom. Got to be there.'

'Doesn't make it any easier. There's probably thirty thousand people in Main Street right now.'

'That many?' Mickleton was genuinely surprised.

'I hope you're not suggesting we cordon off the area. No-one'll authorize that.'

Mickleton shook his head. 'Too risky. These guys are killers. Christ knows how they'll react if they're cornered. Last thing we want is a hostage situation.'

'Any chance of explosives out there?'

'I don't think so. These guys only go for IRA sympathizers and terrorists.' Then he remembered the two innocent Americans killed near Biddy Mulligan's. 'Sometimes,' he added. Then, 'Maybe it's time to give it all a little push. Just turn the flame up and make sure it doesn't boil over.' Mickleton took the Disney man aside and told him his next move.

Fergal Baxter waited in line. The queue, not too long, stretched towards the popcorn and ice-cream vendors. Next to them groups of horse and buggies waited for their next passengers, waiting to transport them past Main Street and the Castle to the small plaza and railway station from where holiday-makers departed for TomorrowLand, FrontierLand, FantasyLand and AdventureLand. He watched Rena and the two kids, full of excitement at being in this place. So different from Belfast and the drizzle and fear of Ireland. So good to see how other people lived. He felt the misgivings build in him again; all this had produced small doubts about what he was into back home. To see the kids this relaxed; to see Rena smiling and laughing all the time. He'd forgotten what ordinary life was like. *Not true*, he corrected himself. He'd never known what ordinary life was like, not even as a kid playing football in the back streets of Belfast. It took this place, this Disney World, to make him wonder what normality was.

The voice over the loudspeakers was so soft he nearly missed it. '. . . Mr Fergal Baxter please report to the nearest Disney information-kiosk where there is an urgent message waiting for him.' It was only the mention of his name that caught his attention.

Rena had heard it too and she swung round, alarmed, scared as she looked to him for comfort.

'Would Mr Baxter please report to the nearest Disney information-kiosk, or to any Disney employee as soon as possible.' There was a click and the metal voice was gone.

Suddenly wary of his situation, Baxter moved deeper into the line of people, crouching as though to speak with his young son, Jimmy. He swung the boy off his feet and stood up, using him as a shield as he searched the crowd. He recognized the searching men immediately, they were walking in pairs, looking over the heads of the crowd for their prey. He could tell they were American, probably FBI. He relaxed slightly; if they got him, all they could do was deport him to Dublin. He wasn't wanted for anything, had no reason to fear them. He smiled reassuringly at Rena, mouthed, '*It'll be all right*.' He knew he had to get away from them, otherwise she'd never give him any peace for breaking their holiday. He beckoned to her and left the queue, melted deeper into the crowd and headed back towards the ferry. Now that he was on his guard, he could identify the searchers more clearly.

The ones he never saw were those who didn't want to be seen.

'Make a fuss and I'll kill the kid,' said the soft British voice beside him.

Baxter froze and looked round, saw his own face reflected back in the man's sunglasses. The man was dressed in holiday gear which was why he had missed him. Any thought of running away was soon dispelled as he felt pressure from the other side. He turned round and looked at another holiday-maker, only this one's eyes were steely cold.

'Tell the wife to be quiet. Now. Then nobody'll get hurt,' said the second man.

Baxter turned round and warned Rena with his eyes. But she was near the edge, about to lose control. He moved closer to her. 'It'll be fine. Just keep quiet or we're all in trouble.' He knew she'd keep her mouth shut. It went with her marriage vows, with her acceptance that he was a member of the Army Council. She believed in the cause as much as he did. In the end, it was what was expected of her. He turned back to the two men. 'What do you want?' There was little point in bluffing, pretending he wasn't who he was. These men knew him.

'Tell her to go to the information-kiosk next to Cinderella's Castle. Say she's Mrs Baxter. That she's worried about you. That you'd agreed to meet near Space Mountain in half an hour. Got that?'

'Can my kids go with her?'

'Just the girl. You keep the boy.'

'I can't see—'

'Insurance, sunshine,' said the man in the sunglasses. 'Or nobody goes anywhere.'

Baxter knew a hard man when he saw one, whether he was a Prod, a soldier or one of his own Provos. These were no idle threats, any more than his would have been in the same situation. He turned back to Rena and explained what she was to do. She tried to argue, but the look in his eyes stopped her. 'Jimmy'll be all right.' Then he kissed her and went back to the two men. He didn't look at her again, just walked back down Main Street and onto the ferry. He heard the loudspeaker once more calling his name, telling him to identify himself. It was too late now; the ferry pulled out across the lake.

The man with the sunglasses played with Jimmy, as though he and Baxter were the best of friends. 'That Tannoy speeded us up, Baxter. We weren't expecting that.'

'Where're we going?'

'To a safe house.'

'You said my kid was in no danger.'

'We just want you, sunshine. The kid's safe. Just hang on to him till we get out of here.'

They left the ferry and caught the tram back from the transportation centre to the car-park. Jimmy wanted his sister and his mum, but Baxter calmed him down, telling him they were getting something from the car before meeting up with Rena. Goofy helped distract the child as the tram approached the car. Baxter saw two more men waiting for them, obviously the rest of the team.

Mickleton waited with Rena at the entrance to Space Mountain. His men were scattered around, watching for Baxter to appear. He had also told the Disney security chief to increase vigilance at the various Disney World exits. Baxter could well have sent Rena on ahead while he tried to escape, although Mickleton thought that unlikely as he still had his son with him. 'We know he's in danger, Mrs Baxter,' he told her. 'We just want to get him off American soil and back to Ireland. Your fight isn't our fight. He's safe once he's in our custody.'

Rena didn't respond. However well intentioned the Americans were, she knew her husband would be dumped by the side of the road if any danger threatened his kidnappers. And there was always Jimmy, not completely out of danger in spite of his infant age.

411

The call from the main gate informed Mickleton that a man leaving the complex had abandoned a small boy there. The child was called Jimmy Baxter and he said his mother was waiting for him at Space Mountain.

A gateman later confirmed seeing a man resembling the photo-identity of Fergal Baxter. What he hadn't seen was Penuel lying flat in the back of the car, the muzzle of his automatic pistol pressed into the back of the driver's seat. The FBI men who were watching Baxter's car never saw the Angels and Baxter leave.

'Easy peasy,' laughed Michael as the Angels, with their hostage, sped back towards South Florida in two cars. He, Lucifer and Baxter, the Irishman still carrying his son, had dodged security staff easily; no-one had been looking for three men with a child. Having left the Disney World complex, they tied Baxter's wrists together behind his back with wide elastic tape, then banded his ankles together. Finally they covered his mouth and dumped him unceremoniously into the boot of Penuel's Thunderbird. As the Thunderbird headed southwards at a steady sixty-five, Baxter considered kicking his feet against the inside of the boot to alert passers-by, but changed his mind when he realized there were no pedestrians on the highway. Anyway, these boyos were professionals. If they'd wanted to kill him, they would've done it by now. Maybe they were British intelligence, after information.

But he knew that was a chance in a million.

It was either a Protestant group or the Angels.

Whichever, they had obviously decided he was worth more alive than dead.

All he could do was wait and see what happened. The last thing he wanted was to rock the boat, have someone open the boot, and send him on a quick trip to oblivion.

*   *   *

412

Michael made the call from downtown Orlando to the *Sentinel*. 'The capture of an Army Council member, Fergal Baxter, was in accordance with the Rules of Engagement as laid down by the Irish Republican Army. In an attempt to fight fire with fire, as the only means now left open to resolve the question of Irish terrorism, Soldiers Penuel, Raphael, Michael and Lucifer, under orders of the Highest Command, carried out the abduction of Fergal Baxter to a safe place. Should the acts of violence by the Republicans continue, then the Highest Command will have no alternative but to order quick and terrible retribution against those who are the enemies to a peaceful and just solution for the Irish situation, starting with the execution of Fergal Baxter.'

Mickleton called the SAC, Confessor Bonnilo, in Miami and arranged for surveillance teams, with local police and Highway Patrol assistance, to be on all the major routes into south Florida. Additional teams were put into all Miami airports and the two in Fort Lauderdale, as well as the AMTRAK railroad station.

'What about Pompano?' asked Mickleton, referring to the RAMS office.

'Dead as hell,' replied Bonnilo. 'You want us to go in?'

'What do you think?'

'Not yet. They might bring him back there.'

'OK.'

'We've had one break. One of the local police officers knew someone who'd been on a RAMS survival course a couple of years back. We followed it up. Looks like they operate out in the Everglades.'

'Can he tell us where?'

'That's the bitch. He was told to report to the Pompano office at night. There were six others taking part. We're trying to trace them, but he only remembers them as executives with various companies. Anyway,

413

they were told to undress, then given some fatigues. They were blindfolded and put in a van with no windows. The blindfolds were taken off and they were driven for between one and three hours, he says, to a small camp in the Everglades.'

'One to three hours?'

'That's how he said it. He was told to take his watch off and leave it behind with his clothes. He's just estimating. Remembers it seemed a long time. Part of the survival training was time and distance disorientation.'

'You got a description of the camp?'

'Getting it now.'

'OK,' sighed Mickleton. 'Anything else?'

'Nothing.' Bonnilo remembered the call from the legal attaché in London. 'Yeah. One of the Angel's committed suicide. In London.' He told Mickleton about the happenings in Elgin Place.

'How serious are the injuries?' Mickleton asked when Bonnilo had completed his report.

'The Company man's OK. But the woman's critical. The Brits have asked that their man come over and observe.'

'Not a good idea.' Mickleton was instinctively wary of other agencies being involved in Bureau operations.

'Washington think we should allow it. They say our man was allowed over there.'

'Not ours. CIA.'

'The Brits have put a very strong request in.'

'Why do they want him over here so bad?'

'I guess they see it's their problem as much as ours. Their terrorists, their ex-soldiers. We'd expect the same.'

'And maybe their operation all along. They want him to cover their tails.'

'The woman who's critical, it's his wife, or girlfriend. I don't think he'll be wanting to go anywhere until she's off the list.'

'Don't believe it. Those Brits are as hard-hatted

as you'll find. Compared to them, alligators can be treated like warm-blooded animals.'

Intensive Care Unit
Hammersmith Hospital
London W6

They allowed Richardson to sleep in the room with Andrea.

The room, a private one, was too small for a second bed to be dragged in, so he asked for some blankets and pillows, then wrapped himself up and dozed in a sitting position, his back against the wall opposite her bed. He smiled ruefully; he often used to sleep on the floor next to his mother's bed when he was young. He was comfortable next to her, felt nothing would harm him while she watched over him. He felt like that about Andrea now. While he was there, nothing would harm her. He would give her the strength she needed. Apart from the doctor-in-charge and nurses, the only visitor was Duggan. He didn't stay long as he had to report back to the Embassy. There was a dressing on his forehead and he looked pale, but his concern for Andrea was genuine.

She was in a coma.

When they first saw her, the paramedics thought her neck had been broken. Closer examination, without moving her, indicated that some vertebrae were probably dislocated, rather than it being a broken neck. They had only moved her after they had put the cervical collar round her neck. The doctor who examined her at the hospital confirmed their diagnosis. She had been struck by a glancing blow; they would never find out that Gabriel had had no intention of killing her. Once the doctor was satisfied there was no sign of any carotid damage, he had her moved from the Casualty department to the small room in Intensive Care.

'I think she'll make it,' he told Richardson. 'Lucky, really. The blow to her neck wasn't complete. It saved her life.'

'How long before she comes round?'

'That could be the problem. Normally, a blow like that causes haemorrhage of the spinal column. Which sometimes means it could be permanent paralysis.' He waited while Richardson pulled himself together from the shock. 'When that happens, we normally find the vertebrae have been dislocated. Sometimes even broken. We've run X-rays on her vertebrae. There's no sign of dislocation like the paramedics thought. That's the good news.'

'And the bad news?'

'May not be any. We just have to build up her strength through IV feeding and wait for her to come round. You see, if there is haemorrhaging in her spinal column, bleeding in her cervical canal, which is what we think is happening, then there shouldn't be enough to cause permanent paralysis. But it could be weeks, even months, before she comes out of her coma and eventually gets back to normal. There may be some slight paralysis – but there's no way of knowing anything definite until she starts to recover.'

'But she will recover?'

'It looks hopeful. But, there is always a small chance she won't.'

It was late evening when Mick Dancer arrived at the hospital. He tried to get Richardson to go to the canteen, but got no joy. He went to the kiosk and bought some sandwiches and chocolate which he shared with Richardson in the Intensive Care room.

'I know you've other things on your mind, but I think you should know what's going on.' Dancer told Richardson about the latest events in Florida which culminated in Baxter's abduction. 'Looks like our boys are hidden

416

in the Everglades. Shit deep with the alligators. Don't know precisely where, but if I know those guys, it'll be somewhere deep and inaccessible.'

Richardson's sixth sense took over. 'Why're you telling me this? I'm out on compassionate leave.'

'They still want you to go out to Florida.'

'No chance.'

'Your country needs you, Sam.' Dancer immediately regretted his bantering approach.

'She needs me more.' Richardson indicated towards the bed.

'They've got her under control. It's only a question of time till she comes round.'

'They're not sure.'

'Not what I was told. The docs feel pretty confident.'

'I want to be here.'

'You'll be back within seven days. Maximum.'

'No.'

'No choice, Sam.'

'No.'

'Duggan's going with you. There's a flight out in nine hours from Gatwick to Miami.' Dancer took an airline ticket out of his pocket and laid it on the floor between them. 'I think you should be on it.'

'Doesn't anybody give a damn?'

'Of course we do. That's why we do the job we do.'

'You know why they want me to go, don't you?'

'It was to protect HMG from the Angels. It goes further now. They want you to make sure Baxter gets out safely.'

'Save a member of the Army Council?'

'That's what they want. Cleans their hands in public, you see.'

'Bastards!'

'Whatever.' Dancer shrugged. 'It's the only way we can go. Help save Baxter. Try and get some information out of him before the Yanks deport him. Then set up a mass of disinformation so that the PIRA don't trust Baxter any more. That'll send the Provos running for cover because they won't know what else he'll have told us.'

'Which is probably nothing.'

'They don't know that. It'll disrupt the PIRA for a while. Until they're reorganized. If they make mistakes during that period, we'll flush them out.'

'What about the Angels?'

'God knows. Usual rule, Sam. Safeguard HMG.'

'Whatever that means.'

'No. Whatever that entails. And no ideas about revenge. Just protect Baxter and HMG.'

'Carter tell you to pass that on?'

'Yes.'

'Scared to tell me himself?'

'I don't think so. Just knows that we get on. You can meet him if you want.'

'No more meetings.'

'One last thing. Fleet's gun, the one he topped himself with, matched the one used at Biddy Mulligan's. Pretty damn conclusive, I'd say.' Dancer stood up. 'I'll come in to see her every day. Stay as long as I can. Make sure someone's here.'

'I'm not going, Mick,' said Richardson firmly.

'It's down to you. They can't *make* you go.'

'To hell with what they can and can't do. Like I said, I'm not going.'

Dancer left the room. Richardson watched him go, angry about what they expected of him. *No compassion, that was the trouble with the bloody services. England expects and all that* . . . He looked down at the airline ticket the MI5 man had left. Then he turned his attention back to what mattered. Andrea. He would wait until he knew she was out of danger.

Sod them. He wasn't going anywhere until he knew she was all right.

BOOK FOUR

HOME TO ROOST

Miami Airport
Florida

The FBI had arranged with customs and immigration
for the two men to come through without any delay.

The flight had been uneventful. They sat side by
side in Business Class, not saying much throughout
the journey. Richardson slept most of the way; Duggan
watched two movies and helped himself to all that was
going. He wanted to talk about Andrea, but held back,
knowing Richardson was under enough pressure as it
was. He would let the Englishman open up and talk
about her when he was good and ready. As he ate his
second meal and watched Richardson sleeping next to
him, he thought back to his departure from England.

He had arrived at Gatwick Airport ninety minutes
before the Virgin Airlines flight was due to leave.
Dancer was already there and the two men went to
the coffee lounge.

'You've got a lot of faith in him,' he told Dancer.

'Expecting him to turn up when Andrea's in a critical condition.'

'He's a professional. He'll be here.' There was no doubt in Dancer's voice.

'You guys want him over there pretty bad.'

'As much as your people wanted you over here.'

'I wasn't told to interfere.'

Dancer grinned. 'Neither is he. Only you did. Jumping in on that funeral.'

'I'll never live it down, will I?' Duggan reddened. 'That wasn't deliberate.'

'I know. As long as you understand that it's easier to get involved than not.'

'In all this, we've forgotten I'm an analyst. That's why I came over. To analyse what was going on. Sam's a different kettle of fish. He's a front-liner. Is that why you want him there? Front-line duty?'

'Does it matter? I mean, the FBI have accepted he's going over.'

'I need to know. Because – I've become part of you guys.'

'Part of our Circle,' Dancer joked. 'Never ask questions, just do any favour that's asked of you.'

'I guess that's right. But it doesn't stop my mind ticking over.'

'And what conclusion has that drawn, Mister Analyst?'

'That he's there to make sure your government doesn't get drawn any further into the Angel scenario. I just want to know how far you expect him to go. And how much I'm expected to help him.' Duggan waited in vain for an answer. Then, 'I'll help Sam, but I won't harm my own people. Not for anything.'

'Don't expect you to. We're on the same side, you know. Whatever my government's involved in will be supported by yours. Maybe not openly because that wouldn't look good in the headlines. Not politically correct. They don't even know the specifics of what's going on. But they'll secretly support it. And you know why, Francis? Because when your lot get up to no good, which they will one day, they'll expect my government to support them. At the end of the day, they're all scratching one another's backs.' Dancer laughed harshly. 'And people like you and me just go on doing our jobs. Keeping our masters out of trouble. That's why I know Sam'll get on that plane with you. Because we don't know any better.'

Duggan suddenly understood Dancer's belief and wasn't surprised when Richardson turned up forty minutes before the flight. The Englishman ignored the two of them and went straight to the check-in desk. Duggan went and stood behind him in the queue; Dancer moved to the side. Nobody said anything until Richardson had cleared his small suitcase. He stepped to one side as Duggan lifted his bag onto the weighing counter.

'Best of luck, Sam,' Dancer said.

'You said you'd go every day,' was the curt reply.

'Don't worry about that.'

'If there's any improvement—'

'I'll let you know immediately. Through their legal attaché.'

Richardson nodded and walked away from the check-in counter towards the Business Class Lounge. Dancer leant over, patted Duggan on the arm in a gesture of goodwill, then left the airport. The American followed Richardson and waited for the flight to be called.

Bonnilo had decided to meet the flight personally. He suspected the Englishman, Sam Richardson, had come over on a specific errand, not just to observe as the British security services had requested. It was what he would have expected if a group of US Special Forces members were holed up in England.

He liked the look of Richardson as soon as he was introduced. Duggan, the CIA man, was tired, his eyes bleary after the exhausting nine-hour flight. But Richardson was awake, his eyes clear, his brain obviously very alert. When Bonnilo suggested they go to the hotel, the Englishman said he preferred to go to wherever Command Headquarters were. He was a professional and that further appealed to the FBI SAC.

'Still no news on your countrymen,' Bonnilo said as they drove from the airport to the field office in North Miami Beach.

'Don't raise your hopes too much,' replied Richardson. 'These boys can go to ground for a long time. Terrain like the Everglades makes it easier. Remember, they're trained to live for months in the heat and open country of the desert, like they did during the Gulf War.' He referred to the SAS teams who had been dropped behind Iraqi lines to pin-point scud missile-launcher positions so that they could be taken out by allied aircraft and missiles. 'A few alligators and snakes aren't going to cause any problems.'

They entered the Special Incident room in the Miami field office at 5 p.m. and Richardson was immediately impressed with the proficiency of the team. There was an instant rapport between him and the black Supervisor, Solomon Jiggs. Richardson was relieved that they seemed to trust him; he appreciated the fact that no-one seemed to be playing games. They were all there to resolve a dangerous situation. Duggan had gone to the hotel and agreed to return in the evening.

'I expected to see satellite pictures all over the place,' he commented to Jiggs.

'They only do that in movies,' came the bantering reply. 'Getting immediate shots of areas is almost impossible,' he went on. 'Those babies up there are programmed before they get dumped into space. You don't just change their angles of coverage that easily, whatever the publicity says.' He grinned conspiratorially.

'No, we've got something better planned. And it's very old technology.'

Richardson didn't push it; they'd let him know when they were ready. He watched Jiggs slot a VHS tape into a recorder and play it. Rena Baxter came up on the monitor; it was her interview with the FBI in Orlando. It ran for twenty minutes and didn't reveal much. The two children kept interrupting her and she was as defensive as you would expect the wife of an Army Council member to be. At one stage she demanded she be released. When the questioner pointed out that they couldn't guarantee her safety, she soon changed tack. Then she insisted she be sent home to Ireland immediately. She didn't budge from the fact that the family had only come over to Florida for a holiday and she stuck to her story that her husband had arranged to meet her at Space Mountain.

'Lying, of course,' concluded Jiggs when the tape finished. 'She knows what happened.'

'Could be a trick?'

'We considered that. Maybe Baxter was meeting someone over an arms shipment or something. Used this to cover his real movements. Even the call to the Orlando *Sentinel* could've been faked. All possible, except for one thing.' He slipped another tape into the machine. It was an edited version of the recordings that had been taken by the Disney security cameras of Main Street and all its approaches. Jiggs freeze-framed a crowd shot and walked over to the monitor. He pointed at a sunglassed holiday-maker in a Los Angeles Raiders cap. Then he came back to Richardson and showed him a photograph. The Englishman recognized the picture as the one sent over to identify Ray Nathaniel. He looked back at the freeze-frame. There were definite likenesses.

'We took it further,' continued Jiggs. 'Took off the glasses and computer-matched the pictures you sent us with the video shot. This is how it came out.' Jiggs pressed play again and another image appeared on the screen. Nathaniel looking out from under the Raiders cap. There was no doubt in Richardson's mind now. He watched Jiggs run the tape on. Another crowd scene, another freeze-frame, another shot of Nathaniel, identical match-up. 'Then we really got lucky,' Jiggs went on. This time the freeze-frame showed Baxter clearly, his son carried in his left arm. The sunglassed Nathaniel walked beside him, as though escorting him. The man on the other side, yet to be identified as Michael, was obviously part of the team. 'We're sending his picture to London. Hope they can match it up and give us another name.'

Jiggs switched off the video. 'We're still staking out the Pompano Beach office. But I don't think they'll be heading there. We're going to have to break in soon and see if we find anything: maps, letters, any clues. No, they're either heading out of the State or into the Everglades. They can't leave the US. They know we'll be on extra alert at the airports and border crossings.' He leant back on his chair, tilting it onto its back legs. 'So tell me how you can help. And why.'

'You're great on technology, but you don't know how their minds work.'

'You calling us technocrats? No good at anything that a computer can't solve?'

Richardson laughed. 'No. But if we had a crazy FBI man running round London and we couldn't find him, we'd turn to someone who understood how he functioned.'

'Go on.'

'These guys are trained in a certain way. Like I am. What is incomprehensible to you, makes perfect sense to me. You and your technology can only go so far. Then you need to get inside their brain. You guys can't do that. Any more than I could if they were FBI men. To help you, I need to know everything.'

'I thought you were here to observe?'

'I'm here to help catch them. You'd be crazy to turn that down.'

'Why?'

'Because to these guys it's not a question of right and wrong. They're doing a job, like any good soldier. Their motives are secondary to that, it's not a moral question. If these Angels get cornered, they'll make David Koresh and his Branch Davidians in Waco look like real angels. I would've thought that was the last thing the FBI wants – all over again.'

Jiggs grimaced. 'You sure know how to hit below the belt.' He considered for a moment. 'Where do you think they've gone?'

'Everglades.'

'Why?'

'Because they're on ground they know. Rule number one: control the terrain in enemy territory. Two: control the MSR – main supply route. Three: have your Forward Operation Base secured and fully operational. And beyond detection. That includes all resources. Weapons, ammo, communications, observation posts, even explosive booby-traps. Four: have an E and E in place.'

'What's that?'

'Escape and evasion. And finally an ERV: Emergency Rendezvous. So you can start all over again with your secondary FOB. Finding them could be the easy part,' Richardson chuckled. 'It could be you'd save a lot of hassle by not spotting them.'

'We could always get our own Special Forces in.'

'Yes. And they're good. But they'll be at a disadvantage. They don't understand that terrain any more than you do. Nathaniel – I'm presuming he's the Head Shed—'

'What's that?'

'Guy in charge – has already spent months, if not years, out there with his men. They'll know every reed, every alligator's copulating period, everything

425

about their patch. If I help, all I can do is tell you what they're thinking, what they'll do in certain circumstances. When you go after them, that is if you find them in the first place, you'll need a small force.'

'How small?'

'Four, five men. And one of them's got to know the area.'

'You count yourself as one of the men?'

'It makes sense.'

'There's some, not far from where you're sitting, who believe you mean harm to the Angels.'

'Don't we all?'

'We'd like them alive. That may not match your orders.'

'Come on,' countered Richardson. 'You don't really believe these guys are going to come out waving a white flag, do you? Look what happened in London. He shot himself rather than be captured. A pretty desperate act. And pretty committed.' He paused. 'That's', he said eventually, 'the confusing bit. SAS are usually trained to hang on, wait until they might get a chance to escape. We know Spetznaz, and organizations they trained, like South Africa's ANC, believe in suicide rather than capture. There's documented incidents of that. But not our regiments, or your own Special Forces. Just not in our make-up. It's things like that you need my contribution on. Otherwise you're just making it unnecessarily difficult for yourselves.'

'I'll go through your views with my chiefs,' Jiggs acknowledged. 'Can't say I disagree with them. But, it's not my decision.'

'In the meantime, can you tell me about the Everglades?'

Jiggs pulled out a Florida map and took Richardson over it. Stretching from the west of Miami, all the way across to Naples and up past Palm Beach on the east and St Peterburgh on the west, it was a natural wetlands

426

that covered thousands of square miles, nearly all a protected nature reserve. Apart from well-publicized alligators and dangerous water snakes, the Everglades was home to a variety of birdlife including wild turkeys, also large freshwater fish, deer and panthers. The main thoroughfare west to east was Alligator Alley, a straight road that linked Miami to Naples. There were small towns in the Everglades, mostly to the south of Alligator Alley. Towns like Everglades City, Marco Island, Florida City and Bonita Springs. Where Marco Island was a major tourist resort and retirement centre, Everglades City was a reminder of Hemingway and clapboard houses and Andy Hardy porches and wooden window-shutters that rattled at night. Most of the Everglades was what America would have been if time had stood still in the forties and fifties. Jiggs explained that the towns were scattered over the region. He doubted the Angels would have made their base near a community. No, it would have been out in the wilderness that they had taken Baxter, like some great lion dragging a deer it had killed into the undergrowth, away from prying eyes and other predators.

Jiggs told Richardson about another group the FBI had shadowed in the early nineties. Cubans. Rebels waiting to overthrow Castro, backed by big business money in Miami. 'The trouble is that the law allows people to shoot off weapons, even use explosives, on private property. These guys had a training camp, about seven acres, where they trained as terrorists to go back to Cuba. Only trouble was, we couldn't prove they had the intent to do that. As far as the authorities were concerned, they were just playing war games on their own territory.'

Jiggs went on to explain how some of the smaller communities, groups of three or four houses built on the small hummocks of firm land that abounded in the wetlands, would be surprised to see men in combat uniform crossing their backyards carrying grenade-launchers, machine-guns and other weapons of equally destructive power. 'It took months to find where these guys were. Then we ran a surveillance on them. Not easy when the ground's all flat and the trees are too thin to climb.' During their vigil, they had realized the Cubans, about thirty of them, lived a regimented military existence and were a highly trained and motivated unit. In the end, the FBI released their findings to a local TV reporter who came out with a camera crew and filmed the Cubans. The result was that the Cubans became more secretive, but at least were now openly monitored by the FBI, local police and local media. It made life difficult for the rebels as they lived their life in a goldfish bowl.

'We have two agents who cover the Everglades,' Jiggs finished. 'If anyone goes in after the Angels, those two will have to go along.'

'Let's find them first.'

'That's being done,' grinned Jiggs. 'Like I said, old technology sometimes comes up trumps.'

Cape Canaveral Airport
East Coast
Florida

It normally took forty-eight hours to prepare her for flight. Most of that time went on the man who would fly her. Long-duration, high-altitude missions required extremely fit pilots. But this was to be a short flight, no more than sixty minutes, no higher than 50,000 feet.

Nevertheless, Lieutenant-Colonel Sirus Leather still had his blood pressure, temperature, pulse and weight checked out by the Physiological Support Division before he suited up in his Dave Clark S1010B full-pressure rubber suit. He spent an hour reclining in an armchair having pure oxygen pumped through his helmet to purge nitrogen from his body, then climbed into the cockpit of a plane that had made its maiden flight on 1 August 1955.

There weren't many left now, U-2s that had once roamed the skies at over 80,000 feet and photographed a hostile land below. Vietnam, Russia, Cuba, Korea, Iraq and probably even Britain had been regularly visited and snapped by the powerful cameras that hung from its slender belly. Long-winged, a sort of 103-foot-wing-span jet glider powered by the Pratt and Whitney J75-P-13B turbo-jet that rammed it upwards with 17,000 lb thrust into the stratosphere. But times changed, satellites took over in space and fast jets like the F-111Fs and F-117A Stealth fighters with their low- and high-altitude cameras now flew missions over enemy territory. The U-2 faded out of service, apart from the few that were kept by specialist agencies.

NASA maintained two U-2s. Occasionally one of them was lent out to a security service, like the FBI.

The Bureau had requested a U-2 to scan the Everglades. Low-level planes and helicopters would draw attention to themselves and send the Angels scurrying for cover. Satellites would take too long to re-programme. Ground forces would never cover all the territory in time and would, as with the low-level aircraft, be easily noticed.

Using the high-level plane had been Mickleton's idea and he pulled strings in Washington as quickly as he could. The National Security Advisor had immediately accepted Mickleton's recommendation and arranged NASA's involvement. Mickleton, with the help of a USAF reconnaissance team, set up search patterns for the U-2.

Lt-Col Leather applied power on the runway and, due to its low fuel load, the slim plane lifted off after 500 feet. The forward speed was slow, little more than 112 knots, but the high angle of climb, 30 degrees pitch, looked to all the world as though the plane was standing

429

on its tail and punching straight up into the sky. Leather kept the power at 95 per cent until he levelled off at Flight Level 500. The whole procedure had been meticulously planned; with such dense air traffic around Miami he had to follow a strict flight plan for his ascent procedure. Below him the outline and topography of Florida, stretching from the Keys all the way to Jacksonville in the north, stood out clearly. He checked his Inertial Navigation System, then turned towards his first run, over South Florida. The indicated airspeed read 170 knots, but, with an outside air temperature of minus 66°C, he knew she was cruising at nearly 500 knots. He eased the power-setting until she was showing 120 knots – 400 knots cruise.

The big circular screen in front of him showed what the primary RC-10 Wild Heerburg camera was seeing. He was coming over the coast south of Miami. The coast, the other cameras, his flight plan and the reporting points for each shot had already been entered into the computer. He set the autopilot as soon as he was in the cruise and the plane picked up the flight management system computer and set about its task. Leather crossed his hands, relaxed and monitored the instruments.

He flew one run over each segment.

The forward camera, the RC-10 Wild-Heerburg, was on a 6-inch lens. His area of coverage was twenty miles square per frame.

An Itek panoramic camera, based in the belly of the plane, scanned a series of multiple exposures and shot a range thirty miles wide by three miles deep.

The rear camera was another RC-10, but with a 24-inch lens. This time each image was ten miles wide and four miles deep, concentrating on areas away from those parts of the Everglades that could be called populated.

The two at the side shot a series of multiple exposures on the latest Long Range Optical cameras. These

LOROPs had a 66-inch focal length and brought individual houses and their environments into focus in areas already specified as potential zones which could accommodate a secret camp.

When the run was completed, the U-2 turned towards its next parallel run and repeated the procedure.

Sixty minutes later, Leather had finished his task and set about his descent into Cape Canaveral.

The photographs were developed, having been shot on positive Echtakchrome, and were on their way to Miami by helicopter an hour later, just as dusk started to settle on South Florida.

Four hours later, Lt-Col Leather took off again. This time he was loaded with infra-red film. As he traversed the same airspace once more, the infra-red film picked up images of body heat and movement that had been hidden during the daytime shoot. Comparison between the Echtakchrome and the infra-red would show if anything suspicious was hidden on the ground. There were, of course, large animals that would also show up. But, in the end, any group of people would stand out, any regular movement would be highlighted.

As the Everglades slept, Sirus Leather worked his automatic plane across the sky and snapped pictures from his secret lair above the earth's curve.

'This guy's taken you in,' warned Bonnilo. 'Even if he does dress funny, like a character out of *The Avengers*.' He referred to the British TV series that had been a cult hit in America. 'Hell, I never seen shiny shoes like that, even in the Army. And a cravat. I thought those things went out with Ronald Coleman.'

'He's an observer,' added Mickleton. 'Nothing more.'

'Don't mean he's not right,' argued Jiggs. 'He's got the one thing we desperately need. An understanding of the SAS operatives. We don't know what they want, what motivates them, nothing.'

'Does he?'

'He's closer to them than we are.'

'Risky.' Bonnilo shook his head. 'Look what happened to Duggan in Ireland. All over the TV screens because of that damn funeral.'

'That'll be nothing if we go in against the Angels and end up re-running Waco all over again. Now that will make great TV. One David Koresh is enough. I agree with Richardson when he says we need a small force.'

'Don't disagree with that. But no Englishman.'

'Who have we got who knows the Everglades?' asked Mickleton.

'Two men. One's retired, but comes in when we need him. They mostly deal with drugs coming into the wetlands. Plane-drops out of the Caribbean and Cuba, that sort of stuff. I've got them coming in tomorrow.'

'Where's Richardson and Duggan?'

'Waiting in the commissary,' said Jiggs. 'I'm going to stand my ground. I want the Brit in with us.'

'We'll see. First of all let's find the Angels. And Mr Baxter. If he's still alive.'

The phone rang and Bonnilo answered it. 'OK, we're coming down,' he said and hung up. 'Pictures are here from Canaveral.'

'About time,' snarled Mickleton. 'What about the infra-reds?'

'By dawn.'

'Can I ask Richardson to join us?' asked Jiggs.

'Why?'

'He might just see something in those pictures which identifies some sort of camp. I don't know what. But every little's going to help.'

Mickleton nodded agreement and Jiggs went to get Duggan and Richardson. 'He's pushy,' said Mickleton when Jiggs left.

'That's why he's good. Never gives up.'

'Yeah, yeah, yeah.' Mickleton laughed. 'Don't know what's so funny. We're going to be up all night going through these aerial shots. How many men have we called in?'

'Fifteen. We've also arranged some portable light tables for viewing these pictures on. Brought down from an old Air Force Reconnaissance store that used to be at Homestead Air Base. A couple of the NASA men are coming down to supervise and we've got two more retired Air Force personnel to help. Both guys worked for AirRecon during Vietnam. With that many, we might just get through the pictures by the morning.'

North of Alligator Alley
Interstate 75
Florida

Ethan West looked out on the flat blackness of the wetlands. It was five-thirty in the morning and he had been awake for over an hour, pottering round the house as he did each morning, cleaning up the mess from the day before. He had always been a light sleeper, needing no more than four hours a night to recharge his batteries.

As he tidied up, he watched the sun rise gently, a shimmering redness over the swamp and hummocks to the east. He stopped and watched dawn break; it was something he always enjoyed, that exciting sense of newness that began each day. He had first visited the wetlands over twenty years ago when he hired a car and drove from Miami towards Naples, along Alligator Alley, on the west coast of Florida. He'd never seen the large reptiles before and naïvely presumed he would see them along the highway that was the only link between the two coasts. There were no alligators; the traffic on the road sent the shy reptiles further into the safety of the wetlands. Tired of the solitary drive along the single-lane, ever-straight highway, he had turned off the road when he saw a sign pointing to the Miccossukee Indian reservation.

The calm of the place, away from the rushing traffic, had immediately made him feel this was where he belonged. The Miccossukee Sioux had settled here after being chased south from Georgia by the white settlers and the US Cavalry. They had come down into the swamps of Florida and fought a long and bitter war until the US Government finally accepted that they could not beat the Indians and sued for peace. The result was the birth of the only area of the USA which still retained certain Indian rights and became accepted as the Miccossukee Sioux Indian Nation. The Miccossukee farmed the area and lived amongst the hummocks of the wetlands, free to live their life in the traditional way. In time, most of them integrated with the whites who had come south and learnt to live as neighbours, not plagued by the prejudices that affected the other indigenous tribes like the Apache and Commanche who had taken on the white settlers and lost.

Within two hours of stumbling onto a small Miccossukee farm and speaking with the Indians, Ethan West was on his way into Everglades City to find a local realtor. The Everglades became his home and he never felt the urge to uproot himself again. Everglades: Sioux language for 'river of grass'. Only the grass wasn't the same as your back-garden variety. It was mostly sawgrass, downward-toothed grass that could tear a man's hand badly if it was gripped and pulled the wrong way.

He was fifty-three now, and retired. After fifteen years in the US Marine Corps, a spell in Vietnam and a final posting with the Special Forces as a full sergeant, he joined the FBI when the Bureau broke from its tradition of only recruiting lawyers and brought in agents with a wider experience in the world of espionage, police work and military expertise. He left the FBI twelve years later, the result of a damaged back which he suffered while on surveillance in New York. He was part of a team watching an American sailor suspected of passing information through an East German diplomat to the KGB. It was a simple operation, the sailor believing he was clear of any suspicion. The ease of the surveillance made Ethan, for the only time in his life, careless. After all, the Berlin Wall had fallen and the spy business was changing, even though the KGB, or the TSRA as it was now known, was still in the market for electronic secrets. Ethan was crossing West 28th Street when the sailor turned and recognized him as someone he had seen before. The sailor swung round and rushed him, surprising Ethan who didn't realize he had been recognized. Ethan fell backwards, across the bonnet of a passing taxi, and cracked his spine as he was thrown onto the pavement. He tried to follow the sailor, but his legs were paralysed and he found himself crawling along the road, pulling himself by his hands. When the ambulance came, he was taken to a nearby hospital. He was lucky; the damage wasn't too serious and after a few months' convalescence he was posted to Washington. That was four years earlier and he now lived on his pension as well as being called in as an adviser to the Bureau when they needed help in the Everglades.

Ethan West was a contented man.

Now as the redness gave way to a wave of early morning light, he saw the panther lying low, its stomach hugging the ground, on the far side of the clearing in front of his house. It was watching some prey, its tail flicking with anticipation as it lay still in the long grass where the hummock ran into the swamp. These hummocks, small areas of trees and bushes, were scattered over the wetlands and were a natural habitat for the Florida panthers, the deer and the turkey gobblers that lived in the area. He moved back into the room slowly so as not to startle the big cat and reached for the binoculars. He focused on the panther, then followed the direction of its stare into the hummock. It was a deer, nervously feeding on its own, unaware of the stalker. Every time the deer turned its back on the panther, the cat moved closer before settling down on its belly again. Ethan watched for nearly ten minutes, watched the panther get within striking distance of the deer. He knew the moment had suddenly come as the panther got ready to spring.

The alligator, which had also been stalking the deer, exploded out of the swamp, just as the panther was about to strike. The startled deer fell backwards, then turned and ran before the reptile could get to it with its vast jaws which were open and ready to snap. The deer escaped into the hummock and safety as the alligator crashed back into the water, causing a mighty foam to swirl about where the water had once been still. *Big bastard*, thought an awed Ethan. *A twelve-footer*. Then it was all over, the water settling down to its flatness once again, the hunter and the prey now departed their separate ways. Ethan turned his attention to the panther. It knew it had lost, and it now licked and cleaned itself, almost as if saying to any watcher, 'I wasn't that interested anyway.' Then the panther jumped up, surprised by some sudden movement, and disappeared into the hummock.

Ethan swung the binoculars towards the swamp and saw Red Snake George. The Miccossukee Indian, in his early thirties, wearing jeans and a black Guns 'n' Roses T-shirt, grinned and waved at him, shouldered his Second-World-War British De Lisle Carbine, and vanished back into the wetlands. The rifle, made mostly of Lee Enfield Mark 3 parts, was built round the 45 ACP cartridge and had clever silencer baffles that made it one of the quietest carbines ever designed, almost silent with a sound that was more of a whiplash crack than the normal boom associated with such powerful weapons.

It was a relic, brought back by an Indian GI who had fought in Europe, and was ideal for hunting in the wetlands, more powerful than a bow and arrow, yet almost as silent as the shadows in which the stalker hid.

He returned the binoculars to their place. He had a good rapport with the Indians; they accepted him as best they could a white man who had no obvious desire either to take what was theirs or pity them for not having taken all the advantages the modern world had to offer.

He went to the big switch panel on the wall and flicked the window and door alarm off. The big board was interspaced with numeric pads and he punched most of them so that the perimeter security alarms were also deactivated. He chuckled as he thought of Red Snake George. All the electronic beams, heat sensors and sound detectors that guarded his perimeter were no match for the Indian; he ghosted himself through the wetlands, but then it was his natural home. Ethan went into the kitchen and prepared some coffee. He put two tin mugs out and waited for his guest, his ears ready to pick up any sudden sound.

Hanging above him were his favourite weapons, a pair of Big Joe and Little Joe crossbows. He envied the Miccossukee Indians their expertise with the bow and arrow. They mostly used guns for their hunting trips, but they had retained their heritage with the wooden bow. Ethan tried to master it but it was beyond him, so he adopted the crossbow and became accomplished with it. The Big Joe was his favourite, a Second-World-War design by the Americans with the fire-power to penetrate a German steel helmet at thirty yards. Instead of a single string, it was powered by a series of elastic strings, connected to a modern trigger and aimed by two pistol grips and a tubular metal butt that gave it the appearance of a carbine rifle. Little Joe was the pistol equivalent of its big brother, with a single pistol grip and trigger.

Ethan West, once the quintessential FBI agent, now wore jeans most of the time and raggedy oil-stained T-shirts. He was never without his cowboy boots; his pride and joy was one pair which he always wore to special functions that he had discovered at the back of a Western shop. The boots were made of rattlesnake skin, and at the toe was the head of a small rattlesnake, its fangs drawn back as though they were about to strike. At the heels of these fearsome boots, the rattlers' tails stuck out, rattling like some awful spurs as he walked along. It was almost as if someone had cut two rattlers in half and wrapped them around Ethan's feet.

The tattoo on his right forearm was his final joke to the world. *Born to Lose* it proclaimed in a serif typeface which had a snarling, multi-coloured rattlesnake sliding through the words. Until he'd injured his back, he'd always been a winner. Now that he'd found his peace, *Born to Lose* was his signature on his life, a man who had fought for what was his and could finally discount all that he had achieved.

To strangers who passed him, Ethan was a tough guy to be avoided. To those he did business with, he was a hard-working nut who never let them down. To the Indians, he was a free spirit, somehow living out life as he wanted to, a soul that had sinned and been pardoned by the gods and was now as much a part of their habitat as the alligator, the panther or the night owl that swooped on the snakes and small creatures.

He heard the creak from the floor-board in the hall and swung round. Too late. Red Snake George was already in the room, his rifle pushed into Ethan's back.

Ethan laughed and handed him a mug of coffee. 'I'll get you one day,' he said.

'You got no chance,' said the Indian, putting his gun down with one hand as he took the mug. 'It's not in your spirit. You settlers just can't hack it.'

'Crap.' Ethan took his coffee and the two men sat at the table. 'That was a big-un.'

'I watched that cat for twenty minutes while she stalked the deer. That gator just went too soon. Too damn impatient. Another minute and he woulda taken her.'

'What're you doing out this way? Didn't expect you till next week.'

'They want you in Miami.' Red Snake George was the Bureau's Special Agent in the Everglades. This was his territory and he spent most of the time gaining information on newcomers, trying to determine when drug runs would take place and helping with the round-up of illegal immigrants. Like Ethan, he had served in the military and been seconded to the Special Forces. That experience, albeit on separate tours of duty, had made the men close friends. They trusted each other. They covered each other's back.

The two men met each fortnight to compare notes and relax with a day's hunting.

'What for?' enquired Ethan.

'Big operation. Here in the Everglades. I got the van about a mile from here. We should be in Miami by nine. Looks like we're going to be stars, Ethan. Looks like our time has come.'

'Hey, I'm in retirement.'

'Part-time retirement. They got Hank Mickleton down from Washington for this one. Bonnilo's involved and Jiggs is running a big team.'

'Drugs?'

'Don't think so. Something else. Big potatoes.' Red Snake George finished his coffee and stood up. 'They want us in soon. They said we should come in together. And bring a tooth-brush.'

That concerned Ethan. What was so important that Miami expected him to spend a night away from home? They'd never asked that before. He shrugged; he took life as it came. No point in changing his ways now.

RAMS Camp
Everglades
Florida

Lucifer and Michael walked under the cover of trees, their shoulders wrapped in reflective material, a silver-coated thin plastic which made it difficult for infra-red detection to pick up body or other heat.

The trees flanked a cleared site on a four-acre raised hummock. The whole area was filled with gravel and, at the south end, there were two rows of three, 3-man, waterproof khaki tents. These tents were lined on the inside with the same reflective material Lucifer and Michael wore. On the west side, next to a deep canal that separated the site from the wetlands, lay a larger tent ready to be rolled up. This had once housed all the supplies needed by RAMS. There was also a wooden stage eight feet by eight feet, a small water-tower, no more than twelve feet high, and a small, green block building with a metal, padlocked door where the weapons and explosives were normally stored. Baxter had been left, still gagged and bound, in this building. Sitting outside the door, a carbine across his knees, wrapped in a reflective blanket, was Penuel. An obstacle course, wooden walkways and rigging nets, had once crossed the centre of the area, running east–west, and the northern half of the site was an open training area. To the north-east, where the two men sheltered under trees, ran a target and firing range.

The tents were being dismantled by Raphael, rolled up and hidden under the trees. The remains of the obstacle course lay littered across the field.

'Would you go like that?' asked Michael, referring to the news they had picked up on the radio a few hours earlier about Gabriel. His death, although partly expected, had come as a tremendous shock to the Angels. Apart from the radio reports, there was no further way they could get news. They had once, a year before, tried a small portable TV, but there were no signals strong enough out here. They were cut off from the world, apart from their tenuous broadcast link, and they had little to rely on apart from their own imagination and experience.

'He was following orders,' replied Lucifer.

'Yeah, but could you do it? I mean, we were always trained to hang on.'

'Don't count on the cavalry this time. He was a nutter, anyway.'

'Only at the end. George was a great intelligence man in his time. You can understand it driving him barmy. I mean, he gave everything he had to the Regiment. Then they fling him because he's too aggressive. And he still came in with us – believed in what he was doing – knew that's what the Army should've done years ago.'

'Still bloody loopy,' dismissed Lucifer.

'Then why bring him on board?'

'Because we're all loopy. Every one of us.' Lucifer snorted with laughter. 'Wouldn't be here, would we? If we were sane. Officers and gentlemen. Jesus! Mercenaries fighting for our own country, that's what we are.'

The two men stood in silence for a while, the heat obtrusive and irritating under their reflective blankets. But they both preferred it to the cramped, humid stillness of the small tents. Their thoughts were broken by a small Piper light plane crossing overhead.

'We don't have a lot of time left,' said Michael as he watched the plane bank towards the east.

'You think it was a mistake snatching Baxter, don't you?'

Michael shrugged. 'Doesn't matter now. He's here.'

'You made your point when we discussed it. Before we went after him.'

'I'll still give it my best. Whatever I feel. This is your command. We're still in uniform as far as I'm concerned. You're wearing the stripes.'

'Do you think we should still change tack?'

'Too late now.' Michael didn't want Lucifer to feel his authority was challenged. He was a good leader, had organized each operation efficiently. 'I just think we've got to move on now. We still haven't completed our mission. Isolate the PIRA from their overseas supporters through fear, through letting them know what it's like being at the receiving end of terrorist action. We're ready to move on from here if the FBI get too close. It's a big country to get lost in, which is why we chose it. Hell, with the funds we've got available, we could run the operation for years without being traced. Baxter's taken away our mobility. His disappearance has put the pressure on the security agencies to find us quickly.'

'Not that easy.'

'Too chancy hanging around here. Listen, they were calling Baxter's name at Disney World. They knew he was there. They could have all our IDs. And they'll link one of us with George. I think we've got to get out of here by the morning. We'd be risking too much if we left together. Too many people watching for us. If they've traced RAMS and Pompano, it'll only be a matter of time before they find someone who came out here.'

'No-one ever knew where this was.'

'We can only run for so long.'

'What're you suggesting?' asked Lucifer.

'Get everything we can out of Baxter, then dump him, split up, and make our own ways out of here. Just spread out over America, get lost in it. Hell, we've got enough safe houses set up. One of us can ring home and tell them what Baxter said.'

'Break up all we've worked for.'

'Just put it on hold. You took the gamble that any information we got out of Baxter would help our security boys. Let's concentrate on that. Maybe it'll give our government the balls to attack the PIRA's primary targets and force the Provos to the conference table without any pre-conditions. That's what all this was about, wasn't it?' Michael started to laugh. 'RAMS wasn't a money-spinner, anyway. Not even a decent living. Even this place was lent to us by that bird you were knocking off. I hope she doesn't put two and two together.'

'She's working in Germany. Not back for another year.'

'We've gone as far as we can. I think the other two'll agree. Arrange to meet up in six months. We'll agree a destination and a time.'

'We need quick results from Baxter.'

'No problem. He deserves it, anyway.'

'These boys are taught to handle pain. Just beating him's not enough.'

'Well, there's pain and there's—' Michael stopped. 'I can get quick information. A Cuban told me. Years ago. In a bar in Miami. We were just chatting and we got on to pain. It was something the North Koreans dreamt up. They passed it on to Castro's lot. Half an hour and we'll have what we want.'

'Didn't know cruelty was your game.'

Michael looked closely into Lucifer's eyes. 'It's what we've become. Outcasts. It doesn't matter what we do any more – does it?' He decided not to search for his own torment any longer. 'What do we do with Baxter afterwards?'

'He's a bonus. Any information out of him will be priceless to London. Let's worry about that when we've got what we want.'

The two men went to help Raphael dismantle the tents. They were all tired. Dismantling the remains of the obstacle course that once straddled the site had kept them up all night. But that's what they were trained to do. Tiredness was part of their life, just as commonplace as the danger they were about to face.

FBI Miami Field Office
16320 NW 2nd Avenue
North Miami Beach

The FBI moved into the RAMS Pompano Beach office at seven-thirty, just before nearby office and shop workers clocked on.

The first agent to enter through the front door was an expert lock-picker. When he clicked the lock, he stepped back and allowed another agent, a bomb disposal operative, carefully to enter the outer office. The operative was wearing a Kevlar bomb-suit with ceramic ballistic tiles, special leggings, sleeves and a helmet, weighing nearly 60 lbs. He moved slowly, checking for any booby-traps that might have been laid. He checked for loose floor-boards under the carpet, checked light-switches, and looked for detonators connected to drawers and filing cabinets. Fifteen minutes later, when he was satisfied, he signalled the armed agents, with their protective bullet-proof vests, into the room behind him. When they had taken up their positions, he carefully opened the second door.

Nothing happened. He moved slowly into this room and repeated the process. When he was once again satisfied, he signalled the back-up team into the second room.

The explosives man followed the same procedure for Room Three and the toilet.

The offices seemed clear.

He took off his helmet and bomb-suit and declared the offices safe.

The rest of the experts moved in, fingerprint and communications men.

They would later find that the offices had been wiped clean. No fingerprints, no letters, no paperwork, no rubbish, nothing to tell the FBI the identity of those who had once worked there.

The communications man realized he had triggered off a warning when he lifted the telephone receiver in the second room. It broke a contact with a transmitter in the base that immediately dialled a number of a mobile phone and emitted a loud, shrill beep. The communications man had to smash the base before he could get to the transmitter and stop it.

In the Everglades camp, Lucifer listened to the shrill echo over the mobile phone handset. He turned the phone off. 'Somebody's broken into Pompano,' he told Michael. 'Probably the Feds or Special Forces. Looks like we're running out of time.'

The two men walked towards the green block building where Penuel sat cross-legged guarding the Army Council man.

Jiggs handed Tom Leese some chalk and leant back in his chair. Richardson, Red Snake George and Ethan West were also in the room. Another agent stood at the back, taking notes and running a tape recorder. Bonnilo had decided that Jiggs should interview the man who had been on the survival course while he and Mickleton concentrated on the aerial photos.

Leese, feeling important because he saw himself as part of an urgent investigation, yet nervous and feeling unnecessarily guilty as people often do in front of officialdom, crossed over to the blackboard in the small meeting-room and drew a rectangle, then started

445

to fill it in with lines, childlike drawings and a few written descriptions.

Richardson half watched Leese; his real interest lay with the two Everglades agents, especially Ethan West. The older FBI man fascinated him, especially his cowboy boots with the rattlers' heads and tails. When Ethan first walked into the room, Richardson recognized the stiff military stance of an old soldier. Only this soldier had let go of the tentacles of his military upbringing and was now as loose as any man could expect to be. Ethan shook hands with Richardson, a big welcoming smile on his craggy face, laughingly warning the Englishman to count his fingers after shaking hands with his partner, Red Snake George.

'Like your boots,' commented Richardson lightly.

'If you ever need a job, I know a few shoe-shine locations you could make a killing at,' was Ethan's reply. 'Like your cravat.' Ethan grinned and moved to the chair in the furthest corner of the room where he sprawled loose-limbed and dangling as he waited for Jiggs to begin.

Richardson scraped up a chair and sat down, annoyingly aware that Ethan was behind him, watching him, observing from the high ground. He grinned; his outfit was probably as strange to Ethan as Ethan's was to Richardson. Red Snake George coiled himself into another chair, pulled out a big wide Bowie knife from a shoulder holster and proceeded to strop it loosely in his palm, as though sharpening it. Richardson smiled; these boys were modern frontiersmen, good people to have on your side.

Leese finished his drawing and turned round.

'That's about how I remember it,' he said to the room.

'Walk us through it.' Jiggs leant forward in his chair. 'I know it was a long time ago, but just try and recall everything you can.'

'It was about five, six acres.' He grinned sheepishly

446

at the men watching him. 'Never was good at drawing.'

'No matter,' supported Jiggs. 'That arrow to the right – what's that?'

'South. I remember that. Worked it out from the sun's path.'

Where did the wind come from?' asked Ethan.

'Don't remember too well. Swirled about quite a bit. Had a couple of days when storm clouds blew up strong gale force winds. Why?'

'If it was from one direction most of the time, you'd've been near the sea. Sea breeze, that's all.'

'Let's not wander,' Jiggs warned the others. 'We're running short on time.' He concentrated on Leese. 'Tell me about the camp. What you remember. Its layout.'

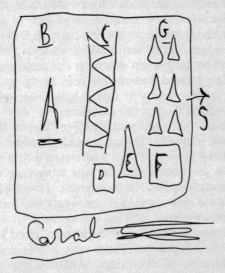

Leese turned back to the blackboard. '*A* was a training and exercise field. About one hundred yards by one hundred and fifty. *B* was the rifle and target range.'

'What weapons?'

'Mostly revolvers and semi-automatics. We had one

light machine-gun. I don't remember the makes. We'd put up targets and fire south to north.'

'Go on.'

'*C* was an obstacle course. Made of wood, tree trunks, netting, a wooden wall about eight feet high. It was a bitch. Included one section where you crawled underground, really cramped, then stayed put for a helluva long time till they called you out. Thought it was all gonna collapse on—'

'About sixty feet long?' interrupted Richardson. 'With stones and sharp points sticking up? And damp, half-full of water? And what seemed like snakes moving alongside you?'

Leese nodded. 'That's about it.'

'SAS training methods,' Richardson told the room. 'The snakes are only short lengths of rope to scare you. For fun, they sometimes put real nasty stuff down there. Even buckets full of worms. Doesn't sound much, but it's mind-blowing when you're in the dark and they're squiggling around underneath you, being squashed in the dark. The theory is that if you keep quiet down that hole, you'll keep still anywhere.'

'It wasn't that bad,' said a relieved Leese. 'Just dark and scary. Anyway, *D* was a small platform. About a foot off the ground. That's where they'd drill you from and give you your orders. *E* was a big supply tent, *F* was a brick building. A dirty green. Had a padlocked door. It's where they kept the weapons. And *G* was small tents we lived in. That was about it.'

'What was the surface of the camp?' asked Ethan.

'Gravel. Chippings. There was a tree-line at the boundaries on all four sides. Although the area was flat, it was pretty well camouflaged by trees. Not too high, but thick enough to shield us from people going by.'

Red Snake George opened a file of photographs and showed them to Leese. Slowly Leese identified a variety of trees he recognized from the camp. Australian Malaleuca and scrub pine. It didn't help; those were the natural trees of the 1.4 million acres of Everglades. 'Ever hear any cars near by?' he asked.

'No. Maybe occasionally, but it wasn't regular.'

'Airboats?' Jiggs referred to the big-prop airboats that skimmed across the Everglades.

'Not really. Not real close, anyhow. I mean, there were a lot of canals in those parts. But I think the airboats go out on the open swamp. Lot of this land looked reclaimed.'

'How wide was that waterway to the west?'

'Twenty, thirty feet across. Oh!' Leese suddenly recalled something. 'There was a water-tower between the supply tent and the green building. Not very high, maybe ten, twelve feet.'

'These guys were all British?' asked Richardson.

'Yeah,' came Leese's reply. 'They all sounded English. I've been to your country. Didn't hear any Scottish or Irish accents.'

'Or Welsh?'

'No.'

'Ex-soldiers?'

'Said they were. Acted like it, too. Confident, knew what they were at.'

'They tell you about themselves?'

Leese shook his head. 'They kept apart from the rest of us. Only time we communicated was when we were on patrol or being trained.'

'Wasn't that strange? Not to discuss normal things.'

'That's how they said it had to be. The chain of command. Unquestioned authority. Necessary for discipline.' Leese clucked to himself. 'Hell, they were tough. One of them, Captain D, he—'

'What sort of name's that?' cut in Jiggs.

'We had to operate under that system. Captain A, B, C, D and E. No names, just rank and letter.'

'You were saying about Captain D.'

'Oh, yeah. There were a couple of snakes sunning on the reeds when we were out on patrol. Big bitches. Poisonous as hell. He said we should wade right past them – you could reach out and touch them. We didn't want to do that. So he stripped off. Everything. Shoes, pants, everything. Then he waded in, water up to his waist, and walked right past them, closer than driving up to a McDonald's take-away counter. He came back again and made us follow him. Shit, were we scared. Even the snakes got pissed off and swam away.'

Jiggs pulled some photos out of a folder and showed them to Leese. 'Recognize them?'

'Yeah. That's them. Three of them.' He pointed at George Fleet. 'That's Captain D.' He then identified Nathaniel and Rush. 'Say, you boys are really getting hold of this.'

'You say you went on patrol?' continued Ethan. 'You see anything around the camp that might help us find this location?'

'No. They always kept us moving in the trees. Thick foliage. Saw one or two planes, nothing more.'

'Coming in to land, or taking off? Maybe there was an airport nearby?'

'No. These small babies just flew overhead. Single-engine stuff.'

'You didn't see any big jets regularly overhead? High up, but slow-moving, maybe on a flight path in to an airport, say, twenty, thirty miles away?'

'Nothing routine, no. I remember a road near by. A white road. We crossed it a couple of times when we were out on patrol.'

'What do you mean, white?'

'Shale. White chippings. But a proper road. Just wasn't paved.'

'Did it lead to the camp?'

'It mighta done. The entrance was always camou-flaged.'

'Any special smells?' continued Red Snake George.

'Like what?'

'Sweet. Like sugar burning.'

'No.'

'Or heavy black smoke? Either in the distance or just heavy, in the air?'

'Nothing like that.'

'That eliminate something?' Jiggs asked.

'It's cane country just south of Lake Okachobee. Hundreds of thousands of acres, all owned by the American Sugar Corporation. Always burning the cane fields after they harvest them. If he'd been in that vicinity, he'd've smelt the sugar. I think that means they ain't in the town of South Bay or anywhere round the lake on the south side.' Red Snake George leant towards Leese. 'You remember anything else about that white road?'

'No. I told you, we arrived there in a van.' Leese defended himself.

'Blindfolded?'

'Not all the way. But the van had no windows. We arrived in the dark, had to be blindfolded again while they led us to the tents. I heard the van drive off and when we came out into the daylight, there was no sign of anything that linked us to the outside world.' Leese shrugged. 'I just know there was a white road that we crossed on patrol. I'm guessing that it went all the way to the camp. We always returned through the trees and the swamp.'

Jiggs turned to the agent who had been taking notes. 'Leave the tape running, but copy that design on the board and get it to the SAC. Tell them about the white road and the water-tower. At least it gives them some-thing to look for with those aerial pictures.'

The agent held up his pad, the drawing already

copied on it. 'Got it,' he said and left the room.

They questioned Leese for another fifteen minutes, but his memory didn't take them much further. He remembered a small, metal footbridge that crossed the waterway and a stone plaque by the roadside that had an engraving and description of the Florida Panther. He also recalled one of the Englishmen mentioning a nearby Alligator and Snake Reserve. When Leese had gone, Jiggs asked the two Everglades agents if they had any further ideas about the location of the camp.

'Could be a thousand places,' said Red Snake George. 'All over the wetlands.'

'But you can't hide a big camp like that for ever. Someone must know where it is.'

Ethan shook his head. 'You remember the Cuban terrorist camp we searched for. Only twelve miles off Alligator Alley. Damn thing took for ever to find. And that was a similar set-up. Six acres, tents, a shooting range. Hell, there's probably a dozen survival camps out there. Privately owned, where men can be soldiers and make like they're Errol Flynn. The only way we'll cover them is by aerial recons, then send agents in.'

'We can't run that play this time, Ethan.'

'Why not?'

'Washington will not risk another David Koresh siege. This time we don't wait for the cameras. Just do the business before anyone finds out.'

'That why me and George are here?'

'It's your territory. Isn't that the action you Special Forces boys like?'

'Hell, I'm retired,' the big man protested, an even bigger smile across his face.

'Yeah. And my name's Edgar Hoover.'

'Who?' came back Red Snake George immediately. The two Everglades agents grinned at each other; it was a gas taking the piss out of the sober suits at Head Office.

'Switch off,' warned Jiggs, 'before you get into jives about wearing skirts and high heels.'

'What? Us?' chortled Ethan. 'Hell, we're real men. Dresses maybe, but not high heels.'

Jiggs shook his head in mock despair. 'Come on. We've got business to get through.'

'We can run a check on stone signs with panthers engraved on them. Florida State Park office may have that. I know the boys down there. The same with South Florida Water Management, too. At least that narrows the search area.'

'Why?' asked Richardson.

'Because the southern Everglades is designated a Florida Panther Refuge area. From Miami across to Naples and fifty miles up. Includes the Big Cypress Swamp and National Preserve. That's where the big cats live.'

'Unless he's feeding you disinformation. Maybe there weren't any panthers. Maybe he wants you to believe that.'

'Why should he do—' Jiggs stopped himself. Richardson had a good point; Leese could be a siphon to the Angels. 'We checked him pretty good. He's a reputable lawyer.'

'No lawyer's reputable,' cut in Ethan, who had a natural distrust of all administrators. 'Could be our English boy's got a point.'

'I'll get someone to go back and check his record. Up to now it all stacks up.' Jiggs changed tack. 'Get any illustrations and locations of panther signs the State Park office has recorded. Show them to Leese. Might just jog his memory. What about the Alligator and Snake Reserve?'

'The whole state's that,' Red Snake George pointed out. 'Unless he got mixed up. Coulda meant an alligator show. Or a farm.'

'Find where they're sited. Then tell the recon room.

They can concentrate on those areas while they go through the U-2 photos. And they can check any white roads with waterways near by that have metal foot-bridges across them. Let's remember the southern Ever-glades tie in with the phone calls to the Angels from Europe. All within half an hour of Big Cypress.' Jiggs stood up. 'OK, let's get to it.' The two Everglades agents left the room as Richardson stood up. 'Don't feel too lost, Sam. When the time's right, we'll find something for you to do.'

'I feel like a spare prick at a eunuchs' reunion.'

Jiggs laughed. 'Come on.' He led the way out of the room. 'I'll show you Florida like you've never seen it before.'

The FBI had converted the biggest conference room in the North Miami Beach field office into a makeshift reconnaissance room.

All the furniture had been cleared from the room and four old light tables, brought down from the old Air Force Reconnaissance store, were set up next to each other. The tables, stock from the Vietnam War, were metal-legged with clear-glass tops, standing 4 feet 6 inches high. Light-tubes illuminated each table from underneath. At the ends of each table were two large take-up spools with handles on them for hand-cranking. The spools were twelve inches wide and accommodated part of the large rolls of film that had been removed earlier from the belly of the U-2. A photo-interpreter worked at each station, a floating stereoscope on the table in front of him. The film, a positive image, was on clear material so the lights could shine up through the table and illuminate the area the photo-interpreter was examining.

Jiggs led Richardson to the second table, where Duggan sat on a stool next to the photo-interpreter. The CIA man looked up and acknowledged Richardson with a warm smile.

'The frames overlap each other,' advised Jiggs. 'You lay two pictures next to each other, with about a third overlapped, and you see it in 3-D when you look through the stereoscope.'

The photo-interpreter looked up. 'Want to see?' he asked.

'Thanks,' said Richardson as the photo-interpreter stepped away from his position. Richardson looked through the two eyepieces and saw a clear 3-D image of an aerial shot of a section of swamp in the Everglades. As his eyes accustomed to the picture he saw a small boat with two men fishing. The clarity of the shot amazed him.

'The optics are so fine that we can read a postage stamp on an envelope from thirty thousand feet.'

'We could've waited for satellite coverage. This may be old-fashioned, but it's cheaper and quicker to get into place,' added Jiggs. 'We don't always demand the resources and budgets you northern boys do,' he joked with Duggan.

'I'm not even responding to such a cheap jibe,' came back Duggan's good-humoured answer. There was always a cutting rivalry between the FBI and CIA. 'Expected more of you.'

'Where're we up to?' Jiggs turned his attention back to the photo-interpreter.

'Nothing to catch the imagination yet. We're concentrating our energies on white roads, canal areas, open five-acre sites that look like a military training camp, all in the southern Everglades.'

Jiggs was aware that Richardson was watching him closely. 'I don't think we should ignore the rest of the wetlands.'

'I'm running three of the tables on the southern area. North of Lake Kissimmee, up towards Orlando, I've got one interpreter working on that.'

'We're aware that Leese could be leading us down

a wrong alleyway,' added Duggan.

'You Company boys are just naturally suspicious,' replied Jiggs.

One of the agents came over and told Richardson there was a call for him from London.

'Take it in my office,' said Jiggs. 'We're going to monitor it, anyway,' he laughed. 'If not here, then the Puzzle Palace will pick it up over the Atlantic.'

Richardson was escorted to Jiggs's office, a small sparse room with a highly polished wooden desk and large executive chair. The agent dialled through to the switchboard, then handed Richardson the phone and left the room. The Englishman waited until the door had closed before he spoke. 'Hello?'

'Hi,' came Dancer's reply. 'We've got to accept this is an open line. Whatever I'm telling you is already being faxed to Washington and Miami from their legal attaché.'

'How is she?'

'Fine. Doing as expected. Still critical, but settling down. They feel confident she'll pull through.'

'Did you spend the—?'

'Most of the night. Sat right outside her room.'

'Thanks.'

'I'll get along there later on. Any change, and I'll be straight on to you. Whatever time of day or night.' Dancer moved on. 'Got some more on our Angels. Pictures are on their way to you. Believe Michael is an ex-captain from Brigade. Close friend of Nathaniel's. David Walker. G3 Intelligence Liaison. Was responsible for surveillance operations. Walker was one of the best. A dedicated soldier, loyal and inventive. Worked closely with TGC.' Dancer chuckled. 'That's Task Group Co-ordinating for them that's eavesdropping. Walker was in constant liaison with all the various agencies, including Special Branch and the Gardaí. Even worked for Box for a while. Immigration have him coming in to Heathrow the day before the Biddy Mulligan's attack. He flew out from Manchester the day after. Direct to Miami. That tells me they were in a rush and they didn't have time to cover Walker's tracks. We know Fleet wanted assistance and Michael was his back-up.'

'One to go. The Dublin bomber.'

'Walker's brother. Damien. Younger by two years. Also gone to ground. Visited America eighteen months ago on a tourist passport. Ex-NI. Explosives man. A squaddie, but responsible and a deft hand for going into tight, secure areas. He would've known about Darcy. Probably worked him when Darcy was giving us information. Any contact between the two of them would've been without our knowledge. But that's how it worked; it was the only protection the supergrass had. Darcy had to deal with an explosives man. It was that connection that led us to find out how to make PIRA bombs. We ran a check on Dublin arrivals. Nothing in the name of Damien Walker. It was a planned operation, probably had a fake passport.'

'Any motives?'

'They're both Barnardo's boys. No family, just each other. Nothing to lose.' There was an electronic pause. 'David Walker lost two of his best friends in Ulster. Both killed in a pub bombing. When the brass told him he was redundant, I guess he had nowhere else to go.'

'That makes quite a team.'

'It does. Nathaniel running the show with all his experience of covert operations. Fleet, Rush and the Walkers. Between them they cover every aspect of covert operations. And each one was bloody good at what he did.'

'But why?'

'There's no obvious reason. You know what I think, Sam? I think they just took sides. That's the trouble with NI. Everyone who comes in contact with it eventually takes sides. After all the killings, all the failed peace

457

initiatives, all the wasted words while the murdering goes on, are you really surprised that someone finally decided to take the law into their own hands? I think that's all it is. I really do.'

Richardson didn't know whether Dancer was telling the truth or feeding a line to the FBI listeners; a deliberate plant to deflect them from the truth that HMG was involved. 'Never asked you,' he heard himself say. 'You a Catholic or a Prod?'

'Left-footer, Sam,' came the soft answer. 'It's not about religion to most people. The Walkers are Catholic. So is Rush. It's more tribal than that. It's about who you want to win.'

'They killed your family, Mick. Why didn't you turn sour like the Angels?'

'Unfair question. I guess I was too funked to cross the line. So I fight back with the law.'

'I'm sorry I asked that.'

Dancer laughed. 'Just be yourself, Sam. It's what I like about you. I'll ring you when she starts to mend.'

The phone clicked in his hand. He put the receiver down and walked out of the office. The NO SMOKING sign reminded him that he hadn't lit up since leaving London. The plane had been designated a no-smoker, as was his hotel room and the FBI building. He suddenly realized he hadn't missed the smokes; somehow he hadn't even thought about it. *Well, girl, looks like you're winning that battle*. By the time he returned to the Incident Room, the photos of David and Damien Walker were already with the FBI and ready to be circulated in the field.

'Is she OK?' a concerned Duggan asked Richardson.

'Looks like she's going to be fine.' As he said the words, he wished he believed what he said.

Dancer didn't tell Richardson he was going to Downing Street.

It was the first time he had been inside. Only he hadn't walked through the famous black front door with the policeman standing on guard outside. He had come in through a staff entrance at the rear and been led up to the Cabinet Secretary's office on the first floor. The two SIS men, Claris and Carter, were already there.

'Anybody else from Five coming?' asked Sir Walter Inger. He was a brusque, bristling type; a throw-back in appearance and attitude to Colonel Blimp. Except Inger was no fool, had avoided any military experience, including the last year of National Service, and was a city financier by profession and instinct. Everything had to make sense on the bottom line. It was the way politics had become. Bottom line was all that counted. You paid your way or you starved to death.

'No, sir,' replied Dancer. The phone call from his superior had been simple. *Listen to what they've got to say. Help where possible. But don't get yourself, or the department, involved. This is SIS's baby. Let them carry the can.* 'I've been responsible for the Angels case. I've been told to give you all the help I can.'

'Are they any closer to finding them?'

'I think they're closing down on the location.'

'Be more specific.'

'I don't know any more.'

'Dammit, man. You've been talking to Richardson. And to their legal attaché over here. They must have said something.'

'Only that they're narrowing the field.' Dancer started to explain about the U-2.

'I know that already,' snapped Inger. He turned to Claris. 'Have Cheltenham picked up anything?'

'No, sir.'

'Not even over American airwaves?'

'We're not supposed to spy on our allies.'

'Balls. We're all doing it.'

'You'd hear before me, sir.'

A frustrated Inger banged his fist on the desk. He leant forward menacingly towards Claris. 'I don't want to be tarred with your brush. We've had enough problems in the past with Matrix and the Iraqi supergun. Now the Press are desperately trying to link us with the Angels. I don't know what you people are up to, but I don't want to see it coming home to roost at Number Ten.'

Claris shifted uncomfortably. He didn't like being admonished in front of Carter, not to mention an even lower-graded MI5 man. 'That's not likely, sir.'

'Can you guarantee that?'

'As far as I can. Sometimes things do get out of hand.'

'Are these Angels part of SIS?'

The question stunned Claris. He hadn't expected something so direct, certainly not in front of Dancer. 'No.'

'I have your word on that?'

Claris wondered whether the conversation was being recorded. It didn't matter; in a special court of inquiry Carter and Dancer would be sufficient witnesses. He realized why he had been instructed to bring Carter along. 'Yes,' he whispered.

'I can't hear you,' growled Inger.

Dammit, it was being recorded. 'Yes,' he repeated.

'The FBI say this Baxter chappie, Army Council man, has been kidnapped by the Angels.'

'That's right.'

'Why?'

'Probably to get some information out of him.'

'And do what with it?'

'Pass it on.' Claris had no choice but to go on.

'Probably to us.'

'It's not the way we expect to get information.'

'I agree. But if it's offered . . . ' Claris left the question unasked.

Inger leant back in his chair. 'Richardson. Does he know what's going on?'

It was a double-edged question. For the record on tape it distanced Inger from ground operations; as a question to Claris it confirmed that the mess was being sorted. 'He's over there to assist and find out why this mess started in the first place.'

'Nothing else?'

'No. Just to assist.'

'And he's been told not to get involved?'

'There were no specific instructions to him.' Claris's palms were damp now. He knew he had to clear himself, the SIS and Inger from any orders he or Carter had given Richardson. 'Just to assist.'

'Does he know some of these Angels?'

'I don't think so. Although Captain Nathaniel was his predecessor in SIS.'

'Well, let's hope he won't get carried away and do something against his instructions. These ex-SAS types. They certainly seem to stick together.'

'As I said, sir, his sole instruction was to assist where possible. His knowledge of SAS methods will be invaluable to the Americans.'

'Good. You understand that the Prime Minister, or any member of the CDOP, would be emphatically against any support by our security forces of these Angels?'

'Yes, sir.' Claris understood where the Cabinet Secretary was coming from. Not only was he protecting himself but also the Cabinet Office Committee on Defence and Overseas Policy. That was the whole team: Foreign Secretary, Chancellor, Defence Secretary, President of the Board of Trade and the Attorney General. Not to

461

forget the Prime Minister. They were whitewashing the truth; even though they hadn't ordered the action directly, they expected it to take place. 'Our men, including Richardson, are aware of that. There's no way we would have been involved with the Angels.'

It was all Inger wanted to hear. He smiled, wrapped up the meeting, and the three security men were led out of Downing Street, once more by the back door. They walked down to Whitehall where Claris hailed a taxi.

'Want to share the ride?' he asked Dancer, who had remained silent since they left the Cabinet Secretary's office.

'No.' As Claris turned to climb into the taxi, Dancer's control blew. 'That was a bastard thing to do,' he hissed.

Claris stopped and turned round. 'I don't know what you mean.'

'You bloody do. We all know why Sam's out there. Not to just bloody assist.'

'You heard what I told Sir Walter. You've got it all wrong,' came Claris's smarmy reply.

'Have I?' Dancer swung round to Carter. 'He's your man. Have I really got it wrong?'

'Don't even bother answering,' Claris cut across. He turned on Dancer. 'Don't think you're the only one with fire in his belly. Don't give me that moral anger of yours. We weren't always bloody desk-wallahs. We've all done our bit in the field, all done things we knew wouldn't be backed up. That's the risk we take. That's our duty. And you should take note of that.'

Claris stomped into the taxi, a worried Carter following him.

Dancer watched the cab drive off. As angry as he was, he realized most of what Claris said was the truth. They were all expendable.

Then he thought of his own Circle, went to the nearest public phone box and called a private number at the American Embassy.

In the taxi Carter finally broke the silence. 'How high does this go? Right to the Prime Minister?'

'I doubt it,' answered a reflective Claris. He leant forward and slid the partition shut between them and the driver. He waited until the driver's eyes had gone back to the road after looking at his occupants in his rear-view mirror. 'Sometimes things gather a momentum of their own. But I understand why now. It's because of all these peace initiatives.'

'They're a farce. Everybody's talking – no-one's stopping the killings.'

'Precisely. Someone on our side is trying to tell the PIRA that we can be as tough as them, unless they lay down their arms and start talking.'

'And they're using us to achieve that.' Carter sat back in the seat and put his hand into the swinging hand-grip. 'Not any more. Sam Richardson. He's the only one who can get us out of this mess now.'

RAMS Camp
Everglades
Florida

Before they started on Baxter, Lucifer and Michael prepared the agenda. The questions were listed on three handwritten sheets of paper. Both men went into the padlocked room and sat on the floor opposite Baxter. The room was empty. A small window allowed some light in, but there was nothing Baxter could use; no old nails in the walls, no protruding steel or bricks; nothing. Baxter curled himself up in the corner under the window, the darkest part of the room. He had removed all his clothes soon after they had untied him and had already started to smear his excrement over the walls in protest. The smell was strong but the two Angels ignored it.

'You can mess this up all you want, Baxter,' warned Lucifer. 'There's no cameras here, no-one to voice your complaints to, no secret army of supporters out there to impress. It's your shit and you can do with it as you want. Just like these are your quarters and you can decorate them in any style that suits you.'

'Where's my family?'

'Safe. I mean, we could lie and say they're hostage until you tell us what we want to know. Only we don't work that way. They're safe. It all depends on how much you want to see them again.'

'You can fuck off.'

'We've a list of questions for you to answer,' came in Michael.

'I told you – fuck off.'

'About your organization. Your plans. Simple sort of stuff.'

Baxter withdrew into silence, put his head between his knees and looked at the floor.

Lucifer took over. 'Maybe I should tell you about your predicament. We're miles from anywhere. In the middle of swamp country. We're all experienced SAS men. And we have absolutely no qualms about getting information out of you. In any way we need to.' He waited, but Baxter ignored him, still held his dismissive pose. 'We'll read you some of the questions. Just so that you can get the flavour of what we're after.' He nodded across to Michael.

'We'd like to start with your knowledge of future targets,' said Michael, glancing at the top sheet as a reference. 'We want to know which selected commercial establishments, like Warrington or the City of London, you've got lined up. What railways? What ambushes of military personnel, any VIP attacks or UDR members you've targeted for immediate reprisal.' Michael paused, waiting for a reaction. There was none, so he continued. 'Then we'd like to know about your ORBAT—'

464

'What the fuck's that?' Baxter looked up suddenly.

'Order of Battle. We want the formation, strength and disposition of the PIRA.' Michael waited again while Baxter shook his head contemptuously and looked down at the floor. 'I want the names and positions of your ASUs. I want the names of the godfathers who direct them and arrange their logistics. I want to know who your explosives engineers are, their ballistic signatures and how specific gunmen work. I want to know where the finance comes from, and who your explosives and weapons suppliers are.'

'You want a fucking lot, don't you!' snapped Baxter. Then he started to urinate, the liquid running out from between his legs and across the floor. 'That's what I think of your fucking questions, you bastards,' he shouted.

Michael waited until he had finished before continuing. 'Then we want to know about who committed acts of terrorism in the past. Who was responsible for Mountbatten's death? Why was it certain occupants of the house refused to join the sailing party when he was killed, the same occupants who are well known in Monaghan as IRA supporters? The same day nineteen soldiers were killed near Warrenpoint. A double bomb incident. We know that South Armagh and North Louth PIRA acted together on this. Their best bomber was on it. He's middle-aged with curly hair, lives in Dundalk. Who helped him, where did the other bomb come from? I also want to know about Enniskillen. Eleven dead, Baxter. Eleven innocent victims on a peaceful procession in front of a war memorial. There's a lot for you to answer, my lad.'

'You'll never know, will you?' challenged Baxter, not looking up.

'I also want to know for sure who sits on the Army Council. Who's on GHQ and we need to establish all the shipments of arms from Gaddafi and anyone else who's supplied you. And how much Semtex you've really got.

We know you're desperate for electronic detonators. Is that why you're in the US? To find new suppliers? There's also the question of unused weapons in your reserves. How many *longs* have you and how many *shorts*?' That's how rifles and hand-guns were referred to. 'And how many support machine-guns?'

Lucifer interrupted. 'I hope you're listening good, Baxter. Because we mean to have answers to all these questions.'

'Yeah.' Baxter kept his head down. 'You and who else? The fucking British government?'

'We want to know how Gerry Adams is viewed by the PIRA. He's a northerner, not trusted by many in the South. Are there any ASUs in areas like East Tyrone and South Armagh who're capable of acting as independent renegades in defence of PIRA Northern Command? And then there's the phantom sniper who's killed so many round the border with his .50 calibre Barret rifle. He's a former US marine, isn't he? All we need is for you to confirm our suspicion.' Michael put the sheet down. 'That's just for starters, Baxter.'

'What, my starter for ten,' came the impudent reply. 'By the time I answer that lot, I'll be ninety years old.'

'If you don't answer them, you won't live to your next birthday,' Lucifer shot back. 'We're short on time. I want you singing within the next hour. I want you out of here within twelve hours.'

'Why? Are the FBI closing in on you?'

'Don't piss me about. I just want it said we gave you a chance.'

'Before what? Pulling out my finger-nails and sticking flaming matches between my toes?' The truth was that Baxter had never faced anything like this before. He'd always kept out of prison and known association with the hard-boys of the PIRA. He was one of them, but had always kept his distance. Until now. He knew answering the questions would bring about his death by the PIRA, if not by these British assassins. Unless he couldn't take the pain and would then plead for a new identity and a new home. That is if his family didn't get back to Ireland first. He knew what would happen then; the Army Council would place them in protective custody. That was one way of making him keep his silence. The trouble was that if he explained his fears to his two interrogators, they would immediately see it as a sign of weakness and turn the screws on. Even if they promised they would protect the family from returning to Ireland, he had no proof that they would honour their word. They were after a quick result and didn't have time to negotiate with the Yanks for his family. He had little choice but to go on. In the end it was what was always expected of him; what he expected of himself. He tried to concentrate on the instructions he had been given in case of torture. Steel your mind for the worst pain imaginable. Whatever happens is never as bad. Like being at the dentist. Imagination is far more dangerous than the truth. Only worry about the immediate act of torture. Don't look ahead at what might be. Commit yourself to overcome the next act. Play it one at a time. Imagine each infliction of pain will be the final one. Pace yourself. Breathe easily. Use your finger-nails to inflict pain on yourself to take your mind off the pain someone else is perpetrating on you. He slowly lifted his head and stared at the two Angels. 'I can't answer any of that. You know that, anyway. You'll probably kill me, but at least you'll find fuck-all out from me.'

'Read him the questions once again,' Lucifer said to Michael. 'This time make them more specific.' He pulled a long, thin, pliable, nylon knitting-needle from his pocket. He held it up, more than twelve inches long, so that Baxter could see it clearly. 'One last chance, Baxter. Before we resort to our alternative method.'

Baxter paled, then lowered his head between his

knees again as Michael started to read through the list of questions.

FBI Miami Field Office
16320 NW 2nd Avenue
North Miami Beach

The U-2 cameras showed three possible sites in the southern Everglades for the RAMS training camp.

Each potential target had been chosen because of its proximity to a series of canals, a white road and a gravel base.

The first was a known Cuban camp, funded from Miami. Although well known to the FBI, it was included because of a potential link between RAMS and the Cuban needs for specialist training. As there were already surveillance points set up for this camp, a small team was despatched to keep an eye on the camp and report any suspicious movement. The satellite pictures already showed that there were men at the camp, although the numbers were similar to those normally found there.

The second site was in the Corkscrew Swamp Wildlife reservation, north of Marco Island and near the west-coast city of Naples. It was a privately owned estate in the middle of the reserve. Not much was known about the owners, a New York-registered, private property company, who dealt in adventure and leisure parks around the country. While the FBI's New York office chased any relevant information regarding the site and its owners, Jiggs arranged for his agents to check round the Naples and Marco Island areas whilst keeping clear of the site itself. This location had four small tents, a structure to the side that could be an obstacle course, a solid building about thirty feet square and an open area that was tarmaced and could be a training or drill ground.

There were two airboats parked in the canal near by. Although the daytime pictures showed no sign of life, the infra-red had picked up enough heat to show there was movement on the location.

The third target was chosen because it was bordered by canals, seemed to have a gravel-based compound, was near a white road and had tents and a small building on it. There was no sign of a tent, firing range or large supply tent. Neither the daytime camera nor the infra-red showed any sign of life. But the site was within forty minutes of Fort Lauderdale and fitted the five-acre layout that Leese had described. The land was traced to a Miami owner who had inherited it, then leased it out to hunters and naturalists. The tents, plentiful in the Everglades, were left standing permanently for those who might want to use them. The camp was surrounded by Malaleuca and large palm trees and was located in the Fakahatchee Strand State Preserve. Of the three targets, it was the nearest to a conurbation; the small town of Everglades City was seven miles to the south.

Jiggs ordered blow-ups of each area, then requested another U-2 flight, this time with video cameras that could be immediately delivered to Miami without any delay caused by further processing time. NASA agreed to land the plane at Homestead Air Base, just outside Miami. The base had been devastated during Hurricane Andrew in 1992, but a small USAF contingent operated from there while it was still being decided what to do with Homestead.

While Jiggs waited for the results, he called a meeting in a small conference room with the two Everglades men, the head of the Miami Hostage Response Unit, Charley Merrill, Richardson and Duggan. Bonnilo joined the meeting while Mickleton went on the phone to the National Security Advisor in Washington to take him through the latest events.

'I thought we'd firm up on where we go next,' started Jiggs.

'No sweat,' said Merrill. 'We don't wait around this time, like we did in Waco. Straight in with an armed unit. That includes helicopter back-up, mortars, airboats, anything we can get our hands on. They either come out waving a white flag or we stick it to them. It's in the middle of nowhere, so there's no innocent passers-by to get caught in any cross-fire. All we need is their location and some idea of their manpower and logistics. It's an easy site for us to take. Open, flat land, very little cover apart from the trees. With our fire-power, that shouldn't be a problem.'

'Not that simple,' said Bonnilo. 'I've a strong hunch that Washington will want it handled differently.'

'Waco *was* different. We can't risk that again.'

'This time they want low-profile action. We don't know who's behind these Angels. Could be Washington doesn't want us to find out. From what Hank was saying earlier, they want a quick hit, effective, with no casualties on our side.'

'Then hit them with an air-strike,' said Jiggs.

'No go. They want the IRA man alive.' Bonnilo concentrated on Merrill. 'Not easy, but that's why we can't go in with all guns blazing. These are trained soldiers. Some of the best. They'd cut Baxter's throat before you hit them with the first helicopter.'

'Then we send in a small squad first. Try and snatch Baxter while a bigger team causes a diversion and goes for the rest of the Angels,' said Merrill.

'You've got to do it the other way round,' interrupted Richardson. They all turned to him. 'SAS training dictates you take out the terrorists first, then you worry about the hostages. That way you get a first-hit. Doesn't give them time to react.' He stopped. 'I'm just telling you how it is. Fleet's suicide in London showed these guys see themselves as expendable. That means they're almost impossible to beat. The only way you'll take them is by infiltrating the camp and hitting them hard. Then, you might just save Baxter.'

'You been in on one of these hostage rescues before?' asked Merrill.

'No.'

'But you believe they'll react in a certain way?'

'Yes. That's standard. That's how I was trained.'

'Take me through it.' There was no animosity from Merrill, no resentment of Richardson on his own turf. Merrill was a professional and every scrap of information mattered. 'Tell me what to expect and how you'd tackle it.'

'Ideally, you need all the targets together in one place. Makes the hit easier. These boys will know that, so they'll split most of the time. One will always be with the hostage. He won't be running around in the open. Either in a safe place, like a solid building with a permanent guard over him, or buried in a hide. He'll be gagged and tied if that's the case. Might even be booby-trapped in case of a rescue attempt. That won't be a problem to them. Penuel, who we think is Damien Walker, is an explosives expert.'

'Will he mine the extremities to the camp?'

'I don't think so. They're somewhere they don't want to be discovered. The last thing they want is an alligator or panther or black bear setting off a booby-trap. Draw too much attention to themselves.'

'They used the place as a firing range once,' cut in Jiggs.

'Not for a while. This time they won't be taking any unnecessary chances. You've also got to remember that they're not conventional terrorists. These guys don't go for innocent targets. They proved that in Dublin when Penuel's bomb only took out the girl. Their enemy is the PIRA. Not the FBI or any other security force.'

'They killed two Americans in London.'

'Sympathizers. Fair game as far as they were concerned.' Richardson went on. 'What they will have is underground hides and safe corridors for a planned escape. That's an SAS priority. Work out every possible escape before you go in. However spontaneous that priority may be. The key thing is to be prepared for all eventualities.'

'How would the SAS go in against the Angels?' asked Merrill.

'Once we've decided the location, we need to assimilate all the information we've got on it quickly. Aerial pics, infra-red line Scans, whatever our two Everglades companions can tell us.' He indicated Red Snake George and Ethan West. 'Then you go in with a small raiding party. No more than six. Teams of two. But each one with a specific instruction. Because we don't know the individual locations of the Angels, each one of the raiding party has to be responsible for a zone. Not easy. Five acres is a big area. Whoever goes in has to have an emotional commitment and be totally ruthless.' He suddenly regretted his words. They were talking about taking out his old comrades, people he would have stood shoulder to shoulder with if he'd been in Belfast at the same time. He forced himself to continue. 'We need diversions. They'll be ready for that. So it's got to be good, realistic enough for one of them not to reach over and cut Baxter's throat.' *Damn*. He was planning the assassination of his own people to save a PIRA terrorist. 'We'll need close-quarter shooting weapons. No need for Claymores or any other stun grenades. No CS gas. No point with all that open ground. What we need is speed weapons, something to hit them with before they can blink. Grenade-launchers will be handy. Especially if they're linked to an assault rifle. And body armour, just not too much so we're too heavy and get sucked down into the swamp. We want good communications in case we need rapid back-up. But we'll have to go in with radio silence. Otherwise they'll have a scanner that could pick up any messages. If it's a night-time operation we'll need flares. Personally I think we should go in the daylight. As long as we have a good diversion. Drop off at night and wait until morning.' He turned to the Everglades men. 'Is that possible out there?'

'Yeah.' Ethan grinned. 'Alligators and snakes eat at night. We'll just have to keep out of their way.'

'In general terms, that's about it. Until we know the exact location.'

'Are the Angels trained in SWAT techniques?' Merrill asked Richardson.

'Yes. I'd be surprised if they're not in some sort of body armour.'

'So we need to get them together, and out of their vests. Wow!' Merrill finished a can of Diet Coke he had brought into the room with him. 'What about helmets?'

'Probably not. But you're unlikely to hit all four of them at the same time with long-range sniper fire.'

'I was thinking of the heat. If they're walking round in body armour and helmets, this humidity's going to wear them out. It's over a hundred degrees out there. With no wind, just a wagon-load of saturating humidity. Maybe they won't be wearing their vests.'

'But they'd have them within reach of wherever they went.'

'OK.' Merrill swung round to Jiggs. 'I guess we've got to wait until we're sure about the location. Then I'd like to go through it with Sam. Just so he can prepare us for anything we might not expect.'

'That's fine.' Jiggs stood up. 'I'll need Ethan and George to go with you. They know the terrain better than anyone else.'

'Suits me.' Merrill got up to leave when Jiggs stopped him.

'I'd like a word in private,' he said to the Hostage Response Unit agent. 'See you all back in the Incident

473

Room.' He waited until the room had cleared, except for Bonnilo.

'I'd like to call in a favour,' said Bonnilo.

'I know. You want me to take the Brit along,' replied Merrill, a faint grin playing around his lips.

'Yes.'

'Why?'

'Don't ask, Charley. I'd just appreciate it that way.'

'He's right about taking in a small team. Is he observing, or part of the team?'

'Officially he's an observer. But if you've got any sense—'

'Which I haven't. Otherwise I wouldn't be holding down such a crazy job.'

'If you've got any sense, you'd arm him to the teeth and make sure he was part of the action. He knows how those boys think. He'll put you between the sheets with them.'

'Do you want them alive?'

'Not particularly.'

'Except for the Irishman.'

'We'd like to send Baxter home First Class, not in a body bag.'

'Is Sam Richardson under orders to take these guys out?'

'He might be. That we really don't know. I understand that Washington would be relieved if these guys didn't stand trial. They'd even like it so that they weren't particularly recognizable.'

'Jesus!' Merrill swore under his breath.

'One other thing,' Jiggs came in. 'These are Sam's people. They come from the same unit. He doesn't see them as renegades, probably applauds what they've done. But he's doing his duty. He'll need your support, when it comes to pulling that trigger.'

'If I agree to let him come in with us.' Merrill faced Bonnilo with his next question. 'Are you ordering me to take him along?'

'No. I can't do that.'

'Do Washington want him to?'

'Not officially, anyway. Politically too sensitive.'

'So you're out on a limb if anything goes wrong?'

Bonnilo nodded. He didn't want to tell the others about the phone call he had received from the legal attaché in London, an old friend who had trained with him at Quantico and taken up a junior post with him in Philadelphia.

'Well,' shrugged Merrill, 'if that's the case I'd better make sure he comes back in one piece. Can't have the boss walking round with his arse in a sling, can we?'

It was the Florida Royal palms that triggered off Leese's memory.

He went over the blow-up pictures once again.

Then it all slowly came back. He was certain he had the right location.

RAMS Camp
Everglades
Florida

Baxter had been a lot tougher than they'd imagined.

After Michael read him the questions the second time and extracted no response from the Irishman, the two Angels left him alone. They left the list of questions on the floor for him to read. Half an hour later they returned. This time he knew time had run out, that these two men meant him immense harm. He closed his eyes and began to lock himself into his own strength.

There were three of them this time. Lucifer, Michael and Raphael. They'd left Penuel on watch, just in case their hunters were getting closer.

The three men were dressed in black rubber wet suits. They wore heavy boots and heavy leather gloves. Each man had a plastic, black helmet on his head and his face was covered with a black visor and respirator. It was an intimidating sight. Raphael carried a flat wooden board, the size of a single front door. He leant it against the wall. Over his right shoulder was a coil of rope; he held four leather straps in his hand.

Lucifer knelt down beside Baxter and picked up the torn sheets of the questionnaire. Baxter had wiped his excreta over it before ripping it up. He gripped it in his hand then grabbed the Irishman by the back of his neck, tilted his head back and forced the torn paper into his mouth. Baxter fought back, but Michael grabbed him from behind, pinning his hands together. Baxter started to choke on the paper and the two Angels let him go. He slumped to the floor and started to pull the paper out of his mouth, his body racked with a spasm of coughing.

Lucifer waited for him to compose himself before he knelt down again. 'It's your filth. Doesn't affect us, the way we're dressed. Never did understand the dirty protests your people had in the Maze. Living in your own shit like that. Showed the rest of us what animals you really were.' He pulled some more paper from his pocket. 'Got plenty of paper. Next time you rip it up, I'm going to let you choke on it. All the way. Now, how about giving us some answers.'

Baxter ignored him. Cursing the SAS man wouldn't get him anywhere, except a clout across his skull.

Michael crouched the other side of him. 'We're a long way from anywhere. If we torture you, then you're going to start screaming. Nobody'll hear you. Only us and some alligators.' He laughed. 'If you push us, not giving us any answers, you're going to end up being fed to them in little pieces. It'll take time because we'll cut those little pieces off slowly. You can sit here, watching the blood ooze out of you into some dirty bandage, and know that the flesh that's missing is already in some alligator's gut. Ironic, isn't it? Responsible for all that killing and now you're going to see what slow murder is really like.' He pulled out a long scabbard knife and held it up for Baxter to see. Then he held the sharpened blade against Baxter's forearm and cut across. The Irishman yelped as the blood flowed out of the narrow cut.

'Give us the answers and you go free,' said Lucifer. 'This isn't our game. But you're giving us no alternative. Don't you see that? There's all this peace-talk going on, all the governments involved, and your lot are still killing innocent people. We need that information. Give it to us, let us bring the PIRA under control, and there'll be peace in Ireland. Because then the talkers can get on with it. Don't you see that, Baxter? You can start the process that brings peace to the whole region. Give us that and we'll get your family into a safe place. Join them, get a new identity and you can start a new life.'

'To promise that, you must be government men,' came Baxter's reply.

'Does it matter? As long as we get you off the hook.'

'What about you lot? You fucking Angels?'

'Lost causes,' answered Lucifer. 'There's nothing can save us. We knew that when we started. But you can be saved. Don't force us to put you through all that pain, Baxter. Think of your family. Think of your kids. While you're lying in this shit here, imagine a warm, clean, bed. With crisp, freshly ironed sheets. With the warmth and comfort of her body next to yours. Just reach out and touch it. Can you feel her with the tips of your fingers, her warmth and smoothness with the palm of your hand?'

'Make it easy on yourself, man,' added Michael softly. 'Make it easy on all of you.'

Baxter spat in Michael's face; the spittle ran across the black visor. Michael wiped it off. 'We won't be breaking your bones, Baxter. Or snapping your nose, or ripping your flesh all over. That's easy pain. We can all, if we've a mind to, put up with that. We learnt the same lessons. Imagine the worst, then the pain's never as bad. Or think about the next attack on your body; always imagine it'll be the last one. What we've planned is worse than anything you've been warned about. This is no rough-knuckle stuff we're talking about.'

Baxter put his head down again, staring once more at the floor. He ignored Lucifer's last request for him to answer the questions. He heard Raphael scrape the wooden board across the floor. Then he felt a punch in his back and straightened up with the shock of it. Two men grabbed him as he struggled, but he was no match for them and they pulled him over and pinned him to the board. Then they strapped him to it with the leather straps, one each across his head, his shoulders, his knees and his ankles. Each belt was pulled tight until he was trapped against the wood. Raphael then freed his hands and tied them with the rope behind the board. Then they let the board fall flat to the ground; the pain as his arms were sandwiched under him made Baxter believe he had broken his bones. In truth, his right shoulder was dislocated.

Michael pulled the long nylon needle out of his pocket and straddled Baxter's waist, sitting sharply down with all his weight and winding the Irishman. The three Angels waited until he had brought himself under control.

'Last chance, Baxter,' said Michael holding up the sharpened needle. When he got no response, he looked up at Raphael. 'Go and keep watch with Penuel,' he said. 'Check the perimeters. Make sure there's no-one out there. Take Penuel with you. And don't forget your reflective capes.' He waited until Raphael had left the small building. 'I've got to say, I'm not looking forward to this.' Michael put his masked face close to Baxter.

'That's the truth. It's not my way. But you're making it necessary. Because whatever I do, if it gets the answers out of you, then I've helped get this peace thing sorted out. Getting close to your last chance, man.'

When he elicited no response, he leant back and placed the point of the thin needle under the lowest rib at the central point of the thoracic cage. With his other hand he felt for the inter-coastal area, where the ribs meet in an inverted V, in that area known as the sternum. Baxter wriggled underneath him and he hit the Irishman across the face with the palm of his hand. 'Keep still, otherwise you'll make it worse.'

'Keep still, you bastard,' he heard Lucifer say over his shoulder. 'Or I'll crack your fucking head open.' Lucifer bent forward and put his arms on Baxter's shoulders to hold him still. 'You remember what that Cuban said?'

'Yes,' said Michael. 'I remember exactly.' Under him Baxter started to sob with fear. Michael took a deep breath, forced himself to go on, and pushed the needle into Baxter, inserting about half an inch into the PIRA man. Baxter shouted in pain but Michael ignored him, knowing that it was nothing to what he would soon feel. Baxter struggled, but he was well secured and there was little movement. The Irishman felt more pain from his dislocated shoulder than he did from the inserted needle.

Michael laid the needle flat on Baxter's stomach, then started to push it upwards, towards his throat. Michael felt the needle hit the first rib, scrape against it as it entered the sternum.

That's when Baxter forgot about the pain in his shoulder and started to scream. The needle scraped along the inside of the chest's central thoracic bone towards Baxter's chin. As it juddered upwards from rib to rib, Baxter forgot about his instructions on how to deal with pain. Nothing he could ever imagine could be as bad as this. It burnt his chest, from inside, as though there was something inside him trying to burst out. He strained his body, stretched it to its extremes as he fought to stop the needle going higher.

Outside, Penuel and Raphael heard the shrieks of pain, but kept walking. They didn't want to know what was going on in the small building; their responsibility was to patrol the perimeter and protect the camp.

Baxter passed out when the point of the needle scraped against the third rib, pushing aside the nerves there, forcing one rib to move from its position. His scream died as he fainted; his face was wet and shiny with tears and the humidity.

Michael waited, leaving the needle where it was, poised to strike slowly upwards in Baxter's sternum, when he came to.

'Tough bastard,' commented Lucifer as they waited. 'Got to respect the sod.'

Ten minutes later, when Baxter finally recovered consciousness, Michael started again. Upwards, slowly and painfully, he manipulated the needle until it was in the centre of the sternum, at its most sensitive point, inter-thoracically against the upper rib-cage central column. Baxter, now in so much pain that he couldn't scream any longer, breathed in great gulps of air, then was violently sick because of the advancement of the needle towards his throat. It was an instinctive reaction and the small meal they had fed him that afternoon discharged itself across his lips. He started to choke on the bile but Michael gave him no respite, just kept pushing upwards, scraping against the inside of the ribs, jerking from one bone to another, reaching the top of the rib-cage. Baxter was trying to arch his back, but the straps held him flat and he suddenly screamed his loudest scream in an attempt to breathe and clear the vomit from his throat.

Michael suddenly removed the needle from Baxter. There was little to show the enormity of what had happened; a small puncture hole in the lower half of Baxter's chest was all that remained.

Michael stood up as Lucifer released Baxter's shoulders. They watched the Irishman turn his head sideways and cough the vomit out onto the board.

When the coughing subsided, Michael once more straddled Baxter and sat on his stomach. He held up the needle, a size-16 knitting-needle. 'Time to start all over again,' he said calmly. It wasn't how he felt inside, but he showed no outward signs of the distress he suffered. He lowered the needle point towards Baxter's chest once again. 'Korean torture,' he continued. 'Taught to the Cubans. Known as the most exquisite pain man can devise. They didn't use this one for ordinary foot-soldiers like me. They reserved this for the intelligence operators. Quite ironic, that. You being head of the PIRA's intelligence.' He slowly inserted the needle once again, just breaking the skin in a new place beside the first puncture. 'Good, isn't it? Very little blood and an even smaller hole. All the damage is inside, you see. I'm told, by my Cuban friends, that some people die when it gets up to their throat. There's so much pain, and so much vomiting, that they choke to death. And those who do survive, when it gets up to their throats, end up in a state of total madness.' He pushed the needle up towards the thoracic bone once again.

'It's up to you, Fergal boy,' said Lucifer as he pinned the Irishman's shoulders down on the board once again. 'Whatever you want. The result is in your hands.'

Then Lucifer averted his gaze once more and looked out of the small window to the clear sunshine above.

Leese sat at the light table, his head bent over the hovering stereoscope, and studied the blow-ups of the Fakahatchee Strand location.

The photo-interpreter stood behind him, waiting for any further recognition. Jiggs and the two Everglades agents joined him.

'He remembers there were palm trees,' said the interpreter. 'That's the only site with them.'

'Of the three, you mean,' commented Jiggs. 'What about other potential sites we've missed?'

'Can I have a look?' said Ethan.

'Sure.' The interpreter picked up another set of blow-ups and overlapped them on another section of the table. He took one of the stereoscopes and held it out for Ethan. 'Focus it until it's right for you,' he advised as Ethan looked down on the map.

It didn't take long for him to identify the trees. 'Florida Royal palms,' he said, stepping back. 'You only find them in Fakahatchee. If he saw palms, then that's where it was.'

'The Cuban camp's near there,' added Red Snake George. 'He'd better check those pictures, too. The two locations are pretty similar.'

'We'll do that now.' The interpreter led Leese to another table where the Cuban blow-ups were and let him study them.

'They've got an obstacle course,' said Leese eventually. 'Only it wasn't the way I remember it. And the tents are in a different position. The whole site is shaped wrong, not as much of a rectangle as I remember. The first one I saw resembles our training camp.'

'The infra-red showed no life there at all. No movements. No body heat.'

'Would it pick up body heat through a tent cover?' asked Jiggs.

'It would.'

'Unless they were wearing reflective capes,' said Richardson, joining them.

'What about it?' Jiggs posed his question to the interpreter.

'Always possible. If they knew they were being snapped.' The interpreter doubted that such precautions would be taken. 'I mean, how did these guys know that a U-2 would be up there, or even satellite coverage?'

'They wouldn't know,' responded Richardson. 'But, they know how high the stakes are, and they'll be taking every precaution.'

The interpreter went back to his own light table and flicked through a pile of photographs. He pulled one out and applied the stereoscope to it. Then he laid a corresponding picture over it and studied it further. 'OK,' he said finally, standing up to face the others. He pushed the stereoscope towards Jiggs, who bent over it. The interpreter took out his pen and pointed to a small section of the overlapped pictures. 'This picture's from higher up. By doing that we can see contours and raised sections a lot clearer than the blow-ups. That line there,' he tapped it with his pen, 'the one that looks like a shadow across the land, that's some form of indentation in the ground. Could've been formed by people running up and down on it, wearing it away.'

'Like the ground under an obstacle course?' asked Jiggs.

'Like the ground under an obstacle course,' came the positive reply. The interpreter moved his pen to the north of the picture, to another expanse of land. 'Those minor indentations there could've been caused by soldiers on drill practice. If you look, the shadows fall in such a way that it defines a square, and quite unnatural indentation in the ground. There's not much of it; probably eroded over time. But the late sun shows it up quite clearly.'

'The water-tower's missing.'

'It was under the trees,' recalled Leese. 'I remember now. Under the palms. They had a funnel system to take the water from the palm leaves into the water-tower.'

'I'll increase the blow-ups,' said the interpreter. 'We might identify something through the leaves.'

'Wooten's is out that way,' said Ethan as the interpreter walked away.

'Who's that?' asked Jiggs

'Wooten's Alligator Farm. About six, maybe eight, miles from there. Didn't you say you'd heard something about an alligator place?' he asked Leese.

'I did.'

'Goes back to the fifties. Started as a sanctuary for alligators that wandered onto golf-courses and new housing developments. It's pretty famous. Hundreds of alligators and snakes. Also got a panther and bobcats and most other things that live in the Everglades.'

'You'd better get down there,' Jiggs said to the Everglades men. 'Check if any Englishmen have been buying provisions in Everglades City recently. George, you talk to your people and see if they've seen anything suspicious. Don't go near the camp. Keep in contact at all times.'

The two men left as another agent came into the room. 'The U-2's just landed at Homestead,' he informed Jiggs. 'Tape should be on its way here.'

Richardson, with time to spare, rang Hammersmith Hospital.

He was pleased to hear that Mick Dancer was there. He waited while an orderly fetched the MI5 man.

'No change,' reported Dancer when he came on

484

the phone. 'That's good news, if you're wondering.'

They spoke about Andrea for a while, then Richardson said they were 'closing in on their target'.

'Good news all round, then,' came the answer.

'I'm hoping to go in with the assault team.'

'Have they suggested it?'

'No. But I'm going to ask.'

'Just be careful.' Dancer wasn't about to break confidentiality regarding the legal attaché on an open line in the FBI office to London. 'Call me if you need any support.'

Richardson hung up and went looking for Duggan. He found him in a small conference room, feet up on the table and a full coffee cup in front of him. He pulled up a chair and sat down.

'I want to go on the mission,' he said.

'They're aware of that.'

'And?'

'"No decision" is how Jiggs put it to me. Trouble is, if you get shot, they're responsible. Create a helluva stink.'

'I'll be a help to the team. I know what to expect.'

'Bonnilo thinks you've been sent in to clear up your government's mess.'

'We've been through this before,' sighed Richardson.

'What other reason could you have for taking part?'

'Because I'm involved. Have been ever since I picked you up at Heathrow.'

'Is that really why, Sam?'

'I'm a tidy man. I just like to finish what I started.' Richardson stood up. 'See what you can do, Francis. I won't do anything that'll compromise your people.' He turned and left the room.

Duggan knew it ran deeper than that; all those in the Miami field office knew that. Bonnilo had already informed him that Richardson, if he wanted to, would be allowed to go on the raid. The FBI SAC had also insisted that he tell Richardson, not Duggan.

Duggan leant his head back and tried to think of Carmella and the children. Somehow, none of it came readily to his mind. His feelings had changed since he got involved with Richardson and the Angels. It was almost as if there was a new purpose in his life, brought on because he was involved in something important. He looked back at what he had become and liked it; there was a sense of urgency, of being useful, that he hadn't felt for a long time. He even softened towards Carmella. He realized she had shared his emptiness, that neither had achieved anything worth while. She had found an outlet to her vacuity by meeting someone else and hoping he would fulfil her. That's how a lot of women were. They lived through their men's achievements. He realized that's why she had rung him after the Milltown episode. Duggan's success had been hers to share. Except he didn't want that. When this assignment was over, when Richardson had packed his bags and gone back to Andrea, Duggan knew he couldn't return to the life he had before. No fulfilment, no buzz. He thought about Belfast and how proud he felt when he saved the soldier's life. He'd achieved something there; made a difference to the world he lived in.

He swung his feet off the desk and grinned.

He had one more chance before going back to his desk at Langley.

Bonnilo had told him that a request had come through for Duggan to go on the raiding party. The appeal from Langley had been OK'd by Mickleton. Duggan didn't know why they wanted him along, but it pleased him that he would be in at the kill.

The briefing meeting started forty minutes later.

Jiggs ran it, but Mickleton and Bonnilo sat near him. The senior photo-interpreter was present, as were Richardson, Duggan, Merrill, two Hostage Response

Unit agents and a pretty, blond, heavily pregnant girl in her late twenties.

'We're pretty sure that the Fakahatchee Strand location is the one we're looking for,' said the photointerpreter. He slid some large-scale photographs onto an easel that had been placed near Jiggs. 'If we look at these shadows,' he pointed with a ruler at a photograph of the site from a distance, 'you can see indentations which confirm Leese's drawing. This area here,' he tapped the centre of the photograph, 'could easily have been the site of an obstacle course. Moving north we can see a squared-off indentation that would tie in with the parade and drill area he mentioned.' He then attracted their attention to the south-west part of the map, next to the solid building. 'The area round here shows a different coloration to that elsewhere. On most of the site, you can see that weeds and grass have begun to grow through the gravel. Not here, where Leese said the supply tent was. No weeds. Because, if a large tent had stood there for a long time, the area would be clear of any growth. When we run the picture through a computer,' the interpreter put a computer-enhanced print-out of the photo on the easel, 'you can see that the coloration enhancer shows pure white where the supply tent was, but a lot of green where the weeds have come through on the rest of the site. The same applies under what would have been the obstacle course.' He moved on, picking up an infrared picture. 'I was pretty sure there was no activity at this camp. Looks like I was wrong. We tweaked up the infra-red image on this picture, then ran it through the same scanner to enhance its image. As you can see, there is a small glow of heat coming out from either inside, or underneath, the solid building here in the south-west corner. We wouldn't normally pick that up, not through a wooden or brick ceiling. Not unless the person inside had no clothes on to shelter his body heat further from the camera.'

'That's quite normal,' said Richardson. 'IRA prisoners often strip off as a protest.'

'I guessed that was where they kept him. That is, if they were wearing protective coats.'

'Would body armour shield body heat?' asked Merrill.

'Not totally. Certainly not their arms or legs. If they're down there, then these boys are wearing some sort of reflective material.' The interpreter moved away from the easel and switched on the TV set in the corner. When the picture had settled, he switched the video player on with the remote. The screen scattered crazily for a moment, then a high-shot of the camp came into view. 'The Fakahatchee camp from forty thousand. The plane's moving at about 350 mph, but the perspective stays the same. It's how the camera's set up.' He waited until the picture became clearer, then hit the freeze-frame button. 'Now look what's changed. Those tents that were there from the previous U-2 pics have disappeared. So has the timber that was lying there, what we took for debris and tree trunks. I think they were poles, the remains of the obstacle run being dismantled. All this work must've taken place overnight. Yet we didn't pick up anything on our infra-red scans. Which agrees with your theory,' he nodded towards Richardson, 'that they're wearing something to camouflage their body heat.'

The interpreter returned to his easel. 'We'll leave the tape for you and get copies of all the blow-ups so you can familiarize yourselves with the location and its surrounds.' He pulled another photo out and put it on the easel. 'Still not a hundred per cent until we saw this. It's an intense magnification of one of the close-ups. You can see, just there, through the palm tree leaves, the top of what could be a water-tower. It's a small construction of some type, and that certainly looks like a rounded edge. Looks metallic. Difficult to confirm exactly what it is. We decided to run through the infra-reds again. Works the opposite this time. We measured the ground heat, then searched for cooler areas. You see that blue there, just there.' Once again he tapped the south-west corner of the site. 'That's the same colour as the canal running alongside. That shows the probability of water. Now, that is either a small well, or an open-topped water-tower. It's in the exact location that Leese said it would be. That's about it. Apart from one thing. When we sent the U-2 up this morning, we also asked them to shoot some more infra-red. If we're right about the hostage being in the solid building, and being naked, then we'll pick up the same heat patterns. I'm pretty convinced this is the camp that Leese went to. I'm also convinced that there have been people working at the site even though we've not picked them up with the infra-red. It doesn't confirm they're the Angels, but if they are, and my new infra-reds back up my theory, then we'll be able to pin-point where your hostage is being held.'

After the interpreter left the room, Jiggs passed the meeting over to Merrill. The agent came to the front and faced the others.

'That's as near as dammit we can confirm it's the Angels' camp,' Merrill started. 'But we can't risk going any closer without jeopardizing Baxter and our own people. If it is the Angels, and they sniff we're on to them, say "Goodbye Baxter" and "Goodbye Angels". I presume they'll have an escape route plotted out?' he asked Richardson. Richardson nodded, so Merrill continued. 'George and Ethan West are out there now, trying to pick up any information without endangering the situation. The only way we'll resolve it is by going in. Hard and fast. Four units. Two-man teams in each unit. I'll lead with Ethan. George can go in with you, Ray.' Ray Meyerschoff, one of the HRU agents, nodded. 'Mike, I want you to take Francis Duggan with you.'

'I'd rather be in there with a pro,' Mike Reynolds,

another HRU agent, wasn't a man to mince words. He swung round to Duggan. 'No offence, but it sounds like these boys are the best. Don't want to be worrying about you when I'm trying to look after myself.'

'That's the way it has to be,' said Jiggs. 'According to Washington this was always a joint operation. They want the CIA involved right up to the last.'

'You're the back-up team,' Merrill told Reynolds. His warning look confirmed that there was no point in arguing. 'Watch for them escaping. We'll work out the logistics of it later on. I only want three teams on the actual assault of the camp.' He turned to Richardson. 'You'll make the third team.' He watched Richardson nod with determined agreement. 'Only I'm having you chaperoned. Say hi to Melanie Downs.' Merrill laughed as Richardson's expression stiffened. 'She's a good agent, member of my HRU.'

Richardson acknowledged Melanie warily. He wondered why they had paired him with a woman, a pregnant one at that. He was sure she was more than capable. But to go against the Angels with her in tow, in her condition . . . He continued to smile as she moved from her chair to one next to him.

'Hi,' she welcomed. 'Don't worry about me. I'm just carrying a big one. Still got four months to go.' She patted her belly and Merrill started to laugh.

Richardson turned to the HRU chief. 'This what you call equal opportunities?' he asked rattily.

'More politically correct,' chuckled Merrill. The laugh became a snort and everyone else, with the exception of Duggan, joined in.

'You guys never were good at keeping secrets,' Melanie said to Merrill. As Richardson turned back to her, she pulled her blouse up and pulled out a flesh-coloured inflated rubber cushion. 'This one doesn't go "whoopee",' she said to Richardson.

Around him the room collapsed with laughter. *They'd*

bloody sent him up. Then he started to laugh with them. He knew he was still paired with her. But the sight of the Browning 9mm strapped to her waist gave him some comfort.

Then he remembered who they were up against. He kept laughing, but his mind started to concentrate, narrow down on his task. He'd have to be SAS again.

He'd have to be the best.

The young soldier's face, running towards him, pleading for him to help, flashed across his mind, taunted him.

Maybe the time had come for Sam Richardson to face his ghosts in the swamplands of Florida.

He laughed louder than anyone else. It was the only way he found he could cope with the fear that was spreading within him.

**Eaton Square
London**

Sir Walter Inger had just dropped off to sleep after a late supper with friends when the bedside phone rang. He reached over and answered it grumpily. His secretary told him a Mr Claris was on the line and it was a matter of some urgency.

'What's the problem?' he asked when Claris was put through.

'You wanted to be informed on developments, sir,' said Claris, starting to apologize for ringing after midnight.

'Go on, go on,' came Inger's impatient voice.

'It looks like they've discovered the Angels' lair, sir.'

'Are they sure?'

'Pretty well. They think they've also identified where the hostage is being kept.'

'Good. What about your chap?'

'They're allowing him to go in.'

'As an observer?'

'Yes, sir. But armed. Just in case he gets caught in cross-fire.'

'That's very good news. At least he'll be in a position to resolve the situation. When?'

'They're moving in now, sir. They didn't make me party to their tactics. Understandable, over the phone.'

'Well, keep me informed if there are any major developments.'

'Good night, sir.'

Inger grunted, put the phone down and went straight to sleep. No point worrying; after all, it was out of his hands now.

A few miles west of Eaton Square, Mick Dancer walked out of Hammersmith Hospital with his MI6 counterpart, Richard Carter. They were both extremely happy; Andrea had finally started to respond. It was only a small movement in her right arm and hand, but it was there for all to see. Just before midnight she finally opened her eyes, regained consciousness for about ten minutes, then dropped back to sleep. The doctor sedated her and said he was encouraged by her quick response. The two men decided not to ring Richardson. After all, he was preparing for a mission that required all his concentration.

'Claris isn't that bad, you know,' said Carter at the top of the hospital stairs.

'You're very defensive suddenly.'

'I feel it. What with Sam out there alone and us unable to help.'

'So why defend Claris?'

'He's the old school. From the days when they all came out of Oxbridge and wanted to do something in the Foreign Office or the Secret Service.'

'Are you lot running the Angels?'

Carter paused for a while. 'No.'

'*Someone's* financing them.'

'Not us.'

'Maybe not directly. But it's coming from your side of the bed.'

'You seem pretty sure.'

'It's my nose, Richard. It gets sniffy when things don't seem right. All that stuff at Number Ten this afternoon. All to protect the guilty.'

'Is that what the rest of Five believes?'

'Funnily enough, we don't discuss this one. We just know it's not our game.'

'Not like Five to keep their nose out of what doesn't concern them.' Carter laughed. 'Not like you at all.'

'If this gets out, there's no way Five wants to be involved. What we don't know can't hurt us.'

3000 feet
30 miles west of Fort Lauderdale
Near Fakahatchee Strand
South Florida

Dawn had nearly broken when the plane, a four-seater Cessna 172 retractable, arrived at its first fix and began to circle some twenty-one miles east of the suspected Angels' camp.

The two occupants didn't say much to each other. They had taken off from Fort Lauderdale Executive Airport and flown to the first rendezvous point as identified on their Trimble 2000 Global Positioning Satellite system. It was the same equipment that was used to help the Allies bomb their Iraqi targets during the Gulf War, accurate to within fifteen feet of any chosen location, finding its position with the help of twenty-seven navigation satellites. This equipment was now freely available to all commercial and general aviation aircraft, some units costing under $1000. They were on radio silence, so they waited for the exact time before moving on to their second position which had already been plotted on the Trimble. As the Cessna kept a 30 degree bank to the left, the pilot re-checked the calculations, taking into account the latest wind-drift, then worked out the time to fly the last twenty-one miles at a ground speed of 110 knots.

Merrill and his ground teams had taken up their attack points overnight.

It had been a long and slow process.

The group, after a final briefing, had left Miami just after midnight. Two unmarked passenger vans, property of the Miami FBI, had driven south along Interstate 95, turned west just past Miami Airport and followed Highway 41, the old Tamiami Trail, out into the Everglades. The road, the original Tampa to Miami thoroughfare, ran through the Everglades towards Everglades City before turning north to Naples and Tampa. With most east–west traffic using Interstate 75, Alligator Alley, Highway 41 was now primarily used by local traffic and visitors to the nearby Marco Island resort. In the back of the leading van the teams prepared themselves for the operation. They were dressed in black assault overalls, long-sleeved to protect themselves from insect bites and the rough teeth of sawgrass. They wore no respirators, only black FBI baseball caps. To keep their faces dark, each agent had covered his face with black grease. Their suits had a number of deep pockets, necessary for their weaponry and equipment. The second van carried the weaponry and other logistical equipment the HRU teams would use.

Although each team had the same weapons, each member had his own job to do. One person carried an M16A2 carbine which had an M203 grenade-launcher attached to the barrel. These could push a grenade over

494

three hundred yards, although accuracy would be lost at distances above two hundred yards. The grenades, packed with 2 ounces of Octol high explosive in a pre-fragmented casing, were essential to the surprise of the attack. The same person carried a Pilkington Image Intensifier to identify targets in the dark, as well as a hand-held thermal imager in case of early morning mist which would render the Pilkington useless. The second agent on each team had an Ingram Mac Ten, 9mm sub-machine-gun. It was an old design and superseded in many special forces by the German Heckler & Koch MP5K. Nevertheless, the Ingram, only eleven inches long, still had many admirers, mostly because of its high rate of fire, small size and ability to fit a silencer. Merrill had decided not to use silencers in this instance; the more noise they made, the more they would confuse the enemy. Both agents carried Franchi Spas-12 combat shotguns and a personally preferred automatic pistol. After the experience of Vietnam, the American Special Forces preferred No. 4 shot in their shotguns as the best compromise on pellet spread and penetration. Ideal for shooting in a darkened area. It was a hard lesson learnt, but one readily accepted by the FBI. All the shotguns were capable of automatic fire, shooting a devastating four rounds per second. Attached to each muzzle was a special device that produced an instantaneous spread of pellets, a function necessary for close-combat firing. In addition to these weapons, Ray Meyerschoff and Mike Reynolds both carried Swiss SIG SSG 3000 sniper rifles. They were only to be used in case an opportunity arose where they could take out the Angels at a distance before going in for close-quarter combat. Both rifles had Orion 80 night-sights attached to them.

Members of the assault team also carried a large-bladed hunting knife, a variety of loaded magazines, spare grenades and a few bars of soft candy, already unwrapped, in their combat-suit pockets. Each person was allocated a body armour suit, including ceramic plates. The suits were carried in the second van; Merrill and Jiggs had decided that each squad-member must wear a fragmentation vest with trauma liner and groin panel, but the choice of the heavy ceramic panels would be up to each individual.

As the vans trundled along, Merrill took the teams through the operation over and over again. As was often the case in similar circumstances, there was very little time to brief the agents.

The plan, originating from Mickleton, had been rapidly drawn up, working on 'reverse planning', which was a step-by-step assimilation of the operation with the starting point being the successful capture of the hostage, Baxter. While the weapons and other paraphernalia of assault were prepared, the teams honed the plan, trying to cover every eventuality. They chose the minimum equipment; the speed of the operation dictated that they shouldn't be slowed down by excessive weight.

Much of the time was given to Richardson and he went through the various SAS systems and routines the HRU team might come up against. He explained how hides worked and their possible positions. He told them of the security patterns the guards would follow; they all realized there could be more than four Angels in the camp. Whatever measures were taken to protect the hostage were covered by Richardson. One good piece of news was that the U-2 infra-red photos had shown that a hot spot, presumed to be a naked man, was still in the solid building. If it was the right camp, then there was little doubt that that was where Baxter was held. As Richardson went into more detail about the extent to which the Angels might have prepared themselves, the enormity of the task confronting the FBI agents became obvious. At one stage of the planning, Bonnilo had asked the men if they would prefer to hand the task to the American army's Intelligence Support Activity.

The ISA, supported by the CIA, had a small team of commandos who were drawn from the Navy Seal and Army Special Forces units. The reaction was swift; this was their patch and they would deal with it. Bonnilo grinned at Jiggs behind their backs. He knew offering to bring in the Army would immediately glue the team together.

The vans stopped three miles from the camp at 2 a.m., deep in the heart of the Fakahatchee Strand. It was a cloudy night; the start of a warm front that was moving across the Gulf of Mexico into southern Florida. That was good for cover, but brought the threat of heavy drizzle and swamp mist in the morning. Ideal conditions for clandestine travel through the wetlands, but not so good for the dawn raid on the camp.

It was stifling as they stepped out from the cool of the air-conditioned vehicles. The humidity and heat of the Everglades was going to be a problem but one the team expected, although it would get worse when they slipped their body armour on. The supply van was quickly unloaded and the vehicles departed towards Naples, just in case there had been Angels' surveillance posts along the road and the vans were reported not to have continued on the route.

Merrill had decided against a waterborne assault, even though it was primarily a riverine operation. Although the site was accessed by several canals, originally created by the US Army Corps of Engineers to help drain the wetlands, each canal was straight for long stretches and afforded little natural concealment. The use of outboard motors was impossible because of the noise factor. Rubber inflatable boats, such as the Gemini and Zodiac, could be paddled in, but would be a hindrance if attacked as they weren't stable firing platforms from which rapid fire could be returned. The final problem was that they would have had to find well-concealed lying-up positions along the bank before first light.

The U-2's photographs proved a great boon in planning. They worked out a track, confirmed by Ethan West and Red Snake George, then plotted the route into their waterproof Magellan GPS Nav1000M hand-held satellite-positioning computers. Each person carried one, just in case they got separated in the swamps and heavy foliage of the area. The plastic and rubber-cased receivers, smaller than a hand-held CB radio set, were designed to withstand extreme temperatures and were set to receive the military Precise Positioning Service which gave them an accuracy of eleven metres.

The group covered the first mile together, then split up into individual teams and made their own way to each attack point. It was slow work; it took an hour to cover the first mile through the soft slush underneath and the thick growth of the woodlands. The teams led by Ethan and Red Snake George made the quickest time. The method used was simple. They followed the directions of the Magellan GPS from waypoint to waypoint. The hardest part was movement across the difficult terrain and the energy-sapping heat. With the exception of Duggan, each member of the group had decided not to take their ceramic panels. Halfway through the second hour, Duggan was near to collapse with exhaustion and Mike Reynolds helped him remove the panels. They buried them near a Florida Royal palm and Reynolds marked the spot on his GPS unit in case it would need retrieving on their return. The two men pushed on; Duggan recovering from his exhaustion because of the lighter weight and his rest while Reynolds had buried the panels. The night sounds of the wetlands were a bigger worry to the CIA man. He imagined alligators swishing in the dark, snakes slithering up trees near him, panthers watching through the foliage, waiting for their moment to pounce. He felt totally vulnerable and the bravado that had come after his Milltown cemetery experience was now replaced by a nightmarish fear of the unimaginable.

It took each team about three hours to reach their objectives.

Merrill and Ethan were the first. They took up their surveillance positions about six hundred yards west of the camp.

Meyerschoff and Red Snake George had further to travel and took up their positions twenty minutes later.

The final group to arrive was Duggan and Reynolds. As back-up, they took a southerly position, once again about six hundred yards from the camp. Their brief was the simplest. Form a hide, take cover and wait until the shooting starts. Then move towards the camp.

Ethan prepared a safe cover while Merrill moved closer to the camp, this time inching his way forward along the ground. When he was about two hundred yards from the camp, according to the waypoint in his Magellan GPS, he lifted himself up, behind a tree, and searched the target zone with his Pilkington Image Intensifier. The water-tower was the first confirmation he had that it was the target. He identified the hostage building, made of brick, then scanned the rest of the camp. He looked back to the building and realized no door was visible; that meant it was on the other side, away from him. He continued to scan the area slowly; no sign of life in the grey images of his Pilkington. He concentrated his efforts on unusual features on the landscape. The mound in front of the brick building seemed out of place. After concentrating on it for ten minutes, he saw it jerk up and down; not a big movement, but enough to know it had moved. He stayed observing it and it moved again four minutes later. He realized it would have been unnoticeable in a general scan. He was convinced there was a man concealed under it; probably an underground hide for whoever was guarding the hostage. Merrill continued his scan. It took another twenty minutes to identify a second man. He was half buried under a Royal palm, his head all that was above ground. It was just like Richardson had described. They'd made a wise choice allowing the Englishman to take part. They'd probably have missed those hides if he hadn't warned them what to search for. As Merrill watched, he saw what looked like a machine-gun muzzle pointing up from the ground, next to the man.

Twenty minutes later, with no further sightings, Merrill made his way back to Ethan's hide, keeping the trees that masked him in line between him and the observer with the Image Intensifier. It had been sheer luck that he wasn't seen; the trees had proved a natural mask. If he had come in from any other direction he would have been spotted and soon put away. He discussed his findings with Ethan and the two men decided not to risk any further surveillance outings, but to move their hide closer by about three hundred yards. When they had completed this next task, they decided their strategy for the attack, marked their individual targets and settled down in the oppressive heat to wait for daylight.

Red Snake George, on the north of the site, located four covered hides through his Image Intensifier, including the two Merrill had seen. Once again, Richardson's notes on tell-tale signs for a hide had come in useful. He returned to Meyerschoff and the two also decided to move closer. They set up their second individual covers some two hundred yards from the camp, at the edge of the Malaleuca trees and swamp water, and sixty yards from each other, creating an area for cross-fire should the Angels break for cover when the diversionary tactic came.

Melanie Downs checked her watch as the sun broke cover in the east and dawn began.

She swung the small yoke to the right and turned the Cessna west, towards the camp.

Richardson sat next to her in tourist garb: Bermuda shorts, long socks, Timberland moccasins and a big loose pink 'Boca is for Lovers' T-shirt. It was baggy and loose because it hid the Beretta Model 92F automatic hand-gun that was taped between the cheeks of his buttocks. The Ingram 9mm sub-machine-gun was taped to the small of his back and a large-bladed knife between his shoulder-blades. *Very Sylvester Stallone*, he thought, *but you should see the girl*. The rest of their weapons lay on the rear seat of the plane, wedged in two small suitcases that also contained grenades.

He watched Melanie expertly fly the plane from the right-hand seat towards the camp. She was also wearing tourist apparel, bright green long pants and a yellow smock. He grinned as he recalled how they had sent him up in Miami. *Pregnant, indeed.* Now he knew more about her, he was pleased that she was his partner. An accomplished aviator, she was also one of the Bureau's top covert agents in the drug wars, concentrating her efforts in Miami and South Florida. She had often chased drugs planes over the Everglades, sometimes in a small bizjet, as the smugglers came into American airspace from the Caribbean.

'You ready?' Melanie asked Richardson as the plane descended from 3000 feet.

'Yes.' He took the sauce bottle and applied it to his face, then smeared her.

'Hope you don't think you're going to personally lick that off,' she teased him.

'No. I like my meat fried, not raw.'

She laughed, then checked her Trimble GPS. 'Whoops,' she said and pushed the nose down further. 'Shut up, Sam. You're stopping a girl from concentrating on what she does best.'

*   *   *

501

Penuel lay in the hide and reflected on his conversation with Michael the night before. The two brothers had always been close, always shared their innermost thoughts. They were both unhappy with the present situation. Baxter had thrown their equilibrium. Torture wasn't something that came naturally to Michael, yet he had been cast in the villain's role. Their brief had been simple. Hit the PIRA and sympathizers until they realize they're at more risk than ever before. After years of trying to bomb the British to the conference table, the roles had been reversed. Now someone else was bombing the PIRA to the peace talks. The brothers understood that. After all, as soldiers they had been trained to take lives in order to save lives. That was a soldier's lot. Only now they were becoming terrorists. Michael had been upset when they killed the Americans in Kilburn. Unnecessary deaths when the real enemy was the gunmen and bombers. Lucifer and the others hadn't known that; it was a secret shared between the brothers. It was the same with the torture. The brothers wanted out, but realized there was nowhere to go. Gabriel's suicide stunned them all. They hadn't looked that far ahead. Is that what was expected of them? He remembered Michael's sad words about their changed tactics from the previous night's discussion. 'Torture, innocent killings. It's their way, not ours. The PIRA have brought this totally on themselves because they won't see any other way to peace. I know what we're doing has got to be done. Trouble is, I don't want to be the one to do it.'

Penuel heard the noise and looked up.

High up, about two miles to the east, was a small plane, its engine at high power. He searched the dawn sky; it was difficult with the sun just breaking the horizon and blinding his vision. He didn't move from the hide; Lucifer's orders had been quite clear. Each man lives in his hide from now on. Movement is minimal and if

502

anyone needs to break cover, they must always use the reflective capes. Each man must be on a constant vigil with night and day binoculars, and all necessary weapons must be readily available in the hide. Raphael was positioned near the brick building to the south whilst the other three were at triangular points from each other covering the north, east and west borders of the camp.

Penuel heard the trouble before he saw it. The engine cut out, then caught again. He listened carefully; it was definitely running rough, almost like fuel starvation. Then it cut out again.

He finally saw it about three-quarters of a mile away, hung in the sky, its propeller stopped. Then it caught again, spun a few times, then jerked to a stop for a final time. It was about a thousand feet high, but descending fast. When it was three hundred yards away he saw the undercarriage was still up. *Shit, it was going to crash. Shit! shit! shit!* He turned and yelled a warning to the others, then watched the last few hundred feet being eaten up as the plane snaked over the tree-line and belly-flopped onto the clear scrub area to the east of the camp. The propeller buckled and the plane skidded along, hurling up spray and dirt. It finally hit an old Malaleuca tree, spun round as it uprooted it, then shuddered to a stop.

A man got out first, obviously the pilot as he was on the left-hand side, and screamed at the other occupant to 'Move it, for God's sake hurry!' To Penuel the voice sounded English. *Bloody tourists.* He saw the man, blood on his arms and face, reach inside and start to pull out their luggage. *Run, you chump, run; run before it blows up.* The man dragged two suitcases from the plane and ran away from the Cessna with them.

Then, finally, the passenger clambered out of the right side of the plane and staggered round in front of the bent propeller.

It was a woman, her face also bleeding from where she

was obviously thrown against the windscreen on impact. *Shit. She was pregnant. Bloody hell.* Penuel still didn't move. His training warned him it could still be a trap. He watched the man run towards him, now no more than a hundred yards away. The woman called to him but he ignored her. *What a bastard!* Then the woman started to run towards the man, not easy when you're that hugely pregnant. She was fifty yards from the plane when it blew.

A big upward explosion, flames reaching in every direction. The man threw himself down on the ground for safety; the woman just kept running. She was almost on the man when a second explosion ripped upwards, this time the fuel tank rupturing its contents into a big fire-ball.

Penuel saw the woman throw herself towards the man, sobbing loudly. The man put his arm round her but kept his own head down in the earth.

'Couldn't get the pin out of the grenade,' Melanie informed Richardson. That had been Merrill's idea. Blow a grenade on the far side of the plane to make it look more like a genuine crash. She continued to sob and shake under his arm. 'See anything yet?' she asked between sobs.

'Nothing. Just play it through. I hope the others don't move too fast.' Richardson was referring to the support HRU teams. Then he pushed Melanie away and stood up. 'Help! Help!' he screamed at no-one in particular.

Melanie stood up and shouted at him. 'You left me to die, you dick!' she shrieked. 'There's no-one here.'

'Help! Anybody, help!' he continued in a blind panic. He reached down to grab the suitcases.

'Your bloody shit's worth more than me,' she yelled at him, trying to dislodge the suitcase from his arms. She clung to his arm; he pulled away backwards. They both continued shrieking at each other.

Penuel sensed someone next to him and swung his

head round. It was Lucifer, broken from his hide but under shelter of the trees. 'Jesus,' he said softly to Penuel. 'All we need.'

'The way he's protecting those cases. Could be drugs.'

'Probably is. God, if she's not careful, she's going to have that baby right here.' Lucifer kicked the base of the tree in frustration. 'If they put out a Mayday—'

'Not if they're smugglers.'

'Enough of a racket, anyway. They were probably on someone's radar and disappeared from view.'

'Doesn't matter,' said Michael, who silently appeared next to them. 'There's plenty of low flying aircraft round here, including floatplanes landing in the swamp.' Out near the blazing plane, Richardson and Melanie were in a weird sort of dance, she hitting him while he kept the cases out of her range and backed away. 'I've told Raphael to stay put. If this is a trick, then he'll take out Baxter before he covers our backs. Jesus, look at that.' They saw Richardson knock the pregnant Melanie flying. She tried to get up, then fell back. She held her swollen stomach, then started to sob again.

'Got to get them away from here,' said Lucifer.

'Stay where you are,' Michael warned Penuel. 'Cover us.' He turned to Lucifer. 'Let's calm them down, then get them out in one airboat and we'll disappear in the other.'

'Come on,' said Lucifer.

Lucifer and Michael walked out from the cover of the trees, sub-machine-guns ready under all-weather clothing, and approached the fighting couple and their burning Cessna. Richardson and Melanie, aware that men were coming towards them, acted as though they hadn't seen them and went on scrapping.

Red Snake George and Ray Meyerschoff stayed in their hides. Meyerschoff's SIG SSG 3000 sniper rifle was trained, with the aid of a scope, on Raphael's hide, waiting for a sighting of his head or part of his body in which the Angel could be incapacitated. Red Snake George's M16A2 carbine was aimed at Penuel's head. It wasn't the ideal weapon for such a small target at this distance, but the FBI man had also uncapped his M203 grenade-thrower in readiness. *Christ, they were good*. He hadn't seen the other two Angels until they appeared next to Penuel, even though they had identified their hides.

Merrill and Ethan moved quickly once they heard the explosion from the plane. They were still some distance from the camp but didn't have the closer cover of trees that the other two agents had. They moved on their bellies, wriggling along on all fours, fast, knowing that they could be taken out by a tree-positioned sniper. But they were low enough not to be seen by Penuel and Raphael. They reached the canal to the west of the camp and slithered into the water. A black snake, a deadly poisonous water moccasin, swam lazily past Merrill, who reacted by stepping back sharply. He trapped his feet in the weeds and slipped backwards and downwards. Ethan kept moving, knowing that the sudden splashing could attract the attention of the Angels. He reached the opposite bank, hoisted his Ingram sub-machine-gun into position and waited for any adverse movement. Merrill caught his footing, splashed around for a moment longer, then crossed to the bank where Ethan had taken up his position.

Raphael heard the splashing and eased himself up, his machine-gun at the ready. He knew whoever it was, unless it was a large fish or alligator, would climb up the bank onto the hummock where the camp started. He waited, hardly showing himself above the hide. His instructions were clear. If attacked, take out Baxter. Don't kill innocent people or official forces, just wound if necessary. Make sure you're not captured; escape as soon as you lose control of your position. He placed a hand-grenade next to the sub-machine-gun muzzle. In case of attack he decided to injure the attackers, then throw the hand-grenade through the small window of the building which imprisoned Baxter.

Meyerschoff saw Raphael's slight movement and sighted his SIG SSG 3000 at the small target that appeared.

Near the plane, Lucifer moved in to break up the fighting couple while Michael held back in case of an ambush. Richardson and Melanie appeared surprised at the appearance of the two men and separated, Richardson protectively gathering up the suitcases which had fallen to the ground.

'Break it up,' said Lucifer, standing between them. Then he saw it wasn't blood; there were no cuts for it to flow from.

He stepped back fast, reaching into his all-weather clothing, and pulled out his sub-machine-gun.

He was too slow.

Melanie brought her Ingram sub-machine-gun from under her smock and sprayed its deadly contents at Lucifer.

He fired off one round before the bullets tore into his chest, flipping him backwards into the soft earth. He was dead by the time he hit the ground.

Michael had been shielded from Richardson and Melanie by Lucifer's body, and he now fired his Heckler & Koch MP5K sub-machine-gun at them, then turned and zigzagged his way back towards Penuel. Red Snake George, although he had a clear sight of Michael, kept his M16A2 aimed at Penuel.

The next four moves happened almost simultaneously.

Merrill scrambled up the bank as the shots exploded and rushed towards Raphael's hide, his Ingram held ready to fire.

Raphael waited until the HRU chief got nearer; he also flicked the pin from the grenade and held it in his left hand, the Heckler & Koch MP5K resting in his right hand, pointing at the man scrambling towards him. He saw that the FBI man was wearing body armour, so he aimed at the upper part of his legs and fired a short, one-handed burst. The Heckler & Koch spattered out and cut down Merrill.

As Raphael had lifted his head to take aim and fire, Meyerschoff sighted the top of the Angel's head with the SIG SSG 3000 and increased pressure on the sniper-rifle trigger.

Merrill and Raphael got hit at the same moment as each other. Merrill crashed to the ground, rolling over as his thighs were slashed and broken by the Heckler & Koch rounds. Raphael only felt a spasm in the back of his head as the single .308 calibre shot disintegrated the top of his skull and killed him instantly. The grenade he had readied for Baxter rolled slowly out of his hand and deeper into the hide.

Penuel, giving his brother covering fire, came out of the hide, his Heckler & Koch MP5K blazing towards Richardson and Melanie, who dived for cover.

Red Snake George had to make a split decision. Immediately protect Richardson and Melanie, or wait for a clear shot and take out Penuel. He opted for the first, dropped his hand to the lower trigger of the M203 and launched a grenade towards Michael as he ran to Penuel. There was a sight on the grenade-launcher, but he didn't have time to sight the shot accurately; he just released it in the general direction of the Angels and hoped it diverted their accuracy when it exploded. Once the grenade was launched, he moved his hand back to the M16A2 trigger and opened rapid fire towards Penuel.

Michael, running flat out towards Penuel's position, heard the grenade whistle past him. He knew what it was as it hit the ground near his younger brother. He threw himself at his brother as the shots from behind crashed round his head, knocking Penuel backwards towards the tree trunk.

The grenade exploded, its fragments erupting across the immediate area.

The second grenade, the one Raphael had been waiting to lob into Baxter's prison, exploded almost immediately after, blowing up Raphael's hide and the body of the already dead Angel.

Michael and Penuel were safe; the tree trunk had absorbed most of the fragmented explosion. They were up immediately, running south, protected from the ensuing fire-power by the tree-line. Bullets crashed around them, another grenade exploded in their path. But they were safe, still running, ducking and diving, their Heckler & Kochs ready for immediate firing.

The bursts of fire galvanized Duggan and the second HRU agent, Reynolds, into action. They spread about twenty yards apart and moved north towards the camp, keeping low to protect themselves by the few trees that grew to the south. Duggan moved more awkwardly than his FBI counterpart; his minimal training had prepared him for nothing like this. His actions at the Milltown cemetery had been a lot easier as he knew his nationality had given him a great deal of protection. It was different here, in the swamp. Here he was the enemy and a well-aimed bullet wouldn't distinguish between the CIA and FBI. He scampered along the ground, frantically trying to keep up with Reynolds as he weaved between the well-spaced trees to keep some semblance of cover. As they broke into the open, a hundred yards from the perimeter of the camp, Michael and Penuel rushed towards them. Reynolds lifted his M16A2 to fire but Penuel's Heckler & Koch slammed bullets into his protected chest, not breaking through the vest but giving enough force to knock him to the ground. Duggan, thinking Reynolds had been hit, threw himself down and landed in a large dirty puddle. The water splashed up and temporarily blinded him as he tried to bring his Ingram sub-machine-gun into play. Penuel reached Reynolds as the agent tried to get on his feet and kicked him in the chest, knocking him down again. The Angel brought his Heckler & Koch up to Reynolds's head and tightened his finger on the trigger. Penuel was furious. *Raphael and Lucifer were dead. These bastards were protecting the Provos. They were responsible for—*

'Don't kill him,' screamed Michael from behind. 'Don't fucking kill him.'

Penuel froze; his brother's warning stopping him from blasting Reynolds's head. Then the anger took hold again. 'Don't!' he heard his brother shout once more. Penuel swore, then pointed the gun at Reynolds's upper legs. 'No unnecessary deaths,' he heard Michael shout again as his brother reached Duggan.

The pause was all the time Ethan West needed. He had scrambled along the side of the canal after Merrill was hit, trying to work his way towards Raphael. He had heard the firing but didn't realize Raphael had been taken out. He waded seventy yards down the canal, moving as fast as he could, knowing that Raphael's position was unassailable from the west, but that he was vulnerable from the south. He slowly came up from the canal bank and crawled along the ground towards Raphael's position. That's when he saw the two Angels break out from the camp, running towards the south. Duggan and Reynolds came from the trees from that direction and firing broke out between the two groups. He saw Reynolds and Duggan go down, no more than forty yards from where he lay concealed. He swung round and brought Big Joe, his Second-World-War crossbow, onto his shoulder. He'd carried it as additional fire-power in case he needed to take out an enemy without the warning sound of a gun. He aimed quickly – the weapon was his favourite and he knew how to handle it fast and accurately – and released the steel bolt as Penuel moved the Heckler & Koch down to Reynolds's legs.

The flying bolt penetrated Penuel's neck as the Angel

pulled the trigger. The spasm of his death kept his finger pressure on the gun and the Heckler & Koch continued to spray its rounds even though Penuel was dead. The bullets cut through Reynolds's legs, then bounced upwards across his chest, penetrating the vest at such close range, slicing the FBI man's neck and head in half. As the Angel fell the sub-machine-gun pumped its final bursts harmlessly into the soft ground beyond Reynolds.

Michael grabbed Duggan and pulled him to his feet, shielding himself from any attacks with the CIA man's body. He knew Penuel was dead, but there would be time later to mourn his brother. All his concentration was now directed at getting away from this place. His escape route was already worked out; he knew every inch of the wetlands round here. He would keep his hostage until he could break cover, get to one of the camouflaged airboats and go deeper into the Everglades where his escape hides had already been prepared.

He kept his eyes averted from where Penuel lay. He sensed it was his fault. If he hadn't shouted a warning, his brother would have killed the FBI man and kept moving, probably still been alive. Michael tried to block the horror of his own actions from his mind. *Escape, get out of here.* That's all that mattered. Get Baxter's list home. *Do something useful to end that terrible NI war.* As he reached the tree line he heard the English voice from behind.

'Leave him, Walker,' said the voice. 'It's over now. You're all that's left.'

Michael dragged Duggan down behind the first tree, still shielding himself with the CIA man. *So they knew who he was, knew bloody everything.* He wondered if those at home who had started this thing were now also finishing it.

Richardson saw him sink out of sight. The Englishman had seen Michael and Penuel break from the camp. He'd moved south, trying to flank the two Angels from the rear, moving into the trees just as Penuel had been killed. He wasn't after them; his orders were to save Fergal Baxter. He'd followed the Angels in case they led him to the Irishman. But that was out of the window now. He'd become part of the game; Michael was escaping and he was the one who would have to stop him. He found himself twenty yards behind Michael, his Ingram sub-machine-gun ready. But he couldn't open fire without the risk of hitting Duggan. For a moment the old fears surfaced as he watched Michael dragging Duggan backwards, the Heckler & Koch rammed into his side. He saw the young soldier running towards him, yelling for cover; he closed his eyes to the sight of the boy being cut down. This time he couldn't fail. This time he had to see it through. He suddenly faced his own cowardice and fear and stood up, the Ingram dangling in his hand. 'I'm here, Walker. You can either take me out or listen.'

'To what?' came the answer as Michael half spun Duggan to shield himself from Richardson. He couldn't see Richardson from where he was hidden.

'Hold back,' Richardson shouted loudly. 'This is Sam. Everyone stay where you are.' He waited for a moment, then turned his attention back to Michael. 'Talk it through, Walker. Just talk it through.' Richardson walked forward slowly, the sub-machine-gun still dangling by his side, as he covered the distance between them.

'Bollocks. I just want out of here.'

'They won't let you go.'

'It'll cost them one of their men.'

'I don't believe that.'

Michael laughed harshly. 'Just fucking try me.' He knew he didn't want to kill his hostage, but they didn't. To them he was just a kill-crazed ex-SAS man.

'They won't allow you out. Not with an American. Take me instead.'

'What for?'

'Because I'm here as an observer. It causes them a bigger headache if your hostage is a Brit.'

'You're a cute bastard.' Michael slowly stood up so Richardson could see him and Duggan. 'Any move to try to take me out now will guarantee this boy's death.'

'Nobody's going to risk anything,' said Richardson as he moved towards the two men, now only ten yards away.

'Show yourself,' ordered Michael. 'If you mean what you say.' He watched as Richardson stepped to the side, not shielded any more by the tree Michael was hiding behind. 'Stay put. And drop that fucking gun.' Michael waited until Richardson had complied. 'You in the service?'

'Was.'

'Is that what they've fucking done? Sent in our own people to slot us?'

'No. Listen, I was in Ulster. I know how you feel. Why you did it.'

'Like fuck. If you cared that much, you'd've done it yourself.' He remembered Baxter's list, that it still had to get home. 'You really prepared to swap places with this Yank?'

'That's what I said.'

'No,' shouted Duggan.

'Shut up!' Michael warned Duggan. The Angel still held Duggan close. 'Come closer,' he instructed Richardson. When Richardson was only two yards away, Michael pushed Duggan hard, sending him sprawling in the mud. With his Heckler & Koch aimed at Richardson's chest, he covered the small distance between them and pulled Richardson into his embrace, the gun barrel now pushed up into Richardson's throat. 'No way out, is there?' he said, a smile playing on his lips.

'No.'

'That's what I reckon. I killed my fucking brother, you know. Looked after him all these years and then got him knocked off.' He pulled back slightly, the gun still against Richardson's throat. 'Don't do anything. Just listen. We did it for the right reasons.' He reached into his pocket with his other hand and took out four sheets of paper. He pushed them into Richardson's side pocket, next to a grenade. 'Naughty. Keeping that up your sleeve, were you?' Michael took out the grenade. He stepped back and pulled the pin, then held the grenade into his chest. 'We always knew, deep down, there was only one way it could end. Fuck Baxter. He just shortened everything. Bitch, isn't it? Your own people shagging you down.' He dropped the Heckler & Koch to his side and stepped further away from Richardson. 'You can slot me if you want. But once I get hit, this grenade's going to make sure there won't be much of me to take back.' He laughed harshly. 'Down to you, Sergeant,' he challenged. Then Michael turned and started to walk away from them.

Richardson picked up his Ingram and aimed it at Michael's back. Then he lifted the gun skyward and released a volley into the overhanging branches. The sound of the short burst reverberated through the trees, then there was a loud silence.

Duggan watched Michael stop, then, once he realized he was safe and that the gun-fire had not been aimed at him, he broke into a run and disappeared through the trees. Richardson walked towards Duggan as the rest of the rescue team, with Ethan leading, burst through the trees. Duggan said nothing as Richardson directed the others to follow Michael, before he checked Duggan and Reynolds. The FBI man was dead; Duggan only bruised and shaken.

The two men made their way back to the camp. Neither mentioned what had happened.

Meyerschoff had radioed the back-up teams ten

miles down the road and they were on their way in. The busy chatter of helicopters from the east soon made itself heard. The helicopters and back-up teams moved towards Michael's last position, trying to cut him off.

Red Snake George was at the green building when Richardson and Duggan arrived. They waited as he brought a naked Baxter out. Baxter was in a state of shock; there was no obvious rationale to the Irishman. His body quivered uncontrollably and all he yelled was 'You bastards! You bastards! You bastards!' over and over again. They tried to calm him, but his eyes never saw them. He just kept on screaming, 'You bastards!' It would take many days before the Miami medical team pronounced him insane. By then he was heavily sedated and had stopped his cursing. They couldn't work out what the Angels had done to him; the only unusual marks were three small, slightly bloody holes near the bottom of his chest. They would never find the size-16 plastic knitting-needle that lay at the bottom of the swamp. Fergal Baxter would eventually be returned to Ireland where he would spend the rest of his life under sedation and care in a mental institution.

Duggan decided not to mention what had occurred between Richardson and Michael, not even the sheets of paper the Angel had put in Richardson's pocket. There was no point; Ireland was a British problem, nothing to do with those who theorized from the safety of their American way of life. If the British had backed the Angels, it didn't matter now. The olive branch had been offered to the IRA. If they rejected it, they deserved everything they got.

An hour later, Richardson and Duggan were on their way back to Miami. Jiggs had arrived with the back-up teams and been debriefed by his own men as well as Duggan. Michael hadn't, as yet, been captured, and Jiggs and Richardson went through the procedures the Angel would carry out. As the Englishman explained the various types of hide Michael would have prepared, the FBI supervisor realized that the Angel may well have escaped capture.

'They want you on the earliest flight out of here,' Jiggs told Richardson. 'Some of the media are already looking for SAS support. I guess anyone with an English accent is going to feed their suspicions.' Jiggs held out his hand. 'Been nice meeting you. Even though one of your Angels escaped,' he said knowingly.

Richardson ignored the comment, said his goodbyes and left the scene. He knew they'd be lucky to find Michael. But that was their problem. He'd done what he was sent out to do. The paper in his pocket proved that.

Richardson and Duggan had a last meal at the airport restaurant just before Richardson returned to London and Andrea. He had spoken at length to Dancer and knew that she was on the mend. He missed her and couldn't wait to get back. He'd already decided they should get married. He wasn't his father and Andrea wasn't his mother. They were different people and he realized it would suit them to spend their lives together.

'You've got to come over and see us,' Richardson said. 'You're really not quite as bad as I thought.'

Duggan laughed. 'I'll do that, macho man.' He decided to clear the air. It was also partly self-interest; he didn't know what Andrea had told, or might tell, Richardson. 'I made a pass at her,' he said solemnly.

'Most men do,' Richardson replied understandingly.

'Did she tell you?'

'No. Nor would she. What about Carmella?'

'What about her? I still want the bitch. But she's not for me. I realized that when I saw you and Andrea. As for the kids, I'm hanging on for myself. Not for them.'

He shuddered as he remembered the gorilla. *David, that was his name.* 'Maybe I can become a friend to them when they get older. Right now they need a settled life. Me being on the scene confuses them. Maybe, and I hate to say it, the shit'll be good for them.' The flight was called over the loudspeaker and they both stood up. 'Will he get away?'

Richardson understood that Duggan meant Michael. 'Should do. He'll stay underground for weeks, maybe months. Then he'll come out and start to rebuild his life. Probably already got an alternative identity in place.'

'Why'd you do it?'

'Because it might have been me out there. As he saw it, he was only doing his duty. Wasn't robbing banks or old ladies. And he'd just seen his brother killed. Fuck it, he'd had enough crap for one day.'

Duggan drove to the road at the end of the runway and watched the British Airways 747 jumbo lift off towards London. He waved, feeling foolish and knowing that Richardson probably wasn't even looking out of the window. None the less, it made Duggan feel closer to his departing friend. *Charisma bypass, my arse.* He wished he'd brought that up. Cocky bastard. He suddenly whooped for no real reason. 'Most men do.' That's what the Englishman had said about him wanting Andrea. *God dammit. That Sam Richardson was one helluva cocky bastard.*

Richardson looked down at the disappearing ground as the 747 pulled away, rumbling as it tucked its undercarriage into its belly. He wondered whether Duggan had stayed to watch the take-off. *The Yank was OK*; telling him about Andrea had taken guts. He reached into his pocket for a cigarette, one of the weak American brands. Maybe if he smoked two of those, they would equal the tar content of one British one.

'Excuse me, sir,' said the hostess. 'This flight is designated "Non Smoking".'

Richardson sighed and put the pack away. A whole eight hours without a smoke. He'd tell Andrea that when he got home. That would tickle her fancy.

The big plane banked to the north and Duggan watched it until it was too small to recognize any longer.

He returned to the hotel, packed his bags and caught the last flight to Washington.

Being a natural worrier, and having decided not to worry about Carmella and the kids any longer, he turned his concentration on his job.

Being a simple CIA analyst was not something he would find satisfying after the excitement of the last few weeks.

The future worried Francis Duggan and he contemplated how he could change it.

The news items were the usual tabloid journalism.

'Angels Fried in Hell'; 'High-flying Angels Crash to Defeat'; 'Angels Mortally Winged in Gun Battle'; 'No Angels with Dirty Faces'; and so on went the headlines.

It was presented as a simple cops and robbers story. The Angels, upset by the loss of colleagues in Ulster and the subsequent breakdown in the 1993 peace talks, had vowed to avenge themselves against the IRA. They would have continued their violent methods for some considerable time if the British and American security services, with the help of the Irish Gardaí and Special Branch, had not quickly rooted out their base and destroyed the Angels in a surprise dawn raid. According to the report, all the Angels had been killed. For the FBI there was one casualty and one critically wounded agent. Rumours flew about that the SAS had sent in a team with the FBI, but nothing was proven. A final note stated that Baxter had been rescued and was retiring to Ireland. The package was sold as an enormous success for international collaboration in the fight against world terrorism.

In Ireland, Baxter's wife was dissuaded by the other members of the Army Council from telling the Press of her husband's predicament. It wasn't good publicity, and no-one knew what information Baxter might have released to his captors. They presumed he'd been tortured. The Army Council initiated moves to safe-guard their operations, but it was too late. Within twenty- four hours of the Angels' destruction, the various authorities, acting on certain secret information received, managed to raid many arms and explosives caches that the PIRA felt were safely hidden in Eire, Northern Ireland and the mainland. The arrest of certain key terrorists, the break-up of secret mainland bomb cells, the confiscation of various funds in false bank accounts, and raids on safe houses helped bring the IRA, albeit temporarily, under control.

Whatever the publicity, the Angels remained heroic figures to much of the British press and their readers. The only blot was the unfortunate death of the FBI agent, Reynolds. Otherwise, all their attacks had been on exclusive PIRA targets. Even the deaths of the two Americans outside Biddy Mulligan's were accepted as they were strong sympathizers to a terrorist cause.

The IRA had refused to support peace talks and had continued their war of attrition with bombs and innocent deaths. Because of the Angels, terrorist action ceased on the mainland and in Ulster. For that, the British and Irish populace were extremely grateful.

The public knew it might not last, but at least it could open the doors for the Provos and the IRA finally to come and join the peace talks.

BOOK FIVE

PASSING THE BATON

Somewhere in Knightsbridge
London

Carter was already at the corner table in the Special
Forces Club dining-room when Claris arrived.

They made small talk until the waiter had given
them their aperitifs and taken their order.

'The IRA are doing their damnedest to convince
the Press it was all down to the Prime Minister,' Claris
reported. He smiled. 'Not doing them much good. This
one is definitely not coming home to roost at Number
Ten, or anywhere else official, for that matter. They've
lost the publicity battle, you know.'

'For the moment.'

'For the moment,' came Claris's taciturn agreement.
'How's Richardson?'

'On leave. Until his woman gets better.'

'Is she going to make it?'

'Yes.'

'Good. I had a call from the Five chap, Dancer.

He was just tying up loose ends, he said.'

'And you said?'

'There weren't any loose ends to tie up. Wasn't an SIS operation. I suggested it might have been a Box special.'

'And?'

'He laughed. Then put the phone down. Cheeky chaps, those Box people.' Claris reached in his pocket and took out a small piece of paper. 'Anyway, the information from Baxter has proven invaluable. Got the old Provos on the run at last.'

'For the time being.'

'It all helps. Until they're prepared to listen to reason.' Claris slid the paper across the desk. 'Slip that in your pocket, will you?' He waited until Carter, without looking at the paper, had done as he was instructed. 'It's a number. Don't make copies of it, just put it in an extremely safe place. You may never have to use it. But it's there if you want it.' Claris sipped from his glass, swilled the Scotch in his mouth before swallowing it. 'Beautiful. First one of the day.' He leant forward so that he could speak quietly and no-one else could possibly overhear. 'It's your passport to promotion. I've suggested you move up in the ranks. Be prepared to take over from me. I retire within the year. You could handle the job comfortably.'

'Thank you.' Carter appreciated the sign of changing times. Once, not so long ago, the top jobs were exclusively for the old Oxbridge men. His new promotion would be a step towards the democratization of the SIS, following on Stella Rimington's new-found television stardom.

Claris waved aside the gratitude. 'The number is a Swiss bank account. Started by my boss in '76. There's a few shillings in it, all raised in the seventies. Commission for another Angel, would you believe?' Claris chuckled. 'A black angel. A very dead angel who certainly didn't go to Heaven. It's not official money. Totally untraceable. Just goes on racking up a very healthy interest. Enough to start a small war with. It's there if you want it. Not personally, of course.'

'Is that what the Angels used?'

'Probably,' came the uncommitted reply. 'No-one knows about it. Certainly not SIS, or anybody in our sister security services. Not the Prime Minister or old Inger. No-one. Just you and me.'

'Really?' came Carter's quizzical reply.

'Well, maybe one or two of the old boys. In time you'll have to trust someone else with the knowledge. A colleague who may have use for those funds. Part of your Circle, possibly.'

'Who dreamt up the Angels?'

'A bit like the old Becket story. The king wanted to be rid of the cantankerous old Archbishop, so some of his knights rode off to Canterbury Cathedral and did in Becket. Nobody asked them to do it; it just needed doing.'

'Inger?'

'Why should that interest you?'

'Because I want to know where the arrows come from – when I take over.'

'Then, yes. Inger's as good as anyone.' Claris took a deep breath before continuing. 'Let's just say it comes up in general conversation. No direct requests on this sort of thing. It's up to you to filter what they require to be done. In the eighties someone in Downing Street suggested we look at a plan to eliminate the PIRA, or at the very least, curtail their activities drastically. The Plan, as you know, was drawn up secretly. At that time it was decided it was too risky to put into operation. It was binned with only a few copies remaining. But over the years things just got steadily worse. There didn't seem any answer to the problem.' Claris shook his head sadly. 'I suppose, when peace does come, it'll come out of the blue. Like the Lebanon, like the Middle East. It's difficult to work out why these things start in the first place, or why they suddenly end. Anyway, as the situation deteriorated, some people started to look for alternative solutions. Which is why the IRA continued bombing and killing into 1994. That's when I was contacted by an old colleague.'

'Nathaniel. Lucifer.'

'Let's leave it at "old colleague". He was in America. Running a small security business. He said he'd like to do something about the Irish situation, now that the peace talks had ground to a halt. He remembered the Cartel Plan. I knew Inger had discussed a similar solution, but couldn't do a thing about it. There was no specific remit. Just a desire to force them to the conference table. I simply arranged a dead-letter drop and let our old friend have access to the Swiss funds. The rest was out of my hands.'

'You trusted him? With all that money?'

'I was right, wasn't I?' Claris leant back in his chair as the waiter approached with their food. He waited until the waiter had gone before continuing. 'The Angels were committed. They believed in what they were doing. Getting hold of Baxter speeded up the operation, but it cost them their lives. They were good soldiers. But they became renegades. They only did what we trained them to do. It's as much our fault as it was theirs. And that really is the end of it.'

'Except one of them's still alive and running around.'

'I'm sure he knows how to look after himself. And who knows, he might even pick up the phone and call you one day.'

'He doesn't know me.'

'No. But the Swiss bank does now. I have, of course, forwarded your name on to them as one of the trustees of the numbered account.' Claris pursed his lips and blew air out slowly. 'I don't know for certain,' he said eventually, 'but it would be unlikely that the only base they had was in the Everglades. After all, they were set for a long campaign against the Provos. The Angels would have realized their Everglades camp had a limited life before the FBI moved in, before Baxter arrived on the scene. I'm quite sure they had alternative bases lined up. Big place, America. Full of deserts and mountains and forests. Easy place to hide, if you're trained to conceal yourself from the world. And God knows, once the IRA have picked themselves up again after the Baxter confessions, they'll be up to their old tricks again. When that happens, unless we see a peaceful solution in the meantime, our man Michael might just contact the Swiss Bank and ask them to call you.'

'Like Nathaniel did?'

Claris chuckled and tucked into his shepherd's pie. Carter watched him, then slowly picked at his steak and kidney. *Right or wrong, it was his baby now.*

'What about Sam Richardson?' Carter asked after a few mouthfuls.

'He's your man. To do with as you want.' Claris paused and put down his fork. 'I'd be a bit careful.'

'Why?'

'That early business in Northern Ireland. When he was with the ground forces. Looking back, I'd say his character was a trifle suspect. Wouldn't you?'

'He did well in America. I'd say he was over it.'

Claris picked up his fork. 'As I said, he's your man. From now on, you stand or fall by your decisions.'

In the rest of the Special Forces Club the old members reminisced about their past deeds and still kept the secrets they had carried with them for all these years.

Claris thought about Reggie Flowers. He remembered the old war-horse and how he had set this whole thing rolling. And soon it wouldn't be Claris's problem any longer. No wonder the old chap had looked forward to retirement so much.

It really could be a dirty game.

He left the hospital earlier than he had on previous nights.

Andrea was better now and he felt he needn't sit by her into the early hours as was his custom.

He drove home slowly in the old Bentley.

He tried to think of his father as the big car idled through the traffic, how he would have taken to Andrea if he'd been alive. But Richardson didn't feel the old man's presence, or his authority.

Once home, he wandered through the flat, touching objects that reminded him of his past, trying to touch those he had loved. But all he felt was an emptiness, nothing was real. He hated feeling so dispirited, not knowing what the problem was that made him restless when all was going well.

He took his shoes off and concentrated on cleaning them. Five minutes later, after intense polishing, he couldn't muster the enthusiasm to continue.

He gave up and went to bed.

Maybe it was the final reaction to all that had happened; to Andrea; to the problems he had faced in Ireland and the Everglades. *That's what it was. Just bloody winding down.*

He pulled the covers over his head and went to sleep.

The boy soldier ran towards him and screamed for help.

Richardson knew he could do nothing, the blind funk of fear wrapped its tentacles round his throat and stifled his warning shouts, paralysed his arm so he couldn't raise his weapon and help the soldier.

As the soldier shrieked and died, Sam Richardson came awake from his nightmare and sat up sharply in bed, his body drenched with sweat.

Yet he shivered in the heat.

He knew now why he was restless.

Nothing he had done had taken away the nightmare of the death he had caused, that he could have so easily prevented.

Sam Richardson slid down between the damp sheets and stared at the ceiling. He felt the twinge for a smoke, but knew she'd probably thrown all the spare cigarettes away.

It didn't matter anyway.

He didn't go back to sleep.

THE END

A SELECTED LIST OF FINE NOVELS
AVAILABLE FROM CORGI BOOKS

THE PRICES SHOWN BELOW WERE CORRECT AT THE TIME OF
GOING TO PRESS. HOWEVER TRANSWORLD PUBLISHERS RE-
SERVE THE RIGHT TO SHOW NEW RETAIL PRICES ON COVERS
WHICH MAY DIFFER FROM THOSE PREVIOUSLY ADVERTISED IN
THE TEXT OR ELSEWHERE.

☐ 13947 5	SUNDAY MORNING	*Ray Connolly*	£4.99
☐ 14227 1	SHADOWS ON A WALL	*Ray Connolly*	£5.99
☐ 13827 4	SPOILS OF WAR	*Peter Driscoll*	£4.99
☐ 12550 4	LIE DOWN WITH LIONS	*Ken Follett*	£4.99
☐ 12610 1	ON WINGS OF EAGLES	*Ken Follett*	£5.99
☐ 12180 0	THE MAN FROM ST PETERSBURG	*Ken Follett*	£5.99
☐ 11810 9	THE KEY TO REBECCA	*Ken Follett*	£4.99
☐ 10050 1	THE DOGS OF WAR	*Frederick Forsyth*	£5.99
☐ 12569 5	THE FOURTH PROTOCOL	*Frederick Forsyth*	£5.99
☐ 13275 9	THE NEGOTIATOR	*Frederick Forsyth*	£5.99
☐ 13823 1	THE DECEIVER	*Frederick Forsyth*	£5.99
☐ 13990 4	THE FIST OF GOD	*Frederick Forsyth*	£5.99
☐ 13598 4	MAESTRO	*John Gardner*	£5.99
☐ 13840 1	CLOSED CIRCLE	*Robert Goddard*	£4.99
☐ 13562 3	TAKE NO FAREWELL	*Robert Goddard*	£4.99
☐ 13281 0	IN PALE BATTALIONS	*Robert Goddard*	£4.99
☐ 13561 5	INTO THE BLUE	*Robert Goddard*	£4.99
☐ 13697 2	AIRPORT	*Arthur Hailey*	£4.99
☐ 13678 6	THE EVENING NEWS	*Arthur Hailey*	£5.99
☐ 13694 8	THE FINAL DIAGNOSIS	*Arthur Hailey*	£4.99
☐ 13869 X	MATILDA'S GAME	*Denis Kilcommons*	£3.99
☐ 12433 8	A COLD MIND	*David Lindsey*	£4.99
☐ 13215 2	SPIRAL	*David Lindsey*	£4.99
☐ 14136 4	THE WALPOLE ORANGE	*Frank Muir*	£4.99
☐ 13771 5	RING OF RED ROSES	*Eddy Shah*	£4.99
☐ 13918 1	THE LUCY GHOSTS	*Eddy Shah*	£4.99
☐ 14145 3	MANCHESTER BLUE	*Eddy Shah*	£4.99
☐ 14143 7	A SIMPLE PLAN	*Scott Smith*	£4.99
☐ 10565 1	TRINITY	*Leon Uris*	£5.99